'An impressively nuanced debut . . . Kemp has a knack for human observation, perfectly capturing the fraught mood between each of the multifaceted characters as they seek to unburden themselves of their hidden pain'   *Book Browse*

'Kemp has an uncommon ability to keep her scenes ticking along, and she's terrific with dialogue, injecting the inter-actions with a brusque, colorful candour at odds with the theme of repression'   *Wall Street Journal*

'A stellar debut . . . Precise, distinctive prose and well-drawn characters make this satisfying tale all the more memorable. Expect Kemp to make a big splash'   *Publishers Weekly*

Nightingale

MARINA KEMP

4th ESTATE • London

4th Estate
An imprint of HarperCollins*Publishers*
1 London Bridge Street
London SE1 9GF

www.4thEstate.co.uk

HarperCollins*Publishers*
1st Floor, Watermarque Building, Ringsend Road
Dublin 4, Ireland

First published in Great Britain in 2019 by 4th Estate
This 4th Estate paperback edition published in 2021

1

ISBN 978-0-00-832650-0

Printed and bound by CPI Group (UK) Ltd, Croydon

For Lalu

'I shall not hear the nightingale
Sing on, as if in pain'

CHRISTINA ROSSETTI,
'When I Am Dead, My Dearest'

I

1

She dreamt of nothing. She woke to the shuddering of train doors, catching only a glimpse of the stark platform and pale white sky before realising this was her stop. As she hurried from the seat, clutching her bags, she had to pull on a strap that had become caught on a rung of the luggage rack. She reached the doors as they were already closing, with a hiss like a punctured tyre. She had to tug her body through them, through their insistence as they clamped around her.

There was no one on the platform except for a woman in a florid skirt and long brown coat, the waxed coat of a farmer. She squinted at Marguerite. She stared for some time at Marguerite's trainers, and then looked back down the platform as if for someone else.

Marguerite dropped her bags and knelt down to take a jacket out of her hold-all. The air was bitter, no warmer than it had been in Paris at seven o'clock that morning, in spite of how much further south she had come. When she stood up to put her jacket on, the woman was standing closer. She squinted again.

'Mademoiselle Demers?'

'Yes, that's me,' said Marguerite. The woman raised her eyebrows, not reaching out her hand.

'I'm Brigitte Brochon, Monsieur Lanvier's *gardienne*. We spoke on the phone.'

'That's right.' Both arms through her jacket sleeves, Marguerite reached to shake the woman's hand. It was given warily. 'Thank you for coming to collect me.'

Madame Brochon shrugged. 'It's my job.' She turned, starting to move towards the squat station building and the fields beyond. 'The car's this way.'

Marguerite picked up her bags and followed.

They drove to the house in silence. When they arrived, Madame Brochon took Marguerite straight inside and through to the old man's bedroom, allowing her time neither to take in her new surroundings nor unload her luggage from the car. The handover was wordless on his part; Madame Brochon stood by his bed as she spoke, sturdy ankles placed wide apart.

'Jérôme, this is Marguerite,' she said.

'Though most people call me Margo,' said Marguerite tentatively, unacknowledged.

'Rossignol may be a grand house but it needn't faze her; she'll soon know her way around. I've left instructions for where all the important things are kept.'

When he opened his mouth as if to object, she swooped straight in. 'The last nurse's notes are all there too so she knows which pills to bring you, and when, and what time you wake and all that. She's got Doctor Meyer's details and she knows where I am if she has any questions. I've left my number in the kitchen' – though this was all previously unsaid, all news to Marguerite – 'and I've told her that it's best to contact me in the morning, early, before Henri and I start out at the farm.'

After the second sentence he had turned to the wall, and started to enact a sort of exercise with his eyelids: drooping them slowly, opening them wide, drooping again, widening them completely and then shutting them tight. The apparently immoveable Madame Brochon twisted her skirt in her fingers, shifted her considerable weight from left leg to right.

When she resumed her speech it was to the accompaniment of his reedy whistle, tuneless and insistent. 'She should get on fine, there's everything needed in the pantry for at least the next few days, and I'm sure she'll not object to the simple things I've put there. They may not be anything fancy but I'm sure she'll find the quality can't be faulted.'

This last comment was, as throughout her speech, directed at the old man in the bed and not Marguerite. And so as Marguerite watched Madame Brochon, Madame Brochon watched the old man and the old man watched the wall.

Total silence took hold of the place from the moment Madame Brochon left. For the first few days, Marguerite barely exchanged a word with Jérôme, taking his silence as her cue. He didn't ask her where she was from, about her background or past experience or suitability for the job. The house was some way from the village, down a forest-lined road that seemed to lead nowhere else. It was many days before Marguerite heard a car pass by, and when it receded the silence came rushing back to fill its space.

She started to explore the house slowly, expanding her radius just a little each day. The floor was stone throughout, and she trod carefully – she didn't like to make much noise. Her own footsteps sounded somehow like an intrusion.

The old man's room was on the ground floor, not far from the kitchen. At first Marguerite spent most of her time in the kitchen, cleaning out cupboards and sitting in an armchair for perhaps hours at a time, staring out into the garden, waiting for him to summon her. As she started to learn the rhythm of his needs, she could afford to spend time exploring the many other rooms. She cleaned them, one by one, taking time to wipe away the blankets of dust over the sinks, the crisp shells of long-dead daddy-long-legs and centipedes in doorways.

He didn't sleep well at night, but often during the day. Marguerite, by nature active but prone to sudden, consuming bouts of somnolence, profited from his naps. Her afternoons often passed by in dull and dreamless slumber, from which depths she would emerge only with great mental and physical effort.

She soon learnt to take these long sleeps early, so that the struggle to come back to the world, to her room's bare walls and sparse furniture, was over in time to face the darkness – when it started to descend – with full strength and clarity. She realised quickly that she was afraid of the nights here, in this house that was never visited by anyone, that it was her charge to protect. The dark was as thick and complete as sleep.

When Jérôme called out or knocked hard on the wooden headboard, sounds that often startled her through the silence, she would go in with a glass of milk or water. At night, he'd stare into the darkness outside the windows before she drew the curtains shut. He might say, 'Totally black, completely and utterly black,' as if to himself; or, 'You wouldn't be able to see the devil if he were standing right outside,' tapping his chin with one of his surprisingly beautiful, fine-boned fingers.

On one of those evenings she dropped the tray after placing a glass and small dish of pills by his bed. Its clattering on the stone floor was a shock to the quiet, and he inhaled quickly, gripping the sheets. When the clatter and its echo died he smacked her arm, pushed the glass aside so roughly that it almost fell too, and turned to face the wall.

'I'm sorry,' she said and he swiped the air without turning, gesturing for her to leave.

He began to speak more, emerging in bursts from his muteness to chide her for taking too long to respond to his calls, or to demand medication, or ask with suspicion what she would be making for dinner. Madame Brochon's provisions hadn't lasted long, and Marguerite took to walking to the village two or three times a week to collect post, fresh milk, medical supplies and – once he had started to talk – the odd request Jérôme might have for something unusual: pistachios, some batteries for his torch, a bag of blackberries.

The route from Rossignol was winding, the quiet road fringed for the most part by forest. Twice, she'd seen a startled deer sprint through the trees. She imagined wild boar and badgers rustling around in the undergrowth too: she knew they must be around here somewhere, since something was digging up great pits on Jérôme's land. What were they digging for? She wanted to know these things, but there was no one to ask. She was unacquainted with the details of rural life: the names of trees, which birds had which call, whether the large oak at the bottom of the garden was dying. Familiar only with the countryside's boredom and silence, she was determined in this job to get to know her landscape, to become self-sufficient.

The people of Saint-Sulpice were not rude, but certainly no one was friendly. Just as it was not an ugly village, but by no means picturesque. It was like the last place she had worked: too close to a town to be remote, too far to borrow any of its buzz. With the same disregard for the old and quaint that she had noticed throughout provincial France, dilapidated old buildings – in fact lovely in their faded hues of rust and lemon – had been spruced up with brazen, teak-bright trellises, garish with orange and purple flowers. A café that might, in Paris, have embraced the tattered charm it would have earned after several decades of service, was here the victim of ruthless stripping, whitewashing and primping. It was filled with the ubiquitous red and white checker of country tabletops; a flock of wooden ducks lined up in polite procession along the windowsills.

She didn't see Madame Brochon on her trips into the village, but there was many a Brochon-like matron. The *grande dame* of the boulangerie refused, even after Marguerite's seventh or eighth visit, to register recognition; she pursed her lips when Marguerite ordered her bread, as if tolerating a young child. But Marguerite had learnt in these places that it was a dangerous thing to look for hostility where perhaps there

8

was mere indifference. She knew it was a trick of the lonely to favour the rude to the simply unmoved; that the loneliest thing in these villages and in this most tucked-away of professions was to elicit no response at all.

She visited the library in her third week. Jérôme had asked for a book to be read to him each night. She had just dried him after an evening bath, the time when he was at his most spitting.

'Can you even read?' he had hissed after bathtime's habitual and adamant silence, punctured only by grunts of indignation and occasional discomfort. Her hands were by his ankle; she was trying to guide one bony foot through the gash of a pyjama leg. His feet were growing soft under her auspices. She rubbed them after every bath with oil, sensed the relief this gave him not in any active words of encouragement but in the absence of the contrary.

'Yes,' she said simply. One foot was through; she started on the other.

'Well, I should think it would do you some good to do some reading,' he said, wincing theatrically as she pulled the waistline of the pyjamas in one swift motion up to his knees. '*Careful!*' he snarled. She inhaled, waited for him to speak again. There was silence. She pulled the soft flannel trousers past his knees – swollen bulbs where stray, sparse hairs stood upright among clusters of moles.

'I should not *mind*,' he continued, looking resolutely at the ceiling as she pulled the trousers up past the shrunken bud of his penis, his soft, felt-like balls, the static fuzz of his white pubic hair, 'if you would find something to read. Before I sleep.'

She tied the trousers' drawstring in a gentle bow at his waist, smoothed the flannel shirt down over his belly. It was distended, hard as a drum. He flinched and flapped his hands.

'All right, all right,' he said. 'Stop fussing.' She stood and he put his hands on her arms and gave her his weight – considerable, in spite of his boniness – as she swung him gently onto his back, lowering him down onto the clean bedsheets.

'Is there anything in particular you'd like me to read?' she asked.

He frowned furiously. 'It's not for my sake, it's for yours. Pick something you can read, only make sure it isn't some ghastly romance. And I don't want poetry. I want something with a real story, something noble. I used to enjoy the classics: Dumas, Hugo, Gaston Leroux. Albert Cohen, even. Just for God's sake no romance or girly tripe.' Then he added, 'Whatever you think you could benefit from.'

And so she found herself two days later in the municipal library. It was as she had imagined, both dim and too bright. The librarian, young and sallow, stamped her books carefully and listed the rules of the place in a flat voice.

'Returns must be made before twelve weeks have elapsed. Extensions can be made only by direct request in person and at the discretion of the librarian on duty. Care must always be taken to keep both food and liquids away from all books issued by this library, and in case of damage you should be prepared to pay a fine of up to twenty-five euros.' Once he had reeled the rules off, he looked a little embarrassed. He secured his glasses, which had not slipped, with one finger, smiling faintly. His nails were chewed right down to the quick, a metro-map of veins across his hand.

'I hope you'll enjoy the three volumes,' he said, turning to disappear back into the solemn darkness of his little booth.

Throughout his monologue, Marguerite had been conscious of being watched, and as she turned to leave she caught the eye of the woman sitting at a table close by. She wore a dark green hijab; her chin was raised imperiously. She didn't drop her gaze. As Marguerite walked past to leave, she said: 'And you are from . . . ?'

'Sorry?'

'I haven't seen you before. Where are you from?'

Marguerite paused. 'I'm working here,' she said.

'Working where?'

'In Saint-Sulpice.'

The woman narrowed her eyes, contemplating her. Then she smiled, a little wryly. 'You're Jérôme Lanvier's new nurse, am I right?'

'Yes.'

'I could tell instantly. You're from Paris?'

'Yes.'

'I knew that accent. Well, you must find it rather different here.'

'Not so different from other places I've worked.'

The woman reached a hand out to shake Marguerite's; she had long nails painted a dark, shiny aubergine. 'I'm Suki. Very good to meet you. How do you like Rossignol?'

'It's comfortable.'

'And Lanvier himself?'

'Fine.'

'That's good. And your name . . . ?'

'Marguerite.'

'Well, as I said, it's good to meet you.' She smiled again. 'Enjoy your books, Marguerite.'

When she left the library, Marguerite stood for a moment to study the noticeboard on the wall outside, to delay the long walk home. A sign for a missing cat, a pamphlet listing a course of dance classes for the previous June, and a notice advertising a babysitter, with the phone number printed several times for people to tear off. Only two had been torn.

' *"What, no wine?" said Dantès, turning pale, and looking alternately at the hollow cheeks of the old man and the empty cupboards. "What, no wine? Have you wanted money, father?"*

"'I want nothing now I have you," said the old man.'

'Tired,' Jérôme said loudly, with a croak as if he had not spoken for days. 'Enough.'

'Are you sure?' Marguerite let the pages fall back, with her finger as a marker. He closed his eyes tight instead of answering. She had been enjoying reading; she hadn't used her voice so much for almost a month. 'Can I get you anything? Are you feeling comfortable?' His response, as so often, was simply to screw his eyes tighter shut.

She rose and took the book he'd chosen from her selection to the table: a 1970s edition of *The Count of Monte Cristo*, its faded jacket showing a large full moon, shivering on the dark surface of water. She folded the corner of their page to mark it and felt a twinge of guilt for doing so; she thought of the librarian and his long list of rules, from which the prohibition of dog-earing a page had surely only been omitted on account of its sheer obviousness. 'Flagrant disregard for the item's longevity . . .' she imagined him saying, and smiled to herself.

Turning to leave the room, she saw that the old man was watching her. He was lying flat on his back, a rigid straight line down the bed, his eyes swivelled to stare at her.

'Don't you laugh at me,' he barked.

'Sir, I—'

'I will not tolerate it.'

'But I didn't—'

'Just get out, now!' He shut his eyes. 'I can send you away the minute I don't want you. Just one phone call and you're out of here, scuttling back to whichever deplorable little hole you came from.'

She felt her cheeks colour; she took a deep breath.

Gradually, she became aware of a whirring in the room: a moth, throwing its body again and again at the ceiling lamp.

The old man was lying stiff and straight in the bed, his fists and eyes and everything clenched.

She watched him for a moment but he didn't speak again and she left the room, walked straight out of the kitchen into the garden, into the blanket darkness. She breathed in deeply, felt the thud of her heartbeat gradually slow. There was a lightness in the air in spite of the cold; she could believe for the first time that spring was here.

She had never had a garden. Her childhood had been spent in an apartment on the fourth floor in the 16th arrondissement – large, with high ceilings and rich, heavy curtains. There was a balcony that they had been allowed to step out onto only under supervision from her mother or the au pair; it looked down over a wide, dappled avenue lined with trees. There was always someone walking a dog – she and her sister would think up names for the dogs they came to recognise.

She didn't like to think of that. The garden here was hers and she wanted to make it grow. She would grow herbs, plant flowers. She would sit in the shade in the narrow olive groves and look over at her herb garden and pluck rosemary to put in little pots around the house. It would be her project.

And then when it was dark – this heavy, enveloping blackness – it would comfort her to think of her plants outside. They could line the house like ramparts.

The vegetables here were huge and beautiful. She had discovered the village market that morning, by chance, and bought red, yellow, brown and green tomatoes, their skins plump. The stall owner had said the green were the tastiest. She ate one as soon as she got home, bent over the sink. Its skin burst under her teeth.

There was a head of curly-leafed lettuce. It was so large, and had splayed open so generously, that she could have worn it on her own head like a bonnet. She washed it slowly, watched with pleasure the water turn black with mud. On a hook she hung a straw plait of garlic, its heads indecently bulbous. They shed veined paper over the kitchen surface.

She would make *poule au pot* for Jérôme's dinner. Infirmity had made his appetite weak, but his eating habits carried the shadow of a once-greedy man: in spite of himself, his eyes widened when she brought in a plate of something he liked. He would gobble fast, with relish. She thought of him

14

as she stood there surrounded by her vegetables, carefully unsheathing spring onions and slicing celery and scattering peppercorns. The chicken still held many of its feathers, which she plucked one by one, with care, thinking of Jérôme's delicate white flesh.

She had started to doze, sitting in her chair in the kitchen as the stock bubbled, when the sound of a car in the driveway startled her. A door slammed, footsteps ground on gravel. No one visited the house; without thinking, she rushed to lock the door.

But it was Suki's face that appeared at the window. She was dressed in a deep, violent magenta, out of place against the silver-greys and greens outside.

'Don't be alarmed,' she said, smiling as Marguerite let her in. 'I've caught you off guard.' She studied Marguerite's face for a moment. 'You've been asleep.'

'No, just – thinking,' she said, rubbing her face.

'Something smells nice.' Suki walked past her into the kitchen, approached the cooker and peered into the casserole. '*Poule au Pot?*'

'Yes.'

'Lovely.' She turned and leant back against the kitchen worktop, smiling, as if she had been there hundreds of times. Marguerite didn't know what to say. She wanted her quiet kitchen back.

'Can I get you something – a glass of water?'

'Oh, please don't trouble yourself. Actually, I can't stay long.' She took a pack of cigarettes out of her bag, and turned to light one on the gas hob. 'I was just passing, and thought I'd come to say hello and see how you're getting on.'

No one passed by the house.

'I'm fine.'

She thought of the cigarette smoke floating through into Jérôme's room.

Suki cocked her head to one side. Her expression wasn't quite friendly, as if it held a challenge.

'Yes? Well, anyway, I thought I'd say hello. And I thought, you're an outsider, I'm an outsider.' She gesticulated vaguely.

'Are you new to the village?'

'Not any more, though I often think I may as well be. I've been here – oh, a long time now. But I'm not from around here originally. Guess where I'm from?'

Marguerite sat down. She didn't want conversation, didn't want Jérôme to be woken by the noise; she wanted to go up to her room and crawl into bed and go back to sleep. And she hated guessing games, the ennui she felt when she contemplated their boundlessness.

'I don't know.'

'Guess!'

'Pakistan?'

'Well, no – Iran. But the right continent, at least. You must be the only person who hasn't guessed Algerian or Tunisian. Everyone just presumes I'm *maghrébine. Maghrébine!* Shit . . .' She rolled her eyes, exhaling a long plume of smoke. 'Oh, can I smoke in here?'

But she was stubbing it out already, in the sink.

'I have to go, I was just dropping by. But you must visit me. I live right next to the doctor's surgery.'

'I can't really leave Jérôme.'

16

'What, you never go into the village? Not even to the library?' She raised an eyebrow. 'Next time, drop by for a coffee. Not before noon, I never wake up before noon.' She walked to the door. 'Goodbye . . . ?'

'Marguerite.'

'That's right. Goodbye, Marguerite.'

She expected to find him asleep when she went into his room to get the book. It was the hour after his lunch; after eating, he almost always fell asleep immediately, as suddenly as a child pretending, his mouth mordantly slack. But today he was lying with the sheets right up to his chin and his eyes wide open, staring at the ceiling. She thought that his look was one of deep fear.

'Don't you know how to knock?' he snapped.

'I'm sorry to have disturbed you. I—'

'You what?'

'I thought you'd be asleep.'

'I see. And so you just wanted to skulk in here and watch me sleeping?'

'Of course not.'

'What did you want then?'

'I wanted to take the book for a few hours.'

'And do what?'

'Read it.'

'Without me?'

'We'd still go back to where we left off.'

'But then you'd be reading those passages twice?'

'Well—'

'Do you think you're humouring me? Is that what you think you're doing?'

'Of course not.' She braced herself for his next question but he looked suddenly weary.

'I'm having some pain.'

'Where?'

'Everywhere.'

'I can't give you more Tramadol.'

'Dolophine.'

'I can't give you that either.' He groaned. 'Let me give you a massage.'

'Don't be ridiculous.'

'I'm not.'

He opened one eye, looked at her warily and closed it again. There was silence, and then: 'All right.'

She approached the bed, pulled the sheet down gently from his chin to his stomach and rubbed her hands together to warm them. Then she pressed his shoulders down, firmly. She didn't rub his skin, she pressed it: his shoulders, his slipped pectorals, the large crown of his thorax. She hummed quietly as she worked.

'Your hands are cold,' he mumbled, his eyes still closed. And then, 'You're always humming.'

'Does it annoy you?'

He didn't answer for a while. She moved her hands to his head, pushed and pressed each side slowly and heavily.

And then, so quietly she could barely hear it, he said: 'No. Not really.'

She lifted his thin left arm, wrapped it in the blood-pressure cuff.

'And?' he asked when it released.

'Fine today. In fact, a little lower than usual. Perhaps you're relaxed from the massage.'

'Hmmm,' he said. And then, meticulously casual, he said: 'You're Parisian, of course.'

'Yes.'

'Why did you leave Paris?'

She sighed as she removed the cuff, the tear of the Velcro the only other sound in the room. 'Why not? It's very beautiful here.'

'But boring. Very boring. Why would you leave Paris to come here? At your age? On your own?'

'Because I wanted to.'

'But why?'

'Why not? This is my job. I came here to work. The position came up, so I applied.'

'But you didn't have to work *here*.'

'No. I can work where I like.'

'So why did you choose here?'

'Why not here?'

'Why not Paris?'

'Because I did,' she snapped. The words came out too loud and too fast. His eyes widened, his shoulders gathered. He watched her intently and she pretended not to notice his gaze, busying herself by going through the drug chart she'd left at the end of the bed. She made a few notes, put the pen in her pocket, made to leave the room.

'I won't ask again,' he said, as she reached the doorway.

She turned around. 'You can ask me whatever you want.'

'Oh, I'm not sure about that.' He closed his eyes, smiling just a little as she turned back around to leave. 'Not sure at all about that.'

2

Henri liked this time of the day the most, when his manual work was largely done and he could afford to slow down a little, to sit on the ground with his back against a fence or wall, feel the scratch of dried grass through his trousers. He could close his eyes and enjoy the thinning of the day's warmth. His hairline was encrusted with sweat; he could rub it, and bits of dirt, and desiccated grass, and what he imagined to be his own refined body salt would fly as if startled into the still twilight air.

The dirt, all of the dirt, was a source of pleasure to him. Meticulous and clean by instinct, he nonetheless enjoyed the day's long accumulation of filth before he headed back to the house on weary legs to take his bath. He dragged the pre-bath moment out as long as possible to build up its eventual release; he would stop at the basin in the kitchen and drink almost an entire beer, usually his only beer of the day, in virtually one go.

Then he climbed slowly into the bathtub that was really too small for his long limbs and he crouched there, only then turning on the taps. He watched the water reach the top of his foot, water that was already swirling brown with dried mud. It reached his ankles, it lifted his large, slack penis. When it reached the base of his back, he started to get to work; he scratched out the dirt embedded behind his nails, scrubbed his long back and torso until they were pink. Then he emptied the bath, rinsed it out, and started again – as many times as it took for the water to be quite clear, long past when it ran hot.

This evening's bath was particularly welcome; today had been hot work. Spring was well underway, the sun swiftly gathering intensity. Henri imagined vaguely the great star's rotation, its heat slowly spreading over Earth, from the Sahara to the Maghreb, over the sea, soaking through the Mediterranean mile by fish-filled mile, reaching the French coast and moving, an inverted shadow, towards the resilient, winter-bitten land around his farm. He had always envisaged it this way, as long as he could remember.

But the bath held a further charm today: the metallic gurgling of the tap, the clunks and creaks the running water set going through the walls of the house, the lightly hissing hum of the rising water level all worked together to drown out the women's voices downstairs. This was one of each week's two or three unannounced visits from Laure, the village *boulangère* and Brigitte's confidante. Returning from the fields this evening, he had caught the small woman's nasal voice just in time to avoid entering the house through the kitchen. That meant no long draught of water, no beer, but it was worth it.

'Henri's bath routine,' he imagined Brigitte saying to Laure in the kitchen below, as she so often did among their friends; 'Henri's *e-lab-o-rate* bath routine.' She tended to give special emphasis to words over three syllables long. 'There are families without water in India and Africa and here is our Henri, using enough water each day to fill an *aquarium*!'

But she also took pride, he knew, in his appearance. When they married, both straight out of school, no one could believe that Handsome Henri – the village's nomenclature, of course, not his own – had chosen Brigitte Arnoult. Plain Brigitte, big Brigitte, dumb Brigitte. Because that was the other thing: Henri was first in the class, always had been. 'A way with words and a head for numbers,' his mother had always said, a regular refrain in the Brochon household as he grew up.

Their courtship and engagement had unfolded quickly. As he leant back in the bath he closed his eyes, imagined his younger self, tall and handsome with his hair combed tidily back, knocking on the Arnoults' door every evening. Every day was the same: he would bow to enter the house through its diminutive doorframe and greet Brigitte's parents, sit down and find his bride-to-be sitting nervously in the gloom. He couldn't imagine now what it was they had found to talk about, sitting each evening in her parents' warm *salon*, drinking milk from her father's cows. Her parents were mistrustful; it was as if he were playing some sly trick.

His own mother had been the first to voice in his presence the question on everyone's lips: 'Henri, for God's sake, why Brigitte?' He hadn't felt cross, or slighted; he had understood her consternation. It's not as if he somehow saw beauty in Brigitte's scant charms – how could he? When he spoke to the girl her face and neck came out in livid purplish patches, she could not meet his eye. He had not failed to notice the great width of her feet, nor the fair but not insubstantial whiskers around the corners of her lips. But there were things about Brigitte that appealed to him that he couldn't explain to his mother, who was so tidily and precisely her opposite.

At eighteen, he chose Brigitte because he liked the silence and reverence she reserved for him, she who was otherwise the loudest and most domineering of girls. He liked her simple way of speaking, her literal reading of everything, her lack of coquetry.

With Brigitte he had sensed refuge, a life left unscrutinised and undisclosed. And hearing her flat, loud voice now rise and fall below the din of the pipes and the water, he had to acknowledge that he had that. In spite of the small-minded prurience with which she had grown to view the rest of the world, despite her endlessly repetitive chiding, he still lived in a home devoid of judgment or enquiry.

He heard one of Laure's whinnying laughs and turned the tap on more fully to drown it out. He leant back against the tub, his legs bent at their extreme right angle in the bath that was too small. He closed his eyes again and rubbed his hands over them, down his cheeks to his mouth; he could taste his salt. Letting his mind drift away from Brigitte, away from Laure, he ran his hands slowly down his body.

Brigitte cracked an egg into a bowl and tilted it to show Laure. 'Do you see the colour of that yolk?'

'There's nothing like your eggs, I always say that.'

'That is the yellowest yolk you can find.'

'You've considered selling your eggs properly, haven't you? You'd put the Bernards right out of pocket.'

'We've got enough on our plate with the dairy and the

24

sheep, we just don't have the scale. Not that you're wrong, of course. You know I'm not one to brag, Laure, but they really do make the very best omelettes. You can tell from an omelette alone how fresh your eggs are.' She continued to crack a further three. 'The secret to a really excellent quiche lorraine is whisking the eggs as long as you can. Whisk them to hell and gone.'

Laure nodded and Brigitte started to whisk with a force she liked to think was almost alarming. 'So Jérôme's latest girl was in the shop again today,' Laure said, 'buying Lanvier's usuals. A baguette and a loaf *aux céréales* to help things get going downstairs . . .' She poked her stomach.

'Laure, you're disgusting,' chided Brigitte, though she loved a good bowel joke as much as the next woman. 'I'm surprised she hasn't been chased away yet, to be perfectly honest.'

'Well apparently not. Though I wouldn't be surprised if she didn't last much longer. She doesn't look like she's cut out for the job.'

'Don't I know it.' Brigitte wiped her hands on her apron and settled her bottom on the edge of a stool. Her ankles ached; she rolled them from side to side. 'She needs a good meal and a stint on the farm. That would sort her out in no time at all.'

'Perhaps I'll throw in a few brioches with her next order – she could do with the extra butter.'

'Do that, then send her my way. I'll show her how we work over here. There's no room for airs and graces when you're having to clear out Vanille's latest blockage.'

Vanille, their eldest cow, had to be 'rectally excavated' – as Henri put it – on a regular basis.

'Forget Vanille's blockages – you'd frighten her away with your egg-whisking alone, Brigitte.'

25

'You bet I would,' Brigitte cried, brandishing the whisk as if to hit Laure with it. She felt a little egg run down her forearm, and wiped it on her stomach.

'I heard she received a visit from our local mystic.'

Brigitte looked up. 'Not Lacourse?'

'None other.'

'I told you how that woman used to turn her eyes at Henri?'

'I could never forget it,' said Laure, who had been there at the time of that great scandal, some fifteen years ago. Nothing had actually happened, but Brigitte had never forgotten Suki's repeated visits to the farm, the stubbed cigarette ends she found in a little pile outside the house, the swish of exotic colours and jangling of metal in her kitchen, and the woman's wretched laugh, false as anything.

'Well let's hope she doesn't get Jérôme's nurse under her wing.'

She poured cream and milk into the bowl.

'Look at that cream,' said Laure.

'Mind you, his nurse won't have time for new friendships. Jérôme's getting worse and worse. He can't move himself any more.'

'And still no sign of his boys?'

'None. They were in touch to give me the bare details of this replacement when the last nurse couldn't hack it any more, and that's the last I've heard from them. Not that I'm surprised. I did tell them a few months back now that he wasn't doing too well and they'd be well advised to come and see him at some point, but they weren't having any of it. They were rather rude, if I'm honest. Told me to get on with my job, and that I was the *gardienne* and not their therapist.'

'I remember. Shockingly rude.'

'I said to Jean-Christophe on the phone – you remember, the youngest – I said, "He is your father, you know," and he told me it was none of my business and that, as I say, I wasn't his therapist.' She let the whisk rest for a moment and wiped her forehead. 'And he's a lawyer! All that education, and still so rude.'

'Well, I'm not surprised really – I suppose he takes after Jérôme. They've always thought they're too good for Saint-Sulpice.'

'Oh, they were such wild boys, don't you remember?'

'How could I not!' said Laure.

'Still, it's dreadfully sad. Their father at death's door and they won't even come and see him.'

A rare silence fell between them. Brigitte stirred bacon into her mixture, and Laure leant over to inspect it. 'Your pigs?'

'That's right.'

They heard water gurgle in the bathroom upstairs; Brigitte rolled her eyes and sighed. She thought again about the nurse: she must go and check in on her and Jérôme. She'd reminded Brigitte of a doll she was given by her uncle as a young girl, which had broken too quickly. She'd been washing its hair and the head just came clean off, with a pop.

This was surely a particularly beautiful evening. As he dried himself, he looked out at his land through the bathroom window. The view was so familiar that he seldom noticed it – no more than the small portrait of Brigitte's mother hanging in the dark corner at the top of the stairs, or the cup above the sink that held their toothbrushes. But today he couldn't help but see: everything was a dark gold, the sun falling but still far from gone, and he could see his herdsman Paul with Thierry, the latest farmhand, still working on the perennially crumbling walls of the olive groves. In this light, only at this point of the day, the silver of the olive leaves was a dark grey – just as only in the searing heat of summer could they appear quite white. The sky was clear and insects whirred and his lone goat let out a shout like a deep hiccup.

He strode over to the window, tucking the towel neatly around his waist, and called out: 'What are you two doing still at work?'

Paul and Thierry looked up immediately, scanning the garden, the porch, trying to find the source of the shout. They were smiling in anticipation. He waved and leant out, feeling with some satisfaction the breadth of his shoulders fill the slim window frame. 'Over here!'

They frowned against the falling light, holding their hands up over their eyes.

'We're just too damn hard-working!'

'We can't get enough!'

Henri laughed theatrically. 'Oh, you can't fool me!' They laughed too and turned back to the wall with some awkwardness, as if uncertain whether the dialogue had ended. He turned too, and his hollow guffawing echoed in his ears, foolish. As he combed his hair in the mirror above the sink he sighed deeply, and his face looked very tired and dull to him then.

'I thought perhaps we could go out today.'

Jérôme turned to look at her, saying nothing.

'It's getting warm,' she said. 'I thought it might do you good to go outside.'

He continued to stare, wearily. Then he turned in bed to face the wall. Marguerite waited for a while, but he remained silent.

'Would you like to?'

'I haven't been outside for over a month.'

'Yes, for at least five weeks,' she said. 'Since before I arrived.'

'You probably expect I don't keep time, just lying here day in day out.'

'No.'

'But I do keep time. I know how long you've been here, I know what day it is. I'm not a prisoner.' He forced out a little laugh. 'I'm not Dantès, raging around his cell with whole years passing by.'

'Of course you're not.'

'I *employ* you. You're not here out of charity.'

'Sir—'

'So don't you think if I wanted to go outside I would have told you to take me out? Or do I strike you as too meek to ask for what I want?'

'No.'

'Perhaps you think I feel like an inconvenience to you.'

Marguerite took a deep breath, waited.

'I suppose you think you're on some mission to rescue a feeble old man from terrible suffering and loneliness.' He turned then in bed, excited. He raised himself up on one elbow. 'I suppose you're living in your own little fairy tale. Our

29

own little Parisian Mother Teresa comes to the countryside to care for a very sad old man who will be eternally grateful.' A fleck of spit had collected at the corner of his mouth. 'Perhaps they'll strike up a wonderfully redemptive friendship and she'll forget all about the shameful life she's running away from and all the people who have rejected her from the day she was born until the day she scurried along to this poor old house. And then the sad little old man will die smiling in her arms, tears twinkling in his eyes.' He licked his lips and stared. 'Isn't that right?'

'No.' Marguerite started to tidy the few belongings on the table. She could feel the whump of her heartbeat; her hands were shaking. 'I was just wondering if you wanted to go outside. I am just doing my job.' She slammed one of the many jars of vitamins down a little too hard. 'I know from your last nurse's handover notes – which, by the way, were entirely perfunctory – that it does you good to get out, and that Doctor Meyer recommends it.'

'Oh, *perfunctory!*' he cried. 'What terribly impressive vocabulary you have, Mother Teresa. Bravo. It must have been that sparkling education you got yourself at nursing school.' She closed her eyes, and he turned back to face the wall. In a low, exhausted voice, he said: 'Now get out please.'

She whispered the words 'fuck you' as she left the room. She walked straight through the kitchen and out into the garden. Now she spoke aloud. '*Fuck you.*' She inhaled deeply, stretched her arms above her head, felt her abdomen pulled from pelvis to ribs. 'Fuck off and die already,' she said, and was surprised to be overcome suddenly with laughter. She bent over to enjoy the sensation, resting her hands on her knees. She felt her hair falling around her face as she laughed. Then she straightened up and rubbed away tears from her eyes.

'I wonder what you'll think, Henri, when you see him. He's gone rapidly downhill.' Brigitte shook her head as she spoke. 'It's very sad.'

'I wasn't thinking I'd go into the house.'

'Weren't you? No, I suppose not.'

'I haven't been in for some time.'

'No, not since – well, I don't know when. Didn't you have to fix his bed that time a few months ago?'

'No, we sent Thierry to do it.'

'That's right.' They had almost reached the village; Brigitte leant forward in her seat to inspect everything. 'That round-about is getting grubbier by the day.'

'Hm,' said Henri.

'It's really a disgrace, actually. I know the weather's only just warming up, but there's no excuse not to have something planted there. Remember when I planted those hydrangeas in the middle?'

'Yes, I think so.'

'Well, those lasted a while at least. But I can't be expected to come to the rescue every time something in the village needs fixing . . . Huh, what a surprise – I can see Fred in the Tabac, already on his second beer of the day, no doubt.' She sniffed, was silent for a moment. 'Laure was saying this new nurse was seen talking to Suki Lacourse,' she said as they passed the Lacourses' house, and she eyed Henri carefully.

31

'Is that right?' He checked the rear-view mirror, indicated to turn right out of the village.

'Well, apparently so. I wonder what someone like that thinks she's doing chatting up some young little nurse.'

'I don't know.'

'Look at the state of that tarmac,' she said, peering out at the battered road leading to Rossignol. 'Well, it seems odd to me. Since she thinks she's such an *intellectual*.'

'Perhaps the nurse is an intellectual too,' he joked lightly; Brigitte snorted.

'I should think not! She hardly seemed capable of stringing two sentences together.'

'Oh dear. Not great company for Jérôme.'

Brigitte was silent for a moment. 'Mind you, you don't have to be an intellectual to be intelligent.'

'No,' said Henri, and he laid his hand over hers. 'Of course you don't.'

Henri pulled the truck into Jérôme's driveway. Rossignol was tired: the once-proud arch stretching high above the gates was covered in rust, the grey paint it used to wear peeling in small patches like sunburnt skin.

'Wait here for a moment,' said Brigitte. 'I'll just check they're both around and awake. If I don't come out in a few minutes, you can presume they are, of course. And pick me up on your way home?'

Henri turned in the driveway and stopped by the tall cypress tree in its centre. It had always been there, as far as he knew. As a boy and young man he had come here often to play with

Jérôme's sons: Marc, Thibault, little Jean-Christophe with his ears like large mushrooms. Henri and his friends would race here from the village on bikes, small stones and flint spraying under their wheels.

He remembered going on expeditions with Thibault, his classmate; they would tie bandanas around their foreheads and take large, pronged skewers into the wild forest around the Lanviers' land. 'We're hunting boar!' they'd shout to Thibault's brothers, refusing to take Jean-Christophe with them despite his pleading. 'You're not big enough yet JC. They might kill you.'

Rossignol had been larger, and grander, and more remote than anyone else's house. When they were teenagers, the surrounding forest was a good place to smoke cigarettes and weed, and get drunk. There was a pool in the garden, long since out of use, into which they'd jump from what felt like lethal distances, hurling themselves in at their most acrobatic angles and dunking each other a little too long.

Yet always hanging over this idyll was the shadow of Jérôme. His sons were terrified of him, even the impossibly grown-up-seeming Marc, whom the whole village seemed to worship. Henri remembered Jérôme coming out to the pool sometimes, in his Speedos, and all the boys falling silent.

'A race?' he'd challenge them. 'Who's man enough for that?'

He'd smile, look around, accept his reluctant contestants. Though not tall, he seemed to the young boys preternaturally strong and fit. And he was, indeed, a faster swimmer – by a breath – than Henri, who was the fastest of them all.

He liked Henri; Henri sensed he approved of him. And so Henri, feeling a little disloyal, liked him back.

'My father's a fucking cunt,' Thibault said once, kicking a wall, fists curled tight by his side and tears in his eyes. Henri felt he could neither agree nor disagree, and said something non-committal; perhaps 'all parents are'. But Thibault had insisted: 'No, you have no idea. My dad's a proper *cunt*.' Then he'd stared accusingly at Henri. 'You don't think so because he likes you. You're exactly what he wishes I was.' And Henri had had to lie.

Brigitte hadn't come out. Henri turned on the engine and made to drive the truck back out onto the road, but he stopped at the sight of a figure standing by the gateway, squinting at him. It was the new nurse, he realised, though he had thought her a teenage boy at first glance. She was younger than he'd imagined, standing long-limbed and straight in plain, even scruffy clothes, her eyes narrowed as she stared at him in the bright sunshine.

He started to wind down the window to introduce himself, but she was already walking swiftly towards the house, keeping a distance from his truck. As she turned the corner of the house to get to the back door, she was the eerie vision of a teenage Thibault.

3

She stood for some time inspecting all the pastries behind the glass. There were glossy chocolate and coffee éclairs, vile-coloured marzipan pigs and frogs that she and her sister used to long for as children. The millefeuilles were impressive, delicately layered and squidgy. There were dark jam tarts, criss-crossed with glistening strands of pastry. It all made her feel a little sick.

She pointed at a pile of *fougasses*.

'Are they plain?' she asked the young woman at the till.

'Yes.'

'No, Julie,' interjected the main *boulangère*, tutting as she looked up from her magazine. She had been reading it standing up, leaning forward onto the counter. Like a hen, thought Marguerite, with her small head, short cropped hair and unusually wide hips. And she blinked a lot, and stared, and jerked her little face just like a chicken. 'That's the garlic and rosemary.'

She watched Marguerite as she paid. Marguerite could feel her small bright eyes on her back as she left, pulling up the hood of her cagoule against the rain.

35

She thought vaguely of going to sit in the library, for something to do, and realised that she was startlingly bored. She couldn't sit anywhere to eat because everything was wet, so she stood under the awning outside one of the closed shops. It appeared to sell pet accessories, exclusively: there were leopard-print dog and cat beds, pink and red and blue collars studded with shiny paw prints. She turned back to the road, the tarmac black with rain. The *fougasse* tasted good. Small crumbs of pastry scattered down her front.

She felt, as always in this village, that she was being observed, though there was hardly anyone around in this weather. And then she heard a whistle. She looked towards it and saw Suki dressed all in black, standing in the doorway of the grand house on the corner, her shoulders a little hunched in the cold. She was beckoning to Marguerite, who could do nothing but cross the street and join her.

'What are you doing out here?' Suki said instead of greeting her. She pushed the door open. 'Come in, come in.'

Inside, the house was dark. Suki led her through a gloomy hallway to the *salon*, switching on table lamps and standing lights. There were strings of coloured bulbs across the old mantelpiece.

'Sit down,' she said, gesturing towards the sofa. 'Will you have tea?'

'I really can't stay.'

'Of course you can.' She walked out of the room, and Marguerite heard her opening and closing cupboards. 'Do you like Persian tea?'

'Yes, I think so.'

The *salon* was a mess. There were heavy, faded curtains

in the same mushroom velvet as the sofa and armchairs. Magazines were piled in columns on either side of the fireplace; there were cardboard boxes around the place filled to bursting, with various words scrawled on them: HOME VIDEOS, PHOTOS MISC., JOURNALS. There were at least eight lamps in a bizarre array of styles: ornate silver antiques, brightly coloured ceramics, a plain beige sphere that could have cost five euros from Auchan. The bookshelves were crammed with cheap-looking paperbacks and chaotic rows of figurines.

'I'm sure you're thinking, *What a mess*,' Suki said as she walked in. Deftly, she kicked magazines off the coffee table to clear a space for the silver tray she was carrying. There was a bowl filled with sugar cubes, a teapot and two matching glasses. The set was exquisitely decorated: dark blue and gold, with tiny pink roses. 'Persian tea is the best in the world. But I'm sure you know that.'

She sat down in the armchair opposite Marguerite, tucking her feet beneath her. She lit a cigarette, exhaled. 'So, you never came to visit me,' she said.

'Sorry – I've been so busy with Jérôme.'

'No apologies,' she said, raising her hands. 'You're under no obligation.' She looked around the room. 'A little different from Rossignol, hm?'

'Yes.'

'I can't live without clutter. It must be in my blood or something. It drives Philippe insane.'

'Is that your husband?' asked Marguerite.

'The one and only.' Suki stood to pluck a photo frame from the mantelpiece, which she handed to Marguerite. She started to pour the tea, all the time balancing her cigarette between two immaculate fingers, its long train of ash undisturbed.

The photograph showed a younger Suki grinning up at a plain, bored-looking man in a suit.

'He looks – nice,' said Marguerite.

'Fat,' Suki said immediately. 'He's so damn fat now. That was taken when he was still young and handsome.' She smiled, finally flicking ash into a little dish. 'Drink your tea.'

Marguerite took a sip.

'Isn't it wonderful?' Suki said. 'Of course, the water should be heated in a samovar. That's the traditional way. But now tell me how you're liking your new job. Or is it new? You've been here some time, I suppose.'

'Almost six weeks.'

'Six weeks! What do you do all day? Aren't you bored?'

'No – it's very busy.'

'I suppose that's a good thing. Keeping busy. Well, six weeks isn't long enough to get really, truly sick of the place. I moved here in '84. So what's that, eighteen years now? I'm no use at maths. All I know is that it's been a long time.'

'Where did you live before?'

'Marseille. Tehran, then Hilversum in the Netherlands, then Marseille. So I was used to life in a big city. I'm like you, I'm a city girl by nature. I'm not made for all this.' She gestured at the window behind her and grimaced. 'How old do you think I am?'

'Oh, I never get this question right.'

'Guess!' she insisted. 'I won't be offended.' She lifted her chin, turned her face a little.

'Twenty-nine,' said Marguerite, lying.

'Thirty-eight!' she cried. 'People are always tricked by my skin, I don't have any wrinkles. Even though I smoke like a chimney, I've got not a single wrinkle. It's genetic.' She leant forward for Marguerite to inspect her face, pulled with one finger at the skin around her eyes. Her eyeballs were a little pink. 'See?'

There were lines, of course, but it was true that her skin was smooth. It seemed polished. Marguerite leant back so Suki didn't inspect hers.

'Anyway, so I married Philippe when I was twenty and came to this little dump. He was very rich, and handsome – you've seen the photo – and I thought I was going to have a terribly romantic life in the countryside. Instead, I sit here all day whilst he works in a technology park. A technology park!' She smiled, looking down at her hands. Her nails were the palest pink, immaculately painted. 'It's not quite the glamorous set-up I had imagined, as you can see.'

'Well, look at my set-up,' said Marguerite. 'I'm aware it's not what most people would choose.'

Suki lit another cigarette. 'And no doubt Jérôme treats you like absolute crap,' she said.

'No, he's fine.'

'Okay, I know what you're like. You're not going to admit it. Very professional. But everyone knows that he's a tyrant.' She topped up their glasses. 'Just a little more,' she said. 'And I suppose you've met the *gardienne*? Brigitte?'

'Yes, of course.'

'And?' She looked sharply at Marguerite. 'All your evil spinster great-aunts rolled into one, right?'

'Well . . .' She paused. 'She's quite stern.'

Then she thought of the woman's visit two days before and felt freshly irritated. Brigitte had walked around the ground floor, inspecting how clean it was. She had peered at the food in the fridge and cupboards, enquired into Jérôme's diet, asked questions about his medication that were nothing to do with her.

'Actually, she's terrible,' she said, and Suki threw her head back and laughed.

'Still waters run deep,' she cried. 'I knew you couldn't be as sweet as you seem. You're right, of course. She *is* terrible. She can't stand the sight of me. In fact, she can't stand the sight of any good-looking female – that's probably why she's nasty to you.'

'I really doubt that.'

'Stop being modest. Look at you! So young. What are you? Twenty-five?'

'Twenty-four.'

'And look at your little waist!' She reached forward as if to pinch Marguerite's waist, but Marguerite wrapped her arms around herself. 'Are you naturally slim or do you diet?'

'I really can't stay,' she said.

'Won't you wait for the rain to stop?'

'I really can't, I have to cook Jérôme's dinner. It's getting late.'

'Don't be silly. I'll give you a tour of the house.'

She stood up and took Marguerite's glass from her hands, putting it down on the table. Then she took one of her hands – her own were smooth, warm from holding the glass – and started to take her through to the kitchen.

Marguerite resisted, pulling her hand out of Suki's grip.

'Please, I would love to see it next time. But Jérôme will wake up and he might be in pain. I have to be there.'

Suki pursed her lips and cocked her head to one side. Then she smiled. 'Okay then,' she said. 'But make sure next time is soon.'

Marguerite was glad to get out of the heat and gloom. In the sullen white light and rain, her stomach uncomfortably full of pastry and tea, she walked home at her briskest pace, almost a jog. The forest on either side of her dripped and crackled like fire.

She could hear Jérôme as soon as she opened the back door, banging repeatedly on his headboard. She dropped her wet jacket and ran through to his room, the stench of shit hitting her before she entered. It was formidable, a wall of smell.

She breathed hard through her mouth as she took him in her arms and raised him up onto his feet. He was wailing quietly, his mouth puckered.

'Let's get you to the bathroom.'

'Where were you?' he cried as they shuffled towards the door.

'Getting food from the village.'

'I don't understand it, I just woke up and it had happened.'

'It can happen to anyone.' She lowered him onto the bidet, removed his pyjama bottoms and was hit afresh by the stench, its unmistakable acrid sweetness. She tried not to look as she folded them roughly, flinging them into the sink. She wiped and cleaned him in the bidet, something he could usually do himself. But he was limp, leaning forwards onto

41

her, his face between her shoulder and neck. His head was very heavy.

'I don't understand,' he said again.

'Don't worry. These things happen.'

He was silent, letting her take his full weight. When she had cleaned him, she pushed him back gently so that he leant against the wall.

'Are you feeling all right? Can you sit like this while I get you clean pyjamas?'

He didn't answer. He sat there with his mouth drawn down, staring at the floor.

She took away the soiled pyjamas, threw them in the battered, ancient washing machine in the utility room. The smell still hung everywhere. When she went back into the bathroom, he would not look at her.

'Would you like a bath?' He nodded slowly. He sat there, naked from the waist down, knees knocked together, hands in his lap as if to cover himself. She wrapped a towel around his shoulders and pulled him up to stand again, very gently, so that he could sit more comfortably on the disintegrating wicker chair in the corner of the room.

'Strong,' he whispered.

'I'm sorry?'

He paused. 'I said you're strong, for a girl.'

She smiled. 'Yes, I suppose.'

She turned the taps on at full force. She fetched vanilla essence from the kitchen and dropped it into the rising water. When the tub was full, she helped him in, folding a towel under his head as he rested back.

'I'll be right next door, making dinner. Just call if you need anything.'

He was silent for a moment, but as she left the room he cleared his throat. 'I suppose the sun is starting to set.'

She stopped. 'Yes.'

'It will get dark soon enough.' He crossed his arms in the water, looked down at his hands. 'Dark, dark, dark.'

'Perhaps I could stay for a short while,' she said, 'and read some of our book.'

He lifted his chin, pursed his lips and gazed at his toes at the end of the bath. 'Well, all right. If that's what you'd like to do.'

That night, in one of her nightmares, she found a small black runt of a kitten with milky eyes; she held it in both hands, wrapped in a blanket. It shivered all over, its little chest bouncing with each heartbeat. She had to find it somewhere to sleep and regain its strength before it was too late, but she couldn't find anywhere safe for them. There were other cats, strong cats, prowling around the barn they were hiding in.

Then she realised that the blanket was smeared with shit; it was all over the kitten too, its fur slick with it. It had collected in the delicate apertures of its ears and around its muzzle. The kitten opened its tiny mouth wide and Marguerite wiped frantically to stop the faeces seeping in.

Disorientated on waking, it was her sister's shit-caked trousers she thought of, not Jérôme's. Until she could wake herself properly and push her memories away, she was cleaning her sister's small thighs and bottom; it was Cassandre's hot head hanging dully on her shoulder, Cassandre's hot arms wrapped around her neck.

She held her pillow to her, squeezing it as tight as she could. 'Cassandre, Cassandre, Cassandre,' she said, over and over, an incantation to keep her safe, as she had done so many times in the quiet of the night.

She spent the morning cooking. It was still raining, though it had abated a little. She had no urge to go anywhere. Jérôme had slept particularly badly, calling her down repeatedly to attend to him. The intervals of sleep she snatched felt febrile, and she woke every time he knocked, or every time a nightmare built to its climax, covered in cold sweat. It collected in a pool between her breasts; her back and shoulders were wet to touch.

He had not eaten his breakfast, and had fallen into a deep sleep after she took the untouched tray away. She had a dull and protracted conversation on the phone with the village doctor, going through Jérôme's repeat prescriptions. When she had finished she went through to the kitchen and prepared a dish she'd learnt as a teenager from their au pair: chicken in a creamy sauce with rice, a sort of English *poule au riz*. She and Cassandre had always loved it, its delicious blandness. Then she made a tart, the lemons stinging her cuticles where they had grown rough and ragged.

There was a low fog; the rain pattered continually, punctuated by the odd torrent coming down from where it collected in the tiles above. She wondered whether the entire roof was made up of Jérôme's tiles, since that had been his business. When she'd met his adult son for her interview, in his glistening office in Paris, he had called the family business, which had gone back for generations until Jérôme sold it, a 'tile empire'. She smiled faintly at the thought of Jérôme as the Tile Emperor. She imagined him standing in a factory amidst piles of tiles, wearing a braided jacket with epaulettes and a gleaming black bicorn on his head. Then she remembered his feeble form in the bath as she'd read to him the night before, and stopped smiling.

She'd opened a bottle of wine to make the sauce, one of five bottles she'd found in one of the cupboards, capped in dust. Now, looking out at the greyness outside, she poured a glass for herself, and the glug the wine made brought her back to some vague memory she couldn't place, an indefinable levity. She sat in her chair and held the glass to her nose, inhaling the earthy, foresty smell. She tried to imagine for a moment that she was in Paris. The pattering of the rain helped to hide the countryside's absence of traffic, voices, sirens. She tried to imagine she was sitting alone in a café where no one knew her and she had nowhere to be.

'What am I doing?' she muttered, and then felt self-conscious, as if she were acting. A plump robin landed on the window ledge and looked in, its head cocked. I'm here, she thought, not in Paris. There's nothing there for me. She took a long sip of wine. This is what I wanted.

She woke up to sounds in the garden. She had a headache and a stale taste in her mouth. Quickly, she got up from the armchair she had been curled up in, and as she stood all the blood in her body seemed to rush, pounding, to collect in her right temple. Pressing one cool palm against it, she heard the clinking sounds again, and a male voice. She looked around, still disorientated, and snatched up the wine bottle and glass, putting them away in a cupboard. Then she went to the door, trying to see through the drizzle and gloom.

There were two young men outside with a wheelbarrow and spades, a few large sacks of manure or earth standing beside them. They were buttoned up against the rain, hooded cagoules fastened to let only their faces show. She locked the door and let her forehead rest against the cool glass; it soothed her head.

Then another man came around the corner from the drive, and they were face-to-face through the glass. Startled, Marguerite stepped back. He jerked his head back a little, as if startled too. He wasn't wearing his hood up, like the other two; even through the glass, and with a metre or so between them, she could see the tiny glass-like bubbles of rain covering his face and hair.

He raised his hand and smiled, signalling an unspecific question – could she let him in, could she open the door, could she come outside? Hesitantly, she unlocked and pulled the door open, not all the way, and stood in the gap.

'I'm sorry to come unannounced,' he said. 'Henri Brochon.' He said his name as if she was supposed to know it, and held a hand out to shake hers. She took it, again with hesitation. It was warm and his grip firm; she looked down quickly at their hands together, hers pale yellow against his brown.

'I'm Brigitte's husband.' He paused. 'Brigitte, the *gardienne*.'

'Yes, of course.' She held her hand to her temple again to try to stop it throbbing. The pain was spreading behind her right eye. 'I'm sorry, I wasn't expecting anyone.'

'No, I'm sorry – Brigitte said she would call you. She asked me to have a look at the oak at the bottom of the garden. She said it's struggling.'

'Yes.' Marguerite tried desperately to think of something to say. 'I thought it might be dying. Do you look after the garden here?'

'No, I'm a farmer. But I can spare the boys for a few hours. Brigitte doesn't have permission to employ a gardener for the Lanviers, but she's responsible for keeping the place running so we do what we can.'

'I see.' She wondered when she had ever said 'I see' to anyone. She waited, and then it occurred to her that he was waiting for her to say something. 'Did you want something?' she said, and then, realising that might sound rude: 'A glass of water? Or do the –' She hesitated to call them 'boys'. 'Do they want some coffee?'

'No, they're fine. I'm going to leave them here for a bit, so let them know if you think of anything else that needs doing. Is everything working okay in the house?' He looked over her shoulder into the kitchen.

'Actually, there are a couple of things,' she said, more to break the silence than because she wanted anything fixed. 'I'll let them know.'

'I can have a quick look now,' he said, stepping forward, but she didn't move. 'Shall I come in?'

'Okay.' She opened the door reluctantly, stepped back into the kitchen. She watched as he crouched down to remove his wet boots. He wore thick, ribbed green socks. They looked very clean and new for a farmer.

'There's a lamp I can't work – here,' she said, leading him to the standing lamp in the corner of the kitchen, by the chair she'd been sleeping in just a few minutes earlier. She eyed the rumpled blanket and indented cushions, hoping he wouldn't notice. 'I've changed the bulb, but I think the whole thing might be broken.'

He nodded. 'Anything else?'

'Well, I can only get two of the gas rings to work on the cooker.'

She didn't want to tell him the other things now; they seemed insignificant and intimate. A broken chair in her bedroom that she didn't need to sit on anyway; the wardrobe door that had come off its hinges and that she had just left resting against the wall instead.

'Let me have a look at these then.' He walked out of the kitchen, into the house, and she scanned the surfaces quickly, wondering how it looked. He came back with a toolbox she hadn't known existed. He didn't look at her but got straight to work on the gas rings and she waited there, unsure what to do. She couldn't leave the kitchen, she couldn't just sit there doing nothing. She switched the kettle on: an old, yellowed electric kettle like the one her au pair had brought from England.

'Would you like coffee?' she asked to his back.

'I'm fine, thank you,' he said, turning only briefly to speak. He bent over the cooker, fiddling with something. He was tall, his shoulders broad; the kitchen felt very small then. She turned and opened a cupboard, rearranging things that didn't need arranging. The kettle's foolish crackling and rumbling started to rise steadily towards boiling, the sound dominating the room. Henri removed his jacket, turning to hang it carefully over a chair. His sweater was also green, green like his eyes and his socks. She wondered if he matched them intentionally.

Finally, the kettle clicked and steam rose. She made a cup of tea she didn't want.

'I'll be right back,' she said, and left the room. She didn't look in on Jérôme; if he was awake, she didn't want to have to explain that there was someone in the house. She went to go upstairs but realised Henri might have to come and find her when he had finished, so instead she sat at the bottom of the stairs and blew into the cup. Steam met her face; she closed her eyes.

It was always strange to be back in the house; practically nothing had changed. Henri could remember countless breakfasts at this kitchen table, when he had stayed the night as a young boy. Madame Lanvier made elaborate breakfasts for her household of males, and she gave the boys coffee. Henri hadn't liked the taste but had drunk it nonetheless because it made him feel mature. He would never have been allowed coffee at home, not at that age.

The kitchen was just as tidy now as it had always been under Madame Lanvier's constant domestic surveillance. He couldn't remember her without picturing her wiping surfaces or washing things. When he was very young, he had watched her hang the family's washing on three lines in the olive groves. He remembered standing against the warm stones of the house, watching her bend heavily to take white sheets from the basket, standing to hang them, very slowly, smoothly, even rhythmically. When she had gone back to the house, he had run over and hidden between the walls of hanging sheets. He'd stood there in a cool, dazzlingly fragrant tunnel of white, until he heard Thibault calling him to some game or other.

His own home had been very dull by comparison. Without siblings, each room was his to enter; there was no friction, no chaos. His mother, adoring, intuitive, had few reprimands for the son she admired without reservation. His father, the best farmer for miles, was a largely silent presence. When Henri wasn't studying, his father taught him, often wordlessly, how to set the cows up for milking, how to nurse suckling runts, how to lop the heads off chickens. The sound of animals and machinery, but little else, had suffused their home. How exotic, then, had Rossignol seemed: the three brothers always fighting or laughing, the great quantities of food consumed, the crude jokes, farts and burps. The chaos would be punctuated and compounded by Jérôme's high-octane outbursts, his fist slamming against the table and doors banging closed after him. Amidst all this Céline Lanvier moved calmly with her slow, gentle force.

He put his tools down and tried the gas ring he'd just fixed; it hissed briefly and then burst into controlled blue flame. A beautiful, electric blue. He turned the gas off and took his tools over to the lamp to rewire the plug, a quick and easy job that most women he knew would have managed with ease.

When he was finished, he put the tools away and the nurse appeared, as if she had been waiting just outside.

'It's all done,' he said, putting on his jacket and boots.

'Thank you.'

'Do let Brigitte know if anything else comes up. It's our

job to keep the place going. I'm sure you're busy enough with your patient.'

'Yes, of course.'

He waited for a moment, wondering if she would say anything else, but she simply looked back at him, very serious.

'The boys will be here for a little while so if you think of anything else, just let them know.'

'Thank you.'

She turned and started to busy herself taking tins out of a cupboard. Henri watched her for a moment, the muscles of her arms flickering under the skin as she moved. He let himself out.

He stood in the drizzle, watching Thierry and his younger brother, Rémy, working in the distance. He let his vision blur a little, trying to imagine they were the young men he had seen so many times here in the past. Marc Lanvier, Jean-Christophe, Thibault. But the Rossignol of his childhood was a place of sunshine and heat; he found it difficult to reconcile that with the grey scene in front of him.

'I'll be back in a couple of hours, okay?' he called out, and they turned and called back, faces small in their hooded jackets. He walked back to the truck quickly, and thought about the nurse as he started the engine and drove out. The place was so cut off, Jérôme so difficult, and she so young. He couldn't imagine what she was doing here.

'Who was here?'

Marguerite placed a slice of the lemon tart by Jérôme's bed, and he stared at it.

'What's that?'

'Lemon tart.'

'It looks vile.'

'You don't have to eat it.'

He picked at it with his fingers, tasted it with a laboured show of reluctance. 'Who was here?'

'When?'

'You know when. I heard a man's voice. I heard you talking to a man.'

She remained silent, took his free arm to take his blood pressure. She always enjoyed the puffing sound of the pump. It reminded her of blowing up balloons.

'Well?' he snapped.

'Monsieur Brochon came here.'

'Henri! He was in the house!' Jérôme smiled, his mouth full of tart, and she watched him carefully. It was the first time she'd seen him look somewhere near happy, even fond. 'A great man. Why didn't you send him in?'

'He didn't ask.'

'Well, that's because he will have presumed I was resting. Next time, send him in. This is my house, you know.'

'I know.'

He eyed her as he chewed. 'Handsome man, Henri, isn't he?'

She turned to put the cuff and pump away. 'Your blood pressure's a little high today,' she said.

'Isn't he?'

'I didn't notice.'

'You must have noticed.'

She took the empty plate from him, brushing crumbs of pastry from his belly onto it.

52

'So the tart wasn't quite so vile,' she said and he scowled.

'Disgusting,' he said. 'Far too sweet.'

She rolled her eyes as she walked out of the room.

'Woman!' he shouted after her, but she ignored him, entered the kitchen and ate a large slice of tart standing up by the counter. It was delicious.

4

Henri leant against the fence, watching Cédric as he examined Vanille. At eighteen, Vanille was his oldest cow and the only one to have a name. She had not been able to produce milk for many years, but Henri couldn't let her go. 'He loves that old thing more than me,' Brigitte would often chide, which irritated him because his loyalty to Vanille felt more elemental than sentimental. It might sound ridiculous – he could guess perfectly well what Paul, or indeed anyone, would think if he knew – but she was the last link between the farm he had now and the farm he had inherited when his father retired. The place had done well under her vigil. It had mutated and expanded, a little colony of industry; Vanille and the house itself were the only things that remained the same.

And now she was ill – slothlike, heavy, sad. He looked at Cédric, trying to read his face. Henri had no instinct for sickness.

'It's not a blockage this time,' Cédric said after a while. 'I can't find anything up there.'

The men stood in silence for a little while. Henri stepped towards Vanille, resting one hand on her head. She didn't flinch, looking up at him blankly, her eyeballs marbled pink.

'Probably just time she went on her way,' Cédric said. Henri let go of her head, resting his palm under her muzzle for her to smell. 'She's what, fifteen by now?'

'Eighteen.' Henri looked into his friend's eyes. They were still their old, deep blue, but Henri noticed his wrinkles now, how deeply they were scored. They had been two of the brightest boys at school; Henri could still remember clearly Cédric going off to Grenoble to study veterinary science, how glamorous that had seemed. 'It couldn't be urinary?'

'Her piss ran normal.'

'Ah.'

'How many productive years did you get out of her?'

'A lot. Ten, perhaps?'

Cédric whistled. 'You're lucky to get more than three these days.' He laid his hand gently on Vanille's back. 'She's done you proud.'

'My girls are all right. They're not a bad lot.' Henri looked at the rest of the herd, grazing calmly, indifferent to the two men.

'Well,' Cédric said, packing up his things, 'I'm afraid I can't find anything. It might be cancer but let's call it old age. At this point it's the same thing really.'

Henri nodded. 'Nothing we can do?'

'I wouldn't say so.' The vet ran his hand again over the big knuckles of her spine and smiled gently. 'They won't get much meat off her.'

'Oh, I won't bother with all that.' Henri stroked one of her ears; she stood there dumbly, not even grazing. He couldn't send her away to die.

'Are you staying out here?' Cédric asked, and Henri nodded. 'I'll see myself out. Send my regards to Brigitte. I'll see you soon.'

They shook hands and Cédric turned and started back towards the farmhouse. Henri watched him go, his figure dark against the pale morning. He turned to Vanille and stroked her muzzle again.

'You pretty old thing,' he said. Then he climbed over the gate; he had to get to work.

The air was warming already: it would be hot work today. The cicadas had started, he hadn't noticed when. It was the same each year, their chorus insinuating its way into the fabric of the days without fuss or ceremony. Once it was there, it was difficult to imagine how silence sounded without it.

Henri turned back as he walked to look at Vanille; she was still watching him. She knew.

'Good God,' Jérôme said when she brought his breakfast. She had barely slept in the night, imagining sounds and the sly movement of human shapes against the black shadows of the trees outside her room. Jérôme was already sitting up in bed, a manoeuvre he managed with difficulty alone; unlike her, he appeared to have had an unusually good night, calling only once for pain relief. 'You look like you've spent the night in a cave.'

'Thank you,' she said, and he laughed. The sound – a real laugh, not a harsh little bark for effect – was so surprising that she turned from arranging his medication to look at him.

He was smiling, his eyes bright, a different creature altogether from the day before.

'But you have slept well.'

'Very well,' he said, tugging at the sheets with a little excitement. 'Like a baby.'

She watched him as he ate, the grinding cogs of his old jaw as he chewed. Sunlight poured through the window onto the foot of his bed. The wind had blown away the rain; the clouds dotting the sky outside were white and bilious.

'Today, I'll go outside,' he said when he'd finished.

'Fine,' she said. She thought with weariness of the effort it would entail. 'Of course.'

'It looks like a good day.'

'It's pretty sunny,' she said. 'It might be a bit cold, but I'll bring blankets.'

'And it'll do me good. As you say.'

'Yes. We can go after your nap.'

'Why wait?' he said brightly. 'Let's go now.'

She brought his wheelchair into the room. It was old-fashioned, more like a grand piece of garden furniture than a wheelchair. She could imagine it carrying young wartime convalescents around country houses in England, or frail, wealthy women in resorts in Switzerland. Marguerite was accustomed to sitting patients up in their chairs for eight hours a day, or as long as their skin could take it; it was crucial to prevent pressure sores and the build-up of fluid in immobile chests. But Madame Brochon had dismissed her request for a modern chair – another thing for which she had apparently not been allocated expenses – and Marguerite relied on bed positioning and the armchair in the bedroom to keep Jérôme upright.

When she wheeled it into the room he scowled, his first unpleasant look of the day. 'I don't need that thing!'

Marguerite stopped. She felt drunk with exhaustion. 'How else do I take you out?'

'You help me walk, it's no different to taking me to the bath or the lavatory. Take the armchair out instead, I'll sit in that. I hate this contraption, I don't need it.'

She lifted him from the bed and they shuffled together through the corridor, the utility room, the kitchen, stopping occasionally so that he could rest against a wall or surface and she could catch her breath. His arm around her neck made her stoop, the long bone of his forearm tight against her throat.

When they got out of the house, he stopped, looking up, breathing hard. The sunshine fell white on his face. They continued to shuffle together, until they reached two particularly old-looking olive trees.

'Here,' he said. She lowered him to sit on the edge of a terrace wall while she went back into the house to fetch the armchair in which she often dozed in the kitchen. She set it down between the two trees and lowered him into it, laid blankets over his lap and chest, asked if he needed a hat.

'I want to feel the sun on my face,' he said.

Marguerite was warm and breathless from exertion. It was still a little windy; the breeze cooled her skin and rustled the silver leaves of the olives. She laid another blanket over the ground by his chair and sat down.

'This is where the washing used to hang,' he said quietly. She looked at him; he looked calm, gazing at nothing.

'Yes?'

He didn't respond. She wondered what ghosts he was seeing right now. A woman, his children, his own younger self. Friends, visitors, maybe lovers. Then she let herself think of home for a moment. Frances, their English au pair, hanging washing in the large spare bedroom. Marguerite hanging a towel over the tops of two chairs so that she and Cassandre could sit under their own little roof; Frances singing funny-sounding songs to them in English, 'Little Miss Muffet', 'Hickory Dickory Dock' with its guttural heft. Marguerite and Cassandre playing *escargot* on their large balcony, taking care to wash the chalk off the ground before their mother came home. Hopping, marking their own squares with their initials, Marguerite always winning. MD, MD, MD, CD, MD.

She looked at Jérôme and wondered about his own painful memories. A man like him must have reams of them. She thought of the son who had interviewed her for the job: evasive, hasty, a little pleased with himself. That unique combination of infallible politeness and unidentifiable rudeness that she had come to recognise in nearly everyone with a privileged background, a background like her own.

He hadn't made a secret of his dislike for his father, though he hadn't openly mentioned it. He'd emphasised that the job wouldn't be easy, that Jérôme had had many nurses leave and that they needed someone who would stick it out. He'd also emphasised that there would be no one else around, no one at all. Marguerite had wanted the silence then, though she was aware now that she had underestimated it. She'd also needed the money – the salary they were paying more than justified the fact that the job was 24/7, without respite.

And of course, crucially, it was far away from Paris. Her

mother and father hadn't tried to contact her when she'd been nursing in Picardy, but they had known she was there. Now – unless they made a little effort, which she doubted they would do – they'd be gratefully unaware that she was here in the Languedoc, surrounded by miles of rural silence, with a dying old man for company.

'I have three sons, you know,' Jérôme said, and Marguerite sat up; she felt eerily as if her thoughts had permeated his.

'Yes, I know.'

'I suppose you met the youngest, Jean-Christophe.'

'Yes.'

'The lawyer.' He looked at her. 'I'll bet he could barely give you five minutes of his time? It's a strange way to work, being paid by the minute. I'm not sure it can do anything except make you think your company is too valuable to share around.'

Marguerite nodded. She had often thought this about her own father.

'And then I have two others. Marc and Thibault. Three sons and me, can you imagine what it was like when we all lived under one roof?' He smiled wryly. 'Poor Céline.'

'Was Céline your wife?'

'Yes.'

'The only woman in a house full of boys.'

He shot her a glance, his softness dissolved. 'Well, I'm sure it was fine. She had nothing to complain about, nothing at all.' He looked at her again, checking for a response, and Marguerite nodded. 'I gave her this house – you might not believe it now, but it was very grand. And I gave her everything she could ask for.'

'I'm sure,' Marguerite said.

'Oh, she had nothing to complain about. You get all kinds of women – and men now, too – complaining, complaining, complaining. Giving a woman a great house, giving your kids skis and expensive bicycles and language tuition, that's not enough. They'll still find something to complain about.' He shook his head, frowned. 'But not Céline. She never complained, not once.'

Marguerite had cooled down a little; she pulled a blanket around her shoulders.

'Are you warm enough?' she asked.

Jérôme turned to look at her again. 'If you ever get married,' he said, 'you'll do well not to listen to any of the crap you pick up in magazines and on television. What men want is a woman with sense and patience. We might think we want the red racing car but we don't really, not in the long run. We need an engine that will keep us going.'

'That isn't a very romantic metaphor.'

'What do you know about metaphors?' he snapped. 'Or romance.'

'I know plenty about both,' she said, irritated, but her words sounded foolish as soon as she'd spoken them. A child trying to show her parents that she's grown up. Jérôme merely grunted.

'Really. Well, your literature teacher must have been terribly disappointed when you chose to become a carer.'

'I'm a nurse.'

'What a difference.'

Marguerite closed her eyes tight, breathed deeply to try to quieten the thudding in her chest. Then she opened them. 'Was working in a tile shop intellectually demanding?'

Jérôme's neck bulged as he turned to stare at her. His eyes were wide; an immediate colour had spread across his face. 'Would you like to repeat that?'

'No.'

'I'm asking you to repeat it.'

'I don't think you misheard me.'

He blinked. 'Have you forgotten that you're working for me?'

'No, I haven't.' She felt the insult of tears forming; she was too exhausted for confrontation. But she couldn't face backing down. 'That's why I don't think it's right that you should insult me constantly.'

'Well! I don't think it's right that you should answer back. Don't forget, just one word from me and you'll be gone, out of here.'

'With pleasure,' she said, very quietly.

'What did you say?'

She didn't answer and he watched her, intently, his shoulders up near his ears. She ignored the crawling of an insect on her neck, determined not to look away, and there was total silence between them as they stared. Then a magpie rattled and Jérôme broke his stare, let out a harsh little laugh. 'You're funny,' he said. 'You know I was just teasing you? You mustn't let me get under your skin.'

'I don't.'

'I was just having a joke.'

'Okay.'

He was watching her again, eyes sharp above his smile.

'And as I'm sure you know, I didn't "work in a tile shop". I owned an extremely profitable business.'

Marguerite didn't reply; she shrugged the blanket from around her shoulders, warm again from the adrenaline. She felt the thud in her chest subside, slowly.

Jérôme laughed again, a laugh that didn't seem wholly forced.

'A tile shop,' he repeated. 'You're very funny.'

The milking clusters detached from the cows' udders and withdrew, clanking and swinging. Henri sanitised the cows' teats, pink and engorged, thin lines of milk still trickling from them like the white sap from figs. He opened the gate for the cows to move slowly out, lowing and nodding as they walked, and then he called Thierry in from the yard to hose the parlour down. When the young man had taken over, Henri pulled off his thick rubber gloves and rinsed them. He would change out of his milky overalls before he saw to Vanille. He didn't want to taunt her with the smell of her youth.

Back in the house, he changed into a fresh shirt and jeans and sat in the study to get some paperwork done. It wasn't urgent, but he needed delay. He went through the accounts for perhaps fifteen minutes until he knew he could no longer put it off. Then he stood up, walked straight out of the house, taking his shotgun, glimpsing Brigitte through the kitchen door and ignoring her as she called out. He strode out to the pasture, where the cows had already settled back into grazing.

Thierry sat with the calves now, feeding them formula, and he looked up and then down at the gun. His head bobbed back slightly, like a tic, and he looked at Henri questioningly, with some alarm, opening his mouth to speak. Henri didn't acknowledge him.

He held the gun behind his back as he approached Vanille, only now slowing his pace. She blinked.

'Come on, my beautiful lady,' he said. 'Beautiful lady.' He let her smell his hand, and she rubbed it. 'Come on,' he said more loudly, even tersely, so that Thierry might hear. Then he led her away, her awkward, rocking gait making him tread more slowly than he could bear. He needed to do it now, could already feel his resolve slipping. Now Thierry had seen him, he had to go through with it. He couldn't turn around and wait until tomorrow.

She was docile, infinitely trusting; he got her with ease into the old stable nestled at the corner of the next field. Standing there beside her, he had to wipe tears from his eyes and cheeks.

'You bloody fool. Get a grip.'

He kissed her head and took it in his hands, turning it so that she was facing out of the doorway, out to the fields. She stared out obediently, not turning even when he loaded the gun. Her cheeks sagged like old elastic; she nodded a little, reflexively. He cocked the gun, took the barrels to her head and pulled the trigger. She dropped in an instant, heavy as concrete. He didn't look at the ground. A fine mist of warm blood settled over his face.

He pressed the heels of his hands into his eyes, pressed until it hurt. Then he wiped his face with his sleeves and strode from the pen, passing Thierry as he made for the house.

'Call the knackerman to come and get rid of that,' he said, gesturing behind him. He didn't look at him, or the cows, or down at the blood he imagined must cover his body. He sensed a silent terror around him, suffusing the pre-twilight air. Everything was silent. Even the cicadas stopped suddenly, for just one second.

Brigitte set his dinner in front of him: lamb and potatoes, and a tall glass of water.

'Busy day?' she asked, but he didn't respond. 'I've finished the feed orders for the pigs and chickens. I found a new merchant, we'll be saving a couple of hundred euros a year.'

'That's great,' Henri said, getting up from the table to get another beer from the fridge. She watched him, glanced down at the bottle in his hand as he opened it. 'Three beers isn't very much, Brigitte.'

'I didn't say anything.'

'Good.' He sat down and took a long draught straight from the bottle. She didn't like that but he knew she wouldn't say anything. Ordinarily, she might tease him – 'farmer by name, farmer by manners' – but he knew that she knew not to do that tonight. He almost wanted her to try.

They sat in silence for a while as she started to eat. When Brigitte felt uncomfortable, she affected a daintiness as she ate that annoyed him. As if the bald eagerness of her darting fork could be mitigated by the small volume of food she picked up each time; or this rare show of delicacy, the repeated wipes of her napkin to each corner of her lips, make her appear less greedy.

'How's Paul's shoulder?' she asked.

'I don't know, he was in Montpellier today.'

'Well I do hope he's seen a physio.' He could hear the moistness of her chewing. 'I wonder how Thierry's mother is.'

'Why?'

'Because she's been ill.'

'What, with a cold or something.'

'Not a cold, Henri. She's had scarlet fever.'

'Scarlet fever?' He leant back and let his chair tip backwards, which he knew she hated. 'What is this, the nineteenth century?'

She frowned; she became embarrassed when he brought up any period of history she couldn't remember from school. As far as he could tell, that left them with only the most superficial smattering of the Revolution to discuss with any ease.

'Well that's what it was,' she said. 'Laure says she's been awfully ill. I did mean to go round there with some things but you know how busy it's been these last few days.'

'Why any busier than usual?'

Brigitte put down her fork and let out a little sigh. 'I've been going through all the re-orders, Henri! It's taken a long time. I've done them all, we're up to date.'

Henri shrugged, took a mouthful of potato and washed it down with beer. He didn't often drink more than one beer and he felt a little drunk already. He let his chair tip back again.

Brigitte took refuge in her food. 'I'll take her something tomorrow if I get a chance.'

'I'm sure she's fine. Maybe it's a good thing; she might have lost a bit of weight at last.'

'Henri!' cried Brigitte immediately, and she looked hurt. Now he had a rise, he regretted his callousness. It was too easy.

'That wasn't kind,' he said, trying to smile. 'I take it back.'

'I should jolly well think so,' she said, and he was freshly irritated.

'But it's true. She's grossly overweight.' He stood up, pushing his plate away.

She stared, eyes wider than usual. 'Won't you eat?' she asked.

'I'm not hungry.' Half-drunk bottle in his hand, he crossed the room.

'Where are you going?'

'For a drive,' he said.

'At this time? Whatever for?'

'I feel like it.'

'Henri!' she cried again, and looked down, her lips pursed tight. 'All right. Of course. Well, I'll leave your food out, okay? I'll wrap it up so Jojo doesn't eat it. You can have it in a little bit. You must need it.'

'Maybe.'

He walked to the truck, pushing aside Jojo as she tried to come with him. He could feel great walls of inevitability closing in on every side, almost tangible. He tried to resist for a moment, considered turning back towards the house. But then he imagined the night ahead of him, sitting downstairs until he knew Brigitte was asleep, crawling into their bed next to her slack snores. That was too dismal, and his hunger too deep.

It took twenty minutes to drive to Edgar's – usually enough time for Henri to question his decision at least three times, but not tonight. As he drove, his third beer and the cool air rushing through the windows made his head light and calm. No more indecision, and no more rage.

He pulled up a little way down the track from Edgar's cottage. The cottage itself was small, tucked away in woodland, and he was able to leave his truck away from the road. There were no cars in the driveway, no guests. Classical music blasted through the kitchen windows: opera, a man's thick baritone, infinitely sad. Henri stood for a moment looking up at the sky, a few stars showing through gaps in the clouds. Then he shook his head and walked to the door and knocked.

Edgar smiled when he opened the door, his eyes only half open, lazy, seductive.

'I've been wondering when you'd come,' he said. He reached out for Henri's waist; Henri tensed his abdominals under Edgar's touch. They kissed. 'Are you going to sit and keep me company for a while, or is this one of your hit and runs?' he said into Henri's ear. Henri groaned, pushing Edgar into the house. He felt sick, and aroused, and relieved.

He lay on the sofa while Edgar sat next to his head, running a hand through Henri's hair. He remembered washing Vanille's blood from it just a few hours earlier, how sticky it had been.

'How's farm life?' Edgar asked.

'Fine,' said Henri. He didn't want to talk. 'How's writing life?'

'Wonderful. I'm eighty pages in and it's flying along. But now you've shown up I'm naturally bound to get lovesick and stop being able to write anything but sonnets. And the world has enough of those.'

Henri turned his head sharply to remove Edgar's hand. 'Can you get me a drink?'

'All the vices are coming out tonight,' he said in the smiling voice Henri couldn't stand. Edgar walked to the kitchen and Henri sat up, flattening his hair down, stroking it firmly into its usual parting. He stared at the coffee table in front of him, covered in books and used cups and glasses. He picked up the book at the top of the pile: *Literary Impressionism in Conrad and Ford*. He flicked through the pages, but could no longer make much sense of the bald, un-accented striations of English on each page. Nor could he remember what Conrad had written, whether he was English or American. His knowledge had receded like Edgar's hairline, eroded under the great seasonal tide of the farming year.

But it was books that had first got them talking, ten or eleven or twelve years ago now, at drinks after a christening ceremony in the village. It was shortly after Edgar had moved there, and for the first hour or so Henri avoided this stranger everyone referred to as an 'eccentric'. 'Pretentious ass,' he whispered to Brigitte when they were first introduced. But then over drinks they began talking, Edgar telling him offhand, as if Henri wouldn't know the first thing about it, that he was attempting a biography of Molière. He had been visibly surprised when Henri reeled off lines of *Le Malade imaginaire*. They went on to discuss Racine, who'd been Henri's favourite at school, and it was enlivening to summon his past knowledge, talk to someone who shared it, let their talk meander down unpractised routes. With everyone else, each conversation was simply a replay of the last.

As the afternoon went on – a violently hot afternoon in mid-August, just before a mistral came and swept summer's intensity away – he felt Edgar's eyes on him, interested and appraising, and felt himself stand taller, hold his jaw more firmly. He left the party reluctantly, to Brigitte's bemusement, since he was usually the one to drag them away from social events. And he drove home drunk, tingling throughout his body, excited and fearful and alive.

Now he was sitting before a stack of books on modernist theory, the Molière project abandoned many years since. Edgar placed a bottle of Chablis and two empty glasses on the table.

'Actually, I should go,' he said, standing quickly to stop Edgar trying to hold him back.

'Would it have been different if I'd brought a Sauvignon?' Edgar asked with a smile, and Henri ignored him. In a drier tone he said, 'And with that, Hurricane Henri sweeps off to other shores, oblivious to the wreckage he leaves in his wake.'

'I left the dog in the car,' he lied, and let Edgar kiss him. Then he left, walking as quickly as possible to the truck.

When he got back to the farm, the house was unlit except for the kitchen. He walked in and saw his uneaten dinner on the side, covered neatly in cling film, with a little note beside it in Brigitte's young-looking hand: 'Enjoy yourself!' He closed his eyes, bowed his head as he leant against the counter. He imagined her writing it, cleaning everything away, thinking before choosing those words. Then walking heavily up to their bed, folding her clothes, moving her large, soft body around their room. Falling asleep alone while her husband ejaculated in someone's mouth. A man's mouth.

He couldn't eat, but he scraped the food into a plastic bag and tucked it towards the bottom of the bin, underneath the rest of the rubbish. Then he walked upstairs slowly, wearily, and crept into the room and lay down beside Brigitte. She wasn't snoring, had clearly not been asleep.

'Is everything all right? What time is it?'

'It's midnight,' he said. 'Everything's fine, my darling. You can go to sleep.'

'Did you eat your lamb?'

'It was delicious,' he said, as quietly and gently as if talking to a tired child.

She didn't reach out for him; she never did. After their first abortive attempts at love-making, when they first married – he twisted his face at the memory of her great pink thighs straddling his hips, the fumbling of her hand around his retracted penis – she had barely grumbled or complained about the largely sexless partnership they maintained. There was the odd time, still, perhaps two or three times a year: in the total dark of night, thankfully free from foreplay or words, when he was driven by privation to indiscriminate urgency. But physical intimacy beyond the most purely anatomical was something she had had to learn to do without.

He wanted to turn to her now, stroke her hair or say something kind, but he felt too deadened, too heavy even to reach out his hand. He lay on his back, apart from her, staring into the darkness.

Marguerite turned her bedside lamp on and sat up in bed, blinking. She hugged her knees to her chest and listened. There was a toad's high rattle like a burglar alarm outside her window; it reminded her of summer childhoods by lakes, where she and Cassandre had been wimps in the face of all the insects and creatures, however hard they'd pretended to be intrepid.

She rested her left cheek on her knees, studying her little room. The broken chair, the empty suitcase under the wardrobe. The tired rug stretched out on the floor.

She had switched the light on to try to escape a constant showreel of memories and images playing in her mind's eye as she lay trying to sleep – as if the light might force them to scatter, like launching a floodlight on a pack of thieves. But the position she was sitting in now – knees to chest, face on knees, ears pricked, bedside lamp on – was too familiar for forgetting. She had sat exactly like this so many times that it almost felt as familiar to her as sleep.

She closed her eyes, the light glowing pink through her eyelids, and let herself slide back into one of the nights before everything changed. She pictured herself from the outside: a fourteen-year-old sitting up in the pristinely elegant cream bedroom her mother had designed for her. The wallpaper was feathered with very slightly raised, pale green swirls. She wasn't allowed to pin or tack things onto the wall so she tried to rebel by covering the bedside table with neon-framed photographs of her and her friends on school trips or at birthday parties. Hiding cigarettes behind their backs, so that the innocuous photos held a secret challenge. She used to hang dreamcatchers and strings of gaudy beads from the polished bedposts; aged ten, Cassandre had already started to imitate this but she couldn't quite get it right. With plastic pony charms and hearts, her arrangements looked too young. If only Marguerite had just given her some of her own.

The night their mother first left them was one of those nights: Marguerite was sitting up listening to her parents arguing. She was used to it by then; she spoke to her best friend Adeline about it sometimes in quiet corners at school, drawing her face in and making it sound much more dramatic than it was. 'I worry for their lives, sometimes,' she'd say, but that was dazzlingly untrue: her father would never have raised a hand against her mother, nor her mother – tiny and skinny, her meticulously sculpted arms weak – against him. Indeed, their lack of physical contact seemed to constitute a great part of the complaints they routinely filed against each other during the day. At night, on the other hand, specific words were hard to make out through the muffler of the bedroom walls; theirs was an amorphous volley of snarling, parodying, occasional bellowing. It was a tidal swell of rage, it came and went through the night, and Marguerite stayed up to listen, mostly for Cassandre's sake. Four years younger, she was not yet sophisticated enough to hear the fights without fear and distress.

Inevitably the door handle would swivel slowly and Cassandre would appear with her little helmet of dark hair ruffled from sleep. She'd stand in the doorway until Marguerite beckoned her in. She had a beautiful face before everything changed; surely it was not just through the prism of an older sister's pride that Marguerite thought that. It was tidy and pointed and neat, her skin a bit darker than Marguerite's, her lips a very perfect bow.

She'd get under the covers at the foot of Marguerite's bed and ask her to sing. Until recently, Marguerite had always sung when Cassandre asked. Usually it was a little ditty she

73

had invented, chronicling the adventures of two unlikely friends: a chimp, blundering yet grandiose, and a nightingale. She improvised the words each time, inventing a new adventure for the pair. Cassandre would join in when the chorus came.

But Cassandre hadn't yet left *école primaire*, whereas Marguerite was already coming to the end of *collège*, starting soon at the *lycée*; she had kissed two boys, she'd smoked cigarettes and tried vodka, she had recently got her period and bought a white bra that she filled carefully with folded tissue. Things were different; she would still defend Cassandre to the death but she no longer sang willingly whenever asked. As a result, Cass had taken to begging, which annoyed Marguerite.

'The Chimp and the Nightingale, Margo?' she asked.

'Not tonight, Cass.' But because she looked sad, Marguerite added: 'I'll sing to you tomorrow. I've just had a really long day: double maths in the morning and double Latin in the afternoon, and I have to get up early to finish extra homework from Madame Garcia because she's a complete bitch.'

'Poor you,' said Cassandre. 'That sounds so stressful.' She had learnt the word 'stressful' from Marguerite, and used it constantly.

'It is. And Monsieur Clerc's an imbecile, and the boys in my class are even bigger imbeciles.' She sighed dramatically. 'Enjoy *primaire* while you can.' Cassandre nodded, wriggling down further under the covers. 'How's your homework, Cass? Are you revising hard enough?'

'I think so.'

'You're a little brainbox.'

'Hmm, I don't know.'

'Well, I do. You're a brilliant little geek. I bet you get the highest marks in your year.'

The toad started rattling again and Marguerite opened her eyes, back in Jérôme's quiet house. She sat completely still, treasuring the memory but also aware that she was inventing the conversation. She always did this: she let her younger self become her ideal of Cassandre's older sister. Always guiding, always supportive. Would she really have been so kind that night? She remembered the slamming of doors, her father coming into the room to declare that their mother had left them all. It was the first time she'd done this, and they didn't know better than to doubt its permanence. She remembered Cassandre crying and her father's willowy frame disappearing back into the darkness; she remembered holding her little sister and drying her tears, eventually getting her to sleep. But she couldn't remember whether she'd sung.

'Please say I sang, please say I sang.' She closed her eyes and shook her head to banish the thoughts and images. She lay back down, leaving the lamp on, hoping that Jérôme would call her down to tend to him. 'Please say I sang.'

5

Jérôme was sick all morning. He refused, over and over, to sit up to vomit, and dragged his weight down in her arms when she tried to force him to. She had to give up, pulling him instead to the very side of the mattress so he could retch sideways into the bin. He hadn't eaten much the night before and there was next to nothing for him to bring up. A senseless, repetitive heaving went on throughout the morning, punctuated by protracted groans like a woman in labour.

As the hours wore on she started to feel angry at the sheer relentlessness of his vomiting. She was rough with him when she pulled him repeatedly onto his side, and almost shouted when he disobeyed her instructions.

'Do you want to choke on your own vomit? Do you think that would be enjoyable?'

He in turn was obstructive and difficult, but she caught a look sometimes in his eyes that was fearful. In regret, she would lower her voice and cool his forehead, but then the heaving and the refusal to get into the right position would start again and her frustration would flare.

Finally the gaps between retching were longer than twenty

minutes, but she still didn't dare leave his room. She let him lie back and close his eyes, and then she sat at the bedroom table, exhausted. She needed to eat, but she couldn't face getting up. She couldn't even face cleaning the bin out; it sat by the side of the bed and the room stank. Jérôme started to snore, a faint and reedy sound.

She was startled by a loud knock coming from the kitchen; so too was Jérôme, who snorted and opened his eyes, glassy and distant, before falling back to sleep. She picked up the bin, taking it from the room as she walked through the house to the kitchen.

'Shit,' she said under her breath as she saw Suki's face peering through the glass of the kitchen door. She tried to smile as she opened the door but it couldn't have been convincing.

'Is it a bad time?' Suki asked.

'Well, quite, yes,' she said, letting her come in. 'Hold on a moment.'

She turned, taking the bin out into the utility room. She took her time to rinse it out with hot water and bleach. You don't just turn up, unannounced, on someone's job, she thought. When she had finished rinsing it out, she took it back into Jérôme's room, setting it down by the bed. Then she turned him, finally malleable with sleep, onto his side. His mouth gaped.

She smelt Suki's smoke before she came back into the kitchen.

'Can you take that outside?' she said. It came out harshly, rudely. 'It floats through the house,' she said, more softly.

'I'm sorry,' said Suki. She opened the kitchen door and stood there, gazing at Marguerite. Half in shade and half in sunlight, she looked more beautiful than Marguerite had realised she could. 'I think I've come at a bad time and you're cross.'

'I'm sorry to seem that way. I'm just very busy. Jérôme's not well.'

'Of course.' She reached down to open the little violet bag that hung by her hip, and took out a folded piece of paper. She handed it over. 'Have a look,' she said.

Marguerite unfolded it: it was a flyer for a spring fête in the village. There were bad illustrations of lambs and ducklings with big eyes and long eyelashes.

'I know what you're thinking,' Suki said. 'Why is Suki giving me an invitation to a ghastly spring fête, I can't think of anything worse. Right?'

'Well, not ghastly.'

'Marguerite!' Suki let her head fall back to look at the sky. 'Don't be so polite! I know perfectly well you would have no interest in a village fête.'

She looked at her, raising an eyebrow in a way that seemed rehearsed, imitated perhaps from someone onscreen.

'Okay, it doesn't exactly sound like my kind of thing,' she said.

Suki watched her for a moment. 'I know I'm sort of foisting myself on you,' she said, 'and you have absolutely no wish for my company.'

Marguerite started to protest but she raised her hands to stop her.

'Stop, don't say anything. But I'm going to keep trying, because I don't think it's right that you're out here in the middle of nowhere with absolutely no company whatsoever.

Apart from Lanvier.' She rolled her eyes and took a last, concentrated drag on her cigarette, little lines appearing around her lips as she sucked. She dropped the butt onto the ground beside her and stamped it out, leaning against the doorframe. 'The reason I'm here is because I need your help.'

'Aha,' said Marguerite. She stood. 'Coffee?'

'Badly needed, yes please.'

She took the kettle to the sink, closing her eyes as she let the water run. She heard cupboards open and close; when she turned, Suki was busying herself shaking coffee into a large, beaten-up cafetière Marguerite had never used.

'I have an instinct for where things are kept,' she said, smiling. 'That had to be a cups and cafetière cupboard. Just as I bet you keep saucepans in that one, down there. Am I right?'

'Yes.'

'You see? It's like I have an instinct for good housekeeping but no knowledge of how to implement it. You've seen my place, it's a total bombsite.'

'It's a great location.'

'Yes and no. I love being able to spy on everyone. And I can avoid them all, I simply wait for the coast to be clear before I walk out the door. But on the other hand, I'm stuck right in the thick of it. I get so claustrophobic there. Sometimes I picture a huge hand coming down and tearing the house from its foundations and carrying it thousands of miles away.'

'Where would it take the house?' asked Marguerite. 'The giant hand.'

'Iran. The mountains. Lorestan province.' The kettle clicked and steam rose; Marguerite made to pick it up but

Suki reached out to stop her. 'You mustn't pour it when it's still boiling. It should be about 85 degrees. I'll do it.'

Marguerite stood back as Suki removed the kettle lid and together they watched the steam escape and thin. Suki took it from its perch, lifted it high above the cafetière.

'You should also pour it onto the coffee from a height,' she said. She poured, let it rest, stirred it carefully with a knife lying in the sink. 'Now we leave it again before we plunge.'

She walked over to the door again and stood there to light her second cigarette. 'What about you?'

'Me?'

'The hand. Where would it take you?'

Marguerite shrugged. She tried hard to think of somewhere, anywhere. 'I don't really know.'

'Surely Paris?'

'God, no.' Suki's eyes focused more intently on her face and she regretted the strength of her reaction. 'Too hectic,' she said, to explain herself. She lifted the cafetière and placed it down on the table. 'Am I allowed to plunge it yet?'

Suki gestured with one hand as she blew out a jet of smoke. 'You are allowed,' she said, smiling. 'Slowly, though. What was I saying before? My house. Yes, it's lovely. But I hate that fucking place.'

Something about the immediacy of the comment made Marguerite laugh. Suki seemed surprised, and laughed too.

'It's all twee little houses and paper-doily curtains and the same small-minded little people wandering around talking about how big their aubergines grew last harvest.' She took a long drag. 'I'm not even exaggerating. That's the kind of thing they talk about.'

'But there must be some normal people,' said Marguerite.

'No, the point is that they *are* normal. Too normal. Paralysingly normal. There are some good ones – little Luc, the librarian. A very smart guy. We have quite a famous writer living in the woods, Edgar DuChamp.' She looked at Marguerite expectantly, but she shook her head; she'd never heard of him. 'And there's Madame Brun, a barmy old woman – three metres tall or something – who only wears black. Have you seen her?'

Again, Marguerite shook her head. 'What about your husband?'

'Philippe?' Suki forced a laugh. 'He's worse than the rest.' She stared into the distance for a moment, scratching her neck with one of her long painted nails, and for a moment Marguerite was reminded of a bird of prey. 'I'm just kidding, he's not that bad. But I get so bored, Marguerite.'

The use of her name jarred, suggestive of an unearned intimacy. As if she sensed it too, Suki threw her unfinished cigarette away and came back to sit at the table.

'I haven't even explained why I'm here,' she said. 'So this fête. Hear me out – it's actually not as bad as you'd think. It happens every May, and it's just the village selling various things and showing off their produce or their latest haircut. And everyone brings their ugly little dogs that look like rats and they dress them up in ugly little outfits.' She smiled. 'I've made it sound dire, haven't I?' Again she laughed, and it occurred to Marguerite for the first time that she might be nervous. 'But anyway, so I'm bored and what the hell, I've signed up to do a stall.'

'What kind of stall?'

There had been a small change in Suki's expression, a flicker of something in her smile. Marguerite noticed a faint blush rising up over her cheeks.

'Last year I ran a fancy-dress stall for the kids. I piled up all the amazing scarves and headpieces and costume jewellery I have – I love collecting these things – and bunged them on the stall and invited all the children to dress up in them.'

'That sounds like a great idea.'

'Well, yes, I thought so too. But the problem is absolutely no one let their kids come and use the clothes. I actually heard one woman tell her nephew not to touch anything from "the mystic's little box of tricks".'

'The mystic?'

'They call me the mystic. I think they think I'm some kind of witch doctor or something.'

'Why?'

Suki shrugged. 'My hijab? It makes me want to shake them. I want to say, there are no witch doctors, there's no voodoo in Iran. We're more civilised than the lot of you.' She looked quickly at Marguerite, watching for offence, and affected a more relaxed expression. 'Maybe they just confuse "Suki" with "Sufi". Though actually they're too ignorant to know what Sufism is.'

'It sounds ridiculous either way.'

'Yes, it is. Ridiculous. And I felt ridiculous standing behind a stall dressed in my most beautiful clothes with the entire contents of my wardrobe displayed in front of me and not a single child even allowed to come near. And they wanted to, you know? I could see it, especially the little girls. They were itching to try on all the pretty things.' She got up and lit yet another cigarette by the door. 'So I'm not making that mistake again this year. This year, I'm running a simple bric-a-brac stall. You've seen my house, you've seen all my things. Well I have piles more hidden away in my attic and Philippe's been at me for years to clear it out, so I thought, right, let's see if they'll stay away from my stall this time. Greedy little shits.'

She was slouching a little as she spoke, staring intently at a point on the doorframe, sucking at her cigarette. The soft beauty Marguerite had caught earlier was gone; she looked sad, shrunken, hard.

'I think it sounds like a good idea,' Marguerite said, though she thought the opposite. If they wouldn't let their children dress up in her clothes, why did Suki think they'd want her ornaments?

But Suki looked at her gratefully. 'You think so? I think so too.' She sighed. 'Anyway, it's probably stupid to bother getting involved, but I just can't bear hiding away in my house pretending I don't know they all hate me. I live in Saint-Sulpice too. I have a right to be there.'

'Of course.'

'So. I want you to come to the fête and I want you to pretend to buy a few of my things.'

Marguerite laughed; she had expected something more onerous.

'I know it's pathetic,' Suki said, smiling ruefully. 'Will you do it though? I have money here, for you to spend.' She fiddled with her bag again, took some notes out. 'Here's fifty euros. You can even keep whatever you buy. I'm basically giving it to you.'

'Okay. I can come, but not for long.'

'That's fine. But you'll definitely come?'

Marguerite felt uncomfortable, constricted, as she always did when she was asked to make a commitment.

'As long as Jérôme is okay.'

'Great. Okay. You'll be there.' She came in to put the money on the table. 'Well, I'm going to let you be now, but thank you. I won't forget it.'

She leant forward to kiss Marguerite on each cheek. Above the smoke, she smelt of vanilla or coconut – something too sweet.

She didn't wake Jérôme for lunch; she let him sleep, and he only called her to him mid-afternoon by knocking on his headboard, so faintly she barely heard it.

'I feel much better,' he said when she went in. But his face was still wax-coloured, and his lips, usually wide and strangely full for a man, were puckered and pale.

'I'm glad to hear it.'

'What are those?' He pointed weakly at a small blue jug she'd placed on the table when he was asleep, holding a cluster of wild flowers she'd found in the garden. He looked at her with an expression she couldn't decipher. It was wary, she thought, but not irritated; there was a softness in his face.

'I found them in the olive groves, growing wild. Someone really needs to take over the garden; it could be so beautiful.'

'It was,' he said. 'You've spent a while outside. You're a little sunburnt.'

'Surely I'm not,' she said, touching her cheeks. 'I wasn't out there for long.'

'Not burnt, a little tanned.' He smiled, the very faintest of smiles.

She brought him bread and jam to eat, and sweet tea. The room smelt rancid from his morning of sickness, and she cleaned it as he ate.

'I'm glad you've got an appetite,' she said and he nodded, opening his mouth to take a bite. Some jam dripped off the bread and onto his chest, but he didn't notice. There was a crumb fastened in the corner of his mouth. These things felt unbearably sad to her then; she came forward to wipe the jam away with a tissue, and he frowned.

'You're forever fussing.'

'I'm going to change your sheets,' she said when she'd taken his tray, and he nodded again. He leant into her arms as she lifted him up and they shuffled together towards the chair. It was odd, she realised, that she knew his smell more intimately than her own.

It was not until the next morning that Jérôme regained his usual strength: he had colour in his cheeks, sat upright in the bed. He was galvanised all the more by hunger; he snapped at her for food, refusing to let her clean his teeth first, and gobbled his toast loudly, flecks of spit collecting in the corners of his mouth.

'I'd like chocolate,' he said when he'd finished.

She smiled. 'I don't think we have any.'

'Why not? Have you eaten it?'

'We haven't had any in the house for weeks. I didn't know you particularly liked it.'

'Well, don't just presume,' he said, his eyebrows screwed together to form a deep, fleshy crease between them. Marguerite noticed that a couple of the coarse white eyebrow hairs had grown long beyond the others, indeed beyond proportion; they strayed up towards his hairline, as if trying to replace the hair that had been lost there.

'What are you looking at?'

'Nothing.' She filled his glass from the jug, gave it to him. 'You must stay well hydrated today.'

But he pushed the glass away, and stared in front of him. 'Get me something else to eat. And I don't mean more bread, I'm sick to death of bread.'

As Marguerite walked through to the kitchen, she realised she was pleased by his bad temper, signifying as it did his return to relative health. She took raisin biscuits from a tin and arranged them on a plate to bring back to him, but when she re-entered his room and set the plate down on his bedside table he didn't even register them.

'I heard a voice here yesterday.'

'When?'

'You know when, come on. I've just remembered, I heard talking when I was drifting in and out of sleep. Yesterday. Come on, I'm not stupid.'

'Of course not.'

'Who was it? Was someone coming to see me?'

'No,' she said, and she saw something slacken in his face. A ripple passed over his forehead, around his eyes and mouth. His shoulders dropped. He stared down the bed for a moment, unfocused.

'It was a woman from the village,' she said, for the sake of saying something.

'Name?' he asked.

'She's called Suki.'

'Suki Lacourse,' he said immediately, his interest rekindled. 'Arab, married to Philippe Lacourse. He's a prime cretin. Why in God's name was she here?'

'Iranian. She just passed by.'

'How do you know her?'

'I've met her a few times in the village.'

'So you're socialising, are you? How nice for you.'

'I'm not socialising.'

'You could have fooled me.'

'I spend every moment in an empty house with you.'

'Henri Brochon was here last week. Suki Lacourse is dropping by on social visits. What next? I'm going to wake up to a party at the end of my bed.'

She couldn't help smiling, then, because it was too ridiculous. He smiled too, unexpectedly; it was a wry smile, a little sheepish.

'So you refuse to tell me why that woman was visiting the house. What could you possibly have to do with someone like that? She's old enough to be your mother.'

'She's not even forty,' she said. 'And anyway, she had a favour to ask.'

He frowned. 'I'd watch out for her, if I were you.'

'Why?'

'She's trouble.'

'Why do you think that?'

'She's – different.'

'You mean foreign.'

He looked at her with irritation. 'No. She makes trouble because she's never adapted to her environment.'

'Has her environment adapted to her?'

'Of course not. Why should it?'

Marguerite shook her head. She didn't have the energy.

'You think I'm talking about her being a Muslim, but I'm not. I'm talking about her aspirations. She's lived here, what, twenty years? But she hasn't accepted anything. She doesn't accept that she's married to a boring man, living in a boring house in a boring village, and that ultimately, for all her exoticism, she's pretty damn boring herself.' He licked his lips and paused. 'You may not think I know much, but I do know that people who don't adjust their expectations cause trouble.'

Marguerite said nothing, and Jérôme smiled again. 'You, for example,' he said, his tone gentler, 'have quashed all your expectations, all your aspirations, and therefore you're no trouble at all.'

She saw, with some shock, that he wasn't needling – that he didn't expect this to offend her at all. But his words caused instant, tangible pain. She felt anger rising up inside her, a rush of it.

'Thank you for your armchair analysis, but you know absolutely nothing about my life.'

'I was joking with you, for God's sake,' he said.

'And the only reason behind people thinking that Suki is "trouble" is bigotry.' He tried to say something, but she interrupted. 'Of course you don't adapt to a place if you're treated like an outsider from beginning to end, and you're left out of things, whatever you do.'

She was inarticulate in her anger; he swiped the air calmly, dismissing her words. 'Let me tell you, Marguerite,' he said, 'the delusion of centrality and the self-doubt involved in *feeling* left out translate into one's behaviour, one's words, even one's body language. All of that renders a person sufficiently unattractive to company that they end up actually *being* left out. It's circular, it fulfils itself.'

He looked up at the ceiling and licked his lips again, satisfied; she imagined clearly how he would have behaved as the boss of his company, how staggeringly arrogant he must have been before old age started to degrade him.

'Thank you for the lecture,' she said, instantly regretting those words. They played themselves back in her mind, immature and empty. He laughed to himself, reaching for a biscuit.

'Silly girl. I found another weak spot.'

She left the room and walked straight through the kitchen, past the stupid little clusters of flowers she'd been arranging. She kicked the door open, swearing, and stopped outside, hot tears starting in her eyes.

She heard a sound, then, nearby, and sensed the men's presence before she saw them. Henri Brochon and his farmhands, lugging the trunk of the ailing oak towards the driveway. So it was finally dead. They looked away, embarrassed for her, and she didn't even try to acknowledge them or gather herself. She walked back into the kitchen with her head down and went straight upstairs to her bedroom, burying her face in the pillow until the humiliation receded, dream and reality becoming fused.

Brigitte had a special way of folding sheets and tablecloths. She'd invented it herself, when she was around fourteen. She didn't like to teach it, in case someone might show someone else and pass it off as their own. That would annoy her, not because she wanted glory but because she couldn't stand anything that wasn't fair.

On the other hand, she had to admit she liked people to see her do it. It was very fast, very effective. She held the two corners at diagonals from each other, and through a series of wrist flicks the entire sheet ended up lying flat, in a diagonal half, on the table in front of her. It could then, with just two further folds, end up as a tidy square of fabric. Fold it once again and it would fit perfectly on a shelf: a slim, flat, unrumpled rectangle.

She felt Laure watching as she applied her method to sheet after white sheet. 'Amazing how you do that,' she said.

'It's a handy trick.'

She smoothed one, adding it to the tidy pile.

'So how many double sheets have we got between us?' asked Laure. 'Fifteen?'

'Fifteen white, and a further two or three if I throw in pink and blue too. We could use the coloured sheets for the flower-arranging stall?'

'That's an idea.' Laure wrote down the figures in her book.

'And an old one for face-painting, because it'll get stained, however washable those paints claim to be.' Laure nodded, and Brigitte kept folding.

'I'm looking forward to the flower-arranging,' said Laure. 'I can't wait to trample over Anne-Marie's dismal collection again.'

'Why does she even bother entering? You beat her every year. It's embarrassing.'

Brigitte was the judge for the fête's flower-arranging competition, so she didn't enter – which was just as well, since she suspected she might outdo Laure's arrangements. Laure's were very pretty – lavish, abundant, scrupulously tidy – but Brigitte simply had a greater variety to work from. The farm gardens were filled with them.

'Speaking of embarrassing,' said Laure, rooting through her sewing basket to find pins for corsages, 'Madame Lacourse is entering again. You know that, don't you?'

Brigitte looked quickly at Laure, who didn't look up, still looking for something in the basket. 'Why didn't you tell me? I had no idea.'

'I thought you knew,' Laure said casually, taking a spool of blue ribbon from the basket and holding it against a band of blue elastic. 'Not quite the right shade,' she said quietly, frowning; then she looked up and blinked. 'Are you bothered? She'll make a fool of herself, like usual.'

'Well, I just would have liked to know.'

'Of course. I presumed you would know.' She looked very serious, then. 'Do you mean she didn't apply to you?'

'No, she didn't.'

Now this was something; everyone in the village applied to Brigitte and Laure with their stall ideas – they had to do so by the end of February so that due planning could be done. And everyone knew to write to them both.

'Oh. That's odd – she applied to me pretty early. She was one of the first, actually. I presumed she would have written to you too.'

'Apparently she doesn't think I'm important enough.'

'Oh you know it's not that,' said Laure. 'She's threatened by you, Brigitte, she always has been.'

'Well,' said Brigitte. She hadn't folded the last sheet quite right; she felt distracted. She shook it out and started again. 'What's the stall, anyway?'

'She hasn't named it yet. As far as I can make out from the description, it'll be a load of her shabby old knick-knacks from Timbuktu to God knows where.'

Brigitte was stuck. She needed Henri at the fête; she had asked him expressly to leave the farm in Paul's hands that day, since she needed him to oversee her stalls while she judged the flower-arranging and artichokes, and to help set up in the morning. But still, though she trusted him, she didn't like the thought of Suki's stall attracting his attention, or the possibility that it might give them a chance to chat. At least fifteen years had passed since Suki's obsession, but it still unsettled Brigitte. She hated the woman's make-up, her painted nails and swaying walk. She hated her cigarettes, her air of sophistication. And while Henri had assured Brigitte that he didn't find the woman attractive either, she remembered just once or twice witnessing his interest in what Suki had to say. She would 'drop by' when she knew his day would be winding up, and sit in their kitchen keeping his attention as he stood by the counter, drinking his beer. She could talk about poets and philosophers and films – things Henri found interesting that Brigitte could never find the time to care about. There was no one in the world but Suki who could get under Brigitte's skin like that.

'Don't worry about it, Brigitte. I'm sure we can make her

stall as successful as last year's,' Laure said, smiling. Brigitte laughed.

'You're awful,' she said, but she felt relieved.

'Poor girl,' said Thierry.

'Yes, poor girl,' said his brother. 'She looked like she was having a breakdown.' He laughed, not unkindly.

'I didn't think Parisian girls swore like that. I should have covered your ears, Rémy. I don't think you've even heard those words before.'

'Shut up,' Rémy said, grinning.

'It was kind of hot actually. Boss?' he asked, leaning forward between Rémy and Henri's seats.

'What?'

'Is the old man really that bad?'

'What do you mean?'

'I mean does he make everyone have a nervous breakdown?'

'No,' Henri said. 'Don't be stupid.'

'It's just, she looked pretty wound up.'

'Be quiet,' said Rémy, looking at Henri. 'It's not funny.'

'Not funny at all, an attractive young woman all on her own, all wound up with no one to vent her frustration onto . . .'

Rémy laughed and Thierry continued, encouraged. 'She must need a shoulder to cry on. Boss, do you have Monsieur Lanvier's number? I could call to just, you know, check everything's okay.'

'I said don't be stupid,' said Henri, too crossly. Rémy's smile dropped; Thierry fell silent. Henri sensed their confusion, but he didn't care. The expression on her face had been one of torment, and Henri was reminded once again of a teenage Thibault, kicking gravel in the driveway at Rossignol, staring out of the gates, eyes glazed with a vision of some other life.

At home, he walked straight through the kitchen, barely acknowledging Brigitte and Laure as they greeted him. He walked through to his study and closed the door and sat down, staring at the wall. He'd been rude to the women, unreasonable with Thierry and Rémy. But it was intrusive, the boys joking about something even he was not qualified to understand. They didn't know the Lanviers or the nurse, had no right to comment.

He leant back in his chair, closing his eyes. He was bored, and frustrated, and the inevitable prospect of masturbation depressed him. He must be the most prolific wanker in the whole of the Languedoc, he thought; literally, the biggest wanker. Handsome Henri, who could have had his pick of all the women, had chosen instead to spend a life of loyal devotion to his right hand. Granted, he cheated occasionally on this life partner, the odd furious fuck coming between them – but deviation only made their relationship stronger, less suffused as it was with sordidness and shame.

He opened his eyes, turned to see his face reflected in the glass of the painting beside him. He didn't recognise his expression as his own: the grim half-smile, the tired eyes. He sighed and unfastened his trousers and let himself wank quickly, without enthusiasm. Then he cleaned himself carefully with a tissue, screwed it into a ball and threw it into the bin. Brigitte wouldn't be best pleased when she emptied the bin out, but she could think what she liked. He'd given up caring.

6

The village was transformed. Usually empty, it was filled with people and noise: an emcee's voice droning on the air over speakers, tinny muzak bleating from various stalls. The stalls filled the central car park, its drab concrete written over with tricolour bunting, flags and white balloons.

It seemed likely, given the size of the crowd, that many more people had come than just those living in Saint-Sulpice. That was a relief; Marguerite had imagined walking into a sparse scattering of people, where she would stand out instantly. Instead, no one seemed to see her at all. She walked into the commotion and let herself wander through the maze of stalls. There was a large food counter serving foods from neighbouring regions: spiky, sculptural *gateaux à la broche*, *herbes de provence* in twee yellow grinders, fatty *truffade*. Woody smoke unfurled through the crowds from a pizza oven.

She passed stalls where children threw coloured balls to win toys or sat patiently to have their faces painted. There were long counters laden with sleek vegetables; they weren't for sale, but genuinely appeared to be in competition with each other. People appraised them, compared their plumpness, their gleam, their colour and size. Marguerite smiled at the shy face of a little girl who had walked into her, and the girl smiled blankly back. Her face was dusted with freckles, like Cassandre's; she wore a headdress of lavender and white carnations, coming a little loose on one side. In spite of the noise and bustle, this felt a strangely peaceful place.

'Marguerite!'

She looked around to see Suki's stall, right at the end of the aisle. Suki smiled, a kind, effulgent smile. 'What are *you* doing here?' she said as Marguerite approached, and gave a theatrical wink.

'Oh, you know, just passing by.'

'Well, what are the chances!' They laughed, though Marguerite was sure neither of them had found it funny. Suki looked serious then. 'What do you think of my stall?'

Marguerite stepped back and took it all in. The stall's metal scaffolding was wrapped in multi-coloured scarves; a string of fake yellow roses hung from the top, under a sign written in indigo ink: WHISPERS OF THE EAST. The counter itself was covered in wares: teapots, small statues, framed pictures, ornate combs and silver trays and misted glass cups. It was shabby, splendid and predictable, a pastiche of an exotic goods store.

'Beautiful,' she said.

Suki narrowed her eyes. Fine, numerous wrinkles spread across the skin around them, like a second set of lashes. 'You see they've put me right at the very end?'

It was true: not only was the stall at the end of the aisle, but it was at a definite remove from the rest.

'Who's they?'

'Brigitte and Laure Richard. The bitch from the boulangerie.'

'You can't be serious.'

'I am!' She took a deep breath. 'But you know what? I don't care today. I just don't care. I'm proud of my stall, and I've had a sale: someone I didn't recognise, she bought an ivory bangle. Real ivory. She didn't seem like she was from around here; she had taste.' She looked around at the fête with a fixed grin. Her lips were deep burgundy, her face immaculate, composed with exquisite care. 'I think I'm going to get a lot of interest throughout the day. They'll see.'

'I'm sure you will.'

'Why don't you keep wandering around? Come and buy something when you need to go.'

'Okay,' said Marguerite. She had come simply to fulfil her promise to Suki and leave, but now she was here she felt no urge to hurry home to Jérôme. It felt odd – unsettling, faintly thrilling – to be among so many strangers. She had seen no more than two handfuls of people for months.

She bought a cone of small *beignets* from a stall manned by two young teenagers, clearly a brother and sister. They counted her change carefully, earnestly. Marguerite imagined herself at that age, doing that job; she knew she would have sneered at it, and regretted that.

She sat on a low wall to eat, the sun warm on her face. Different radio stations vied with each other, blaring out from the many stalls, but she recognised none of the pop songs playing. A fly attempted repeatedly to land on the edge of her cone and inspect the sugary contents; she batted it away, and brushed crumbs from her mouth.

The recorded blare of a trumpet sounded three times, the emcee announcing the annual flower-arranging contest, and a crowd formed quickly around one stall. Marguerite recognised Brigitte Brochon standing at the centre, taking a microphone. She was wearing a furious shade of pink, and with her yellow hair and rosy cheeks she looked like well-cooked gammon.

'This really was a very tough year to judge . . .' She started to reel off the relative merits of five contestants, and Marguerite stopped listening. She stood up and threw away the empty cone, heading back to Suki's stall. She would buy something and leave; she wanted to get back now to check on Jérôme.

'Back so soon?' called Suki, waving to her. She had been talking to the librarian, who turned and greeted her shyly. In a low voice, she said to him, 'Marguerite's also here for entirely neutral reasons, like you,' and the three of them laughed. She sucked hard on her cigarette. 'Just as I suppose Laure and Brigitte were nothing but entirely *neutral* in instructing people to avoid my stall.' Her eyes darted to the librarian, and he shrugged. 'You think I'm being paranoid?'

'I didn't say that.'

She sighed. 'Men always think we make this shit up. Anyway, I don't care today. I have you two customers, don't I? Marguerite, will you be tempted to buy something?'

'What's this?' she asked, turning a purple jar in her hands. It was the first thing she'd seen.

'You put wishes in it. Write them down, roll up the paper,

put it in the jar.' She frowned. 'It's just something silly. Don't you want a scarf? A nice green one to set off your dark hair.' She unwrapped a pale green silk from one of the poles and held it up to Marguerite's face. 'So stunning. The colour is perfect, you look like a film star. Don't you think, Luc?'

'Of course,' he said, looking away, and Marguerite could see Suki smile in preparation to tease him.

But they were interrupted by a voice, and Marguerite turned to see the *boulangère* standing behind her. She was wearing a lilac rosette affixed to her lapel with '1st place' on it, as if she'd taken part in a gymkhana.

'Mademoiselle Demers, isn't it?' She cocked her head to one side, lips pursed tightly. 'Monsieur Lanvier's nurse, am I right?'

'Yes,' said Marguerite.

'Laure Richard,' she said, smiling tightly, offering a hand to shake. 'I work in the boulangerie. I'm sure I've seen you in there once or twice.'

Three times a week, thought Marguerite, but she said nothing. Laure nodded, her little eyes flicking back and forth over Marguerite's face, and then she smiled again.

'Well it's wonderful to see that Monsieur Lanvier is so much improved.'

'Improved?'

'Well, clearly he must be very well for you to be taking a day off to visit the fête,' she said. 'It must be such a relief for you to know he's getting better.'

'I'm not taking the day off,' Marguerite said.

'Just coming here for a few hours, then?' she asked, still smiling tightly, head bobbing.

'Very briefly, in fact,' she said. 'I've come to get our usual supplies.' Marguerite was aware that she was like a child in trouble, making excuses. Laure raised her eyebrows as if she'd heard something extraordinary.

'I didn't realise Jérôme's usual supplies included fashion scarves and trinkets!'

Marguerite didn't know how to respond; she didn't want to explain herself, but felt somehow compelled. She turned to look at Suki, but couldn't catch her eye; Suki was staring down her nose at a fresh cigarette, flicking a lighter into flame in a cupped hand. Her nostrils were flared, her perfect eyebrows in a tight frown. Luc had moved away.

'Should I send Monsieur Lanvier your regards?' she asked Laure, turning back to her.

'Oh no,' she said, beaming; 'please don't worry. I'm sure I can send them via Brigitte. She's the *gardienne*, of course. It's a shame I can't see her now,' she said, turning to scan the crowd behind her, 'otherwise I know she'd be so interested to see you here too. I'll be sure to mention it.' She gazed steadily at Marguerite; her little eyes blinked, again and again. 'Well, goodbye,' she said. 'Do enjoy your day off.'

She walked away and Marguerite turned to Suki, who didn't meet her eye.

'What was that?' Marguerite asked, and Suki looked up then, frowning.

'What was what?'

'That interrogation. What does she have to do with Jérôme?'

'Isn't it obvious? She's just trying to destroy my stall again by making a fuss.'

Marguerite stared at her for a moment. She wanted to ask

how Laure's interrogation had had anything to do with Suki's stall, but the questions she tried to form felt too petty. She had a child's sense that she was missing something, that the other women understood something she didn't.

'Well, I'd best be going,' she said then, and Suki nodded.

'Thanks so much for coming,' she said. She handed the green scarf over. 'Take this as a thank you.'

'No.'

'I insist.'

'I can't take it. And I owe you your money back.' She took the euros Suki had given her a few days ago and put them on the table. Suki didn't look at them but smiled vaguely, looking over Marguerite's shoulder as if a new customer might be coming. Marguerite suspected there was none.

She left the fête by walking behind the backs of the stalls, avoiding the bustling aisles full of people. But she stopped when she heard, very clearly above the music and general din, Jérôme's name being spoken. It was Laure's voice, surely less than a foot away; they were separated only by the white tarpaulin of the stall's rear wall.

'Jérôme's nurse, chatting away to Lacourse, laughing away as if there was no sick man alone in his bed at home. I mean it, Brigitte: anyone would have thought she was on holiday here.'

Marguerite stayed there, behind the tarpaulin; she was too curious to move on, too appalled to intervene.

'I don't believe it,' said Brigitte's voice; 'I just don't believe it, Laure.'

'And she was so arrogant, Brigitte! Not even the tiniest bit embarrassed to be caught out.'

'I knew it. I thought it right from the beginning, I said to myself: this girl can't be bothered with the job, her heart's not in it.'

'Poor old Jérôme.'

'What's happened to Jérôme?' A new voice now, a male voice.

'Well hopefully nothing, darling,' said Brigitte. 'But Lord knows how long he'll last with his current nurse. I must do something.'

'What's happened?'

'Laure just saw her buying clothes and gossiping at Madame Lacourse's stall!'

'What's wrong with that?'

Marguerite breathed out just a little. A skinny little grey cat slinked towards her.

'What's wrong with that,' said Laure's voice, 'is that she's supposed to be tending to a dying man.'

'As I understand it,' he said, and Marguerite recognised something of her own in his voice – weary, almost deadened with irritation – 'the Lanviers employ just one nurse and she's allowed to come and go from Rossignol when necessary. They don't even provide a car, so presumably they're happy for her to be out of the house for reasonable stretches of time. How else does she get anything?'

Marguerite felt something at her foot, looked down to see the cat weaving its body through her ankles. Its fur was a little crisp; it looked up with its deadened eyes, whoreish, and mewed loudly. She bent to bat it away.

'Henri! I don't believe you're defending someone you don't even know—'

'And you're criticising someone you don't even know.'

'With all due respect, Henri, I think Bri might have good reason,' said Laure.

'What reason?'

'Well, the girl's – sniffy,' Brigitte said; 'she barely speaks when spoken to—'

'And God forbid anyone should value silence, Brigitte.' It was quieter and biting, a parting shot; Marguerite knew that he had walked away. The stillness he left behind him felt loaded. She waited, still squatting by the cat as it rubbed itself repeatedly against her legs.

'Bri, don't worry. Men never understand these things, they don't realise we have an instinct for girls like that.'

'It's because of that stupid woman,' cried Brigitte, and her voice was trembling.

'No, Brigitte.'

'Yes, it is – I'm telling you. It's because we said she was at Lacourse's stall when you saw her, he gets all defensive over her, I swear it.'

Marguerite stood, then, and moved away from her spot. Unsettled and confused though she was by their vitriol, she felt calmer than she could account for.

At the end of the *parking*, as she started to cross the road in the direction of home, she saw Henri Brochon leaning against a stall, looking down at his feet as he listened to another man. He looked up, then, and caught her eye. Neither of them smiled, but as she started out on her long walk home she wished that she had.

Jérôme was quiet, even docile, and she wondered whether he regretted his insult the previous day. She sat on the stairs outside his room as he ate his lunch, replaying the conversation she'd overheard at the fête and the interrogation she'd had from Laure. She was struck by the clear animosity they had for Suki – she had wondered, previously, whether Suki had been a little paranoid. And she thought about Brigitte's words about 'that stupid woman', the threat of tears in her voice, the implication that their mutual enmity had its roots in something tangible, not just Brigitte and Laure's prejudice and parochialism. Suki had never alluded to anything untoward between herself and Henri. Marguerite tried to imagine the couple they might make, if Brigitte's suspicions were founded, but found that she couldn't – even if, tall and handsome, he made more aesthetic sense with Suki than with his dour wife.

She wondered about their clear animosity towards her, too: Laure's brazenly accusatory manner, barely concealed behind cold jollity; the outrage with which Brigitte had objected to her presence at the fête.

But Henri had defended her; that thought lingered around the edges of everything else. She was used to hearing people whisper about her: it started when Cassandre had taken ill. At nursing college, too, and in hospitals, and at the care home in Picardy, she'd walked in on broken conversations, caught snatches of things she didn't want to hear. But she couldn't remember hearing someone speak in her favour, like Henri had.

She shook her head and stood up. She wouldn't think any more about it, she was no good at trying to understand codes and nuances: they left her feeling tired, emptied out. She went through to see if Jérôme had finished lunch. But his food was only half eaten on the tray on his lap, and he was asleep, chin resting on his slightly pigeoned chest, his shoulders and spine curled forwards like an ammonite. His jaw was so slack, the skin drawn so tightly up to his cheekbones, that she had to wait a moment to check that his chest was still rising and falling with breath.

She felt deeply unsettled as she left the room, conscious once again of the remoteness of the house, how vulnerable they were. And she wondered now on a practical level what she would do if Jérôme died under her watch. He shouldn't die for some time still; he had the right medication, and he ate well. But he was deteriorating. He was less able to tolerate some of his medications; he was losing weight quickly, sleeping more and more.

She walked back out into the garden, trying to stem a rising sense of horror. She shouldn't feel so anxious: she had supervised many deaths, even if she had never been the only medically trained person there, the only person responsible for a dying patient. That hadn't worried her before today. She wasn't afraid of handling Jérôme's body, of the litany of deathly ablutions: cleaning him, changing him, tying his jaw to keep it from dropping, placing padding around his anus and urethra to absorb the life that would leak out minutes to hours after death.

Until a doctor or coroner arrived, she would be the only living human for miles. But nor was that the full source of the horror settling around her as she walked through the garden, the clouds plump and grey above. This was the feeling she had at night, when she woke up from nightmares about Cassandre or saw shapes in the thick darkness outside. She'd first learnt it when she was fifteen, when Cass took ill. There were times in those first six months when she would awake in the night and gain access to the full nightmare of reality. She would sit up in bed, panicking, for fear it would crush her chest; she'd clutch at her face and head to try to wake up out of it.

There was no waking up out of it, she had learnt. It was simply a matter of acclimatising yourself. She'd worked out, through night after night, that horror can't be excised from reality. All life is lived alongside death, right next to it, hand in hand. She liked to think that her realisation had been something more than the banal existential conclusion drawn by most fifteen-year-olds: it had been visceral, not academic. What other friends had deduced from Camus she had learnt first-hand from Cassandre. She'd chosen a career centred around it.

She walked further than before, to the end of the olive groves, which she now realised wasn't in fact the end of the garden. Coming to the final terrace, she looked down to find an enormous rectangular pit in the ground – what must once have been a very large swimming pool.

The deep end was filled to perhaps half a metre with murky, viscous-looking water. A debris of leaves formed a patchy scum on the water's surface, its brown broken only by the faded red-grey of a Coca-Cola label that had long since come loose from its bottle. The walls of the pool, moistened by algae, must once have been tiled all over with small green cubes. They had crumbled away in misshapen patches, revealing dirty cement underneath. The patches of tiles were like islands and continents on a dark grey ocean.

She stepped down to the poolside and tried to imagine it as it might once have been, an expanse of limpid water looking out onto green terraces and silver-leaved trees, backed by thick woods. There was a ladder at one end, rusted and precarious, trailing off sadly into empty space. She imagined being able to step down the ladder slowly, feeling sunshine on her back, and launching off into cool, clear water.

She sat down on the paving, itself cracked and broken. In Jérôme's house, this derelict garden and decayed pool, she was witnessing the deterioration of more than an old man. It was the site of a whole life in decay: a large family, a huge garden filled with the ghosts of what had once been Jérôme's world. She could imagine the voices that used to fill these spaces; their echo seemed to hang in the air.

She wondered, not for the first time, why his sons were not here, why they did not come. There were no friends, no relatives, no noise. She was inhabiting the great, sprawling fossil of a whole family.

She noticed a little movement on the scummy surface of the water: some insect had moved, or perhaps a frog. There was a slight chill in the air; she stood up to walk back to the house. When she climbed up from the poolside back onto the terraces she became suddenly aware of the abandonment behind her, the pool and thick wood, and in spite of herself she broke into a run.

Jérôme awoke within an hour, calling her to him by knocking loudly on the headboard. She welcomed the sound.

'Where have you been?' he said.

'Waiting for you. You were asleep.'

'Was I?' He frowned. 'Where's my lunch?'

'I took it away. You fell asleep before you finished it.'

'Then you should have woken me.'

'Are you hungry? I can bring you a snack.'

He nodded, rolling his eyes, and Marguerite returned to the kitchen, coming back with a plate of crackers and Comté.

He plucked at a cracker. 'It's stale,' he said.

'I'm sorry.'

'Don't drop your standards.'

He ate a piece of the cheese, chewing noisily.

'You have your energy back,' she said softly.

'I know.'

He took the glass of water in both hands, shaking, and stared into the bottom of the glass as he drank, like a child. He kept drinking until it was almost finished, then pushed it towards her and leant back in the bed.

'I'll get dinner ready early, since you didn't have much lunch.'

'That seems reasonable.' His face and voice had softened a little.

She smiled. 'I came across the disused swimming pool,' she said. 'In the garden.'

His eyes narrowed as he looked at her. 'Yes. And?'

'I hadn't realised it was there. It must have been a huge pool.'

'Yes. It was. And?'

'I just—' She wondered now why she had mentioned it. 'I hadn't realised it was there.'

'As you just said. But what's your point?'

'I was just interested. I just – I have no point.'

'Yes, that's right. No point. But thank you for reminding me of the pool and its "disuse". Most tactful.'

She shook her head slowly, irritated now, and turned again to leave the room.

'Bring me those flowers,' he said. He pointed to the jug on the table with his shaking right hand. 'I would like to smell them.'

Marguerite brought the jug over: a pretty jumble of the wild, unearthly-looking flowers she'd picked, flowers she associated with the Alps more than these parts. They wouldn't smell of anything, but she brought them to his nose for him to try. In a swift, precise movement, he swiped the jug from her hands and it dropped, smashing into blue pieces and water and tangled stems on the floor by her feet.

When she cooked dinner that evening, she did something she'd always considered apocryphal: she spat into his spaghetti. She stirred it in, part appalled, part amused.

As he ate, she knelt by the bed to sweep up the wet mess of the broken jug and flowers. When he'd finished eating and she took away his tray, he said, 'It was my jug.'

She didn't bother to respond.

She dreamt she was underwater. The walls of the pool were glass, though she couldn't see through them; they were very grimy, the water greasy. As she swam, trying to reach the end of the tank, she felt something ice cold on her foot and knew that it was dead. She didn't look back, didn't want to see it; she tried to shake her foot free.

She kicked so hard that she woke up, pulling her legs up in the bed and scrambling to sit up, still feeling that something was trying to hold on to her. She switched on the lamp and, squinting, looked around the room. Her left foot throbbed; she must have kicked the cold radiator. Her mouth was furry, and she remembered that she'd been a little drunk when she'd gone to bed. A headache was spread like someone's palm across her forehead.

She rubbed her feet to warm them, and as she held them it was Cassandre's icy feet she imagined. Cassandre had come in at around midnight that night, burning with a fever, flushed and blotchy. She ached all over, she said; her head was agony. Marguerite let her crawl into her bed and lie head to toe as she so often did when she was ill, like tonight, or their parents were fighting, or she was scared of something and couldn't sleep. But tonight Cassandre wriggled and squirmed, turning from one side to another, restlessly. Her teeth chattered and she tugged the blankets constantly around her. At first Marguerite sang to her and stroked her burning face, but eventually she became tired and impatient. 'I have vocab tests tomorrow, Cass, I've got to sleep. Just try to stay still.'

But still she squirmed and shuddered, and every time Marguerite started to slip away into sleep she was awoken by Cassandre's feet; it was like someone pressing large blocks of ice to her arm or back or shoulder. Finally, she ordered her back to her own room. 'For God's sake,' she snapped, irritated in spite of how ill her sister was. 'Get your feet out of my face. They keep waking me.'

110

'I'll stop moving,' Cassandre said, and Marguerite had said the words she could never forget.

'*Just go away.*'

And Cassandre had gone away. Too scared to wake their parents, she'd gone back to her own bed. Marguerite could never know what loneliness and pain and fear she'd suffered from then until the next day, by which time she'd slipped into a coma. Marguerite watched from the door of their building as Cass's body was rushed away in an ambulance, their mother in the back instead of Marguerite, even though Cass was her little baby more than their mother's. She watched the ambulance disappear and knew that this was, in entirety, her own fault.

If Cass's feet hadn't been so cold, if her shaking hadn't kept waking Marguerite, surely she would have been less cruel, surely she would have let her spend the whole night there. She would have woken up when things got worse, when Cassandre had a seizure or whatever it was that had happened; she would have prevented her descent. Cass would be a healthy young adult now, able to walk and talk with precision. She and Marguerite would be living together; as soon as Marguerite had finished school, she would have found a job – not as a nurse, perhaps far away from death and sickness – so that she could take Cassandre out of their parents' noxious apartment and rent somewhere small of their own. She would work while her little sister attended university, studying science or philosophy or literature: intelligent, a brilliant student.

Or was this fantasy, as ever? Who could vouch for the fact that Marguerite would have taken Cassandre away from their parents when she was old enough – she who had sent her back to her own bed the night of her illness, who had told her, rough and impatient, to *go away*? Unspeakably, brutally stupid, she'd failed to see how gravely ill Cassandre was, how she shook and shivered, how her blotchy face wasn't right. She hadn't paid attention. She had been more interested, in those years – on the surface at least – by the attention of boys and the approval of her female classmates than the blind devotion of that elfin little girl.

After that night, Cassandre's feet were never the same again. Before the illness they were pretty, soft from the family's carpeted lifestyle, surprisingly long for such a little girl. 'It means you'll be tall,' Marguerite had told her once or twice.

Her arches were not as pronounced as Marguerite's, but that changed after meningitis. At first, her feet were limp and lifeless. And then, slowly but unstoppably, her left foot started to curl until it was pointed constantly, even when she slept. Within a year the right foot had followed suit, and finally they became a gross parody of a ballerina on pointes.

When daylight began to creep in between the shutters, she dressed and left the house. She moved like a sleepwalker down the track, looking down, watching her trainers step one after the other and again and again and again, of their own accord. She felt at a remove from her body, as if she were still drunk.

She thought of the word sleepwalker as she moved, let it plod out its heavy, muffled consonants in her head: *somnambule, somnambule*. It was a tired word. For a moment she thought: *I am so tired*. What she wouldn't give for someone to come along now and put her in a car and drive her somewhere, let her sleep. She didn't want to be in the house with that tyrant of an old man; she didn't want to be in the village, among its dully vicious women; she didn't want to be back in

Paris, nor a new nursing home in some forgotten corner of this country. She was out of options.

Jérôme was quiet when she brought him his lunch, patient as she helped him up to piss and then settled him into his chair. As he ate, she tidied his bedside table and emptied the pan by his bed into the loo. They would have to come up with a new approach soon: he could no longer sit up unaided. For now, he could call her each time he needed to piss – but it wouldn't be long, she knew, until he couldn't hold it for as long as it took her to come.

When she came back with the empty pan, he looked up.

'This stew is very good.'

She didn't answer; she had barely spoken to him since he'd smashed the jug of flowers. He watched her, chewing slowly.

'I had a dream this morning,' he said. 'I tried to get out of bed to walk through to the garden, but I fell. I had forgotten how to walk.'

She sat at the table, looking over his charts.

'I was like a beetle.' He took a shaky spoonful of the stew, spending time to fish out a coin-shaped chunk of carrot. Then he looked up, waiting for a response, and she pushed the charts away and cleared her throat.

'It doesn't sound like a pleasant dream.'

'Well, obviously,' he said, frowning, and she waited for the customary outburst. But instead he gazed into the distance, his frown fading. 'It's funny, what reminds you of things you might have forgotten. I woke up remembering the way woodlice try to get onto their front when they've fallen the

113

wrong way.' He glanced at her. 'I used to flick them off the wall sometimes, to watch them struggle on their backs until they worked out how to get up. That's what young boys do, you understand.' He rested the spoon on the edge of the bowl, was quiet for a moment. 'Anyway, they can't simply turn over onto their front, woodlice; what they have to do is curl up into a little ball, and only then they can sort of roll onto their legs again. Every time, it takes them a while to work it out afresh.' He took another spoonful, chewed the meat carefully before swallowing. 'Why was I talking about woodlice?'

'Your dream.'

'Yes, that's right. Anyway, the fact is—' He paused, and she could see that he was picking his words with care. 'I thought, if you'd been here when I'd fallen – in the dream, that is – you would have helped.' He sniffed then and frowned. 'In other words, I might get rather angry but I'm afraid that's just the way I am.' Marguerite waited, and he continued to stare ahead of him, his expression imperious. 'After all, what I'm saying is that I am grateful for your care.'

Then he exhaled loudly and started to eat again, scooping up his stew more quickly and steadily. She stood there, aware that she must speak now.

'Thank you,' she said. He batted her words away with an impatient gesture.

'Oh shhh shhh,' he said, and she turned and left the room.

7

The light was falling, soft as felt, when she heard a car pull into the driveway. She had been lying on her bed, eyes open but reading nothing, and she got up and walked to the large bedroom at the front of the house. Through the window she watched Suki emerge from her car, slam the door, straighten her clothing, turn towards the house. Marguerite stepped back, but not quickly enough. She thought Suki had seen her watching.

She walked heavily downstairs, pulling her cardigan around her.

'Hello,' she said when she opened the door.

Suki leant her head to the side, smiled ruefully. 'Am I interrupting?'

'No. Come in.'

She took the kettle from its perch to the tap, watched the little flakes of limescale swirling as it filled with water.

'How are you, Marguerite?'

'I'm fine.'

'Good. I'm here to say a bit of a sorry.'

Marguerite looked at her as she replaced the kettle. Again, the rueful smile. 'Why?'

'I felt a bit bad after the fête. I felt like I should have stuck up for you when Laure was doing the Spanish Inquisition on you.'

'It's fine.'

'Really?'

Marguerite paused. 'I felt a bit confused by the whole thing. It was – unclear. There seemed to be something going on that I didn't know about.'

'Yes, there was. Thank you for being honest. I thought you were just going to say it was fine and bat me away.' She leant her head to one side again and looked at Marguerite intently. As so often, there was something staged in the gesture. 'Laure hates me. Laure and Brigitte hate me. They claim I made passes at Henri Brochon, Brigitte's husband, and they claim that's the reason they hate me. But they always did, ever since I arrived in Saint-Sulpice. You might think I blame too much on prejudice, but I don't. I arrived five years before *l'affaire du voile islamique* kicked off. You remember, the schoolgirls in Creil? Shit, you probably weren't even born.'

'I was. I was a child, but I know about it.'

'Of course you do – I forget you're actually educated, unlike these peasants. Anyway, when that came to a head they stopped even trying to pretend they liked me. Most people around here behaved badly, but them more than most. So it was way before the thing with Henri started.'

'And what was the thing with Henri?'

Suki frowned. 'Nothing happened. Okay, to be completely honest with you, I developed a crush on him. I was bored

116

in a way I had never even imagined could be possible. Even more bored than when we moved to Hilversum.' She got up to light a cigarette by the door. 'We went from a huge, magnificent house in Tehran to a hideous high-rise in North Holland. Hilversum, Europe's most depressing city. All of our assets stripped, my childhood home taken. We went from living like kings in the country we knew to living like trash, seen by everyone as outsiders. But that's a whole other story.'

She took a deep drag of her cigarette. The kettle hit its climax and clicked off, but neither of them moved.

'I was talking about Henri. Yes, and boredom.' She rolled her eyes with exaggeration. 'I was *so bored*. Philippe was never around – still never is, actually. I had no friends. And Henri and I got chatting once and I realised he wasn't just a brainless farmer; he was actually very sensitive, very smart. Educated. And of course it helped that he was devastatingly handsome.'

She smiled, a little wickedly.

'I'm here to apologise to you, so fuck it, I'm just going to be completely honest. I fell head over heels. I went over to their farm all the time, tried to talk to him about anything and everything. And I think he liked it, I think he liked the attention and the flattery and, God, just having someone more interesting to talk to than his tedious wench of a wife.'

Marguerite laughed. 'You have a point.'

'Anyway, this is an incredibly long-winded way of telling you: Laure and Brigitte hate me, and it goes back a very long way, and it's rooted in this huge perceived slight to Brigitte as well as in their racist ignorance. They're threatened by me, by the fact I'm attractive and confident and educated.' She dropped her unfinished cigarette, grinding it with her foot, and came back to sit at the table. 'But for some stupid, stupid reason, I did the fête again this year to try to show them I'm not beaten down by it, and that they haven't won. And—' She looked at Marguerite, now, with real awkwardness. 'And actually, when Laure was having a go at you, I didn't really want to be swept up in it.'

'You didn't want to be tarred with my brush,' Marguerite said, smiling.

'Don't put it like that,' Suki said. 'Do you think I'm terrible?'

'No. I really don't care. You shouldn't be worried about it.'

'Well, I have been. Because I really value getting to know you, and I want us to be friends.'

Marguerite felt herself recoil. She went to the sink and filled a glass with water, her back to Suki. 'Really, don't worry about it any more,' she said.

There was silence between them for a while as she drank the water; she was conscious of the glugging in her throat. When she put the empty glass down and turned around to face the table, Suki was pulling a bottle of wine from her bag. 'Now let's have a drink,' she said – and Marguerite must have looked confused, because she grinned. 'Yes, I drink. How could I survive here otherwise? I smoke, I drink, I flirt with married men.' She held both hands up, in mock defence. 'Don't judge me.'

'Okay,' said Marguerite, and smiled. 'I'll try not to.'

She went to get glasses and a corkscrew. 'What happened, by the way, with Henri?'

Suki looked up.

'You don't have to answer that.'

'Nothing happened. My theory,' she said as she pulled the cork out with a quiet pop, 'is that he's asexual. Or just incredibly, boringly moral. He obviously fancied me, but he just wouldn't take it any further. I think, deep down, he lacks imagination. I was projecting too much onto him out of sheer boredom. That's my theory.'

She poured two glasses, right to the top.

'*Santé.*'

'There's nothing out there, you know.'

Brigitte's words brought Henri back to the kitchen. He turned, and leant back against the counter. 'I was in my own world.'

'And some.' She was polishing their brass; pots and ornaments were laid out along the table, on newspaper. The smell of the polish filled the kitchen, gradually snuffing out the tang of garlic that had lingered from dinner. Henri loved the polish's petrol headiness. 'I couldn't be blamed for thinking there was a carnival going on outside or something, the way you're staring out.'

'That would be fun.' He looked over at Jojo, asleep in her bed in the corner of the room. 'I'm going to take her out,' he said, nodding towards her.

'Will you check on the lambs?'

'Yes, why not.' He whistled and Jojo opened her eyes and watched him. 'Come on, madam.' She sprang up and shook herself and went to wait by the door.

'I've almost finished these but I'll wait up,' Brigitte said.

'Great.'

The night was cool. Henri strode from the house, Jojo trotting ahead. He dropped his head back and looked up at the wide dark blue above him, stars edging out between teal clouds. There was a plump, waxing moon – he barely needed his torch to show the way. As they climbed the gentle hill towards the field, he called out to the sheep, telling them he was coming. Jojo yipped alongside him.

The lambs didn't need checking, really – they were two months already, and thriving – but he felt happier going to sleep this way. He liked to stand in the pasture and look down at the house and the cottages half a mile beyond it, their lit-up windows winking back at him when Paul and Thierry were in. Exhausting as lambing season was, in the months afterwards he half missed checking on the ewes in the middle of the night. Brigitte pitched in, too – she'd go before midnight, he'd go up at four. If there was frost on the ground, his boots would crunch as he made his way to the lambing barn; otherwise, there was no sound at all until he was close enough to hear the cries. That silence was good for you, he was sure of it.

The ewes blinked in the torchlight as he approached. Some were feeding, some lying half asleep, their lambs curled up next to them. He tucked the torch under his arm and checked his thinnest ewe, pressing his hands over the hard bulbs of her backbone, behind her ribs. Usually large and robust, with good milk supply, she'd had triplets this year and had been whittled down through the relentless feeding. Though the lambs were eating grass now, taking much less milk, she didn't seem to have gained any weight back.

When he set off back down to the house, he saw the lights blink off in Thierry's cottage. Could he be going to bed already?

He wondered whether he brought girls back from the village, or whether his brother and their friends visited the cottage and they stayed up drinking together, perhaps playing video games, or cards if young men still did that. Perhaps he ate dinner with Paul and his wife in the next-door cottage, free to come and go as he pleased.

He felt a terrible sadness then, and stopped walking. When this feeling came it was tangible, a tearing in the centre of his chest. He thought it might help if he could weep, as if somehow it could allow the tearing to stop, but tears never came. He took a deep breath, kept on walking. He imagined for a moment how things might have been if he had gone to work somewhere else when he finished his degree, rather than starting straight out at their farm. Perhaps he might have lived for a time in the town, with some friends. Jesus, maybe he might have allowed himself to have a relationship with one of them.

When he and Edgar met, they had for a time something resembling a relationship. For some months the vision opened up before him, forbidden and hidden but laced with a sort of hesitant joy nonetheless, of a different kind of life: long conversations at night, dinner plates left on the table long after they had finished eating, pushed to one side so they could concentrate on a bottle of good wine in the middle of the table, play cards, lean forward occasionally to kiss. Waking up full of desire from a night slept in sub-conscious proximity to someone he wanted; reaching over to pull Edgar's body towards his own. Allowing himself, just sometimes, to believe in the approval, the esteem of someone whose opinion he valued. He'd felt himself grow, allowed himself to believe in being a good man, a great mind. Brigitte's unfaltering high opinion of him only made him feel more worthless; he knew he didn't deserve it. With Edgar, for that short while, he could believe that he did.

It wasn't tenable, though; it couldn't last. There was the farm, there were his parents, there was Brigitte. There was everyone who had ever known him and believed in the dream of handsome, dependable, normal Henri. Henri the man, not Henri the faggot.

That reality had slowly poisoned their relationship. Edgar sensed it, and held on more tightly; this irritated Henri, burdened him with further guilt. Then Edgar became snide and arch. Their tussles became a competition, feints for power and dominance. Edgar had the great power of knowledge – the knowledge of Henri's secret – and Henri resented that. It could not make their partnership equal. He had stopped seeing Edgar, only ever catching a tense glimpse when they passed each other in their cars, or across a road in the village. And then, after over a year, the visits had started up again, different now. Purely physical, purely for the sake of release.

'Everyone all right?' asked Brigitte, looking up as he came in. She had put away the cloths and brassware; the large urn on top of the fireplace gleamed.

'Apart from Thirteen and her three. I'll get her on some extra food, try to get her condition back up.'

'I was wondering whether that might need to happen.'

Henri sat down opposite her at the table, and they each leant on their elbows and looked at each other and then away.

'Will I make a chamomile, or are you going to go down for the night?'

'Go down,' he said. 'I'm tired.'

122

'Me too.' She lifted herself heavily from the table, with a sigh, and he waited a moment and then did the same. They headed upstairs, switching off lights as they went, and he imagined the ewes in the field watching the windows snuff out to black, one by one, the moon and distant roadside lamps the only lights left in the valley.

8

She had to run from Jérôme's room to vomit. She managed to get to the sink in the utility room, where she brought up water and bile. Pain pounded behind her eyebrows. She rested her head on the side of the basin, still standing hunched over it.

'Are you all right?' Jérôme shouted from his room. She didn't answer; she took deep breaths. 'Hello?'

'I'm fine,' she called.

'You don't sound it.'

'Shut up,' she whispered into the sink.

She had always suffered terribly from hangovers, even as a teenager. On weekends, as a seventeen- and eighteen-year-old, she would go to bed very late, to sleep only for three or four hours; then she'd wake early to go and visit Cassandre, mouth dry and hair stinking from all the cigarettes she'd smoked the night before. 'Ponn-kyy,' Cass would stammer with her one eye pointing inwards and one eye out, trying to wave her hand in front of her nose. Curled like a rosebud, it didn't look like a hand waving away a smell. Sometimes, Marguerite would have to dash out of Cass's room to vomit in the large wet-room across the corridor. Then she'd rest her forehead on the cool porcelain of the toilet until she had the strength to go back.

'You've been sick,' he said when she returned to his room.

'I know.' She took his empty glass, filled it from the carafe on the table. She fought the urge not to drink it herself.

'If you were a different kind of girl, I'd say you were pregnant.'

She laughed, then, handing him his glass, but he looked entirely serious.

'I mean it!'

'What kind of girl?'

'One with a little more of the devil in her.'

'What does that mean?'

'You know what it means. A girl with a bit more—' He paused. 'You know what I mean, anyway.'

When he fell asleep she walked into the kitchen and lay down on the floor and closed her eyes. The ground was hard under her back; she felt her spine uncoil. The floor felt clean and cold as porcelain. The room was still spinning but it was gentler now. She could manage this.

Snippets of conversation from the night before slipped into her mind. She remembered the bizarre story of Suki's meeting with Philippe: her seventeen, living with conservative parents, him thirty-two. Suki had said her parents had never reconciled themselves to the match. Her face had stilled when she'd spoken, briefly, of the fact she saw them only twice after her marriage. 'Of course I'm not saying I regret anything,' she'd said. 'How could I regret Philippe? But nothing's worth losing your parents for.' Marguerite had thought briefly of herself and her own parents – how they'd all three of them lost each other, and how easily.

She remembered flashes of stories about various people in the village: the gay poet in the woods who'd had an affair with some minor politician; the raucously loud sex Laure the *boulangère* apparently had with her husband; the teacher at the local school who'd been discovered with child pornography; the woman who worked at the petrol station and was always turning up to work with a black eye or broken finger or fingerprint-shaped bruises on her arms. Sordid stories that Marguerite had enjoyed last night but that now made her feel complicit, uncomfortable.

She got up, very slowly, very carefully. She went to the loo, closed the door, sat down and pissed. A dark, sleek centipede made swift progress across the skirting board. She watched the occasional drip of the tap. Still not fixed. And her herb garden, still not planted. When would she do it? She'd do it tomorrow, she decided. Tomorrow, when she had her health back, she'd kick into action, stop sleepwalking.

She heard the sound of bottles clinking in the kitchen as she walked back towards it and she stopped. There was a clink again, and footsteps: someone there.

'Hello?' she called out, and edged forward, though her instinct was to run. And then she heard a loud, angry sigh and water gushing from the tap in the kitchen. She walked in and there was Brigitte dressed in a large pea-green shirt with short sleeves, her back to the doorway, standing at the sink.

'Hello,' she said again, and it was only then that Brigitte turned. Her lips were pinched tightly together, her eyebrows arched with the great strain of unsaid words. She turned back to the sink.

'I just thought I'd clear up some things you seem to have left out,' she said finally. She rinsed and shook the two wine glasses dry, resting them on the rack by the sink. Then she turned around, dried her hands on her hips. She stared at the empty wine bottles Marguerite had left on the table.

'You didn't need to do that,' said Marguerite. They stared at each other, steadily. Brigitte's top lip twitched a little.

'I must say, it looks like you've been entertaining,' she said.

'I had some visitors,' said Marguerite, before realising she didn't need to explain herself. And then she wondered – did she, in fact?

'So I see. And does Jérôme know about this?'

'I don't know. It's not a secret. He usually knows when someone comes into the house.'

'A lot of people come, do they?'

'No.'

'I'm not sure, Mademoiselle Demers, that someone in your position should be entertaining, let alone drinking on the job.'

'Oh, I haven't drunk a drop,' she said.

Brigitte blinked, her eyebrows raised high. 'And how is Monsieur Lanvier?'

'Fine,' she said. 'On very good form today, in fact. He's asleep right now.'

'I see. That's convenient.'

Marguerite couldn't respond to that. Her headache was back, pounding furiously behind her eyes. She rested her weight against the table. 'Can I help you at all?'

'Well, I was just coming to see how you were doing,' said Brigitte. She sniffed. 'To see if I could help with anything, in fact. See if you needed anything. But you seem to be getting along perfectly happily.'

'Yes, I'm absolutely fine,' she said. 'I'm fine, Jérôme's fine. Thank you for checking.'

They stood there again for a few moments of total silence, gazing steadily at each other. Marguerite clenched her toes in her trainers, hoping, pleading that Jérôme wouldn't call for her, bang the headboard, make some noise. To compound the situation, she was quite sure the next great wave of nausea was coming, and she wasn't at all sure she'd be able to keep it down. And then Brigitte broke the silence.

'Well, I'll be back again soon,' she said, turning. 'I'll take these out for recycling, will I?' She picked up the bottles with one hand, their necks gripped between her fingers. 'You do recycle?'

'No need to take them,' said Marguerite. 'I'll do it.'

Brigitte stared again and then she put them down carefully and opened the door. 'Goodbye.'

'Goodbye.'

Marguerite watched her pea-green bulk turn the corner of the house, heard the scrunching of her footfall on the gravel, the slamming of a car door, the chug of an engine. She sank into her chair, pressed her hands over her eyes.

The strange thing was that he had been thinking of Thibault just that morning. Out of nowhere, striding across the yard, the sun barely up, he remembered a day they'd decided to ride their bikes as far as they could take them. It was the summer they'd just finished school; he remembered that most of their friends had gone on a trip, they'd all hitched rides to Italy. Henri's father wouldn't let him go away from the farm for so long – not when he was just about to start agricultural college – and Thibault had fallen out with Jérôme over his exam results, which Jérôme said weren't as good as they should have been. And it's true, they weren't – Thibault hadn't worked enough, intelligent as he was. After their fight Thibault had a swollen mauve cheekbone and a limp; he threw an empty beer bottle at a wall so that it smashed and said that he was going to go to Italy anyway, fuck his dad. But when it came to it their friends all left and he didn't, and Henri didn't refer to it.

They set off before dawn, and by noon they were sodden with sweat, slow and heavy as donkeys on their bicycles. They were miles away from home. Henri was ahead on the empty road, surrounded by flat yellow fields, when he heard the thud behind him and turned to see Thibault in the ditch, his bike collapsed away from him.

He shouted out and pushed his own bike aside and ran over to Thibault's body, which was rigid and twitching. Brown as he was, his face was a pearly sort of blue, eyes rolled back into his head. Henri shouted his name, shook his shoulders, shouted his name again and then not much later Thibault opened his eyes and blinked and his great black pupils contracted and he fixed his sight vaguely, cloudily on Henri.

'What the fuck is happening?' he said, and Henri let out a tentative smile.

'I think you passed out.'

Thibault licked his white lips with a tongue that looked

129

dry. He had dirt in his wet black hair; still he didn't move, though he looked around from side to side.

'I've been here before,' he said. Then he raised himself up, slowly, onto his elbows. His face was yellow, a little colour coming back. He looked around himself again. 'I've been here exactly. This has all happened already. I've lived a whole life already.'

His expression was very calm. He fastened his eyes back on Henri, and then he smiled.

'Dude, that was weird.'

Henri laughed, relieved. 'You're talking total shit, asshole.'

'You're the asshole. I'm serious.' He was still smiling as he pushed himself up to a sitting position. 'Seriously, listen. I went way, way, way forward into my future. Years into my future. And now I've come back to this shitty road. With you.'

He smacked Henri around the head, lightly.

'Right, right,' said Henri. 'So what happens in this future of yours? All these years you've gone forward. What happens all the way over there? You're a millionaire, right? Surrounded by models?'

'Shut up,' he said. 'I don't remember what happened. But I know I lived virtually a whole lifetime. I mean it. Jesus.'

He was serious again then, and stared past Henri, into the distance. Henri looked at the crease of his frown, a firm line between his thick eyebrows, the stray hairs there where they almost joined. And underneath them the thick, dark eyelashes that he thought unutterably beautiful. He looked away.

'Well, you're a massive pansy,' he said, standing up. 'I can't believe you just fainted.'

'Oh, piss off,' said Thibault. 'It was trippy. It was like the best acid trip I've ever been on.'

He stood up, a little shakily, and wiped himself down. Henri didn't bother pointing out that Thibault had only taken acid once.

Thibault ran his hands through his hair, squinting as he looked into the distance. Then he turned to Henri. 'I don't know about you but my mouth's drier than an old man's anus,' he said, and they laughed again.

'Let's find some water,' Henri said, walking back to his bike.

'And food.'

'And beer.'

They set off again, Henri taking care to ride at a slower pace, but Thibault overtook him, riding too fast, showing he was fine.

'So long, sucker!' He flew past and ahead, wheels whirring, and Henri thought that that was fine, that he'd stay right here at the back to make sure nothing ever happened to him again.

He'd been remembering all of that only that morning, God knows why. Out of nowhere. And so now, when Brigitte told him over lunch, trying hard to seem calm with the news since she knew he hated gossip, that Thibault and his brothers were coming back to Saint-Sulpice the coming weekend, he felt like he had just been kicked, very hard, in the stomach. He stopped listening to what she was saying, took a long drink from his glass of water, felt it gurgle in his oesophagus as it made its way down.

'About time,' she was saying, 'for more than one reason.'

He looked up. 'What do you mean?'

'Well,' she started, and paused to take a delicate bite of her beef. He realised that there was more to the story than what she'd just said, that she was bursting with news. He couldn't stand it; he stood up to affect indifference and she caved, as ever, and spoke with her mouth still full.

'Well, first off, it's about time those sons visited their sick father. But secondly, I think they need to check out the very serious situation he's in with that new nurse.'

Henri took a beer from the fridge; he could feel the adrenaline pulsing through his body. He poured the beer calmly into a glass, took the glass to the table, sat down. She eyed his beer; he didn't usually drink at lunch.

'What are you talking about?' he asked.

'I went by Rossignol today,' she said, 'to tell them that Jean-Christophe had called, that the three of them would be visiting from Paris.'

'When do they arrive?'

She laid down her fork. 'I've already told you, Henri. On Friday. For the weekend.' She lifted the fork again, started to arrange her next bite. 'Anyway, so I went to Rossignol to check on things and see if I could do anything to help, and of course to let them both know the good news, and you just won't believe what I found. I walked in and she was nowhere to be seen but the kitchen table was *littered* with bottles, glasses, you name it.'

'And so?'

'Henri! *And so this nurse*, whose job it is to care for a dying old man, is clearly not only an alcoholic but has been entertaining people at a house that isn't even her own. And she didn't even deny it!'

'That she's an alcoholic, because she drank some wine?'

'No, Henri, she didn't deny that she'd been entertaining.'

'Come on, that's hardly a crime. Surely it's a good thing she's got friends?'

'Henri! You're being impossible, on purpose!'

He leant back in his chair and she frowned.

'She shouldn't be entertaining on the job, it's not her home and anyway she's on duty, and she certainly shouldn't be drinking alcohol, which she quite clearly had been. And there were only two glasses, which quite frankly leads me to think that she's entertaining a male visitor.'

'That's completely unfounded,' said Henri. He pushed his knife and fork together and stood up from the table. 'What did Jérôme say when you told him about his sons?'

'Well, I never told him. He was asleep.' She was quiet for a moment. 'Actually, I didn't tell her they were coming.'

'What?'

'I decided not to, Henri, and I think you'll understand why. It's in his sons' best interest that they get the full picture, so I think it's best she doesn't have any warning. Just like she didn't have any warning I'd be there today. I can tell you, those bottles wouldn't have been sitting there like that if she'd known I was coming.'

'That's ridiculous,' he said, and she blinked.

'Henri!'

'You've withheld that information from her to catch her out? It's absurd. And of course Jérôme needs to know.'

Brigitte's eyes had watered as they did easily, at the slightest recrimination. 'I'll go and tell them this evening,' he said. 'If you haven't already.'

'But Henri!'

'There's no discussion.' He drained his glass and slammed it into the sink. 'I've got to work.'

He ignored her sniffing and walked out of the door, Jojo at his heels. It was hot and overcast, so he had been covered all day in a film of sweat. He strode up the hill to the left of the house but he didn't go straight back to work: when he reached the top he lay down on his back on the grass, looking up at the muggy white sky, letting his irritation ebb away. Jojo lay down next to him, waiting. He could smell the heat coming off her and the dark, breathing soil, its minerality and fecundity and pulse.

Another memory came to him from that summer. The two of them, lying together on the grass somewhere under a dark sky and stars. Their heads together, so that when they turned to speak to one another their faces almost touched. Stoned and teenage and happy.

'Why do you want to leave so badly?' he had asked.

Thibault was silent for a while.

'Why do you *not* want to leave?' He turned to look at Henri and their eyes were dizzyingly close. Cross-eyed.

Henri turned back to the stars. 'I like it here.'

'You want to get married and run the farm and breed.'

They laughed.

'I want to run the farm. I think I'd hate living in a city.' He flicked the lighter, the flint hot against his thumb. 'I like it here,' he repeated.

'And I hate it.' That was mildly wounding to Henri, but

not as much as it might have been. Just as, when he thought about Thibault moving away, he didn't feel as sad as he should have done. He hadn't realised, then, everything it would entail, the total separation. He'd vaguely envisaged regular weekends spent back in Saint-Sulpice, and the kinds of family holidays his own family had never had: cycling, skiing, sailing trips abroad.

'You mean you hate your dad.'

'What's the difference?' Thibault sat up, then. He hugged his knees. 'I want to get so far away from him that he's just the size of one of those stars.'

Henri sat up like Thibault had all those years ago, and gazed down at the farmhouse. He thought again of Thibault pedalling fast ahead of him on that country road and Thibault arriving here in just a few days. The dog jumped up and panted with impatience and he lifted himself to his feet and gave her a gentle slap and they set off. He allowed himself to whistle as he walked, happy and afraid.

It was no longer dark in those hours after his dinner, when she read to him. The light this evening was soft, low pink-grey clouds dissolving into dusk. The smell of roast chicken still hung faintly in the room, though she'd taken his plate away. He was calm and clean and sharp-eyed, staring attentively into nothing as she read, interjecting occasionally – 'He'll show them sooner or later', or '*Yes*, Monte Cristo!'

It was a shock when the phone rang. They looked at each other, alarmed or confused, and then he said,

'Well, come on. Haven't you ever answered a phone before?'

'Of course I have,' she said, leaving the room. But she didn't want to. It was an intrusion.

Brigitte's voice was flat, distant. 'I just realised I'd forgotten to tell you earlier that Monsieur Lanvier's sons will be coming here this weekend. They called me last night to let me know, which is why I came over earlier today.' There was silence. 'I *never* normally forget anything, but I was too distracted by—' She paused again, the silence full. 'They'll be here on Friday, anyhow.'

After Marguerite had put the phone down she waited, head bowed, thinking about what this would mean for them. When she came back to Jérôme's room his neck and shoulders and face were tensed and alert.

'Well? Who was it?'

'Brigitte Brochon.'

'Oh, for God's sake,' he said. 'What did the old bat want?'

'She had a call from your sons.'

Jérôme blinked, his eyes enormous. 'And?'

'They're coming to visit. This weekend.'

'Oh, are they now!' He frowned and she saw his jaw working a little, lips moving as he thought. 'Well well well. Finally feeling guilty, I suppose! Or perhaps they're hoping I'm about to pop my clogs.' He looked at her then. 'Did she say anything else? Did she say why?'

'No, nothing.'

'You should have asked her.'

'I didn't think to.'

'That doesn't surprise me.' He took a deep sigh. 'Ah well. It is what it is. Perhaps they just feel like a break from work.'

'Perhaps they just want to see you?'

'Huh!' He laughed. 'No one ever *just wants to see* someone.' He drummed his lovely fingers lightly on the sheets, mouth still working away at something, eyebrows drawn into their deep frown. And then he shook his head, fastening his gaze back onto her. 'In case you're getting the wrong idea, you're not going to be able to have a dalliance with any of them. They're all married. Well, apart from Thibault, but he won't be interested. He only asks out fashion models as far as I can tell.'

'I'm not looking for a "dalliance".'

'You can't fool me. I know women. Especially your age, it's biology. Time to push some children out.' She started to object, but he interrupted, tapping the book in her hands with a finger. 'Well? Come on, where were we?'

She rolled her eyes and started to read again, and as she went on she noticed his face start to soften, his eyelids become heavy. She closed the book, put it away, turned off the overhead light.

'You've lasted a lot longer than I thought you would.' He looked up at her as she leant over him to tuck his blanket in.

'You haven't always tried to make it very easy,' she said, and to her surprise he nodded.

'I thought you were a lot weaker than you are, actually. Now I realise you've got a bit of backbone, for a Parisian.'

'Oh,' she said, smiling. *'For a Parisian.'*

'Yes. I'm quite serious.' He frowned. 'Your lot are mostly pampered and pompous. Equating the countryside with ignorance, small villages with small minds, when the fact of the matter is we're all as base and desperate as each other. Take how my sons have turned out. They could have been strong, sensible fellows and now – well, you'll see for yourself this weekend. Jean-Christophe is an arrogant little lawyer. Thibault's wet, he wastes all his time and intelligence picking up women. Marc's all right but he's ended up with a wife who spends all his money and thinks we live in the sticks down here, that we're all cretinous and inbred. She's only been here three times, can you believe that? And their children are all odious, spoilt little creatures.'

'You can't really think that.'

'I can! And I do. They're pampered little lap-dogs who've never had to experience one day of hardship.' He blinked slowly, looked down at his hands. 'Not that you can ever guarantee how they'll turn out. Céline and I gave our boys everything: education, great holidays, all the latest sporting equipment. I've told you, this place was quite something – it was the grandest house in this whole area, hands down. But I didn't spoil them. I always showed them the merits of hard work. I made them sing for their supper, just like I had to as a boy. Céline, of course, she was softer than me, she thought I was too hard on them sometimes.' He sighed. 'Maybe she was right. I don't know. Maybe she was right.' His voice was very quiet now. 'If she was still around, they'd be down here once, twice a month. Don't think I don't know that. Don't think I don't know the only reason they don't come is because they just can't stand me.'

'I think you're being hard on yourself.'

He looked up at her, and she saw that he was trying to work out whether he could believe her.

'Oh, maybe I am. I don't know. She was too soft sometimes. I don't know.' He clasped his hands together. 'My back is very painful tonight. Right at the bottom. Can't you give me something for it?'

'Yes, I can.'

'Give me something that will knock me out.'

As she prepared his medication she tried to think of something she could say to him, something to make him less sad. 'I think your sons will enjoy their time here, you know. Maybe they'll start coming back more often after this.'

'Don't pity me,' he snapped. 'I'm not a fool.'

'I don't. I mean it,' she lied.

'You don't mean it. You're pitying me. The only person you should be pitying is yourself.'

She sighed, and he shook his head.

'They won't start visiting more often. You know as well as I do that the next time they come down after this weekend, I'll be fastened up tight in a wooden box.' He looked at her, and his face softened again. 'And you'll be off to your next job, God knows where, God knows why. Wasting your youth on miserable old buggers like me.'

He took the pills she handed him, held the glass of water to his lips. He looked very tired then.

'You're not a miserable old bugger,' she said.

'I will be if you don't piss off now and stop being so soft.'

He smiled a little wryly and she smiled back and wanted to say something else, but didn't.

She felt unusually peaceful when she went to bed that night. She felt peaceful, too, when she woke in the morning, after a quiet night from Jérôme. But when she had left him with his breakfast, when she was settling into her chair in the kitchen with her coffee, silence soft and thick around her, the telephone rang again. It was the youngest son. His voice was too loud in the receiver, so she had to hold it away from her ear.

They'd decided, he announced, to come sooner than the weekend; they were about to set off in the car, would be arriving that evening. In his quick monotone he told her what time to expect them, which bedrooms they'd each be taking, asked her to make beds up. She accepted all of his orders without thinking, realising only as she ended the call that she was Jérôme's nurse, not their housekeeper, and that she'd just agreed to move out of her own room because it used to be Thibault's.

When she told Jérôme they were coming sooner he was furious, blaming her and then Brigitte for getting the timing wrong. And then he barked for the pan because he needed the loo and he shat immediately, with urgency, and she realised that he was nervous, that this was a response fuelled by adrenaline.

'You'll have to put me in some proper clothes when they arrive. Not these wretched pyjamas again.'

In the afternoon, she left him to go and start moving her belongings out of her room. She had to sweep and scrub; she fetched new sheets and towels, put on a wash. She looked at the room that would now be hers, the small sagging bed. The view from the window was blocked largely by one of those dark, priapic cypresses. She didn't like their gloomy stature, how they refused to rustle in the breeze.

When he slept she went down to the empty pool and sat on the cracked paving in the sun, her legs dangling down into what would have been cool, clear water. She rolled up her jeans, let the sun warm her legs and face. It was a great shame the pool was no longer in use – she could swim every day. Things would surely be a lot nicer, generally, if she could do that.

A wasp became interested in her, perhaps attracted to the sweat in her hair; it started to come and go, buzzing close and then retreating. There were huge ants wandering back and forth around her, bodies black and shiny as mica. She ducked again from the wasp as it hovered near her face. She should check on Jérôme anyway. She stood, and as she walked away from the pool area she saw something and froze – a thick, metre-long snake stretched out against the wall. It was dead; its face was dry and ashen, eyes blanched, skin flaking like loose pastry. But it made her shudder. She wouldn't come back down here.

Jérôme was already awake. He was silent and watchful as she took his blood pressure, gave him pills, cleaned and tidied about him. But as the shadows lengthened in the room he became restless, fidgeting constantly, plucking at his blanket.

'Let's have an early supper now, get it over and done with. And then let's have me sitting up in the chair,' he said. 'I won't be in bed when they come, I think.'

He ate very little. After she'd cleared the tray away she combed his thin hair into a side parting and dressed him in a pale blue shirt and navy jumper. It was a nice jumper, with a zip at the collar. But the clothes were far too big for him; his collar fell away stiffly from his neck.

She took him to his chair and he sat with his shoulders tense, up near his ears, staring intently before him. She offered to read to him to pass the time but he shook his head quickly.

'I can't bear to listen to that bloody book right now,' he said. 'In your plodding voice.' She left him then. She went upstairs to her tiny new bedroom and lay on the bed and waited.

She wasn't used to sleeping on such a small bed; she woke up at the point of falling off. It was completely dark outside. She sat up, trying to work out where she should be and what she should do. Then she remembered: Jean-Christophe, the sons, Jérôme, it must be past half past eight, they must be here already.

But she heard nothing when she came down the stairs. It was eleven o'clock and the house completely silent. She checked the kitchen before seeing to Jérôme, but it was empty. She went to the large window by the formal front door, which overlooked the drive. No car.

She looked into Jérôme's room then; there he still was in his chair as she'd left him, chin on his chest, drool collecting at the front of his bottom lip where it fell away from his gum and spilling gently onto his swollen stomach. He was sparrow-like in the big chair, in his smart clothes. She approached him quietly, knelt before him and rubbed one arm to rouse him.

He woke and looked around immediately, sucking in the drool, pulling his head painfully upright.

'I just nodded off,' he said. He cleared his throat. 'Just for a moment.'

'I know.' She stayed there, kneeling before him. He blinked a few times, pulling himself back into his surroundings as she had just done upstairs on her bed.

'What time is it?'

'It's eleven o'clock.'

'So where are they? Why didn't you wake me and show them in?'

'They're not here yet.'

His head jerked back a little; he looked away, focusing on the door. He moved his mouth, he breathed in and deeply out. When he spoke again, he didn't look at her.

'Take me out of these stupid clothes.'

'Okay.'

'And get me out of this chair. It's uncomfortable, I despise it.'

She lifted him and he leant all his weight into her as she did. She felt as if she might tear his arms from their sockets. They made slow progress to the bed. Then she pulled the jumper over his head and with some difficulty took his arms out, one by one. She unbuttoned the shirt from the top to the bottom. She unpeeled the vest he'd worn underneath, lifting it gently over his head, brushing her hand against the woolly white hair at the back.

'You always smell rather nice,' he said quietly, and she heard something horribly sad in his voice.

'Really?' she asked. 'Of what?'

'Oh don't ask me what of. It's just quite nice.'

The tight fists of his spine were red, rubbed by his position in the chair. She got some cream and he sucked in when she applied it.

'Cold,' he whispered.

'Sorry.'

She buttoned him into a clean pyjama shirt and gave him a pill and let him piss into the pan. It was a slow, reluctant trickle. Coffee brown. She laid him down and he turned over in his bed to face the wall.

'Goodnight,' she said, but he didn't answer.

She cooked while she waited for his sons to arrive and it felt strange and pleasant to be cooking so late at night, somehow illicit. She took out stumpy sweet potatoes and a bowl of firm, quivering stock from the fridge. A few tiny green chillies, a sprig of browning thyme, a bunch of smart baby tomatoes, bouncing from the vine.

While the vegetables were cooking she opened one of the windows above the sink and leant forward to listen to the night. A very loud toad or frog was burping – it must have been his mating call. It sounded proud, as if it might have its chest thrust out, sizing up the competition. She thought then of Cassandre. These were things she might have told her to make her laugh.

But only when she was little. Not after the illness. Even though in many ways she became younger with her injuries – that spider's web of injuries that had amassed and spread and colonised her, gossamer fine but immoveable – she didn't revert to the young mind, fearsomely discerning and delightful and quick, that she had had as a child. She became a child, yes, but a different one. The new child was passive and slow and pubescent. A child who gained weight and became spotty because of medication and lack of mobility, but also because of the hormonal havoc wreaked by her injury – because beauty, too, is governed by the brain.

She heard the distant sound of gravel prickling under

tyres and the humming whoosh of a good engine before it switched off. Silence, and then doors slamming. She wondered where to stand when they arrived. Greeting them at the door would be servile, as if she should curtsey and take their bags and coats. She turned to the hob instead, busied herself with the stew.

There were voices and a quick knock on the glass and the door opened, and she turned.

Jean-Christophe came in first – shorter and chubbier than he'd seemed to her in Paris, where he'd been impatient and remote, squeezing her interview in between meetings. The other two were dark where he was fair: one very tall, almost bear-like; the second black-haired with a sharper face, wide cheekbones, dark eyes.

'Hello,' they said in echoes of each other. They threw down bags; the tallest closed the door behind him. No one came forward to greet her but they each held hands up in a perfunctory sort of wave.

'I hope you haven't waited up?' asked Jean-Christophe, but didn't wait for her answer. 'Such a long drive. I suppose the old man's asleep?'

'Yes, he's asleep now,' she said, and she noted the relief on their faces. They removed jackets, threw them onto the low sofa to the left of the door, which she never used. Jean-Christophe sat down right there, letting out a loud sigh as he did. Another – they still hadn't introduced themselves – trampled over to a cupboard, took a glass, went to the sink and filled it up and drank it down. The other sat at the table, leaning back, looking around. She remembered as she saw them do these things that they knew this place, it was their place.

'We'd been hoping to get here sooner but we got caught up on the way,' said the tallest.

'Was the journey all right?'

'Yes, fine. I'm Marc,' he said then, reaching a hand forward to shake hers. 'You've met Jean-Christophe. And this is Thibault.' He gestured towards the son at the table, who smiled stiffly but didn't move.

'Nice to meet you,' she said, and felt stupid. She couldn't think when she had last spoken in front of more than one person.

'Nothing's changed, hey?' said Jean-Christophe, addressing his brothers. He rubbed his hands over his face and blinked, looking round. They were small hands, not like Jérôme's. She could see nothing of Jérôme in him: rosy, healthy-looking cheeks, a small chin. Soft shoulders and plump soft neck, pale eyes and eyebrows. 'Drink?' he said.

Marc and Thibault grunted, and Marc walked through to the pantry; she heard cupboards open and close, bottles clink. 'There's a very old-looking whisky,' he called out.

'Bring it through,' said Thibault.

'I'm shattered. It's a long time to be on the road,' said Jean-Christophe. He took out his phone, a shiny BlackBerry, and scrolled. 'Oh for God's sake,' he said. 'The office is already after me. I've told them not to bother me but this always happens. They can't help it.' He spoke fondly, as if of a friend.

'That's because you're just *so* important JC,' said Thibault, and Marc laughed as he came through with the bottle, ducking his head instinctively in the doorway. Marguerite turned back to the hob.

'There's some stew here, in case you're hungry,' she said, turning to look at them.

Jean-Christophe was typing busily, muttering with a frown about the poor mobile reception; Thibault leant back and stretched his arms out, a taut golden stomach showing as his T-shirt lifted. 'I'm fine,' he said.

Marc grunted, pouring whisky into three glasses. 'Me too. Thanks very much,' he said, looking away awkwardly, and she realised he didn't know her name. She hadn't introduced herself, and now it felt too late.

Jean-Christophe looked up, finally, and blinked.

'That's incredibly kind but I'm actually stuffed, we ended up stopping by a friend's for dinner along the way. That's why we're a bit later than we'd hoped, I'm afraid.'

She thought of Jérôme waiting up for them in his smart clothes, falling asleep with the knobs of his spine grinding into the chair, and she felt her toes clench in her shoes.

'Erm . . .' said Marc, looking at her. 'Would you like a drink too?'

'I'm fine. Thank you.'

He looked relieved.

'*Santé*,' they said to one another, raising their glasses.

'Home sweet fucking home,' said Thibault, looking sideways at Marguerite. She turned back to the hob and switched off the gas and put the lid back on the stew.

'I'm going to go up,' she said, and they all looked at her.

'Yes of course,' said Jean-Christophe. 'I do hope you didn't wait up for us.'

'No, I was up anyway.' But she wouldn't have been.

'Goodnight,' said Marc, and Thibault nodded and raised his glass.

'We can catch up properly tomorrow on what's been going on,' said Jean-Christophe, cheeks becoming neat and round as he smiled, like a marionette. Then he looked back down at his screen.

They'd said Friday and arrived three days early, she thought as she cleaned her teeth. They'd said eight thirty, and arrived close to midnight. She wondered, spitting into the sink and rinsing her mouth, splashing her face and drying it roughly, whether this was all manipulation – whether, like their father, they simply intended to pull her around on strings.

II

9

She woke very early, sensed that Jérôme was awake too. She lay there for a moment, listening. It was a particularly silent morning, she thought, a beautiful thin white sky following dawn. She struggled to open the window; it was stiff and groaned as she struggled with it. But then it gave, and a panoply of smells tumbled in: wet, fresh, herby like tarragon. Her new room looked over the other side of the house from the kitchen, adjacent to the driveway. If she looked to the side of the cypress she could make out, just over the tops of the trees and hedges that cut the house off from the world outside, the hint of distant hills, each layer less blue than the one before until they disappeared as if into smoke.

She dressed more carefully than usual: trousers instead of jeans, clean blue sweater. She brushed her hair, noticing in the mirror that it was getting too long. It would need a cut, God knew where.

She walked down the landing and stairs carefully, loath to wake their intruders. She opened the door to Jérôme's room quietly in case he was asleep, but he was just as she'd known he would be, awake, eyes wide to greet hers.

'Good morning,' she whispered.

'Morning.'

'Are you okay? Did you sleep?'

'Mostly.' He was whispering too. 'Did you?'

She was embarrassed by the question; he had never asked it. 'Yes, thank you,' she said. 'I'm going to go and make some coffee and then I'll come back.'

'I'll be waiting.'

She hated the big, rusty cafetière, the unwashable grime in its filter, and so she used a percolator to make coffee here, something she'd had to learn at the beginning of this job. She remembered swearing at the various parts, trying to work out how smooth coffee came out of them. They had winked smugly at her, unwilling to share their knowledge. Now she loved the ritual of it, unscrewing the top from the base and taking out the filter, pulling away the parts like a matryoshka. And the smell when the water started to rise up through the filter, like magic. She took hers black but she heated milk to add to Jérôme's. Then she took them through, with some buttered toast with jam.

'Delicious,' he said. He looked up. 'You can stay here while you drink your coffee.'

'Okay,' she said. He'd never invited her to do that before. Sometimes she just did, so she could wait for him to finish eating and then get straight on with his medication. But she'd never been invited.

'They're here now,' she said, sitting down, and he flapped his hand and scowled.

'Oh, don't talk to me about them.' He took a bite of his bread, and looked at her. 'You know what I'd really like?'

'What?'

'A croissant. But a fresh croissant, straight from the boulangerie.' He wiped the corner of his mouth. 'Really buttery. I'm not asking you to go and get me one,' he added. 'But I suppose that's the shame in not having a car here, isn't it?'

'Yes,' she said. 'I'd like a croissant too.'

'Perhaps we'll think about getting you a car.' He frowned then. 'Nothing special, I mean. We could just see if someone in the village has an old one they're not using, someone who wants to make a few euros. There's always someone willing to sell what they've got, especially in this place.'

He ate the rest of his toast in silence, staring fixedly into nothing. When she took the empty plate from him he said, 'I don't want any visitors this morning. I need to rest.'

'You mean—'

'Yes, I mean I don't want those louts to come in. You're allowed, of course,' he said. 'But no one else. Oh yes, I may be stuck in bed but it doesn't mean they can just swan in and out as they please.'

She took his blood pressure, his temperature and heart rate, made a note. He was doing okay.

'What should I tell them?' she asked then, and he didn't answer right away.

'Just tell them I'll see them later,' he said. 'If I feel up to it.'

Jean-Christophe was the first to wake, joining her in the kitchen as she cleaned.

'Morning,' he said. 'Sleep well?'

'I did, thank you. And you?'

'Like a baby.' Clean and fresh with his neat wet hair, she thought how just like a baby he looked. 'Any instant coffee or do I have to grapple with this thing?' He nudged the percolator, peered inside it. 'There's only dregs left in there.'

'There's a cafetière.' She turned from him to rinse out her cup and looked at their three whisky glasses in the sink, unwashed. He sighed, loudly, and she heard him patter through to the larder and rummage around.

'I'm going to have to pop out to the village to get a newspaper and some breakfast things,' he said when he came back in. 'There's only old sliced bread here.'

'I find I can't get it fresh each morning.'

'Quite.' He sank down into the sofa where he'd sat the night before, next to the jacket he'd thrown there and hadn't yet moved. 'Strange not to have Grenouille here.' He gestured at the space beside him, and she must have looked blank. 'Our dog. He used to spend his life curled up right there. Someone took him when Mum passed away. Dad said he couldn't bear the sight of him any more.'

Marc came in then, his face crumpled with pillow lines, and he raised a hand at Marguerite. 'Good morning.'

'Good morning.'

'Any coffee?' he asked Jean-Christophe, and there was a little silence.

'You can make some, I can't be bothered. And there's

absolutely nothing to eat. We'll have to go into the village to get everything.'

'Well, that's to be expected,' he said, and nodded at Marguerite. 'How's the old man?'

'He's okay.'

'Let's go,' said Jean-Christophe. He turned to Marguerite. 'Will Dad be up when we get back, do you think? Does he usually sleep in this late?'

'He's been awake since dawn,' she said, and she thought for the first time that Jean-Christophe looked uncomfortable. 'I was just going to go and check on him.'

'Don't check on him on our account,' said Marc. 'We'll head into the village now and say hello to him when we're back.'

'Okay.'

She watched them leave, the absent way they pulled the latch and swung the door to, muscle memory. She leant back against the hob. She didn't know where to go – the garden was no longer hers, the kitchen certainly wasn't. She went to check in on Jérôme; he was asleep now, as she'd thought he would be. And so she left the house and walked through the driveway and out of the gate, turning left for a change rather than right towards the village. And she broke into a jog, surprising herself, and then again she started to run faster. She felt her calves spring in that old, familiar way, let the balls of her feet propel her from the ground, her concentration fastening onto the rhythm of her breath. Her core was locked into position; her cheeks started to burn; the whoosh of passing air felt good against her temples. These were all things she used to love.

The door to her room – Thibault's room – was still closed when she got back to the house, and she was quiet as she moved around the small new room and across the landing to the bathroom. She filled the bath halfway with tepid water – she had imagined wanting it to be ice cold, but it was too much to bear – and lay back in it, letting her face throb against the cool that rushed to surround it. She felt her heart rate slow, her breath regulate. She wondered why she hadn't done this before.

When she came out of the bathroom in her towel, Thibault's door was open and he walked out, eyes skimming over her quickly as he pulled a T-shirt over his head. She realised she'd known that this was what would happen.

'Morning,' he said, lazily, and she murmured back, trying not to look as if she were hurrying back to her room. She shut the door behind her and sat on her bed, feeling compromised, somehow tricked.

Jérôme was watchful and wide-eyed. When he was in one of these moods he was like a vole, listening out for predators, ears flexed, whiskers quiveringly alert.

'So they're all here? What are they doing with themselves? Have they asked to see me?'

'Yes I said you were resting.'

'Don't say I'm resting! Say I'm not ready to see them yet.'

'Okay.' She rolled up his sleeve, pulled Velcro from Velcro, wrapped his arm in the blood-pressure cuff, pumped. 'They think they can just swan in and out,' he said. 'Just as they wish. No warning. Arriving late. Are they even awake?'

'Yes,' she said, letting the pump go with a soft whoosh. 'Mouth.'

He opened it, let her slot the thermometer under his tongue, closed his mouth around it. He watched her as she moved about the room, rinsing his glass and filling it, taking his pills from the cabinet, selecting them one by one, laying them in the little saucer.

The thermometer beeped and he took it out himself.

'Normal.'

'Good.'

She took it from him, made notes.

'I'll listen to the radio,' he said. 'You can tell them I'm wide awake, listening to the radio. And I'll have some lunch soon please. I'm ravenous.'

'When would you like to see them?'

'Make sure they know you're taking my lunch to me.'

'Okay. When would you like to see them?'

'Oh, I'll decide when,' he said, and she sighed as she turned to leave the room.

It wasn't until sunset that he announced he would see them, one by one. She'd had to placate them all day, saying he was tired but they could see him later, pleading silently with him to let them in. When he finally said he would, she exhaled heavily. She couldn't have stood keeping them out until the next day. She already felt uncomfortable, possessive, like his gatekeeper.

He asked for them in what she understood to be order of age: Marc, Thibault, Jean-Christophe. Each looked grim before

157

they went in and light when they came out, little schoolboys waiting to be seen by the headmaster after being caught playing truant.

'He was fine,' Marc said when he came out, clapping Thibault on the shoulder. 'He wants to see you now.'

'Bizarrely cheerful,' said Thibault when he was done. 'Though he looks like a skeleton, Jesus.'

Even Jean-Christophe looked apprehensive then, but when he came out he seemed lighter too. 'He's obviously pretty sick, but his spirits are high, huh,' he said, and they all murmured in agreement.

'I was shocked at first, but . . .'

'I mean, I kind of expected worse, the way Brigitte has been banging on.'

'It's still pretty bad.'

'Yeah, for sure, but he was in a really good mood.'

'If you've got energy to be in a good mood you can't be too sick.'

It went on and on like that as they tried to keep their relief at his mood in proper line with his clear deterioration in health. Marguerite listened to it all though she pretended she didn't, and they didn't try to keep it from her. They could have left the room to speak but they didn't, sitting sprawled around the kitchen table as she cooked.

When she took him his dinner, a bowl of pasta with ragu, he too seemed lighter, calmer than she had expected. He ate with relish, splashing little drops of orange oil against the napkin she laid across his stomach and chest. When he was done he licked his lips.

'Delicious food tonight, chef,' he said.

'Thank you.'

'You can read to me later. Go and relax for now.'

She widened her eyes to herself when her back was turned; he'd never told her to do anything of the sort.

When he had undressed for his evening bath, before he stepped into the tub to turn the tap and let it fill, Henri kicked his clothes aside and dropped to the wooden floor to do press-ups. The floorboards creaked rhythmically as he dipped down and rose up, dipped down and rose up. It was the sound of sex. When he had done thirty he lay for a moment on his front, catching his breath. Just as the blood had rushed to his face with the effort, now it rushed to his groin. He closed his eyes.

There was a sharp knock on the door and he pushed himself up and stood in a rush, the room spinning for a moment, and wrapped a towel around his waist.

'Henri?'

He turned the tap; the water started to gush. 'What is it? I'm about to have a bath.'

'I heard lots of movement,' she said, and he heard the uncertainty in her voice. He went to unlock the door and she was standing there, her eyes wide.

'What's wrong?' he asked.

'I just . . .' She looked at his naked torso and then away. 'I wanted to check you hadn't fallen or something.'

'I was just doing my exercises,' he said, and she nodded and turned.

'Sorry, darling. I just wanted to check you were okay. I'll see you downstairs.'

'Won't be long,' he said, closing and locking the door. He got into the bath and stared at the water as it spewed from the tap.

She was excited when he came down to the kitchen.

'I just spoke to Laure,' she said.

'Okay.'

'The Lanvier boys are already here.'

He turned away, went to get a glass from a cupboard. He cleared his throat. 'I thought you said they were coming on Friday.'

'That's what they said! But Laure saw Marc and Jean-Christophe in the village this morning.'

He waited, just a moment.

'And Thibault?'

'Well, presumably he's there too. Probably too lazy to help with the shopping.' She was watching him carefully when he turned around. 'They had bread but they didn't get it from Laure. Isn't that strange?'

'No.' He set the glass on the surface. 'I'm going to go and do some paperwork.'

'I thought you'd be more excited.'

'Why?'

'Well, he's only your oldest friend,' she said, unable to keep away the special tone of disapproval she kept for any reference to Thibault.

'Yes, well, I already knew they were coming. I'll go and see them tomorrow. Or later.'

'But you'll have your dinner here?'

'I don't know, Brigitte.'

He went into his study and sat down and pulled papers towards him but he couldn't think. He felt, he realised, immensely happy. He pulled the phone towards him, cleared his throat, dialled the number – he still knew it by heart. And he knew Jean-Christophe's voice as soon as he answered, though it had been years since he'd seen him.

'JC?'

'Henri?' Jean-Christophe laughed. 'News travels fast! How are you?'

'Great. I heard you and Marc were in town.'

'All three of us mate, all three of us.'

'Welcome back,' he said.

'Thanks very much. We're just about to crack open a beer – are you going to come over?'

Henri paused, ran his hand through his hair. 'Yeah, sure, why not?'

'See you in a bit.'

He put the phone down, leant back in his chair. He looked at his reflection in the painting hanging beside him; the falling light struck one side of his face, nose very straight, jaw very solid. His hair, still a little wet, had risen in its slight curls. He didn't look too bad at all, just now.

'Who was that?'

They had all heard the conversation, Jean-Christophe's too-loud voice bouncing into the kitchen from the hall.

'Handsome Henri,' he said, smiling, as he came in. 'I've asked him over for a beer.'

'For fuck's sake, JC,' said Thibault, standing from the table. 'What?'

'Just – I thought we were going to have at least a night just easing ourselves back in. Now you're inviting everyone over for drinks?'

'It's only Henri,' said Jean-Christophe, frowning.

'Yes, who we haven't seen for what, five years?'

'Don't be a grumpy old shit. God, one day back here and you've turned into our father.'

'Shut up.'

Thibault left the room and Jean-Christophe looked at Marc, his face a mask of incredulity. 'Is he on his period?'

Marc winced at Marguerite, and she turned back to the washing-up.

'It'll be nice to see him,' he said. 'Nice we still have a friend or two around here.'

'That's the spirit. Now, what are we going to eat? I'm getting hungry.'

Marguerite remained quiet as she scrubbed a pan, unpeeling the ghosts of onion skins with steel wool.

'It's not dinnertime yet.'

'It will be soon.'

'So let's go get a takeaway.'

'From where?'

She had felt churlish as she'd packed the leftover ragu away in containers for the freezer.

She turned, now, sighing quietly. 'There's some ragu you can have,' she said, 'though I meant to freeze it for your father.'

162

'Perfect,' said Jean-Christophe, banging the table with one hand. 'Much easier.'

They insisted she eat with them, and she couldn't think of a way to refuse. She sat there looking at her food, finding it difficult to speak when they asked her questions. Her voice sounded meek and ineffectual to her; she felt their attention like a spotlight.

Henri's arrival was a great relief, then. She watched the three sons each get up to greet him, the cursory, informal way they hugged. They must all be roughly the same age, she thought, and as she watched them she tried to imagine them as young boys. Thibault was smiling, the anger he'd shown only an hour ago apparently diffused. Marc brought a fresh round of beers to the table, offering one to her too, but she refused and she was relieved when they turned from her again.

'What are you up to these days, Henri?' Jean-Christophe's cheeks were bright with beer, polished like wood, and his voice even louder than before. 'What does life look like for you?'

'Same as ever, JC,' said Henri, leaning back in his chair and cradling the back of his head with his hands. 'Nothing changes, I just get older.'

'So still on the farm? Still making Brigitte the happiest woman in the Languedoc?'

'Definitely not the latter,' he said, the sides of his eyes creasing as he smiled. 'But yes, still on the farm. We've expanded quite nicely but I'd say we're a medium size. I considered going bigger about five years ago, but you've got to get so much manpower. It's more trouble than it's worth. But yes, it ticks along.'

'God, you're like Dad's wet dream.'

They all laughed, Henri shyly, she thought. He looked down as he smiled, as if he were smiling to someone else.

'Apart from the no kids part. He wouldn't like that.'

'JC, you're a dick,' said Thibault.

'Why?' Jean-Christophe looked around innocently. 'I'm serious though. Why did you never have kids, Henri? I always pictured you having a big strapping squadron of them.'

Again, Henri laughed shyly. They were all watching him. 'What can I say, JC?' Marguerite noticed the softest flush spreading over his face. 'I've got a big strapping squadron of cows instead.'

They all laughed.

'That sounds far less trouble,' said Marc. 'Mine are becoming teenagers. Give me ten cows over a teenage girl any day.' He looked at Marguerite with embarrassment. 'No offence.'

'She's not a teenager,' said Jean-Christophe.

'You know what I mean.'

'God, it makes you feel old, doesn't it?'

'Having teenagers? Yup.'

Silence fell between them, then, and Jean-Christophe turned to her. 'And what about you, Mademoiselle Demers?'

'Marguerite,' she said.

'What's your story? What do you like, what do you do, what makes you tick?' He was affecting a pompous, caring tone. Some impression of someone the others knew, perhaps. 'Apart from nursing our dad, of course.'

164

'She goes for long runs,' said Thibault, watching her sideways, and she worried she might blush.

'No, but I mean what's your actual *story*. You're from Paris, right? Have you got a handsome man waiting for you there?'

'Shut up JC,' said Marc.

She tried to smile. 'Yes, I'm from Paris. But actually I haven't lived there for a while. I was working in Picardy before here.'

'Urgh,' said Jean-Christophe. 'Poor you.'

'And you, JC?' asked Henri. He leant forward now, crossing his arms on the table. They were long, broad forearms. 'Commissaire Maigret. What's happening in your life?'

Marguerite watched his face as he spoke. When he caught her eye, she looked away. She thought she noticed Thibault look from her to Henri.

'Happy to answer any questions you fire at me,' he said. 'Sophie is doing very well at work. She's a bit of a hotshot these days. The kids are fine, pretty good really. Ah, and we've moved—'

'Into a grotesquely expensive apartment in the 16th,' said Thibault.

'You can hardly talk.'

'I can. Mine's a studio in the Marais.'

'A huge studio. On one of the trendiest streets in Paris.'

'Please never use the word trendy,' said Thibault.

Marc cleared his throat, looking again at Marguerite. 'They don't usually spend their time comparing real estate,' he said.

'We're not comparing real estate,' said Thibault.

'And more to the point,' said Jean-Christophe, 'I'm sure Mademoiselle Demers lived rather a nice life in Paris. Didn't you?'

'It depends what you mean.'

'I never asked much about you. What's your background? You're well spoken. Where were you brought up?'

'Avenue Raymond-Poincaré.'

'There we go. 16th arrondissement born and raised.'

'Jean-Christophe, why don't you shut up?' said Marc.

'It's nothing to be ashamed of. I could tell. So are Mum and Dad still there?'

She could feel herself flush. 'Not on Avenue Raymond-Poincaré.'

'Divorced?'

'Yes.'

'So – 16th upbringing, rich parents – excuse me for asking, but I know we're all wondering – why on earth have you ended up as a live-in nurse?'

The silence was total. Marc and Thibault picked up their beer bottles and drank from them. Henri cleared his throat.

'Because the job interests me,' she said. 'Why have you ended up as a lawyer?'

'To make money.' He slapped a hand on the table. 'I make no bones about that. It's well paid! And I needed to make money.'

'I like the profession. I like caring for people who need it, I like helping them where I can.'

'Didn't want to become a doctor?'

'I've become a nurse.' She heard that her tone was squeezed of warmth, of any pretence at boisterous banter, the words bouncing around the room in a silly, angry voice.

Jean-Christophe held up his hands, smiled broadly. 'Hey, I'm just asking,' he said. 'No offence meant. None at all. I'm just interested in people.' He looked around. 'Right, guys? God, if I had more patience I could have become a psychotherapist.'

'With all due respect, JC, you'd be a terrible therapist,' said Henri, and the others laughed and the conversation turned and moved on. She sat there trying to smile along with it but all the time felt hatred pulsing from her towards the small, big-eared man at the head of the table.

She waited until the earliest moment she could leave without letting him feel like he'd won. When she closed the kitchen door behind her, she stood for a moment in the darkness of the corridor. She heard their voices erupt into another bout of laughter, muted by the thick wood of the door, and wondered if they would talk about her now.

Jérôme was awake.

'I was just thinking about you,' he said when she sat down. 'Wondering how you're getting on with a houseful of lads.'

'It's not too bad,' she said.

'That makes it sound bad,' he said.

'It's fine. And it's not for long.'

'And then we can have some peace and quiet again.'

She nodded. 'Monsieur Brochon is here tonight.'

'He is?' Jérôme's eyes widened. 'I'd like to see him. Not now though, not when I'm in bed. Ask him to come over again, in the daytime. It'd be a pleasure to see the boy.'

'Of course.'

'Make sure you ask him when the others are around.'

'Okay.'

'Now, how about some of that book?' he asked. She tilted her head to one side.

'In spite of my plodding voice?'

He looked rueful, even a little embarrassed, and flapped his right hand. 'Oh, never listen to me when I'm in one of those moods. I didn't really mean it. Actually, your reading has improved.'

She rolled her eyes to herself, though she didn't mind. Of all the things. She read to him until he was asleep and then she stood and placed the book down on the table quietly. She walked with care towards the door, pulling it to behind her. Then she walked to the bottom of the stairs, and stood listening for a moment to the voices and laughter rising and falling from the kitchen, but she couldn't make out a word.

'Now where's that little nurse got to? I was enjoying winding her up.'

'Well there's your answer,' said Thibault. 'You wound her up.'

'What do we make of her?'

'Not much. She's fine. Quiet. Great legs.'

Thibault smiled with one side of his mouth as he drank from his bottle. Henri remembered that half-smile, the sly expression he made when he spoke about girls. Faux-sly.

'Stop being a letch,' said Marc.

'He can't,' said Jean-Christophe. 'But I mean, as in, what do we make of her and dad? And what's her deal?'

'What do you mean, what's her deal?'

'She's what, early twenties? Wealthy upbringing. What's she doing here?'

'She probably just flunked nursing school or whatever and didn't have much choice. Stop being suspicious of everything, all the time.'

'But she didn't. She had excellent credentials, great references – that's why I hired her. So why come here?' He turned to Henri, who had been gazing at the table, leaving the conversation to them. 'Henri, you must know more about her. What's your impression?'

Henri looked up and shrugged. 'I don't get involved with the house too much,' he said. 'It's Brigitte's job. But she seems good. I think she's nice.'

'But what does she *do*? A pretty young girl, stuck in this dump.' He smiled at Henri. 'No offence. But I mean, does she have friends? A boyfriend? I don't get it.'

'I mean it is quite weird,' said Thibault, and Jean-Christophe nodded.

'Right?'

'But I wouldn't get too het up about it. She's lasted longer than most, right? Dad seems to be happy enough, he would have told us immediately if he wasn't.' Thibault stretched, yawned. 'Maybe she just doesn't like people very much. Maybe she had a bad break-up, needed some nice stagnant country air.'

Henri looked down at the beer in his hands, tried not to notice the words 'stagnant', 'dump'.

'Maybe she's a bit simple,' Thibault continued.

'But you see that's the thing,' said Jean-Christophe. 'She seems quite smart.'

'Oh for God's sake, JC.' Thibault rolled his eyes. 'This is tedious. Stop trying to work everyone out, constantly. You're not very good at it.' He finished his beer and stood up. 'Let's get pissed. Whisky?'

Henri was already pissed. He watched Thibault turn and walk through to the pantry, still with those narrow hips, still slim. Other things had changed: the flecks of white hair at his temples, the bulkier arms. His gait was indolent, he leant his shoulders back as he walked.

'Anyway,' he said as he came back in with the bottle. 'We don't need to worry about her being bored. I'm very happy to provide her with some entertainment.'

That half-smile again, and as his brothers laughed and groaned Henri realised that, though he'd seen it before, hundreds of times, it didn't look right now they were no longer teenagers. Perhaps it was no longer faux-sly; it was just sly.

'You wouldn't be able to,' said Jean-Christophe.

'I absolutely guarantee I will. I'll bet you a hundred euros.'

'Thibault, no.'

'You won't bet because you know I'll win.'

'No, I won't bet because you're what, twenty years older than her?'

'I reckon fifteen at a push.'

'I'm not going to make a bet on whether you shag our dad's nurse or not.'

'Scared you'll lose.'

'No – just not sleazy enough.'

'You! I think we could all name at least five occasions that disprove that.'

Laughter rippled among them, and Thibault handed out their glasses of whisky.

'Are you alive, Henri?' Thibault looked at him now. Stand-

170

ing there, head tilted back, his expression was something new.

'What?'

Thibault sat down. 'Just very, very quiet, aren't you?' He held Henri's gaze, not smiling. 'Does our chat offend you?'

'Don't be ridiculous,' Henri said, laughing, and the others laughed too, and the conversation moved on, but he felt Thibault watching him for a long time after that.

He was too drunk to drive, really, but he couldn't stay. Jean-Christophe had enjoined him to spend the night on one of the huge dusty sofas in the drawing room but Henri had reminded him that they weren't young any more, plus they might be on holiday but he had to wake up at sunrise to work. Thibault hadn't stuck around to listen to his reasons and now they rang in his head as he drove, glum and middle-aged.

Other things: discussing women and Thibault looking sharply down the table at him – 'You were never that fussed about girls, were you?' Thibault yawning when he talked about the farm, a big loud yawn, surely not deliberate but still making clear, absolutely clear, that Henri's life was a dull and distant prospect to him. As far removed as possible from Thibault's world of beautiful men and women, advertising, the anecdotes about nights out that would roll far into morning, the casual references to cocaine and warehouse parties and work trips abroad. The regular mention of names Henri had never heard of but clearly should have.

He cut the engine and sat in the car for a moment, looking out at his dark, lifeless driveway, the squat farmhouse with only one light on, the gloomy shapes of the barns just visible against the night sky. The total absence of noise, of humans. He imagined Thibault sitting next to him and seeing these things and saw how repetitive, how crushingly unimaginative it all was.

And on top of that he had an uncomfortable feeling that Thibault was seeing him differently not just for the boring life he led, not just as a dusty relic of Thibault's claustrophobic youth, but for something else. Casual references to the many gay neighbours he had on his street in the Marais, casual in tone but with that sharp look, those darting eyes, that watchfulness from his end of the table. That question, replaying itself again and again in Henri's mind: 'You were never that fussed about girls, were you?'

Thibault's arms, the edges of firm muscle under his T-shirt, a strong thin neck. The raised black freckle under his ear. And then the curl of his lip in that smile; his dark, darting eyes, his intentionality. Thibault's eyes, Thibault's thick eyelashes, Thibault's quick humour. Thibault. And not Thibault.

When Henri walked up the stairs to bed, he noticed the little framed photo of Brigitte's mother at the top. She had big bovine eyes and a heavy jaw and yet she looked small, afraid. Provincial, he supposed. And he wondered, as he cleaned his teeth and looked around the familiar bathroom, the primrose-painted walls, the rusty patch around the plughole in the sink, if that's how he looked too. Small, in spite of his size. Afraid of life outside.

10

When he woke at five his head throbbed and he was bathed in icy sweat. He splashed cold water over his face and stared into the mirror above the sink. His eyes were bloodshot. He took two aspirin, drank two glasses of water and then leant his head over the sink, eyes shut, for a moment or two while his stomach rose up in protest and then sank back down.

Then he was striding out of the house and over to the sheep, where he checked on his skinny ewe and her triplets. He examined her and thought that perhaps she had gained a little weight already, wasn't necessarily a cull ewe as he'd thought she would be by the time the lambs were fully weaned.

It was Paul's day off, which he was glad for; he wanted the rhythmic, familiar work of the milking parlour. As he entered the parlour the lovely stench of milk and disinfectant reached up into his nose and down his oesophagus into his stomach, curdling with the whisky, and there was a certain grim satisfaction to be had in that acrid feeling, just as there was in the sweat that was soon breaking out in his hair and across his back as he worked. After ten minutes he was overtaken by gripes and he removed his gloves and made for the outhouse for his morning shit.

When he came back to work he imagined that the whisky had left his body. He felt lighter and better and he worked mechanically, pushing aside remembered words and looks and moments from the night before, pushing out the sense of dejection he'd felt on his way home, setting his mind against the insipid self-pity he'd nursed as he took his drunken body to bed. Fuck Thibault, he thought, but then: no, it wasn't Thibault's fault, it was him, it was Henri, it was this boring little life he'd chosen for himself. And he'd chosen it so fuck it all, nothing to be done but get on with it and keep this great machine of a farm running because it was no mean feat, and he was a good farmer, and that took work, and if it was boring and bored other people then so be it, he'd just be boring, that was his life, there was no other option now. He'd missed his chance for something different a long, long time ago. For a moment a terrible image came into his mind of another version of himself, strutting down a street in the Marais in the clothes of a dandy with a mincing gait, and he shook his head and looked over his cows and then down at his strong fore-arms and hard-working hands in their gloves, and thought, No, I made the right choice, it was too dangerous to go down another route; I've saved myself at least from that ignominy. No, he would just be boring and Thibault could think what he wanted; those days were over, that was fine.

But later, when he and Thierry sat eating sandwiches at the table in the barn, wiping sweat from their faces and grunting half-chewed comments at each other, he felt a momentary slice of elation cut through him: Thibault was in town, his

Thibault was here and he could see him today if he wanted to. Perhaps, perhaps he was over-exaggerating, had been drunk and over-sensitive, perhaps Thibault wasn't so very different, his feelings for Henri hadn't changed so very much. Then the dread he'd felt was laced with hope: perhaps they'd spend time together and speak properly, that easy friendship would come back, he wouldn't feel like this.

He finished his sandwich, scrunched the foil into a metal ball in his fist. Then Thierry asked something about the relative efficiency of herringbone versus rotary milking parlours, and Henri heard the question through Thibault's ears and the whole process started again: the mortification, the crushing feeling that opportunities had been missed and something else had been lost, something deeper and more momentous than just opportunities. He stood up and smacked the table, 'Let's go, come on,' and Thierry looked up, a frown passing swiftly over his face as he stood and hurried, still eating, to walk beside Henri out of the barn.

Jean-Christophe made a big deal of being hungover, rubbing his face and moaning, though she could tell he felt fine. He opened the fridge and poked his head in, lifted the layer of foil from the bowl of soup and placed it back roughly, took out some cheese, turned it in his hand, put it back.

'Nothing to eat,' he said, as if to himself. He went to the pantry and came back with a family pack of crisps. He opened it and laid it on the table in front of him but didn't eat any. There's bread, jam, ham, cheese, she thought. What was his point?

When they had all emerged, they sat around the table and grazed lazily, like it was a Sunday morning, while she prepared a quiche for Jérôme's dinner.

'I'd forgotten how boring it is here,' said Jean-Christophe at one point and Thibault looked up from a book and then down again. Mostly they were silent, eating and flicking through yesterday's papers. At one point, pulling tomatoes from a vine, she noticed Thibault watching her. She caught his eye and he didn't look away but didn't smile either, and she felt something stir inside her, both pleasant and unpleasant. As she moved around the hob and the worktops, chopping and pouring and measuring, she felt not only his eyes on her at various moments but a sort of palpable confidence he was putting out into the room, a thick, solid presence, until she almost found it difficult to move.

'What's the deal with dad then?' asked Jean-Christophe, and she turned.

'What do you mean?'

'Can you give us an update on his health?'

'She's busy, JC,' said Thibault.

'Of course I can,' she said. 'This can wait.'

'Well, we don't need the full debrief right now. At some point I'd like you to do that, and we'll want to see all your notes, get the full medical picture.'

'Of course.'

'But just for now, what's the general outlook?'

'He's stable. He's frail, as you can see. He's in a lot of pain, though we're managing it relatively well.'

'How's his mood?' asked Marc.

'Up and down. Relatively okay at the moment,' she said.

'That's pretty good, for Dad.'

'Or a bad sign,' said Thibault. He was smiling, darkly. 'If his mood is relatively okay, he must be really ill.'

'How long do you reckon he's got?' asked Jean-Christophe, and Thibault snorted.

'God, JC,' said Marc. 'What the hell?'

'I'm just saying it like it is.'

'You don't have to say it like that.'

'Everyone wants to know. I didn't say I'm looking forward to the end, I'd just like to know when it'll be.'

'It's impossible to give you an accurate answer,' she said.

'And you don't have to,' said Marc.

'But a rough estimate?' asked Jean-Christophe, and then the banging came, three knocks on Jérôme's headboard, strong and firm. They all looked at the door, the three of them, and then Thibault let out a barking laugh.

'Bang, bang, bang,' he said. 'Knocking at the castle doors.'

'What the fuck, Thibault?' asked Jean-Christophe.

Marguerite washed and dried her hands, and as she walked through to Jérôme's room she smiled to herself. She'd enjoyed the look of fear on their faces.

'Almost lunch?' he asked when she came in.

'Yes, almost lunch.'

'Splendid. Sort my hair out, won't you? Make it a bit smart.'

She filled the sink, dipped his comb in the water. Then she combed his thin flossy hair back, gently over the speckled pink of his scalp. It curled a little behind each ear.

'Come on then,' he said, patting the bed with both hands. 'I'm starving. And get those boys of mine in here, if they're even here.'

177

With the three sons in the room, arranged awkwardly in a crescent of chairs around the side and foot of his bed, the air contracted. She opened the windows wide. The ripe, sludgy smell of pea soup filled the room; a fly came in, bumped itself against the open windowpane, flew back out. She made to leave but he stopped her.

'Marguerite, do sit down. You're not a stranger here.' His tone was formal and seemed odd to her. She didn't want to stay but she saw that leaving wasn't an option, so she sat at the table, behind the men. She laid out her notes in front of her, so that she could pretend to keep busy.

There was silence for a while as Jérôme started to eat, slowly and carefully, but then he stopped, laid the spoon on the side of the bowl, took the napkin she'd spread over his chest and stomach and wiped each corner of his mouth.

He looked up at them all.

'So, I've caught up with each of you.' He smiled grimly, without his eyes. 'You all seem to be doing fine. Jean-Christophe, I'm not going to congratulate you on your various successes at work because you've obviously mastered the art of self-congratulation.' He affected a chuckle, which Jean-Christophe echoed. 'Marc, I still can't quite make out what it is you do and I won't pretend it doesn't sound astoundingly boring, but then, most good honest work is, isn't it?'

There was a little spray of stale laughter from Marc and Jean-Christophe, dutiful, like guests at a wedding. He eyed Thibault. 'Certainly my job wasn't the most engrossing from the outside. No, it wasn't a rip-roaring glamorous roller-coaster ride from the outside. But it was engrossing to me. It was fulfilling. Good, important, straightforward, commercial

178

work. Supplying a product as well as a service, keeping up standards. Providing jobs for good, honest people.'

Thibault raised his hand up over his mouth and nose, cocked his head. His eyes were beautiful, almond-shaped, bored. He was trying, she saw, to make clear he wasn't impressed. She saw the glint of danger in Jérôme's eyes.

'As for you,' he said to Thibault. He paused, for effect. And then his face lightened. 'You seem to be doing fine too.'

He smiled, looked around.

'So in summary, all seems fine for the lot of you. Am I right?' There was a ripple of yeses, and Thibault, who was sitting at the foot of the bed, turned to look at her. She looked back down at her notes. 'And as for me, well, I'm doing all right. I'm sure I don't look a terribly pretty sight to you lot, but then a lot changes in, what, two years? Is that when I last saw one of you?' Silence. 'But here you are now. And it's always better late than never, isn't it? Isn't that what they say? Yes, here you are now for a nice impromptu visit. Out of the blue. And all three of you together! What a delight, what a nice thing, for a sick old father to get an impromptu visit from his terribly impressive, busy, important sons.'

He looked at Marguerite then, and they all turned to look at her too.

'This one's been doing an absolute sterling job. She's a Class-A nurse. Great girl. Jean-Christophe, you employed her, didn't you? That's one thing you do deserve congratulations for.' To her relief, they turned back to Jérôme. 'On a serious note. I couldn't be doing this well without her. Thibault, call Brigitte Brochon this afternoon. I want her to source a car for our girl. It's high time she had a bit more freedom. Exhausting for her to lug the food back and forth from the village twice a week or whatever. It's been a great oversight; one of you should have sorted it out much sooner.'

They each glanced at her again.

'Thank you, Monsieur Lanvier,' she said.

'See?' he asked. 'She's a saint. But you shouldn't be thanking me, Marguerite. You should be chastising each and every one of us for not getting you one sooner. And that brings me onto another thing.' He paused again, looked around, weighed the air around him with his eyes. 'Jean-Christophe, see to it that she gets a pay rise.'

Jean-Christophe's head moved back involuntarily. The brothers took swift looks at each other and then back at Jérôme.

'Well?'

'Fine,' said Jean-Christophe. 'How much?'

'We'll discuss details later. That's enough business for now; off you go. Let an old man get back to his soup, eh?'

He smiled at them all broadly, eyes glinting, and they stood up, scraping their chairs back and leaving them in disarray around the bed.

When they were gone, she got up to pull their chairs against the wall.

'Great soup, this,' he said, not looking at her.

'Thank you, very much—' she started, but he held one hand up.

'Don't thank me. A pay rise was due. I used to hate spending money but what's the point in hoarding it all away now? What am I going to do with it? Buy another radio? A new set of bed linen, a mobility seat? A spanking new pair of pyjamas?

Anyway, you've earned it. Mind you, don't let it go to your head. You're not so very special.'

He smiled, feeling relaxed and expansive, she could see, and she felt then that it was all odious, what was going on in here, and in the kitchen where the men would have re-congregated, and in the whole house.

'Like a bunch of bloody schoolboys seeing their teacher,' she heard as she took his tray down the corridor. She stopped, waited. 'Why do we act like that? Why don't we tell him to put his fist up his own arse?'

'Thibault, it wasn't that bad.'

'It was. Games. Power and games. It's not even him I'm pissed off at anyway, it's us, sitting there with our dicks tucked between our legs like . . .'

He didn't finish; she heard them lapse into silence. She walked quietly back down the corridor, laying the tray outside Jérôme's door, and then she climbed the stairs to go and close herself away in her dark room.

She left the house quietly, leaving from the front door for the first time. Her legs felt bruised from the run she'd taken yesterday; it was good to walk them out, to work warmth through them as she took the road down to the village. She jumped lightly a few times to try to loosen out her bunched calves, but she liked the ache really, it reminded her of athletics at school as a girl, the lovely milky blur her thoughts took on by the second lap, when her parents and the sick blight of what she'd done to Cassandre could stop existing for almost an hour at a time. The warm rubbery smell rising from the asphalt, the tight belt of her abdomen, the constriction of her chest, the silence but for a pat pat pat of her feet as they pushed off the track.

It became hot as she walked, but there was the heady smell of pine, the whisper of cool from the forest on either side. She brushed a small spider from her arm with a little shiver, and as she did she thought about Thibault's glances, his surely clear messaging of sexual interest, and wondered how long it had been since she'd last had physical contact with a man who wasn't a patient she was nursing or examining. Not since before Picardy. There were all the nameless, virtually faceless young men she'd encountered at parties, their young thin strong bodies in dancing crowds. There was Robert before that, the boyfriend who had been kind to her, who'd seemed to understand her pain without trying to probe into it, who'd let her be silent. And then the time she'd seen him parodying a 'spastic' to their friends, the grotesque accuracy of his impression. The look on his face when she caught him had shown that he knew about Cassandre.

She became distant from him, as she did from the friends of hers who became maudlin when they were drunk or high and talked about all the pain in their lives, which in most cases amounted to the divorce of their parents and not much else. '*Putain*, it's all a fucking farce, I can see my mother's eyes are swollen from crying and yet she puts on this fucking bourgeois bullshit show of being happy'; 'I used to hear him, crawling home at 3 a.m. and her shouting about where he'd been.' She understood that they saw glamour in pain, and that they clung to the dissolution of their parents' shoddy marriages and their affairs as if all of that were anywhere near the full extent of tragedy. For her, all those divorces were just another layer of the banal grimness of life, of relationships, of faulty people trying to share faulty lives. And in any case, tragedy wasn't glamorous. It was grimy, sordid, exhausting.

She dreamt often about sex: vivid, pleasurable dreams. But the impulse behind them was physical, surely nothing more. When she actually considered touching another person, merging and melding into their space and they into hers, it felt almost laughably impossible. A rupture to her long-held status quo, of almost mythical implausibility. No, she didn't want anything with Thibault, surely: she didn't like his darting glances and his swagger. She wouldn't have anything with anyone. She'd made that decision; it was okay.

Suki's face cracked into a look of absolute pleasure when she opened her front door. She held a hand up in front of her mouth.

'I'm going to die of shock,' she said, laughing. 'Come in, come in.' She gestured Marguerite down the hall, waiting for her to pass so that she could close the door behind them both herself, as if she didn't believe Marguerite would stay if she weren't marshalled in.

She cleared an empty space on the sofa.

'Let me fix us a tea,' she said. 'I won't be a minute.'

And she bustled out, leaving Marguerite to sit in the cluttered salon. When she came back with the tea, there was a flash of red on her lips that hadn't been there before.

'Sit, sit,' she said, though Marguerite was already sitting, 'make yourself comfortable.'

She laid down the beautiful tray with the matching tea-pot and glasses. She lit a cigarette quickly, inhaled deeply and blew it from one side of her mouth as she took a saucer of *madeleines* off the tray and handed it to Marguerite.

'Delicious. Thank you.'

Suki sat down. 'I was just thinking about you yesterday,' she said, lifting her feet up onto the seat so she was hugging her knees. Her feet were small and pretty. 'And now you're here, visiting me as I have enjoined you many a time to do.' She tilted her face as she spoke, sing-song. 'A silent apparition at my door.'

Marguerite laughed too. 'Am I such a ghost?'

'No, no, nothing ghost-like about you.' She blew a long jet of smoke, smiled. 'I'm teasing. I just didn't think you'd ever actually come over without me forcing you to. It's nice, it's a nice surprise. Now tea, it'll be ready.' She leant forward to pour the tea into glasses and Marguerite remembered her telling her to pour the water into a cafetière from a height. She thought that Cassandre would have liked that. She loved to learn a grown-up trick, perform it like a solemn and scientific ritual.

'It's jasmine tea. Great for cholesterol.' Smooth amber water, dark buds unfurling. 'You should give some to Jérôme. How is the old boy?'

'Not bad actually,' said Marguerite.

'Well let me give you *my* news. Philippe's away on busi-ness, which is always quite nice. I stay up late watching telly and reading and it's divine. No snoring to keep me awake once I get to bed.' She closed her eyes luxuriously, opened them with a flick. 'Oh, and I was invited over to Edgar's house in the woods for dinner last week. Edgar DuChamp. He's gay, a poet, and hilarious. Did I already tell you about him? Well, I was telling *him* about *you*. You two have to meet.'

Marguerite nodded, but she struggled to imagine Suki telling anyone about her. She could have had nothing to say.

'You don't believe me.' Suki laughed. 'You're very transparent for such a private person. But I did; I was telling him about the Lanviers. He didn't really know anything about them. He arrived in Saint-Sulpice long after their great fiefdom had ended.'

'Were they really so fief-like?'

'Yes. A lot more money than everyone else. Rossignol was thought of virtually as a *château*. The boys were handsome, well, two of them anyway, very superior and just different. Everyone was terrified of Jérôme, like they still are, really. When his sons each left for Paris, it was very apparent that they thought Saint-Sulpice was just a dump. They never hid that.' She put out her cigarette lighting another immediately. 'They were right, of course. I personally never minded them. I'm sure we would have got on well if we'd had the chance, though we never really got to know each other. They'd hardly be Philippe's idea of fun, or vice versa. I told Edgar that he would have loved them. We're all urbanites at heart, trapped in the sticks. Like you.'

'I don't know whether that makes anyone superior to anyone else.'

'I think it does. It's about culture. These bumpkins here have no culture. They're ignorant.'

'I don't have culture.'

'Oh, you do,' said Suki. 'You just don't realise it.'

Marguerite took a sip from her tea. It was too much effort, to keep disagreeing. 'It's funny you mention his sons,' she said. 'They've come to visit.'

Suki's eyes widened; she put her glass down. 'What!'

'They arrived a few days ago.'

'*Why* haven't I heard about this already! I always hear about this kind of thing. A few days ago?' Her posture had changed; she perched on the edge of her chair, one foot tip-toed on the other. 'And? What are your impressions?'

'They're . . .' She paused, wondering how much to say. 'I suppose they're quite like you say.'

'In what way?' Suki leant forward, rested her chin on her palm.

'Their accents are fully Parisian, for example. I wouldn't have thought they were from these parts if I didn't know.'

Suki looked bored. 'What else?'

'And they're quite snooty. Quite superior, as you say. Not Marc – he seems fine.'

'I bet they love having a pretty young lady around.'

She hated comments like that, felt an urgent sense of duty to deflect them.

'I don't think so. That's partly why I'm here, actually,' she said. 'To delay going back to the house.'

'Why?'

'It's just, it's full. I don't want to intrude.'

'So they make you feel like you're intruding.'

Marguerite squirmed. 'Not exactly. It's just, it's awkward. I have my routine there, and it's a big adjustment having a lot of people around.'

Again, Suki was bored by her response. And why was she being so guarded? Who would Suki tell?

'I feel uncomfortable around them.'

'Yes, they do that. They make people feel uncomfortable. Mind you, you must be used to it with Jérôme.'

Marguerite laughed. 'True.'

Suki leant back then, looked at the bookshelves for a moment in silence.

'So the prodigal sons have returned,' she said. 'I wonder why.' She looked at Marguerite. 'How ill is he? Is it a case – dare I ask – of vultures, circling?'

Marguerite wouldn't talk about Jérôme's health; Suki should have known that. She caught herself frowning.

'Don't answer that,' said Suki. But something had shifted; Marguerite felt uncomfortable, realised she should get back.

'I need to get back to him now,' she said. 'I was just popping by to say a quick hello.'

To her surprise, Suki didn't protest.

'Of course.'

They stood, Suki bending to grind her cigarette out into the ashtray and then rising to follow Marguerite out of the room. 'Thank you so much for the visit. Please come again, even just for a few minutes. It's the loveliest surprise.'

'Thank you for the tea.'

Suki smiled, swiped her thanks away with one hand. 'I've scared you away again.'

'Of course not.'

'I thought of you yesterday.' She leant against the wall as Marguerite stood in the open doorway, squinting a little into the light. 'There was a little black cat in my garden,' she said. 'Tiny. Very cute. So I went out with a little saucer of milk for it, I was very quiet, I didn't approach it too fast. But scoot, it was off.' She held up a fist, exploded it into a star. 'Gone. Just like you.'

Marguerite grimaced. 'I'm sorry you feel I'm like that.'

'Don't be sorry. That's just you.'

When she got back to the house, the men were playing football on the grass in the sun. They waved to her as she came around from the driveway and ducked into the kitchen. As she was unloading her backpack onto the kitchen table, Marc came in.

'Do you need some help with that? We could have given you a lift.'

'It's no bother at all,' she said. 'Don't worry.'

'It definitely makes sense for you to have a car,' he said, and he opened the fridge, leaning in to take out a can of Coke. They'd taken their shirts off to play football, and she saw that he had a bit of a gut on him, folding into soft layers, fleeced with dark curly hair. His temples and back were wet with sweat. When he straightened up, she noticed him sucking his stomach in. He gestured his can at her, and she shook her head.

'No, thank you.'

He nodded and left, and when she had finished packing the shopping away she went to check on Jérôme. He was listening to the radio, looking grim.

'Everything okay?' she asked.

'Fine. Just fine.' He barely bothered to look up at her. 'I can hear them outside,' he said. 'Shouting, hollering. Whooping. Are they drunk?'

'No,' she said. 'They're playing football.'

'Playing football,' he said, with derision. Then he turned to the wall. 'Turn that thing off. I'm going to sleep.'

A kestrel was whooping, a high lonely 'ooooo', when Henri woke. He shivered; the sweat laced in the threads of his shirt had cooled.

He'd been working in the ferocity of the afternoon sun when he'd been struck by the unfamiliar, overwhelming urge to sleep. He'd had to come and lie down by the little old root cellar building, stretching out in the shady grass to close his eyes, to let the throbbing of his headache still. He couldn't remember the last time he'd slept in the day. He couldn't get away with late nights any more, he thought, or excessive drinking. He was too old for it all.

He got up now and crossed the field, looking away from the old stable where Vanille had fallen to her side with a whump in the echo of the shot, and he imagined he could still smell her blood. He'd have a long glass of water, an early bath. With coffee he'd get through his paperwork, and then when evening came he'd have a quiet dinner with Brigitte, be kind to her. They'd go to bed early. He'd check back in with Thibault over the weekend, concentrate on work until then.

Brigitte, the phone tucked between her neck and shoulder, was washing her hands up to her elbows in the kitchen sink, and she looked up, cheeks flushed, when he came in.

'One moment, Laure, one moment,' she said. She dried

189

one hand to hold the receiver, straightened and stretched out her neck; 'Oh, Henri,' she said. 'Thibault Lanvier called.' Then she tucked the receiver back into her shoulder and plunged her hands back into the water. 'Yes,' she said, 'yes, well exactly.'

'What about?' asked Henri, but she didn't answer. He stepped closer, said louder, 'What did he say?' but she frowned, mouthing, 'I'm on the phone,' and then 'Yes, oh gosh, oh I'm so sorry to hear that, Laure,' and continued. He felt a burst of fury.

'Brigitte?'

'Just *wait*,' she mouthed, a pantomime whisper, and she pulled the plug out and watched the water level fall, nodding and yes-ing into the phone.

He left the room, slamming the door, but by the time he'd reached the top of the stairs his anger had dissolved. Thibault had called. Of course he had been imagining the derision and suspicion, the change between them. No, not the change – things *had* changed, they couldn't have stayed the same – but it was just that: change, neither positive nor negative. Theirs was his oldest friendship, and Thibault's oldest friendship too, and that meant something. Perhaps he'd go over again tonight; he wouldn't get so drunk or be so quiet. He'd be himself, whatever the fuck that was.

The kitchen was empty when she went in to prepare Jérôme's meal. She filled a glass with water, looking out of the window at Marc and Thibault in shorts and bare feet, still kicking their ball around in the falling light, each holding a beer bottle in one hand, chatting as they volleyed. Jean-Christophe was in a deckchair she hadn't known existed, asleep. Thibault was nimble, a practised-looking player. Marc's shoulders were soft and sloping, Thibault's straight and proud. She realised that Thibault must work a little, a man in his late thirties or early forties, to keep his physique in that condition. His back and stomach were beautiful, all their muscles moving in subtle unison as he talked and walked and kicked. But she didn't want to find him attractive. She went to get the quiche out of the fridge, along with some sad-looking green beans that would need topping and tailing.

And then he was in the room, and she felt his presence like a tightening of air.

'Hi,' he said, and he rested both hands on the back of a chair. 'I was just getting some beers. Would you like one?'

'I'm fine,' she said. 'Thank you.'

She continued cutting, and he was silent for a moment. She heard him open his mouth to speak but exhale, as if unsure.

Then he said to her back, 'We're grateful to you.' She looked at him, over her shoulder. 'I mean it. God knows you don't have an easy job.' She turned to face him fully, and he smiled. His cheeks were flushed; he was a little tipsy, she thought. 'I don't know how you do it.'

She smiled back.

'I'm sure—'

'I'm glad he's been good with you,' he said, interrupting, looking down at the table with concentration, 'and that he's showing you approval.' He looked up, looked at her steadily, solidly. 'That probably sounds basic or patronising or some-thing, but with him, it's very rare.' He gave a wry smile, his lip curling, and he couldn't keep the bitterness out of his voice. 'I didn't even know he knew how to do that. Show approval.

191

Of anything. Perhaps he's actually learning some things in old age.

'Anyway, I suppose it's just – I'm sure you don't need me to tell you he's an impossible father. When we were growing up, he was . . .' He looked into the distance for the words, gave up. 'He was a very difficult father. But it's still a good thing to know he's being looked after well, by someone like you.'

'I'm glad you feel that,' she said, and he smiled again.

'I think I'll stop being so serious now, don't you think? And please have a beer.' He gave a look of exaggerated concern, humorous – leant his head back a little, to one side, as if imploring. 'You're allowed. You have permission. You're not on sole watch for once, and frankly anyone who's spent more than five minutes with my dad deserves a drink.'

She hesitated and he went into the pantry, coming back with three open bottles. He passed one to her and she felt the atmosphere of the house crack, soften.

'I'm following your orders,' she said.

'Absolutely,' he said, and they clinked the necks of their bottles and took a sip. 'Now let me get this to Marc.' He walked out of the kitchen and she went back to trimming the beans. She could hear the foam pop on the surface of her beer.

Jérôme was awake, cross.

'Well, are they on holiday or are they here to see me?'

'I think they're probably waiting for you to ask for them,' she said, reading his blood pressure.

He eyed the gauge. 'How's that?'

'A little high,' she said.

'No wonder!'

She made notes, folded the cuff and popped out three different pills for him.

'Tomorrow,' he said, nodding as he stared down the end of his bed. 'I'll have you take me outside so I can get some air.'

'That's a good idea. The weather's lovely.'

'Oh, for God's sake,' he said, glancing at the window. 'I can still see, you know.' He bit his top lip, furrowed his eyebrows together. 'See how they enjoy frolicking in the garden then, with their old man watching. A bloody holiday. They'll see.'

'Shall I say you'd like to see them?'

'I didn't say I'd like to see them,' he hissed. 'I said, Aren't *they* supposed to be here to see *me*?'

She took a deep breath. 'I really think they were waiting for you to rest.'

'Taking their side, are you?' He stared at her then, studied her face with his keen eyes. 'Warming to them, are you? How's that alley cat Thibault appear to you? Caught a whiff yet? Sniff sniff sniff, hey?'

His lips were wet, his sneer like a mask.

'I'm not warming to anyone,' she said. 'I'm here to help you.'

'Yes, well don't forget that. You haven't got your car yet.'

She turned, then, and left the room. When she got out to the garden, she didn't have to call out to them: they all looked over.

'Your father's awake,' she said. And then, taking pleasure in disobeying his orders, 'He said he'd really like to see you.'

She saw the collective body language change, felt the atmosphere constrict. Thibault's face closed down, he kicked the ball with violence at the tree and it scudded up it, made a silly loop in the air and came to rest, abandoned, on the grass. They grabbed their shirts and put them on as they filed past her.

'Are we all going in together again?' asked Jean-Christophe.

'Yeah, come on, it's better that way,' said Marc.

She followed them, stepping into the utility room to take some sheets out of the wash, and to listen.

'Hi Dad,' she heard Marc say. 'Did you sleep well?'

A few laughs, some carefully friendly comments in jocular tones. Their gradual silencing, the low drawl of his voice. She imagined them, Thibault leaning back indolently in his chair to signal that he wasn't buying into it all, Jean-Christophe laughing like an underling in a board meeting, Marc affecting a bland, unperturbed smile. She went back and finished her beer at the table. Then she went and took out another. She sat on the low sofa in the kitchen for the first time, flicked through one of the newspapers they'd got, drank her beer. Something moved in the corner of her eye and she saw a pigeon, fat and beautiful, peering into the kitchen window. Then it was off again, with a kerfuffle of wings.

Thibault and Jean-Christophe drove out to pick up pizzas for dinner. They bought one for Marguerite, too, and she joined them around the kitchen table and ate and listened in on their conversation, getting up occasionally to take medication to Jérôme, read to him for twenty minutes, put on a wash, get a jumper. The men became sturdily, sleepily drunk. She felt the edges soften, around her vision and her body. She spoke more easily. When she was in the pantry to check that there was enough bread for Jérôme's breakfast, Thibault came in to get some more beers and it didn't seem awkward when he stepped into her space, smiling, smelling of dried sweat and beer. He tugged her gently towards him, a finger hooking one of the belt loops of her jeans, and looked at her mouth, mumbled 'Lovely Marguerite,' breathed her in, kissed her forehead. She felt that old, familiar ache at her cervix, heat rising up into the base of her abdomen. His hand held her hip, the top of her bottom, holding her into his space. She closed her eyes and they stood there for a moment, swaying very slightly, and then he stepped back and they both laughed lightly and she turned away, busied herself opening pots and jars. He rested one warm hand on the back of her neck as he opened the fridge, and then he bit the cap off one of the bottles and placed it on the counter next to her and smiled and left, joining in the conversation again at the lovely detritus of the kitchen table.

He got into bed next to Brigitte. She wasn't asleep, but neither of them spoke. He turned onto one side but his knees felt in the way; he turned to the other side and his shoulder dug into the mattress. He lay on his back and opened one hip out, resting his hand on his stomach. His lips felt full, they ached: he'd kissed Edgar urgently and insistently, holding the back of his head tight, closing his eyes as they rocked together, back and forth, back and forth, on the cool firm of Edgar's mattress, the windows wide open to let in moonlight and early summer air. They'd lain next to each other afterwards and he'd kissed Edgar more, seeing how long he could draw that moment out, before the hatred stole into the space between them. It would come crawling from his mind down the column of his spine, through the tentacles of his nervous system and into his bloodstream, every inch of his body. When it did, he rose and dressed and left.

Brigitte shifted and huffed and he wanted then to push her from the bed, push her stupid body face-first down into the floor. Her flat voice quivering high with excitement when she'd finally relinquished her prized information: 'Oh, he wasn't calling for you. Sorry darling, I didn't realise I'd been unclear. No, he was just calling to ask me to organise a car for that nurse of Jérôme's.' A sniff as she said, 'I suppose she needs one, though I do hope she won't be drinking when she drives.'

He drew his knees up to his stomach, pressed his fists into his eyes. Fuck every single one of them. Fuck Brigitte, fuck the nurse, fuck Edgar. Fuck Thibault. And then, no, fuck Henri, Henri the secret faggot, fuck him in the mouth until he chokes. Then he got up because there was no way he was going to sleep yet, and he slammed the bedroom door behind him and went downstairs and took Jojo and a torch and pulled on his boots and walked out naked into the night.

He wanted to shout and roar up at the sky, but he couldn't: there was Brigitte, there were Thierry and Paul and his wife, there was propriety. Inhibition. He strode up to the sheep and flashed his torch in their watchful blank faces. He sat on the wet grass and felt it tickle, cold, against his haunches. His skin rose in goose-bumps with the cold. He wanted to cry. He could imagine, vaguely, how it would feel to let the tears out, to ease the frantic, angry white noise inside his chest in great sobs. Jojo ran a circle around him and came to sit next to him, watching him, waiting for his next move. She yipped, quietly.

11

She didn't wake until ten. She could hear someone's voice in her ears, left over from a dream, but she couldn't remember whose. The room was very warm; outside was the steady, insistent racket of cicadas.

Inside, the house was quiet. When she got downstairs, she looked in on Jérôme, surprised to find him asleep. She found the kitchen empty, the door to the garden open; she startled a cat, and it dashed outside in a blur of browns. She thought of Suki's story of the black cat, and how much she and Cassandre had wanted one. She went to the door to look for it but it was nowhere to be seen. Perhaps, once they were gone, she'd try leaving a saucer of milk outside each night.

The cat had been denuding the leftover pizza slices, which were nothing now but glazed, lumpy dough with the faintest traces of tomato. The kitchen was a tip, pizza boxes and beer bottles and now she noticed breakfast plates too, scraped with butter, crumbs, jam. A fat tear plopped from the tap into the sink; she tightened it. She looked out at the empty garden littered with a few bottles, the football, two deckchairs. And then she saw a note stuck to the glass with two stickers peeled from apples: 'Out for the day – back this evening. Thanks!'

She sat down at the table, a layer of dread settling over the room. She'd have to tell Jérôme. She remembered he'd wanted to go outside and she groaned aloud: how could she tell him they'd taken off, that he'd be sitting outside on his own, among the scattered remains of their game? What were they playing at – why go for a day trip now, here?

And there was something else there, another feeling: irrational, something like humiliation. She felt a little sick when she remembered standing with Thibault in the pantry. How had she let him come into her space like that, rest his lips on her forehead? And what a strange way to approach her, with what strange familiarity had he hooked the loop of her waistband. She forced her mind to slide around it, settling on the mess of the kitchen instead, and she got up to clear it all away.

Jérôme pretended not to believe her at first, asked her to repeat it. Then when she'd started he held his hand up – 'Enough! I get it!' – and turned to the wall, hissed at her to leave him alone.

The silence in the house felt eerie now. She went outside, turned left out of the driveway and broke into a jog. Soon her muscles stopped hurting. She felt spooked, occasionally, by the emptiness of the road and the rustling not-quite-silence of the forest. It made her run faster.

Jérôme didn't want lunch. He asked for the strongest pain-killers though he didn't seem in much pain, and she refused him. She watched her refusal stoke his fury, the tightening of his jaw, shoulders, neck.

'I can't,' she said, and he mimicked her, wailing it like a child.

She decided to make bread, as Frances had taught her to do, but halfway through the dough mixture she became bored. She threw it all away. She went outside and lay out on the grass in the sun, but then she felt things crawl and prickle under her neck and it made her flinch. She got up, pulled a deckchair out, curled her body into its tired linen.

She thought of the stories the men had told last night, the girlfriends they'd had from the village, the illicit rural raves they'd apparently organised in the early 1980s, when they were young: the heady drunkenness, the recreational drugs, many of which she'd never heard of, the ecstasy. And she thought of the first time she'd taken MDMA. Seventeen, and they'd measured out the right quantities into cigarette papers, wrapped them up into little balls. When they were in the club, they swallowed them with water. Half an hour or so, said one of their friends, until the stomach starts to break down the paper and absorb the drug.

She waited but half an hour passed, then forty-five min-utes, and nothing happened. Perhaps she felt a little drunker, but they'd drunk a lot. Her friends' eyes had started to bloom into inky pools. 'Are you coming up?' 'Have you come up yet?' She started to accept that she wouldn't come up. Everyone around her looked even further away than usual, locked away in the intensity of their happiness.

Then after an hour, when she'd given up, the air started to rush in, cool, around her face. As she danced, she started to hear all the many strands in the music, pick each one out, each sound separable like sedimentary layers in a textbook diagram. She thought she could touch them. She'd never realised, she said into her friend's ear, pulling her closer, how had she never realised, you can feel music with your face? Her friend had nodded, chewing gum, smiling, taken Marguerite's face in her hands and kissed her cheek. Marguerite felt the lovely electronic ripples of music like cool fingertips on her cheeks and mouth and temples.

Later, she started to see Cassandre in the crowd. She was sitting on people's shoulders, dancing, smiling, turning round to gaze at Marguerite. The shiny helmet of dark hair she'd had as a child swinging gently as she moved. 'It's all okay, you see?' said a friend into her ear. 'Everything's totally okay, don't you see?' Marguerite had smiled, yes, and they'd laughed together, dancing and laughing at how obviously okay everything was.

When they all spilled out of the club into a clear, rosy dawn, Marguerite had taken a bus and another bus, straight to see Cassandre. She huddled into her leather jacket so that her body was warm but her face still cool, that lovely coolness. She knew it was the drug that made everything seem okay but she also felt strongly that there was some truth in it, and as she walked into the care home, her legs light as if she were floating along the corridors in spite of her tiredness, she realised that there was an answer. A real, practical solution to her and Cassandre's predicament. The way that she would, finally, be able to rescue her little sister.

She was startled to find their mother in Cassandre's room.

It was 7 a.m., and a Saturday; she'd never imagined her mother came this early. On her way to aerobics, surely, she thought, a convenient stop-off on her journey to the gym. Her mother turned, shocked to see Marguerite. Caught out.

'Margggggo,' slurred Cass from her wheelchair and Marguerite went to her, wrapped her arms around her, whispered into her ear, 'I know what to do. I've got the answer. You don't need to worry any more.' Cass looked confused but happy when she pulled away; her eyes, unaligned, roamed over Marguerite's face. Her breath was warm.

Marguerite held Cass's face in her hands, though it was difficult with the headrest and the strap Velcroed across Cass's forehead, and she kissed her on her cheek, firmly and softly, like her friend had done to her not so long ago. Her sister's skin was warm and oily, smelt faintly of peppermint.

Her mother was watching them. Then she stood, took Marguerite's face in her own hands. She snorted and rolled her eyes. 'Oh, for God's sake, Margo,' she said.

Her hands were very cold. This close to her mother's face, Marguerite could see the pale powder blotting out her pores. Her thin lips twitching. She dropped her hands.

'Like flying saucers. Go home and sleep that off.'

It felt like a slap. As she walked out, she heard Cassandre ask in her new language why Margo couldn't stay. For a moment, the happiness of the night felt as if it might come crashing and splintering inwards.

But by the time she had got home she didn't feel sad at all. She had the answer.

They returned in a great slam of noise, a little drunk again, wet towels shed in a pile on the kitchen table. They gave cursory hellos and Thibault didn't seem to notice her. He filed straight out and upstairs and when he came back five minutes later he was naked but for a towel, hair wet, torso still a little jewelled from his shower. She busied herself cooking. They'd spent the day at a lake, Marc explained, some two hours from here, a favourite if theirs when they were young. Briefly, she imagined taking all her clothes off, jumping into cool water.

'Is the old man all right today?' asked Jean-Christophe, and she spoke without turning to face them.

'He's been okay,' she said, though he hadn't; he'd been foul.

'What she means is that he's pissed off with us because we went out,' said Thibault, and still she didn't turn. There followed a little symphony of practised phrases, excuses, them rationalising and reassuring each other: 'We came here three days earlier than we were going to, so one day out is fine.' 'He must know we need a little holiday, it's not often we take this time off work.' And finally, 'He seems to be asleep most of the day anyway. Let's go see him now.'

At this last, she spoke.

'He said—' She paused, stopped chopping, turned around.

'He said we can't,' said Thibault and she looked at him and felt the blood rush to her face. She turned back to the vegetables.

'Yes.' She waited for the flush to run its course and recede again. There was silence, and then they became anxious, repeating the well-reasoned phrases they'd spoken just before.

Then they took beers and went outside, and she watched them spill across the grass, Thibault still with just a towel wrapped around his waist.

When she took Jérôme his dinner, he seemed softer.

'Well, this looks good,' he said. He was docile as she took his obs, complimented her again on the food when he'd finished. When she'd cleared everything away, he asked her to read to him.

She pulled out their book and he cocked his head attentively as she read. And then there was a knock, very soft, at the door.

'Didn't you tell them I wouldn't see them?' he hissed.

'I did,' she said. The knock came again, and the door opened slowly: Jean-Christophe, poking his head around the door, his expression studiously benign.

'Hi, Dad,' he said.

Jérôme looked away, mouth clenched. Jean-Christophe came in, looked at Marguerite and down at the book in her hand. 'Sorry to interrupt. I know you're tired, but just thought I'd say a quick hi.'

'Get out.'

Marguerite squirmed, looked down.

'Dad, I hope you're not put out that we went out today?'

Jérôme's head snapped around. 'I said get out,' he said.

Jean-Christophe looked pained, but he left. Jérôme tutted when the door clicked shut. 'You can't play with people like that,' he said, not quite to her. Then he looked at her. 'Coming to visit me unannounced one day, off without saying a thing the next. Are they here on bloody holiday or what? Or just waiting for me to die?'

A fat fly flew in and his eyes darted to it, startled. Tiredness swept across his face then.

'Well, go on. Keep reading.'

They were cooking pasta when she came back into the kitchen.

'I hope you don't mind, we opened a pack of this,' said Marc, holding up an empty box of fusilli. It was boiling furiously on the hob.

'Of course.'

'We're going to sit outside,' said Thibault.

'We do hope you'll join us,' said Jean-Christophe. 'Are you allowed?'

Marguerite frowned. 'Of course.'

'Splendid. Glass of wine?'

'Perhaps in a bit.'

'Ah, perhaps in a bit. Very sensible.' He poured one for himself. 'So was he being as badly behaved with you as he's been with us? Or are you exempt from his moods?'

She couldn't see a way to respond. 'He—'

'You don't have to answer that,' said Marc.

Thibault was watching her. When she caught his eye, he smiled. Without warmth, she thought.

'Well you've been doing a majestic job,' said Jean-Christophe. He raised his glass. 'To Marguerite, the saint, for looking after our dear old father with apparently inexhaustible patience.'

They raised their glasses, and she tried to smile. Thibault stood and took out an empty glass, filled it and passed it to her.

'Go on, take it,' he said. 'You deserve it.'

When the pasta was done – overdone, she thought, looking at it – they piled it onto plates and took them outside, sitting on the grass to eat. Sunset had forged forward into dusk; the sky was violet, the grass a little wet. As they ate, the focus moved from her and they swapped stories about their lives in Paris and people they knew. The tension crumpled. Thibault sat cross-legged, like a yogi. Jean-Christophe and Marc lay on their sides, heads propped up on an elbow. She finished her food and waited for a polite amount of time, and then rose to take her plate inside.

'You're not going to bed, are you?' asked Jean-Christophe, mock-expansively. 'Stay, stay.'

'Stay,' echoed Thibault.

'We're only just getting to know you,' said Jean-Christophe. They were playing. He pouted like a little child.

'She can go if she wants,' said Marc.

'But she doesn't want to go,' said Thibault. 'Does she? She wants to stay with us.'

He smiled, almost sweetly, and she sat back down.

'There we go.'

'We need light,' said Marc.

'We'll get candles. Lanterns.' They were drunk, but there was an air of joviality to their drunkness. She thought she didn't mind staying a little longer.

They were lighting the lanterns, the darkness settling softly around them, when they heard an engine approach and slow, gravel prickling under tyres. They looked at each other; Marc and Jean-Christophe got up, chests a little puffed, walked around to look. They came back and sat down.

206

'Some woman?' said Jean-Christophe. 'Headscarf.' He gestured around his face. They all looked at Marguerite. 'A friend of yours?'

'I didn't – I'm not—'

Suki came around the corner from the drive then, braced to head into the kitchen but her attention was caught by the lights.

'Oh!' she said, holding one hand to her chest, walking towards them. 'You gave me a fright!' She approached and everyone stood. 'You must be Lanvier's sons, am I right?' she asked. She looked majestic in loose green scarves, her lips dark in the sparse light. 'I had no idea you were in town!' She leant forward to kiss Marguerite on each cheek. 'I was just coming to check up on you,' she said. 'See how you're doing.'

But that's a lie, Marguerite thought, and felt unnerved.

'Hi Suki,' she said. 'How are you?'

'Suki,' repeated Marc. 'We've met, a long time ago.'

'Yes,' she said, narrowing her eyes as if trying to place them. 'I know we've definitely come across each other at some point or another over the years . . .' She looked to each of them, smiling brightly. 'Please excuse my rudeness, but I can't remember your names?'

'JC. Jean-Christophe.'

'I'm Marc, this is Thibault.'

'Lovely to meet you properly,' she said.

There was silence, then Marc spoke again. 'Would you like to join us?'

'Absolutely,' she said, looking down at the lanterns. 'What a romantic set-up.' They sat back down a little awkwardly, one by one, and she settled herself easily on a hip, legs tucked to

207

one side. She reached in her little bag for her pack of cigarettes, offered it around.

'I shouldn't,' said Thibault, reluctantly.

'What?' Playful, exaggerated surprise in her eyes and voice. 'Four Parisians, and none of you smoke?'

She lit her own and then Thibault gave in, gesturing to her. There was silence for a moment as he lit it, took a deep drag. Jean-Christophe was watching Suki carefully.

'Aren't you married to Philippe . . . What's his name again?' asked Jean-Christophe then.

'Lacourse,' she said, and Marguerite caught a glimmer of embarrassment. 'Do you know him?'

'Not really.' Jean-Christophe smirked a little. 'I mean, everyone knows everyone.'

'Very true,' she said.

'I mean I know who he is but we wouldn't have overlapped at school or anything. No, it's just I remember him marrying someone – a lot younger than him,' he said. 'Not meaning to be rude.'

'Not at all.' She blew out smoke, batted it with a hand.

'Can I get you a glass?' asked Marguerite, and Suki smiled and nodded.

'Bring another bottle?' called out Thibault as she walked back into the house. As if he knew her, as if they were all friends. She opened a new bottle, got an empty glass for Suki. She looked out of the window to see them, dark figures around little boxes of light. Why had Suki come? But she knew, of course. She didn't judge her for it at all; she just couldn't understand how she could lie in front of Marguerite like that – 'I had no idea you were in town!' – without being crippled with embarrassment. And Thibault, the way he acted like nothing had happened last night, to the extent that she had doubted momentarily that it had. Would he reach out for her body again? Would she let him? She didn't want it, she thought. But still she hadn't insisted on leaving them after dinner; she was staying.

When she got back to the group, Suki was holding forth. She made them laugh when she referred snidely to Brigitte; she filled them in on the most outlandish things that had happened in the village over the years, and Jean-Christophe was rapt. But after a while, Marguerite noticed Thibault start to become bored. He gazed to one side, long fingers fidgeting with the grass.

When Suki saw that, she stopped. 'But you must stop me. I can keep talking for hours.' She smiled at Marguerite, a lovely film-star smile. 'Marguerite will back me up on that.'

'I'm sure,' said Thibault. He looked from one to the other. 'So are you two friends?'

'Yes,' Suki said.

'It's nice you've found an ally in the village,' said Jean-Christophe to Marguerite. 'So you're not *completely* alone.'

'Oh, Marguerite's very independent,' said Suki. 'I force my company on her, really.'

'Well as long as she has some sort of human interaction,' said Jean-Christophe, and Marc coughed. 'I was starting to worry she might be a robot.'

'Jean-Christophe,' said Marc.

Thibault looked amused.

'No offence, no offence,' said Jean-Christophe, smiling. 'I mean it in the best possible way. I just – I mean, you have to

209

admire it. I don't know how you do it. All the hours you must spend staring into space.'

'She's too busy looking after your father to stare into space,' said Suki.

'The women are ganging up on me,' said Jean-Christophe to the others.

'You like goading people,' Suki said then, smiling. 'Ruffling feathers. I get that.'

'*Thank* you,' said Jean-Christophe. 'At last, someone who understands me.'

Thibault and Marc rolled their eyes. 'Don't encourage him,' said Marc, and they all laughed, though weakly. The conversation moved on, back into the men's lives. Marguerite caught Suki's eye a few times, smiled. Suki kept sipping from her glass, refilling it and everyone else's. She smoked continually, reaching her pack out to Thibault, who took one every now and then. She listened to their jokes and stories with great attention, flicking from one face to the other as if watching a tennis game, laughing and smiling with them.

At some point they spoke about a man called Grégoire, and when Jean-Christophe referred to his teeth falling out, Suki joined in the laughter.

Thibault shot her a sharp look. 'Why are you laughing?'

'What?' she said, still smiling.

'You don't know Grégoire,' he said.

But the others ignored it.

'He's aging at an accelerated rate because of his wife,' said Jean-Christophe. 'Belly, teeth, grey hair . . .'

Marguerite watched Suki's face, how she kept it composed. She wanted to reach out and touch her hand.

She watched their volley of anecdotes: quick puns and wordplay, a bank of shared stories. They had a language and a repertoire all their own. Suki and Marguerite sat on the outside. She begged, in her mind, for Suki to get up to go, so she too could leave, head upstairs to the safety of her room. But Suki kept watching and listening, still smiling, though laughing less.

When there was a silence in the conversation, Suki leant in. 'How is it to be back at Rossignol?' she asked, and then, before they could answer: 'And how *is* your father?'

It didn't sound authentic, the knowing sympathy in her tone. Marguerite could see Thibault bristle.

'Well, we haven't seen much of him,' said Jean-Christophe.

'Oh?'

'Marguerite doesn't let us in. She's like a sentinel at his door.'

Suki looked at Marguerite.

'Cerberus,' said Thibault, and Jean-Christophe laughed.

A quick, vague montage of myths flashed through her mind, things she'd learnt some time at school: harpies, rocks that came crashing together, deadly whirlpools. She couldn't remember who or what Cerberus was.

'I can think of kinder comparisons for Marguerite than a three-headed dog,' Suki said. She cocked her head to one side, gazed at Marguerite. 'Oh, for me, you're one of the sirens.'

Three-headed dog, she thought. She remembered Thibault's words the evening before: *Lovely Marguerite.* She set her glass aside. She didn't want any more. She wanted to go.

'I have a question,' said Jean-Christophe, looking at Suki. He swirled a finger twice around his face. 'What's this about?'

There was momentary silence; Marc looked away, Thibault's eyes darted from one face to another.

'You mean this?' asked Suki, smiling politely. She touched the emerald silk around her face. 'It's a hijab.'

Jean-Christophe looked irritated. 'No, I mean I know what it is. I'm just interested – please, do tell me to back off if I'm being rude—'

'No, it's fine. You don't approve of us wearing them?'

'Oh, I don't care about that. I mean, I'm pretty sure it's a symbol of oppression, but each to their own. I just, as you can tell, I say things as they are. I'm just interested.'

'That's fine, ask away,' said Suki. She wasn't smiling any-more.

'I just, you know, you smoke, you drink – I'm interested, are you actually a Muslim?'

'I think Suki is too polite to tell you that you are actually being quite rude,' said Marc.

Jean-Christophe's eyes widened, innocently. 'Is that so?' he asked.

'It's fine,' she said.

'Do you always wear it?' he asked.

'Yes.'

'But why? You're clearly not – again, please correct me if I'm wrong or overstepping the mark – but, here you are, un-chaperoned by your husband, smoking, sharing salacious gossip, drinking alcohol, so why the hijab?'

'It's fashion,' said Thibault. 'You don't have to be—'

'It's not fashion,' said Suki, sharply, and there was total silence. 'It's my identity, my heritage. It's . . .'

She struggled for the words.

Say something, Marguerite told herself; say something, say something. But she couldn't find the words either.

'Fair enough, fair enough,' said Jean-Christophe, holding his hands up. 'I was just interested.'

Marguerite wanted to reach over to Suki, suggest they go inside or say a kind word about the incredible earrings that swung, pendulous, when she moved her head. But Suki wouldn't have liked that. She didn't need Marguerite's help.

'Cigarette, Thibault?'

'No thanks.' There was silence.

'You really can smoke, can't you,' said Jean-Christophe.

'Yes, I can,' she said. Her voice was hard. 'I can't believe that none of you does,' she said, repeating herself. 'I'm with four Parisians, and not a single one smokes!'

'Our mum died of lung cancer,' said Thibault. He stared at her.

'I'm sorry,' she said, and Marguerite spoke then, finally.

'She didn't know.'

Thibault looked from one to the other, a flicker of tongue on his lip.

'I'm going to have to go to bed,' she said. 'I have an early start. Suki, will you be staying longer?'

'No,' she said. 'I'll head with you.' She collected her cigarette butts together with her perfect fingers and nails. She emptied her glass onto the grass, shovelled the coiled butts into it. 'Well, good to meet you all,' she said and they raised hands.

'Good to meet you,' said Marc.

Marguerite and Suki walked back to the house together. 'Are you okay?' asked Marguerite.

'Of course,' said Suki, smiling bravely at Marguerite. 'Why wouldn't I be? Are you?'

'Yes, fine,' she said. Marguerite wanted to reach out through the unspoken words between them and tell her she thought they were all assholes, and that Suki should never even have bothered making an effort with them.

'See you soon?' she asked instead.

When she came out of the bathroom on the first floor, teeth cleaned and face washed, Thibault was standing there, leaning in the doorway to his room.

'Are you going to bed?' he asked. His lips were wine-blackened on the inside; it looked like dried blood.

'Yes,' she said.

'Sure I can't tempt you to stay up just a little longer?' he asked, stepping forwards, his face softer than it had been all night. She reached her doorway and turned.

'Yes, I'm sure.'

Closing the bedroom door behind her, she thought she heard him laugh.

12

Marguerite left the house early. She'd get fresh croissants for Jérôme today. The ground was still wet when she set out, the light high and thin.

The village was different at this time: there was a bustle of industry. Bleary-eyed men in overalls leaning on the high tables in the boulangerie, drinking foul-smelling coffee in tiny plastic cups. Was there a factory near here, she wondered – where were these blue-smocked men all going on a Saturday morning?

There was a thin, stressed young woman in the queue in front of her, buying enough bread for a large household. Her daughter, perhaps three or four, looked up at Marguerite, a little coquettish. Practising her smile. Marguerite smiled back and the girl hid her face in her mother's bottom, then turned back to take another peek. I don't find you sweet, Marguerite imagined saying. Stop smiling at me. You have nothing on Cassandre.

On the way home, she stopped to sit by the side of the road. She had become used to seeing a flattened toad there, stretched like a large sticker on the broken tarmac. It had been there, in varying degrees of decomposition, ever since she started the job here; finally someone had removed it. She looked closer to see if there were any remnants of its body, but found nothing but slight discolouration.

She took the claw from a croissant, then ate the whole thing. Then she ate another. She only got to her feet when she heard a distant engine. When she heard it coming closer, she said aloud, 'Oh, piss off.'

Henri was driving too fast. He only realised he was when he saw the nurse appear suddenly at the side of the road; he slowed and she turned, a bald look of irritation on her face. He lowered the window, came to a halt.

'Marguerite?'

'Hello,' she said. Her scowl dropped and she smiled politely, squinting a little into the gloom of the car.

'This is your new machine,' he said, and he thought she looked embarrassed. 'Can I give you a lift the rest of the way?'

'Oh,' she said. She removed her backpack, opened the door, got in. 'Thank you.' She put the bag on her lap, fastened her seat belt. Slow and methodical. A stick of bread poked out of the top of her bag. She hadn't even looked at the car.

'The morning bread run?' he asked, setting off again.

'Yes.'

'Well, you'll be able to drive next time.'

'Yes.'

They drove the rest of the way in silence; he noticed her

hands fidgeting with the bread. Pulling off little flakes of crust. She only spoke again when they pulled up in the driveway.

'Oh,' she said. 'I just remembered. Will you be staying here for a little bit?'

'Can do. I have to wait for Thierry to drive over and pick me up.'

'Great. If you can, Jérôme said he'd like to see you.'

'Okay,' he said, though he didn't want to. He thought of his own father's sickbed. He had struggled to reconcile the stale, talc-sweet, inhuman smell with his always immaculate dad. The head he knew so well emerging from his diminished neck like a big lollipop.

'I'll need to check with him first,' she said. 'Check that it's a good time.'

'Of course. I'm happy to wait.'

'Thank you for driving the car over,' she said as they walked towards the house, but still she didn't turn to look at it.

Jérôme had been excited at the news. He'd asked for a shave and a shirt, and she'd combed his hair carefully. When she'd brought Henri into the room Jérôme had barked out a jovial laugh.

'Henri, old boy. Great to see you.' They'd shaken hands, and Henri had taken the chair she offered him. 'Bigger than ever, I see,' said Jérôme, 'or is it just that I've shrunk? Excellent to see you.'

She'd left them then, door ajar, and sat in the kitchen, listening out for signs of life from upstairs. She flicked through

217

one of the papers she'd already read. Then she got up, walked out and around the corner of the house to the driveway to look at her little car. She liked it: small, dark green, tired-looking. She liked that Henri had given it to her, not Brigitte or one of the sons. She imagined getting into it now and driving away for miles and miles. Perhaps until she found the sea.

And then what, she thought. She heard the clanking of pipes from inside the house and headed back into the kitchen. She'd have to find somewhere in the house to spend the day where she wouldn't have to speak to any of them.

Jean-Christophe was the first to emerge.

'God, I do not feel pretty this morning,' he said. His face was puffy. 'Beer and red wine is *not* a good combo. Where's the coffee?'

He poured the dregs from what she'd made for Jérôme and Henri.

'Henri Brochon is here,' she said. 'He's visiting your father.'

'Is he now!' Jean-Christophe shook his head as he sliced a baguette. 'I didn't know that had been arranged. Looks like Dad's got all sorts of new friends.'

She didn't say anything, didn't want to explain that he'd come to bring her the car.

'Well,' he said. 'Good luck to him.'

When Henri came back into the room, bowing his head elegantly under the low doorframe, she thought again that she caught something shy in his expression.

'Henri!' said Jean-Christophe. 'Good to see you again. Why haven't you been over? Can you stick around a bit today?'

'A little while, sure.' He rubbed the back of his neck. 'Your father asked to see whichever of you was up,' he said, and Jean-Christophe gulped his bread.

'Here we go.'

Henri smiled at her when Jean-Christophe had left.

'Oh, here are your car keys.' He took them from his pocket and held them out to her. 'I almost forgot.'

'Thank you very much.'

'It must be strange having the house so full.'

'It's okay, it's fine. It's not for long.'

He was leaning against the dresser, looking around the room. 'I've eaten so many meals in this room,' he said.

'Really?'

'I used to spend most of my time here, when I was a young boy.' He shook his head. 'It used to drive my mother mad.'

'So you were good friends with the Lanviers?'

'Yes,' he said quickly. He cleared his throat, pushed himself away from the dresser. 'Could I make another coffee?'

'I'll do it.'

'Thank you.'

Jean-Christophe came back into the room, didn't speak. He had his BlackBerry in one hand, scrolling through it. The kettle clicked, and she let it rest as Suki had instructed her, measured out fresh coffee, left it for a moment. Then she realised that Jean-Christophe had stopped scrolling, and was staring at her.

'It's funny,' he said. 'My father's just asked me to arrange a visit from his lawyer.'

She frowned, poured the water in. She forgot to do it from a height.

'He wants, as he put it, to "review certain things in his will".'

'Who's his lawyer?' asked Henri. 'A local?'

'Yes, ish. A Monsieur Richoux.' She started to plunge. Jean-Christophe was still watching her.

'Did you know anything about this?'

She looked up. 'No, of course not. I'm just his nurse.'

'Hm,' he said. 'He hasn't mentioned anything to you?'

'No.' She poured the coffee into Henri's empty cup, passed it to him. 'But I don't see why he would.'

'No, quite,' said Jean-Christophe. 'One wouldn't *think* that his will should have anything to do with you.'

She looked at him, then. What are you saying? she thought. Just say it. She could feel that she'd become flushed.

'I'm going to get on with the washing,' she said, addressing Henri. She tried to slow her step, not to run from the room as she wanted to. She had a flash of a memory: staying at their uncle's big house in Provence as a child; exploring the cold, spidery basement until she became spooked, then sprinting down the corridor and up the stairs until she emerged back into the light of the house, her breath ragged.

'What do you think of the nurse?' Henri asked.

'Marguerite?'

Thibault looked over to the house, thought for a moment. They were sitting on the low wall surrounding the old pool area: Thibault's suggestion that the two of them come outside, 'catch up'. Henri could see the stump of the old oak tree he had had to lop down. 'Oh, she's a total nut job.'

'What? Really?'

'Yeah. Come on, she's twenty-four, clearly very well-to-do, and she's decided to leave Paris for *this* job? She barely speaks. She sees no one all day, every day, lives in the middle of fucking – forest and shrubs, in a decaying old house. Wiping my father's arse. Though I must admit, she does seem to have worked some Svengali shit on dad. He loves her.' He pulled a little piece of the wall away with his hand, crumbling it in his fingers. Like a little boy, Henri thought.

'JC thinks she's snivelling around for inheritance money, of course. Classic JC conspiracy theory. Though there may be some truth in it. If she's not a masochist then she's certainly the patron saint of patience. There's got to be something in the situation for her.'

'I think that's a little unfair.'

'Of course you'd think that,' said Thibault, his voice bored, and he smiled to make up for it. 'Always seeing the best in people, aren't you, Henri?'

'No,' he said. 'Not at all.'

'My theory is that she's running from something.'

And what about you? thought Henri.

'What's it like, coming back here?' he asked instead.

Thibault stared into the distance for a moment. 'Weird. Really depressing actually.'

Henri tried to suppress the feeling of hurt, the light punch to his stomach. 'How so?'

'Well, we're getting older, aren't we. Like it or not. I'll be forty next year. And this place just reminds me of being young. Don't get me wrong, I hate the place, it's full of painful memories. I can see Mum everywhere, for one thing. But we were also right in the prime of everything, weren't we?'

'Yes. I know. I feel like that too when I come back here.'

'But it wasn't your house,' said Thibault, eyes darting to him.

'Yes, obviously I don't feel the same as you.' Henri frowned. 'But I still associate a lot of my youth with Rossignol. We spent some amazing times here.'

Thibault relaxed, nodded. 'We certainly did.' He gestured at the pool with his chin. 'You know JC lost his virginity in there?'

Henri laughed. 'Yes! To that girl – she was actually quite hot.'

'Camille Brun. She was extremely hot. I still can't understand how he pulled that one off.'

'I'm sure he still can't understand it either.' They laughed, shook their heads, and Henri remembered other things: the bursting pulse of his lungs as Marc dunked him, the sting of chlorine in the back of his nose as he gasped back up into the air, the run-up and jump into a neat somersault, whipping around quick enough to enter the water cleanly, feet first. Strong young bodies. Sunburn and tight, aching muscles.

'And now look at the dump,' said Thibault. They stared at what it had become, this big empty decaying coffin. Then suddenly Thibault jumped to his feet and for a wild moment Henri thought he was going to dive in. He jumped up to stop him, but Thibault ran to the side of the pool and then came running back waving something at Henri: a huge rope, like a snake, he thought, and then: yes, a snake, and involuntarily he yelled and held his hands in front of his face as Thibault flung it at him.

It was dead, though it thrashed as it landed on the floor by his feet, the impact lending its body a last tug of movement.

Henri stepped back quickly, squeamishly away from it, and then he stood there and looked up at Thibault, whose head was thrown back in laughter, and he was flooded with fury. He kicked the snake into the pool, heard it splash as it hit the murky water that had collected at the bottom.

'What the hell, Thibault?'

'The look on your face!' Thibault gasped, through gulps of laughter. 'Ah, priceless!' He leant over, hands on his knees, straightened up with a few stray chuckles. 'Henri the big brave farmer.'

'You're a dick,' said Henri, though he was starting to see the funny side. He breathed out, felt his heart calm in his chest. Then he laughed, stepping forwards to peer down into the pool. The brown, scuddy surface was rippling.

'Thing is,' said Thibault then, eyes darting over at him, sly. 'You love a bit of snake in your face, don't you.'

Henri felt his shoulders square, his jaw clench. The adrenaline came soaring back into his body.

'What?'

They stared at each other. Thibault's eyes were serious, locked into Henri's. And then his face cracked into a smile.

'Relax, buddy, I'm making a joke.' He clapped him on the shoulder. 'Chill. It's just a joke.' He stared into the pool. 'There it is. Big motherfucker.'

Henri looked at Thibault's sharp profile and thought that it was too sharp. And he realised with the sudden clarity that comes with adrenaline that he didn't like the man standing next to him. A wave of exhaustion came over him then.

'Come on, let's go,' he said. 'I've got to get going.'

'Okay,' said Thibault, in the same tone of voice in which

he'd told Henri to 'chill'. As if Henri were making a scene. They left the pool area and walked up the grass towards the house in silence.

'Say goodbye to the others from me,' said Henri. He would walk into Saint-Sulpice, call the farm for a lift from there. He couldn't face going back into the house. 'It's a shame I didn't catch Marc today.' He didn't want to look at Thibault's face again, but he made himself look him in the eye.

'That man could sleep for France,' said Thibault.

'Well. Good to see you.'

Thibault half smiled, raised one hand and called out his goodbye over his shoulder, already in the threshold of the kitchen. 'Till the next time, buddy.'

Henri poured himself a whisky when Brigitte went to bed, even though he was exhausted. He felt emptied out. Sitting at the kitchen table, swivelling the whisky in the glass, he let himself picture Thibault's face by the pool: the sharp lines of his profile. The too-short, too-sharp nose. The thin top lip. He tried to put the features back together in the way he used to see them – in a softer, fuller way – but he couldn't manage it. He couldn't see the face he'd seen before.

And he remembered a time when they'd been ten, eleven years old. It was the end of a long, hot summer; they'd spent almost every day together and most nights and they'd run out of humour. They were ready to go back to school, oppressed by the heat, the moronic whir of cicadas, the long, repetitive days. Thibault with closely cropped hair, still mousy. The soft, blonde fur on his face like the fuzz of a peach. He'd squatted next to Henri on the baking-hot tiles outside the house, sullen, setting large ants on fire using a magnifying glass. There was the smell of plastic burning as the Tupperware he'd collected them in melted too. Burning plastic and something else.

'Stop it,' Henri had said, twice. Thibault ignored him. He said it a third time. '*Stop it.*'

'Piss off.'

'I mean it. Stop it. It's just cruel.'

Thibault had turned to him and stared. And then he'd thrown his head back and roared with laughter. 'Stop it,' he said in a whiny voice. 'Save the darling ants, Thibault. It's so *cruel.*'

'Shut up,' Henri said.

'Can't you just go home, Henri?' He tapped the magnifying glass on Henri's face, between his eyes. 'I am so, extremely, *bored* of you.'

Then they were entangled on the ground. Henri's face scraped across the tiles; he twisted Thibault's arm back and then they were biting, hissing, puce, a pair of stag beetles locked to each other. It had taken Jérôme and Marc to pull them apart.

It was too hot; she couldn't get comfortable in the bed. There was a sort of spasmodic pulsing in her feet and legs, as if her nerves were twitching. She imagined Jérôme's life, confined perpetually to the dull flatness of a mattress. The irritating weight of sheets and blankets on his legs.

He hadn't eaten a thing this evening, had barely spoken. He hadn't asked about Thibault, though he must have realised that he'd left.

'He's even worse than he ever was,' she'd heard Thibault say to Marc as she stood, hiding, in the utility room. His voice was hoarse with the threat of crying, and then the thud of a kick against something: a chair, a door. 'It's like he's compensating for not being able to lash out physically any more by nailing the art of ripping you apart with words.'

'Thibault, one more day. That's all we have to get through.'

'Not me. I'm going to get the train, I've got an hour. Drive me to the station?'

'You'll regret it. Stay, I'll make sure you don't have to speak to him on your own again.'

'I won't regret it. Honestly, Marc. Thank you, I appreciate your concern, but I'm beyond regret. I never want to see that cunt again.'

She'd had to watch their confrontation. Jérôme had insisted she stay in the room, sitting in the background by her table, as he'd called in each of the sons one by one. The interviews with Marc and Jean-Christophe were innocuous enough: the usual needling, the thick tapestry of things left unspoken. Thibault came in last. By that time, she was sickened and exhausted by these exchanges.

'I must go now,' she'd said. 'I need to start preparing your dinner.'

'No, we won't be long, Marguerite. I insist you stay.'

He'd kept her there to make his sons more uncomfortable, she supposed, having to enact an intimate scenario in front of a stranger. And beyond that, she sensed that in an indirect way she was there for back-up: some adult version of the playground principle of two against one. She made him somehow stronger, bigger, legitimised.

He'd asked Thibault a little about his job. About his salary: 'Decent enough, Dad, put it that way.'

'Not going to give me the actual figure?'

'As I said, it's decent enough.'

'Fine, fine.'

He'd asked him if there was a particular woman in his life.

'There might be,' he'd said. Marguerite remembered his warm kiss on her forehead, the easy affection with which he'd rested one hand on the back of her neck.

'Not going to tell me about that either?'

'I don't want to jinx it. Surely you understand that.'

'All right.' Jérôme had sniffed. They'd jabbed and feinted and blocked, a guardedly civil back and forth. Thibault stayed determinedly calm. She could see Jérôme thinking, working out how to get a rise.

'I saw Henri today.'

'So I hear.'

'He wanted to visit. We always got on very well.'

'I know.'

'Henri Brochon,' he'd mused, gazing ahead of him. 'Now that's a man.'

'Here we go.'

'Here we go with what?'

'You just—' A sigh; remembering to be calm, she thought. 'You don't need to worry that you haven't already made it clear that you think he's better than me.'

'I haven't—'

'Yes, you have. You were always very clear, Dad, more than clear enough, that you wished I'd been more like him.'

'Well, you could have been. If only you'd applied yourself, if only you'd ever had an ounce of discipline.'

'Ha! So I could become a farmer? That's what discipline and application get you? I'd rather die than live Henri's life.'

'Oh, how very snooty you've become. I didn't realise a good, honest job like farming was beneath you.'

'Stuck in this dump, counting sheep. With a hideous wife. Thanks, but I'll take my lot over that.' Silence for a moment, and then, in a smiling voice: 'And anyway, Dad, if you really want to know, I'm 99 per cent sure your precious Henri is a fag.'

Jérôme had snorted. 'Of all the jealous, filth-slinging things to say, Thibault. How utterly ridiculous.'

'Fine, fine.' Thibault's tone was as if amused, but there was no humour there. 'But get the full picture before you start lamenting how you ended up with the wrong son and how much better it would be if I was like him. He's buried alive, look at him.'

'And look at you!'

'Okay, okay. Let's look at me.'

'Yes. Let's look at what you've become.'

'What have I become, Dad?' Still pretending to smile, but she could see the anger quivering in the set of his shoulders, his neck, his face.

'You've become a smarmy little city boy.'

He laughed, harshly. 'I'll take that.'

'Ha. Just like you take everything. Take, take, take. That's all you've ever done.'

'Fuck off,' Thibault muttered, looking away.

'What?' Jérôme's eyes were glittering. 'At least be man enough to say it to my face, if you're going to.'

'I said fuck off, Dad, I don't need to listen to this.'

'Well, you will, because this might be the last conversation we ever have.'

Thibault had shaken his head. 'And do you really want the last conversation we ever have to be like this?'

'Of course I don't want it to be like this. I didn't ask for you to hate me.'

'I didn't say I hated you.'

'What *do* you say, then? What's your great grievance, Thibault? Come on, you bring it in here, you walk in here and look at me full of reproach, your shoulders visibly *weighed down* by it.' Marguerite had stood, tried to leave. 'Stay right there,' said Jérôme. 'I'm not afraid. Let him say it. Let him have his audience. What's the accusation, Thibault? What's Daddy done so terribly wrong? Fiddle you, did he?'

'Dad!'

'Well there you go then. He wasn't a paedophile, he wasn't a rapist. So what was he? Hey? Just a little bit too strict?'

Thibault had stared at him for a long time. His face was set; he was no longer trying to affect levity. She saw him weighing up the words.

'Where do I start?'

'Wherever you like.'

'For one, you treated Mum like shit.'

'Oh yes?' Jérôme's face came forward, his eyes wider. 'And how would you treat a wife, if you had one? Hey? A nice, sweet, tolerant wife – would you be a nice, sweet, tolerant husband, Thibault? Bring her flowers, would you? Pay her compliments?'

'No one said you had to bring Mum flowers. You just didn't need to bully her, relentlessly. You didn't need to humiliate her with your affairs.'

Jérôme barked out a little laugh, high in his throat. 'And what's the longest you've ever been faithful to a woman?' Thibault stared at him. 'Hm? At least man up and answer me, you pious cunt.'

Thibault closed his eyes then, his lips pulled tight together. When he opened his eyes, Marguerite could see tears shining in them.

'We're more similar than you think, matey.' Jérôme smiled, grimly. 'Except that I think you're going to have a little weep.'

'Yes,' said Thibault, his voice breaking. 'Yes, I'm going to have a little weep. But look at you, Dad. Are you happy? Your entire existence is based on how to make everyone around you feel small. You think I buy all this crap with Marguerite?' He swiped his hand towards her. 'You think I don't see that you treat her like shit too? She's your dream punching bag.'

Keep me out of this, thought Marguerite. She stood again, stealthily, but Jérôme looked up.

'Stay here!' he hissed, a ball of spit shooting out onto the sheets, and she sat back down, stared at the table. 'I spend all my time making people feel small, hm? And what's *your* existence based on, Thibault? Don't you ever like making people feel a little small? Because for someone who claims not to do it, you're pretty damn well practised.'

'Fine, Dad, we're more similar than I think. I'm just as bad as you. I get it, trust me. You've made your point.' He'd wiped the tears away from his eyes, leant back in his chair. And then he came right forward, elbows on his knees. 'But you don't scare me any more, Dad. And yes, you know what, I do hate you. No, that's not enough. I *loathe* you.'

'There we go,' hissed Jérôme, every muscle of his face alive, straining forward from the bed. 'An honest word. Finally.'

'No no,' said Thibault, shaking his head. 'You don't get to absolve yourself of responsibility for this. I *wanted* to love you. I tried, and tried again. But you made it impossible.'

'What a sentimental pile of crap. You've never loved anyone in your life apart from yourself.'

'That's bullshit. I loved Mum. I still love her.'

'Stop bringing her into this.'

'And you know what? I love Marc and JC too. They're my brothers. They would miss me if I died. But you? You'll have no one to miss you; no one will mourn. No one will even spare you a moment's thought. No fond memories, no tears.' He bit his lip. 'That's the honest truth, since you're asking. The honest truth, Dad, is that not a single human on this great earth will miss Jérôme Lanvier.'

When he'd got up, standing in the doorway, he'd snorted in mock laughter. 'Just the redemptive final goodbye I always hoped for.'

Jérôme had leant his head and neck back against the wall, a boxer strung out backwards across the ropes. She'd waited for a few minutes, her heart fast in her chest. He didn't see her when she stood, then walked slowly and quietly out of the room.

III

13

Those days after the sons left began to feel endless. She'd longed for the house to resume its silence, to be able to reclaim the spaces of her kitchen, her previous bedroom. But it felt like Thibault's bedroom now, and she still imagined their mess and noise filling the kitchen. Marc's muscle memory as he ducked to enter the room, Jean-Christophe flinging his jacket on the sofa. It was theirs.

Jérôme was restless and lethargic; he barely spoke. She could only get him to eat when his pain became unbearable. Then he would eat some bread, just enough to take the pills. He lay in bed, eyes half open, listening to the radio.

The lawyer visited, as Jean-Christophe had arranged. A quiet, grey-looking man, he stayed in Jérôme's room for almost two hours and then he left and took off in his small grey car, and the silence rushed back into the space he'd left like water. Jérôme was exhausted from the effort of sitting up and talking for so long, and she put him back in bed earlier than normal, cleared away the lunch he refused to touch.

She worried about him. His pain was much worse than

normal. He was constipated, his lethargy was unsettling. He needed a lot more food than he was having. Withdrawn and passive, he was asking very little from her.

Taking out the rubbish, changing the bin liners in the kitchen, washing the sons' sheets, set by set, sitting on the tiles outside the kitchen in the sun with a cup of coffee, watching the odd skinny little lizard flicker by; she began to feel that these things were all she'd ever do and know. Endlessly, on repeat.

She didn't use the car when she went into Saint-Sulpice. She couldn't bring herself to, yet. It would feel hubristic. Igniting the engine would feel like too large an affront to the surrounding stillness. She felt too small to break the silence.

On the fifth morning, Jérôme's blood pressure was markedly higher.

'This isn't good,' she said. She looked him in the eyes, tried to get something from him. She watched him brace himself against another spasm of pain, his lips white.

'You're hypertensive.' she said when it had passed.

'So what? Don't you have pills for this kind of thing?'

'You're already on them.'

'You're the nurse. Sort it out.'

'I can sort out your blood pressure, but my concern is what's causing it.'

'Let's not worry about it.'

She stared at him, but he looked away.

'I do worry about it.'

'So do something!' He flapped a limp hand at her. 'Stop

bothering me about it. You're going to raise it even higher with all this fussing and whining.' He tried to turn in the bed but he winced with pain again, squeezing his eyes shut.

'I'm going to give you some of the strong pills. But I don't want you being sick. You've got to eat.'

'So I'll eat.'

'Can you tell me where the pain is?'

'Everywhere.'

'Specifically?'

'Shoulders, back. Under my ribs. My stomach.'

'You're constipated.'

'So I'd noticed.'

She got him to eat a little muesli, lumpen with milk. She watched it mulch through his teeth, some of it trickling down his chin. He didn't seem to notice. He ate mechanically, his eyes staring into nothing, and then he belched, wetly, and pushed the spoon and bowl away.

'No more,' he said.

She cleared it away, wiped his chin clean, gave him his painkillers and laxatives and lowered him down into the bed.

'I want you to try to get some sleep now,' she said, taking his pressure again. 'And I need you to try to relax. If you're feeling stressed, or anxious, that will be raising your blood pressure too.'

'I wonder why I'd be feeling stressed or anxious.'

She sighed.

'Try not to think about negative things.'

He snorted as she left the room.

He didn't eat lunch; he said he felt too nauseous. In the afternoon she had to give him more of the painkillers, the strongest she had. She stayed in his room, skim-reading one of their library books, as he slipped in and out of sleep, in and out of pain. His breath was shallow, particularly when he slept. His mouth caved open, rending a deep hollow between his cheekbones and jaw. Lying there with his hands curled like claws in front of his chest, he looked like the dead mouse she'd once found in the pantry.

By the evening the pain was back and with it his blood pressure began climbing again, steadily. He could no longer keep medication down, vomiting harshly into the bucket like a barking fox, and she saw that this wasn't going to go away now, that he needed to be put on intravenous morphine. She began to feel sick with dread. She couldn't get him to the car on her own, she didn't think, but she wouldn't call an ambulance. She knew that was irresponsible but she just wouldn't risk that they might leave her behind, watching as they took him away.

He reached out one of his claws, wrapped them around her wrist.

'What did he just say?' His voice was thin.

'Who?'

'Thibault. What did he say?'

She paused, looked down at his face.

'Something about the telephone,' he said. 'Oh, never mind. I thought he was saying something about the telephone.'

She went to the telephone, then, and took out Brigitte's number.

'I need someone to help me take him out,' she said when she got through.

'Henri will come right away.'

She packed a bag with his medical notes and medication, and heard the wheels on gravel within fifteen minutes.

'Tell me what to do,' Henri said when he appeared at the door, and followed her through to the bedroom.

Jérôme didn't seem surprised that he was there.

'You're a bit early, old boy,' he muttered. 'Well, no matter.'

She maneouvred him into a sitting position, swivelled him round so his feet touched the floor. He smelt different. She tied him into shoes, his ankles emerging from them like onions. Henri took him under one arm, she took the other. They lifted him and she felt the cobbles of his back under her palm. He hung heavy onto them as they shuffled with him, step by step. Panting.

'I could carry him,' said Henri.

'Let's keep trying like this.'

They grunted as they moved, glacially slow.

'Of course you'll have to wake the others,' said Jérôme. 'Tell them we've only just got here.'

'Yes, okay,' she said, looking at Henri.

'I've no idea what they've all been doing' – he paused, panted – 'upstairs. While we were gone. It's no use leaving them all alone, in any case.'

'Hm,' said Henry, eyeing her. 'No. But it's nothing to worry about.'

He had parked his truck at the very closest edge of the

239

driveway; they hauled Jérôme into the back seats and then stepped back, catching their breath. Then she sent Henri inside to get the bag she'd packed, so that she could climb straight into the back seat next to Jérôme. She leant her face over his to look at him. His eyes weren't clear.

Henri returned, slammed the car door, started the engine.

'Pain,' Jérôme croaked as they drove, fast, down the lane to the village.

'Where?'

He lifted one hand to his chest, tapped it once, weakly.

'Here.'

Fuck, she thought.

'Is it radiating to your back, or down your arm?' she asked, but he closed his eyes, tight. 'How far?' she asked Henri.

'Twenty minutes.'

'Hurry,' she said, even though she knew that they already were. He caught her eye in the rear-view mirror and accelerated a little more.

At the hospital, Henri stopped the truck and got out, slamming the door shut. 'I'll get someone.'

She watched the hospital doors slide open for him, swallow him up.

'You okay?' she asked Jérôme.

'Yes, yes,' he said weakly. His breath was more even.

'Not long now.'

'No, not long, if the trains are running. Did you manage to get through to Céline, too?'

She rubbed his arm, the thin mouse flesh under his shirt.

'Yes.'

'Everyone's got the memo?'

'Everything's fine.'

They came out with a stretcher, a small team of them, and she gave his history to the paramedic in charge. And then they took him and she had to stride behind them, to keep up. She wouldn't lose him.

She had to stay out of his room while two of them wired him up to an ECG, set up the IV and ran tests; it was too small for 'non-personnel'. She sat on one of a chain of plastic chairs, fixed into the floor, and waited. It was a good, clean place. They seemed like they knew what they were doing. But she couldn't stand not to be involved: sitting on the hard plastic just waiting, like all the relatives she'd seen when she was working. She knew very well the guileless, gormlessly anxious set of their faces. Occasionally she could see they were acting, that their concern wasn't real – but mostly they looked as if they'd crawled right into a hidden part of themselves.

Just as she would have looked once, waiting for Cassandre. She'd sat holding Frances's hand that first time, sinking her teeth into her own shoulder. Her father circling and circling, her mother tinier than ever, leaning back against the wall, pelvis forwards, the only time she'd ever seen her abandon her posture. Then, she'd imagined her little sister in a brightly lit room filled with shining metal, nurses and doctors milling around her supine body like silent, ingenious, blue-clad ghosts. She knew now that the reality would have been harsher, quicker, louder, messier. Now she knew exactly what it was like to see a young child drugged and dwarfed on a high hospital bed. Aged fifteen, she'd sat in the waiting room imagining only that Cassandre was struggling between life and death. She hadn't understood then that those weren't the only two possible outcomes.

She didn't see Henri until he was standing in front of her. She noticed his boots first, sandy with dried mud, incongruous against the fridge-white linoleum. When she looked up and saw his face and heard his voice – 'Is everything all right?' – she realised she'd forgotten about him altogether, had simply left him with the truck and not given him another thought.

'Fine. They're just running some tests.'

He sat down, leaving an empty chair between them.

'Then they need to get his pain under control.' She felt ashamed that she hadn't been able to.

'I'm glad you called us.'

'Thank you for coming so quickly.'

'That's what we're here for.'

That's not really what you're there for, she thought.

'Any time of day or night,' he said.

'Thank you. Please don't feel you have to stay,' she said. 'I'll be here for a while. I'll call a taxi when we need to go home.'

He frowned. 'No.' Non-negotiable. 'I'll wait until we know what's happening.'

One of the nurses came out of Jérôme's room and gestured to her. 'You can go in.'

She saw immediately that the pain had gone. But he looked smaller than ever in the hospital bed, sheets pulled up to his distended trunk, bare chest patterned with electrodes. His shoulders were hunched, bird-like. He was afraid; she could see it in his eyes.

'Marguerite,' he said, and she flushed at the warmth and relief in his voice. 'I kept asking where you were. I was worried you'd gone away.'

'Of course not,' she said. 'I was right outside.'

'Are we going to be all right?'

'Absolutely. Everyone's going to bring your blood pressure right down to normal and manage this increase in pain, and then you and I can go home.'

'Good. I kept telling them, I wasn't there when it happened. They'll have to ask someone else how it all happened.'

'No,' she said. 'But nothing happened. We had to get you here to make sure you were completely safe. And you are. Surrounded by lots of very helpful people and good equipment.'

'But we won't be leaving for home any time soon.'

'We'll go back home. We're just here for now.'

'So I'm not—' He smiled, weakly. 'About to pop my clogs.'

'No,' she said, and it was a relief to her that he was making some sense. 'You are absolutely not going to pop any clogs at all. We're just making sure you're as safe as can be.'

'What's the time?'

'Eight thirty.'

'In the morning?'

'At night.'

'Do you need to go back with Céline now?'

She paused. 'No.'

'So you'll stay here.'

'So I'll stay here.'

And she did, sitting by his bed, watching his heart rate on the screen above him while he closed his eyes and dozed. And then they came to take him away for a chest X-ray, and she followed him out of the room and saw Henri sitting there waiting, two Styrofoam cups on the floor by his feet.

'I think it might be cold,' he said as she sat down, handing one to her.

'It'll still do the job. Thank you.'

She downed the cold coffee, blackly thin and bitter, and tried not to wince.

'I admire what you do,' he said after a while. 'I can't think of many scarier jobs.'

'Really?'

'Yes, terrifying. You're there the whole time, responsible for your patient at every moment.' He shook his head. 'I'd be terrible at it. I'm no good with sickness.'

'I never really questioned it,' she said. 'I had a lot of informal experience nursing, when I was growing up.' She stopped, surprised that she'd given that away. He nodded, waiting, and she liked and appreciated that there was no question on his lips. 'It just seemed natural to go on and train properly.'

She, who had never been much of a successful student, had excelled at nursing college. The work came naturally because she already knew intimately the rhythms, the subtle language of care. She knew how to position a body to prevent sores, and how to suction someone who couldn't cough of their own accord. She knew how to feed someone via the PEG in their stomach, how slowly to flush the tube with water afterwards so they wouldn't get gas and cramp. She knew where to position

244

scopolamine patches to slow down excess saliva production. She'd cleaned up shit, vomit, drool, mucus, blood. The rest came easily.

'So this is a normal environment for you.'

'Yes. But I still hate hospitals.'

He grinned. '*You* hate hospitals?'

'Yes.' Long corridors, too much activity, and death as a sudden cessation: violent and undue. She had chosen to work with a different kind of death: a slow, timely snuffing-out. 'I hate them. I couldn't wait to start my community training so I could leave hospitals behind.'

'That makes me feel better. I don't feel like such a wimp any more.'

She smiled. 'I'd probably be terrible at what you do, too.' Then she realised she didn't know the first thing about what he did. She vaguely envisaged tractors, hay bales, the lowing of cows. A flat cap and a pitchfork. Tediously large, loud, muddy machinery. Repetition and discomfort.

'Yes,' he said, looking out at the waiting room. 'Probably.'

She liked that. It was true, he was right, and she liked that he hadn't bothered to decorate the truth. It caught her by surprise.

It wasn't until they were sent home that he saw the nurse flounder. Until then, he'd watched with interest how calmly she'd dealt with everything: leaving Rossignol, liaising with the hospital staff. Whenever she could be with Jérôme, she was. He liked the way she channelled her fear into efficiency.

But later, when Jérôme had been sedated and they'd been

sent away, he saw her composure crack. Her reluctance to leave the hospital had met with a firm response from the nurse in charge of Jérôme: he would be out cold, they didn't like relatives to stay overnight, she would be needed tomorrow. He'd driven her back in silence, and now, turning into the driveway at Rossignol, he saw clearly her fear, noticed how like a tense rabbit she peered out into the dark. She didn't want to go into the house alone, and he realised that there was no way he would want to either.

'Will you be able to sleep?' he asked, cutting the engine.

She exhaled, made a 'pffff' with her lips. 'Probably not.' She had her hand on the door handle, but she wasn't pulling it.

'Me neither.' He paused. 'You won't want to fetch him tomorrow in your own car.'

She turned to him.

'It'll be much better if someone else drives, so you can sit with him again on the journey back here. And get some help carrying him in'

She nodded.

'I'll call a taxi.'

'No, call me again.'

'Okay.'

He watched her hand rest again on the door handle.

'Unless.' Her hand dropped. 'They might call for you in the middle of the night.'

'They might.'

'If you're happy with this,' he said then, realising how much he wanted her to agree with the idea, 'I'll crash here, sleep on a sofa. Then I can take you the minute you're needed.'

'I can't ask you to do that.'

'You haven't. But it makes the most sense.'

She hesitated, and he could see she wanted to say yes.

'You could sleep in one of the spare rooms.'

'Fine. Even better. But the priority is you getting to Jérôme whenever you need to. And back here with him.'

'You're sure?'

'Of course.'

He was filled with a great lightness at the prospect: a bed that was all his own, no Brigitte, sleep broken only for good reasons: help, duty. And, yes, being able to spend the night once more at Rossignol.

He made the bed up with the sheets and blankets she'd given him, and then he undressed and turned off the light and lay in the dark in Marc's old room. He could hear the creak of the floorboards on the landing, the bathroom door close. The thud of pipes, a distant hiss of water. When he heard her go back to her bedroom, Thibault's bedroom, he imagined her putting away her things, moving around the room in her distinctive way: unhurried, precise.

He thought about himself at that age, and what it would have taken for him to be able to live entirely alone, so far from everything he knew. He was sure he wouldn't have been able to do it, would have been scared by the prospect. Funny, because he'd thought of himself as so grown-up, so responsible and independent: qualifications under his belt, a wife, his head bursting with ideas as to how to streamline and then expand his father's already successful farm. Around that time he'd temporarily stopped worrying so much about his private sexual feelings and urges, vaguely thinking that with children they would dissolve in a blazing heterosexual epiphany. Handsome Henri. He would have a son he could train up on the farm himself, as his father had trained him. A clever little daughter.

He thought of Marguerite getting into bed – the very same bed in which he'd topped and tailed with Thibault so many times as young boys, then as teenagers. Waking up with a foot in his face. Tussling for the duvet. Sleepless, surrounded by the sense of Thibault's wild, animal warmth. He pictured her pulling the sheets up, switching off the light, and he felt a dart of sadness. She was very young. What a strange, deprived existence she'd chosen here.

'A total nut job,' he heard then, clearly, in Thibault's stupidly inflected voice. What a load of crap, he thought. What a perverse, miserable way to view the world. And he felt again, as he had since their goodbye on the Saturday, a sense of dizziness, precariousness. He was disorientated. That space he had kept inside himself, filled to the edges by Thibault for as long as he could remember, was suddenly empty. Its contents had just dropped right out. He would have to work out how to re-align himself now, without its familiar weight.

The kitchen smelt of coffee already; the cafetière was steaming. The door to the garden was open and she saw Henri outside, standing in the lovely dawn. He turned at the sound of her, a cup in his hand.

'Morning.'

'Morning.'

'I'm ready whenever you are.'

'Thank you.' She felt a little snap of irritation; this was her job, she didn't want to be made to feel as if he'd been waiting for her to get going. But then she thought, he's just being helpful. He doesn't even need to be here. Still, she poured herself a coffee and sat down. She'd set the pace.

'Did you manage to sleep?' he asked, sitting down opposite her.

'I did, strangely.'

'Me too. It's so quiet.'

'Is it quiet where you live?'

'By this time of day, things are already kicking off at the farm. And there are the animals. But yes, it's very quiet there at night.'

Unbidden, an image came into her mind of him and Brigitte sleeping next to each other in the dark, curled on their sides, back to back. She stole a look at him now and tried to understand how they worked as a couple. He was almost embarrassingly handsome, almost a cliché. And Brigitte surely hadn't just 'let herself go', as her mother would say: she could never have been attractive. But perhaps this was a shallow way to look at people; perhaps Henri saw something beautiful in Brigitte's character, though admittedly – based on every encounter she'd had with Brigitte – she thought that, too, seemed wildly implausible. She remembered the conversation she'd overheard at the fête, when she'd hidden behind the tarpaulin screen. He'd stood up for her against Brigitte and Laure.

She drained her coffee, a few pithy grounds on her tongue. 'We should go.'

249

'Absolutely.' He stood, took car keys from his pocket, and she noticed that he took both their empty cups and set them down in the sink. How strange it was, seeing someone do these little things.

Jérôme was still asleep when they arrived. He'd slept through the night, he was stable, his blood pressure was right down. No troponin in his blood, nothing abnormal on the X-ray. And yet Marguerite felt overcome with dread. She'd felt okay last night and this morning and on the way to the hospital. But now Jérôme was out of immediate danger, she could only wonder how long he'd stay out.

Jérôme wouldn't be discharged for a good few hours, if at all today. She told Henri he must go and that she'd call when they needed the lift back, and this time he didn't demur. He'd left before she realised she hadn't thanked him.

Brigitte didn't like it; she just didn't. How convenient, that the nurse should need Henri to stay over. Of course, she couldn't simply have called again this morning, when she needed another lift; or, better yet, used her own car – which had, indeed, taken some time for Brigitte to find; or even, if it was really as urgent as she seemed to have made it out to be, have called an ambulance in the first place.

No, she didn't like it. She took an emptied shelf out of the fridge, dipped a cloth in her bowl of vinegar and water. She wiped it over the shelf, working out the scum with the warm liquid. She shouldn't have sent Henri over with the car in the first place, she should have taken it over there herself, only Henri had been so keen to see the Lanvier boys.

And she knew the girl's type. The empty bottles and glasses, the casual clothes – jeans and scruffy trainers, in a medical career, when hygiene was surely supposed to be the number one priority – and then, of course, the standoffish manner. At first she'd thought the girl was just a bit dim, like the last one, and that was why she kept so quiet. But since then she'd grown to suspect there was more going on in that head than she'd first expected. She rinsed the shelf, left it on a dish towel to dry, took the next one out of the fridge.

Hanging around with Suki, too, Laure had said. A most interesting pair. And frankly, she wouldn't have been surprised if Suki had set the girl up to go for Henri – out of spite, because – Brigitte was almost 100 per cent sure – Suki had never been able to get her own hands on him. Not for want of trying, certainly.

There were those nights he just took off after dinner, but that was different. Men were different from women like that. She'd never asked Laure outright about it, but she was pretty sure César must head off out on his own too. Sure, she might not like it, but she knew Henri of all people needed his time alone, whatever that involved. Without it, he got antsy. And she also knew there must have been times when he'd gone off and, well, 'got off'. Men had their needs. Not that she didn't have her own, admittedly – but it was different with men. Biologically.

If he'd gone off and got off in the past, she might hate the thought of it, it might make her feel sick, but it was simply best she didn't think too much about it. The odd one-off, surely, was all it would ever have been. Scratching an itch, she thought. Only, let it never have been with a specific someone. Dear, gentle God: never let there be an actual something with a real, specific someone. She didn't know what she would do.

Marguerite spent most of the day at the hospital, waiting for them to discharge him. As the afternoon stretched on, she began to dread that they might keep him in another night. If they did, she wouldn't leave – she couldn't go back to the house on her own, they couldn't make her. She'd insist on sleeping in the chair in his room.

He was sleepy and placid. She thought he was rather enjoying the fuss made of him, until she crept out of the room to get a sandwich for her lunch and he opened his eyes, fixed them on her.

'Don't let's stay any longer.'

She went to his bedside. 'You want to leave?'

'Oh, for God's sake. Of course I want to leave.'

She smiled. Right now she liked his crossness. He was lucid again, his confusion and placidity dissolved.

'I'm trying. They want to have had you here for twenty-four hours.'

'For God's sake.'

'I know.'

'You're the one who knows best. Why don't you just over-rule them?'

'I'm doing what I can.'

'Well, try harder. I'm sure you can be assertive if you just put your mind to it a bit.'

But it wasn't until the evening that they were able to go. She couldn't call the Brochons, she thought, couldn't ask them again to help. She asked the staff to call a taxi and they helped Jérôme into the car when it came, but she dreaded having to take him into the house when she got there. She wasn't entirely sure she'd be able to do it, if he dragged and staggered now as much as he had yesterday.

She did manage. Slowly and painfully, so painfully that once she'd got him onto the bed she could feel the twang of a headache reverberating from her lower back right up to the base of her skull.

'Just us again now,' he said, leaning into her as she pulled on a pyjama shirt, buttoned it up one by one.

'Much better, isn't it.'

'I hated that place.'

She took a breath, swivelled him around to lie back on the bed. She pulled his trousers down, shuffling them over his hips. He seemed to have lost a lot of weight just in the last few days, since his sons had left. His pelvis emerged enormous, like a riding saddle.

'You hated it that much?'

'I loathed it.'

'Well, now we're home. And if you don't want to go back there,' she said, pulling his pyjama bottoms up to his knees and over, 'you need to eat more and concentrate on getting yourself calmer and better.'

'For God's sake. You sound like my mother.'

'Well. Would you have done what she said?'

'Depends. Depends on how sensible I thought she was being.'

'And you know I'm being sensible.'

'Yes, all right. All right.' She shifted the seat of his trousers under his bottom. 'But don't you start gloating.'

'So you'll eat something now?' she asked.

'Anything to shut you up.' She smiled and left the room, but she felt tense as she prepared a small bowl of stock for him, with pasta. She tried not to think about how bony he was, how fragile this all was, how dark it would be in another hour.

14

To celebrate Jérôme being better, she drove into the village. She couldn't remember when she'd last driven a car; it felt strange and lovely to whizz down the long road to the village.

She bought an array of little treats to tempt him: raspberries, nectarines and plums, tiny iced éclairs, a miniature tarte au citron. The kind of things she would have bought Cassandre when she was little.

She drove past Suki's house when she left the village, its curtains drawn. She should drop by when Jérôme was fully recovered, she thought; she felt as if she ought to, after his sons had been so foul. As she changed gear, turning off out of the village, she remembered Henri's hand on the wheel when he'd brought the car to her. He had no reason to come back to the house now, of course.

'What is all this?' he asked when she brought in a tray with yoghurt, stewed fruit and pastries. 'You're trying to fatten me up.'

'Exactly.'

'Well, let's have a go then.'

They both watched in silence as she took his blood pressure; he sighed with relief as the cuff sighed and released.

'Much better,' he said.

'Indeed. Let's keep it like that.'

'I don't want to go back to that place,' he said. 'That's the whole point of having you here. You're not cheap. But what's the point in working your whole life, accruing a pretty considerable amount of money, and then getting thrown into a care home to waste away your final days? Much as my dear sons would love that.'

She thought about the old people's home she'd worked at before this. The stale, lunchbox smell of the corridors. Sloppy grey food and jaunty music playing continually, a sequence of twelve songs playing on an eternal loop in the day room. Worst of all, for Jérôme, would have been what they called 'Happy Hour' on Tuesday and Saturday mornings. All the residents were gathered after breakfast into semi-circles in front of that day's Happy Act: am-dram farce performers with sad eyes, community volunteers playing the recorder. He would have got himself kicked out.

'No, I refuse to go anywhere. I'll die right here in my own home, thank you very much.'

'No need for that kind of talk,' she said.

'Die, death, dying,' he said. 'I'm not afraid.' She didn't respond. She'd seen enough from him not to buy that.

The fields were splendid, emblazoned by the sinking sun. And yet he realised he hadn't really seen anything for the past fifteen minutes, walking on autopilot. He was supposed to be checking that the maize looked healthy and good – these fields were the lifeblood of his cows, and so the lifeblood of the whole farm – but he'd have to do another fieldwalk in a couple of days. He hadn't been concentrating.

His mind's eye had been in the grand central staircase at Rossignol. It had always been quite a surprise that the top floor of the house wasn't bigger. You'd imagine eight or nine rooms up there, perhaps a hidden corridor leading to a spindly staircase and capacious loft. It was a bit of a disappointment.

Downstairs, though, those rooms the family had never used too much: the formal salon leading off from the hallway, the virtually forbidden little maze of other rooms, including the rarely seen study in which Jérôme had spent much of his time. Those rooms were dusky and imposing, entirely undisappointing. He'd loved them as a boy. They had felt gravid with intrigue and secrecy.

How different from the light and noise of the family room, which had now been converted into a one-man ward for Jérôme. And the kitchen, that boisterous refuge presided over by un-boisterous Céline. He supposed that was the kind of house in which he'd always imagined, indistinctly, bringing up a family of his own.

Not, he supposed, that it was absolutely a physical impossibility that they could still have a child. They didn't talk about that kind of thing, but he knew Brigitte still got her period: he knew the muddy, cereal smell of it. So it wasn't absolutely unfeasible that they'd be able to conceive. But then, they never had. And he didn't, really, suppose that they could. He couldn't remember how long since they'd had sex, though he imagined it might be well over a year. She'd stopped bothering him with the children question a good few years ago: she'd just suddenly stopped asking. As had everyone else, thank God. Though there was Jean-Christophe last week, he thought, and then again he was back in that kitchen, remembering what it was like to be folded up into their noise.

He'd go there now, he thought. He should check that all was all right there after Jérôme's scare. If he'd been asked to judge, he would have guessed they'd been driving Jérôme to the hospital to die.

Brigitte wasn't happy when he told her he was off.

'I won't be long.'

'But Henri! Why are you going there? It's nothing to do with you.'

'Brigitte, I thought Jérôme was going to have a heart attack. I had to race to the hospital with what looked like a dying man in the back of the truck.'

'But it's not appropriate for you to go.'

'Surley it's inappropriate for me *not* to go.'

'Why?'

'Just – calm down, Brigitte. I'm going to check how they're doing. That was an emergency, there, just two days ago. I was part of it.'

'But—' And then she stopped, mouth set. 'Well, I hope you'll not be long.'

She wasn't surprised when she heard wheels in the drive, and then saw him coming around the corner. He was wearing a deep blue shirt, thick and soft-looking, a fabric she couldn't place. She was aware of her shabby grey cardigan, the holes at the cuffs where she tugged them.

'How is everything?'

'It's okay. Thank you for coming to check.'

'Not at all.'

Jérôme looked something like happy when she told him Henri was here. 'Send him in, send him in, of course! Wonderful.'

She walked behind Henri, watched him duck as he entered the room. He made Jérôme look even smaller.

'Can I get you something, Henri?' she asked when he'd taken a seat. 'A glass of water?'

'Get the man a beer!' said Jérôme, eyes alive. 'Do we have any? Or what drink do you take? I'd join you, but God knows what this one would say if I tried.'

He cocked his head at Marguerite and they all laughed, dutifully.

'We have beer left over . . .' She trailed off. She didn't want to remind Jérôme of his sons' stay. 'Or a glass of red wine.'

'Look at this! It's the Hôtel George V!'

'I'd love a beer,' he said, turning to Marguerite. 'Thank you.'

'It's for us to thank you, actually, Henri,' Jérôme said then, and his tone shifted a little. He raised his chin, stared down the length of the bed. 'From what I hear, you did us a good service the other day. I was a bit out of it, you understand. No, I'm not young any more, you can see that.' He turned back to Henri; his voice pinged back to a tone of levity. 'But it's

259

nothing to worry about, nothing to worry about. Look at me now, I'm fit as a fiddle. Go and get the man a beer.'

She brought beer and then she left them, but it wasn't long before Jérôme knocked and she went back through to his room. She saw that he was exhausted but pretending not to be; he was pale and grey, his lips thin.

'Now, Henri, do you have to go straight back to the old battleaxe?' He looked from Henri to Marguerite, back again.

'I can stay a bit longer if you'd like.'

'No, not with me,' he said, 'not in here. I'm afraid an old codger like me needs his sleep. But why don't you stay for supper with Marguerite? God knows the girl could do with a bit of company for once. What do you say?'

Henri looked at Marguerite; she saw that he couldn't say no in front of Jérôme.

'No need for that,' she said.

'I don't want to impose,' he said.

'Nonsense!' said Jérôme. 'Stay, stay. She's a magnificent cook. Or stay at least for a drink. Go on.' He looked from one to the other again. 'Hell, why don't you have a drink yourself, Marguerite? Just one, mind you. I don't want you wiping out on me.'

When they left the room, they danced around Jérôme's words.

'You really don't have to stay.'

'I'm free, it's up to you.'

'I think Jérôme just likes the idea of company in the house.' Though that wasn't true, she thought.

'I'm happy to leave you be, you must be exhausted.'

'You must want to get back.'

Then he stopped dancing; she saw him make a decision, saw it in the set of his face.

'It'd be nice to stay for another drink.'

So she opened a bottle of wine. She poured two glasses and they sat together at the table, in the warmth of the kitchen.

'I'm glad he's doing better.'

'Me too.'

'What was—' He stopped himself. 'No, don't worry.'

'It's okay,' she said. 'You were there, so it's hardly confidential. As far as we can tell, it was the pain alone that was causing the hypertension. I was worried it was hypertensive emergency – your blood pressure can get so high it starts affecting the vital organs. Heart, lungs, brain. But it doesn't seem to have got that far.'

'Will it happen again?'

'I hope not. I'm going to request a pump and IV line to have here, for when the pain next gets that bad. We can get some morphine on prescription.'

He nodded. 'It's a very interesting job.'

'Oh,' she said. She tilted her glass, straightened it. 'Mostly it's not. It's very unglamorous, very repetitive. Banal to most people. But I couldn't do anything else.'

'Just not in a hospital.'

She laughed. 'No. Not in a hospital.'

'Running a farm is like that. Extremely unglamorous. Banal and repetitive, not just to most people, but to me too. But there's no way I could do anything else.'

She'd never met a farmer before. She'd never really thought of it as a profession you might choose, more a category of person: a Canadian, a toddler, a farmer. It belonged in her personal experience to farmyard toy sets and nursery rhymes – or the low, sturdy buildings on rural plains seen from the window of a moving car, driving from one city or destination to another.

'What kind of farm is it?' she asked, and wondered whether that was a stupid question.

'Dairy, predominantly. But we've expanded it to have sheep too, and Brigitte keeps a few pigs and chickens, though they're not for commercial use.' He looked a little embarrassed, she thought. 'See? Banal.'

'Not at all.' She smiled. 'So – you kill your pigs?'

'I'm afraid so.'

'Okay.'

'Are you a vegetarian?'

'No. Though my mother is.'

'Is she a nurse too?'

'God no.' He looked surprised by her vehemence. 'No, she thinks it's a terrible career.'

'Really?'

'Yes. She was miserable when I became a nurse.'

'Why?'

'I don't know.'

She'd said enough; she was surprised to have referred to her mother at all. The word was a novelty on her tongue.

He stayed for another glass after he'd finished his first, and she heated leftovers for them to eat. It became dark all of a sudden, as it did here among all these trees, and the air coming in from the garden was warm, swaying with cicadas and frogs, the hum of the oven adding another layer to their song.

She asked him about growing up in Saint-Sulpice, and he

told her about the school he'd gone to, along with everyone else he knew. He'd played tennis and football, particularly enjoyed history, maths and literature. She knew from the way he spoke of school that he'd been a good student, that he'd been a success. She pictured a charmed existence. Tanned, healthy young boys and girls doing wholesome things. Unlike her own school in Paris, how sophisticated they'd all tried to be: girls trying to be anorexic, boys trying to be druggy.

And, not drunk but with the edges of the night softened just a little by the wine, she surprised herself by talking a little about her own childhood. As they ate, she talked about school, mentioned her English au pair, the immaculate apartment. She made him laugh when she told him the whole codex of rules that had governed their home: no second-hand or library books (they were dirty), all newly purchased clothes to be washed before they were worn, no apples (the smell too pervasive).

'Have you inherited any of these rules yourself?' he asked.

'No,' she said. 'You can eat apples wherever you like. No, I don't think I've inherited any of them. I mean, look, I have holes in my clothes.' She pushed the sleeves of her cardigan up to her elbows. 'My mother would not approve of that.'

'Well, I'm sure she'd approve of this pie,' he said. 'It's delicious.'

'She wouldn't have eaten it.'

'Ah yes – meat.'

'Actually, I was always a great disappointment to her.'

He frowned. 'I can't believe that.'

'I was.'

'On what account?'

'Everything.' She smiled, to show it was all right. 'I was a

263

difficult pregnancy – she was very ill the whole way through, in and out of hospital. I think the disappointment started then. She told me it was like I was a parasite, trying to kill her.'

'But that's irrational.'

'She got pregnant again four years later with my sister, who was apparently much kinder on my mother's body. Even the birth was easy; my parents claim she came out smiling.'

'And how is she now?'

Marguerite stopped, caught short. 'She's wonderful.'

'So she survived your mother's strictness?'

Survived.

'Yes. She's very intelligent, very successful. The opposite of a disappointment. Particularly to me.'

'You must miss her.'

'Yes,' she said. 'Very, very much.'

She reached out, added salt to her food. How had she mentioned Cassandre, how had she talked about her mother? What else would come out if she kept talking?

When the phone rang, she knew it would be Brigitte; of course it would. She didn't wait for Brigitte to say much more than her name; she called Henri into the hall and he spoke to his wife and she left him, went back to her food. When he returned, she saw the irritation on his face again. There was a deep wrinkle between his eyebrows, like someone had drawn a line there with a pen.

'Thank you so much for letting me intrude.'

'You haven't intruded,' she said. 'Really. Jérôme would have been furious if you hadn't stayed.'

He smiled. 'I can visit him again,' he said. 'If you think it's good for him. I mean, to have visitors.'

'He'd definitely like that.'

He nodded and she thought he looked shy. She felt shy then, too. Now the food and wine had been consumed, they were just two strangers.

She lay in the bath for a very long time, filling it now and again with more hot water. The mirror was steamed over, the flesh of her body flushed pink. Her fingertips and toes became wrinkled, like walnuts. As she stared down over her body, she waited for the first stirrings of shame to start within her, as they always did when she spoke about things that felt private to her, but they didn't come. And yet how openly she had spoken to Henri about her mother, with what ease she'd mentioned Cassandre.

She hadn't, of course, told him the full extent of her mother's disappointment in her, in who she had become. She had made her decision when she was seventeen, that great epiphany as she walked into Cass's care home, still high on the remnants of the drug she'd taken the night before: she would become a nurse. But not just any nurse; she'd become Cassandre's nurse. For Cassandre, she would sacrifice the careers she'd considered pursuing; that was the least she could do. She'd finish school and go straight into nursing college. She'd work, for once she'd really apply herself and work hard, get qualified in the shortest possible amount of time, specialise in acquired brain injury and disability patients. And then she could take Cassandre out of the care home within a few years – take her to an apartment of their own, hire a rota of orderlies to help her with positioning. Apart from the orderlies it would be just her and Cass, living together, forever. She would be her sister's servant. She'd dedicate the rest of her life to giving Cassandre the best possible care a girl in her position could get.

Never again would a stranger undress and handle her sister's body, turn her roughly, leave her in soiled nappies for hours. Never again would Marguerite have to worry about the long hours of the night in the care home, when the orderlies and nurse on duty slept instead of heeding Cass's cries. All of that would end.

'I know what to do. I've got the answer. You don't need to worry any more.'

She remembered Cassandre's expression when she'd said that. She hadn't known what Marguerite had been talking about, but she'd known that finally her big sister was doing what she should have done all along. What she should have done the night she'd come into her bed with a fever, her feet like ice. She was taking care of her.

Her mother had laughed when she first voiced the idea. 'Don't be ridiculous. You're not going to become a nurse.'

'Why not?'

'For many reasons, Margo.'

'What reasons?'

'This is ridiculous, I'm not going into them.'

'Why not?'

She would have sighed, creased her lips. Then given the reasons: that it was a waste of a good education. That no one they knew became a nurse, it wasn't for people like them. And then, when she'd realised that Marguerite was actually serious, she'd told her she'd make a terrible nurse, that it would actually involve difficulty and hard graft and dealing with 'real' people, that Marguerite didn't have that in her. And finally she'd said, pushed by exasperation, that the only reason Marguerite wanted to do it was out of guilt.

'And guilt will only take you so far. Then you'll realise it's a career for a stronger kind of person than you, Margo, and you'll quit.'

She was too warm when she got into bed, the blood in her face and feet still pumping, hot, from the bath. As she lay on her side, waiting for sleep to take over, she imagined Henri lying on his side behind her, one arm around her waist, his breath cool on her neck.

He knew what was happening when he turned his keys in the ignition, Jojo on the seat beside him. He'd known what was happening when he'd got into the bath after work, filling it with water and draining it and filling it again until the water was cold but clean. He'd dressed in the green shirt he knew looked particularly good with his eyes, and he'd known why he'd chosen that one. But still, as he drove down the winding track, Jojo excited, her head out of the window to taste the warm summer evening, he didn't let himself look properly at what he knew. He let it sit there, untested, unexamined, and he was surprised by how easy that was.

He spoke to Jérôme about the farm, and then he let the old man talk, watched his posture change as he spoke about his former career, at length, until the colour in his face and the volume of his voice changed, very suddenly, his exhaustion clear.

He saw that he'd brought Jérôme pleasure, by visiting again.

And it was with pleasure that he walked back through to the kitchen, placed his empty glass on the table, looked through the window in the twilight to see Marguerite throwing something to the dog. She threw well, like a boy.

It was painful not to go back the following evening. The evening stretched out before him, unutterably dull. Brigitte was unusually quiet over dinner, which he found a relief. He didn't care that she was sulking about something; she would get over it. He could hear the squelch of her mastication as they ate and he wanted to get up and take his food outside and eat it there, in silence, but he didn't.

He planned to go the following day, but a few of the ewes became ill and he had to call Cédric to check it wasn't something sinister. He managed to get him to stay for dinner afterwards, and then he suggested a glass of whisky after that but Cédric looked tired, excused himself – he had an early start the next day. Henri poured a glass anyway, stayed up on his own when his friend had gone and Brigitte had thudded her way up to bed.

But the next day he told Paul and Thierry he'd be out; he needed to get a new milk pump. And he did, he drove to the dealer and looked at a replacement but decided not to get it just yet, that the current one was old but would hold out a little longer, and then with a feeling of lightness he got back into the truck and left, driving it in the heat through the forest, to Rossignol.

15

She could barely meet his eye when he arrived. She was cooking, making béchamel for lasagne, and was relieved to be able to turn her back to him, stir the sauce. She felt his presence behind her. She felt as if every hair on her face and neck were alive with it.

'I'm afraid he's just gone to sleep,' she said. She lowered the heat, took a breath and turned. He was standing, one hand resting on the table. She thought that he looked embarrassed.

'I'll go,' he said. 'Perhaps I can come back over the next few days.'

She thought, wildly, for a reason to keep him. 'That oak tree,' she said. 'The one that died. Was there a disease – in the tree? Will it spread?'

She hadn't even thought for one moment about the tree since it had gone.

'No, I don't think so.' He looked serious, frowned. 'But I can take a look.'

'I don't want to trouble you.'

'It's no trouble. While I'm here, I may as well.'

They walked down the garden together, the air thick and delightful around them. She sat on the grass, waiting while he examined the stump of the oak. She dared herself to look at his face while he examined it and then she was too embarrassed, in case she might see that he was only pretending.

He came to sit down next to her, and she looked at him briefly and then away.

'It doesn't look like it was anything pernicious,' he said. 'I hadn't thought so originally, but it's always worth checking.'

She nodded. She couldn't find a single word to reply. He was sitting right beside her, on the grass, the closest they'd ever been to each other. His body, right there beside her.

'I spent some of my happiest days here.' He reached forward and plucked a cornflower from the ground, gently, rotated it between his forefinger and thumb. She imagined him as a teenager: clear-faced, uncertain.

He handed the flower to her. 'It's from the same family as a *marguerite*.'

'I didn't know that.' She thought that her voice sounded scratchy, unclear.

'Yes,' he said quietly. 'I think it's the second biggest family, there are tens of thousands of different species within it.'

She rotated the flower as he had done.

'We have *marguerites* growing throughout the farm,' he said.

She laid it on her knee. Her jeans were thinning at the knees; the cotton was wearing through. She looked at the cornflower, looked down at her trainers, breathed in and out. She couldn't think about anything at all apart from the sense of him, his presence beside her. She closed her eyes and exhaled.

She opened them and turned her face very, very slightly towards him, still not looking at him. She could feel the still air between their faces, between her right and his left cheek. The space was full. She tried to imagine it closing, and the skin of his cheek against hers.

She breathed in and out deeply, took the flower from her knee and stood up. 'I must check in on Jérôme.'

He didn't respond; still sitting there, still staring in front of him, he nodded. When he finally looked up at her she had to turn away.

'I'll see you soon,' she said. 'Goodbye.' She spoke slowly. Each word felt heavy, a stone on her tongue. Then she walked towards the house, left arm wrapped around her waist, right hand holding the flower to her mouth.

Henri got into his truck and pressed his hands over his face. He breathed hard.

He imagined her now in the house, tidying or nursing Jérôme, her still and private gait as she walked about each room. He knew she was thinking of him. Whatever she was doing right now, she was thinking about him. He knew it incontrovertibly.

He imagined walking in, taking her upstairs, not into Marc's old room or Jean-Christophe's, but into Thibault's. Holding her small stomach. Kissing her throat. He tried to imagine taking off her jeans and touching what was there, the foreign nothingness of her groin. He tried to imagine entering her there, at the front, but then he let himself turn her around and find her from behind.

He opened his eyes and breathed out. He shook his head, banishing images more confusing to him than the very first thoughts he'd had about Thibault, as a boy.

He was startled when another car came through the gates, and turned his key in the ignition, shifted the gearstick, eased up the handbrake. He peered into the other car: Suki Lacourse, who looked as surprised by him as he was by her. He raised a hand, turned back to the gateway and drove through, leaving Rossignol behind.

He went straight to Edgar's without letting himself think. Edgar was outside, reading on a bench. He looked up and smiled, the surly smile Henri had never liked. He pretended to finish his passage as Henri approached him; calmly, he placed a bookmark at his place and looked up again.

He wasn't in the mood for kissing or talking or foreplay. He fucked Edgar immediately and wordlessly, pinning him by his hands up against the outside wall of the house. He came within a matter of minutes. He stood there for a moment to catch his breath, then withdrew. He zipped his trousers, fastened the belt. And then he dropped down onto the bench, closed his eyes, leant his head back against the wall. Edgar pulled his trousers back up and sat beside him.

'Well . . .' He laughed. 'Good evening, I guess?' Henri didn't respond. 'Will you have a drink, or is this a purely social visit?'

'I have to go,' he said. 'I can't stay.'

'For fuck's sake, Henri.'

'I'm sorry.' He tried to think of something further to say, some casual word of explanation for his presence.

But Edgar touched his shoulder gently. 'Are you all right?'

Henri pressed the heels of his hands into his eyes, feeling his face break as the tears finally came.

'Hey, hey,' Edgar said softly. 'You're all right, big guy.' He rubbed Henri's shoulder as you might a young boy. Henri let himself cry soundlessly. Finally, he thought, these tears had come – but they brought with them no relief.

He stood, breathed out hard, dropped his hands and raised his eyes to the sky. He willed the tears to stop. He imagined, as so often he did, what his father would think if he could see him now. He looked at Edgar finally, smiled lightly. 'Sorry about this.'

'Don't worry. I'm here if you need to talk, you know. Are you sure you don't want a drink?'

'I really can't,' Henri said. He patted Edgar's shoulder now, tried to be matey. 'I've got to go. I'll see you.'

'Will that be any time soon?'

'Things are extremely busy on the farm.'

Edgar stared at him for a moment, and Henri thought his eyes were wet now too. 'You know what?'

Henri waited, willed him to speak. He wanted Edgar to stop watching him. He thought that Edgar could see something despicable in his face.

'I'm not sure I can play this game any more.' He smiled sadly. 'You're not such a magnificent lay that you can simply turn up and fuck me every time you're too exhausted by your heterosexual scam. And then scuttle back to it until the next time you need some.' Henri said nothing, and Edgar shook his head. 'That came out too harshly. I'm sorry for your unhappiness, and your confusion – I really am. But I'm damned if I'm going to keep sitting around, just – waiting for you to see the light. I can't be just this for you, the mechanism of your self-disgust.'

A ready, well-oiled phrase, Henri thought. Edgar would have thought it up some other time, thinking about Henri and their predicament on his own. It was, of course, bang on. A mechanism was all Edgar had become to him. He nodded, staring at the ground, and Edgar let out a little gasp of incredulity.

'Of course, not even a response. God forbid you'd pay me that final compliment.'

Henri looked at Edgar. Unremarkable-looking, not tall, chin a little weak, shoulders narrow. But he looked handsome now, full of conviction. Henri felt the very opposite, standing there with his head bowed: small and stupid, diminished by cowardice and denial.

'Well, goodbye Henri.' Edgar picked up his book, turned, walked towards the house.

'Goodbye.' Henri made his way back to the truck, replaying Edgar's words in his mind. And then he heard Marguerite's 'goodbye', too, the barely perceptible whistle in the back of her teeth as she spoke: 'I'll see you soon.' He wondered if he could see her again, remote as she was on the other side of the vast chasm that separates the pure from the sullied.

He drove fast back to the farm, letting the truck hurtle through the quiet roads.

'You're a grown man,' he said aloud. 'Come on.' He turned into the driveway to the farm; Jojo was already there, barking excitedly. He stopped the truck, removed the keys from the ignition, inhaled deeply and exhaled. 'Get a fucking grip.'

274

Marguerite sat in the kitchen, slumped forward so that her chin rested on her arms on the table. She twisted the corn-flower between her thumb and forefinger, brushed her palm with its petals. She felt aware of every part of her body. She felt as if she were cocooned by something – as if anyone who saw her right now might see a halo or aura surrounding her. She heard footsteps then: he was back.

But it was Suki standing at the door. She had a cigarette already burning between her fingers, hand hanging down by one hip. She didn't come in.

'Hi,' said Marguerite, sitting upright and smiling. But Suki didn't smile back, and Marguerite realised then that she looked angry, very angry. Her eyes darted to the discarded flower on the table.

'Been picking flowers?'

'Are you all right?'

Suki rolled her eyes, flared her nostrils, took a long drag. Looked out at the garden as she exhaled, looked back at Marguerite.

'You think you're so safe, don't you? Hidden away behind your grief.'

Marguerite felt herself flush. 'What grief?'

Suki flapped a hand vaguely. 'All that pain you hide behind. Whatever you left behind in Paris. Whatever it is that's made you opt out of the world.'

'Why are you being so unkind?' she asked. She stood. 'Why are you angry with me?'

Suki laughed. 'You don't even get it, do you. You can't step out of that little locked-up world of yours. Although, what am I saying, you clearly can for the right kind of people.'

'I don't understand.'

'Do you remember me? Remember who I am?'

'Of course.'

'But you haven't seen fit to come and see me this week, have you? Check I was okay after the Lanvier boys ripped me apart?' She started to cry, angrily, and Marguerite was appalled. She looked like a child, standing there with one hand over her face, her shoulders hunched. 'Didn't feel the need to stick up for me at all that night, did you, and then you haven't even followed up once.'

'I'm sorry. I was going to come by your house, as soon as I had the chance.'

'Oh wow, great, that's okay then. Thank you for making such a huge effort.' She shook her head, wiped away the tears. 'You know what, it's not even your fault, it's just – God, I don't even know why I bother. Just – have fun with Henri, okay? The two of you, just, have a great time together. It makes much more sense anyway.'

'I don't understand what you're talking about.'

'No, of course not. No one ever does.'

'I'm really sorry about Jérôme's sons. I knew you were hurt, I knew I was useless, but I just couldn't—' She paused.

'Couldn't what?'

'I couldn't think of the right words. I never can.'

Suki rolled her eyes. 'Sure.' She dropped her cigarette, stamped it out. 'It's not rocket science, sticking up for someone. But then, what would you know about other people. You don't even know real friendship when it hits you in the face.'

She wiped inky tears from her eyes, took a deep breath

and walked away, around the corner into the drive. Marguerite followed her, called out as she got into her car, but Suki didn't stop. She turned her head to guide the car out in reverse and then she held her hand up in a stiff, perfunctory wave, and was off.

A milky, opalescent sunset. Pink, peach, violet, fabric-conditioner blue – a spectrum of pastels that would be kitsch if put together in any context other than the natural phenomenon of nightfall. Edgar looked away to examine the tomatoes sprouting plumply in front of him. He pinched a few, gently. Then he plucked the four ripest, carried them in his plastic bowl back into the cottage. He heard a few dogs howling somewhere: they sounded like greyhounds. Not Jojo.

Edgar realised he'd been holding his breath. He forgot to breathe deeply most of the time. When he remembered, like now, he'd take a really huge breath in and out, try to expel all the gunk he imagined got stored up inside with all that shallow breathing. He'd done a weekly meditation class for a while, God, six or seven years ago now though it felt like just a few; time here had a way of curdling. He remembered the scrawny teacher with her flaccid grey curls, breasts like long slippers under her tank top, telling them to envisage breathing *in* all the good (through the nose), *out* all the bad (through the mouth. Bad mouth). It never quite worked for him, though. He'd imagine breathing out all the bad and then realise it didn't have time to waft away from his face entirely before he inhaled again – so all the allegedly positive air he breathed in would be contaminated with the dregs of the negative that he'd just concentrated so hard on expunging. So really you should probably exhale, he thought, hold your breath entirely, walk into another space full of clean air, and only then feel free to inhale. But of course, it was all a load of crap.

And now, exhaling deeply as he washed his tomatoes, he could feel that at the end of the breath there was absolutely no sense of relief: still the big, hard rock in the pit of his lungs. Henri: self-loathing, arrogant, beautiful Henri. And he wouldn't let that self-loathing and lovely sadness make him pity the man, either. Look how far that'd got him. He must think about what he'd tell a friend in his position: sweetheart, you're a big, fat fool, that man doesn't give a toss about you, he's got you wrapped around his little finger. Scapegoat for his heterosexually brainwashed shame. His brainwashed *sham*. No, no more pity.

But it wasn't as easy as that, of course. Because the man was suffering. And he had a great deal of loveliness inside that stupid big bulk. In another time or place he would have made one hell of a splendid queer.

Nonetheless, this was a good thing. It was. He'd needed the impetus to put the cottage on the market and get himself back to Paris and here it was now. Time to go, time to move. There'd be no more beautiful plump ripe tomatoes to grow in his own garden like a veritable bucolic wizard, admittedly, but there would be people, company, bustle. How ironic: he'd come here to get away from the terrible noise of the city, but after all these years the silence of the place had become even louder.

There was Suki's car, parking up under the lovely trellises. No more trellises in Paris either, presumably, unless he could find an apartment with a pretty balcony. He'd need a great big grant to make that happen. For a grant, he'd need his book proposal to be somewhere near credible-sounding. For that, he'd need to work out how to find the early modernists interesting again. He watched her get out of the car, slam the door. How would she take the news that he was leaving? They'd only just become friends and now he was heading off, leaving her all alone with the chubby little husband in his nylon suits. She wouldn't be happy at all.

He came out the door and they kissed on each cheek and he took the bottle she was holding, inspected the label.

'Divine,' he said. She sat down heavily on the bench, and that big hard rock ground down inside him again when he thought about Henri bending him over it just a few hours ago – their final fuck, he thought then for the first time, oh Jesus, could that really be it? – and she stared up at him and clicked her fingers.

'What's up with you?'

'What *is* up with me?'

'You were a million miles away.' She fumbled in her bag, took out a cigarette. 'You'll have to forgive me, I've had a horrible day.'

'That makes two of us.'

'What happened to you?'

'Oh, nothing too bad.' Sadness soared, a physical thing, from his gut up to his throat. 'Writer's block. The usual.'

'Too bad,' she said, inhaling. She leant her head back against the wall, her face framed in electric blue. The colour was a bit too strong for her, he thought. A bit hard.

'And you? Actually wait, let's do this with a glass in our

hands.' He went in with the bottle, came back out with two glasses full of the local red he already had open in the kitchen. In truth, he wasn't absolutely 100 per cent sure about the Merlot she'd brought. They could open it later, if need be.

'So what's wrong?'

She rubbed her eyes and he thought then that perhaps she wasn't just being dramatic. She genuinely looked upset. 'It's not that big a thing,' she said. 'I may well be being stupid. I'm just—' She lifted her face, looked him square in the eyes. 'I was feeling a bit better, and now I'm feeling just a whole load worse.'

'About what?'

'My life. For some reason, I've been feeling a bit happier recently. I've been seeing you a little bit, I've had some nice me-time with Philippe away, I thought I had a couple of new friends – not just you but that girl I was telling you about, Marguerite.'

'Okay.' He would have to delay telling her that he'd be moving.

'But, I don't know, Philippe's back, which is obviously great, obviously I missed him terribly, but I just – I don't know, he's come back in a bit of a mood, the work trip wasn't great, you know how it is. And then there's this girl. Marguerite.'

'The nurse.'

'That's it.'

He would entertain her. While she was here, and he was making her feel better and making her laugh, he might just forget about his own sadness for a few hours. He screwed his eyes closed.

'Wait wait wait, let me remember: young waif, fled from

city, nursing ogreish man. Said ogreish man troll-like in the extreme. Sitting, one might surmise, on piles of shimmering treasure. Young waif stuck against will in house of great former grandeur, haunted by ghosts of handsome sons.'

'Ha, yes. That's the one. Only, you might need to revise your description of the sons.'

'Intriguing. New intel?'

'Well, they were *here*. Only a few days after you and I were talking about them. Very strange. Anyway, I met them again, and they're not handsome any more. Well, one is, sort of, but in a crafty sort of weasel way. You'd probably like him.'

'Oh. Because of my great penchant for weasel-faced men?'

'He's just – yeah, you'd definitely fancy him.'

'And you're only just telling me he's here *now*?'

'They've left. But anyway, my point is that they're total assholes. Racist, arrogant assholes.'

'Ah. Less attractive.'

She smiled, drank some wine. 'So anyway, they were rude to me, rude to Marguerite. And obviously I stood up for her. And it's not the end of the world, but she didn't stick up for me when they were ripping me apart. And that's fine, I know it's not her being unkind—'

'Sounds unkind to me.'

'Honestly, I don't think it is. I felt irritated but – okay, maybe they weren't exactly ripping me apart. They were just – I don't know, they made me feel literally this small.' She held her thumb and forefinger up, a tiny gap between them. 'And she could have stepped in a bit more. But that's just her, I think. She retreats into herself and it's almost like the rest of the world doesn't exist.' She took a last long drag of her cigarette and dropped it, grinding it under one foot. 'But the thing is, I honestly have tried so hard with that girl, trying to coax her out of her sad little shell, and I kept making a little headway and we actually, remember I told you, had a really fun, drunken, silly night together, and I just felt like – yes, this is good, this could be a friend. Most importantly, I can be a friend to *her*, because God knows she must need one.' She sipped her wine. 'Anyway. The little sneak, actually. Because today – this is having heard absolutely bugger all from her since the night of the Lanvier asshole sons—'

'We'll call them gargoyles,' he said. 'It fits the narrative better than "assholes", I don't remember there being many assholes in any of the folklore I've studied.'

'Shut up.' She batted his arm. 'Okay, gargoyles.'

'Great. Go on.'

'I *had* kind of been waiting, wondering whether she might surprise me by seeking me out. She doesn't, of course. But then I think, look, she's stuck there nursing the troll, ogre, whatever, I'll go see how she's doing.' She lit another cigarette. 'And this is the thing, all jokes aside now Edgar, this is the thing that really stabbed me in the gut. Henri Brochon' – and at this point his ears sharpened, stomach turned – 'who she *knows*, because I opened up to her and told her all about it, who she *knows* I had this thing with . . .'

What the actual fuck, thought Edgar. Well now. What the actual, actual fuck? 'You had a thing with that farmer guy?' His voice was leaden, he could hear it, but she didn't seem to notice.

'Yes. A while back.'

Breathe it all out, he thought, hold it just out of range.

Wait until you can step back and look at what it is, examine it from each angle.

'Anyway, I get there today and he's there in the driveway, just sitting in his parked car—'

'What time today?'

She frowned. 'Oh, I don't know. Around three. Whatever.'

Around three. And here Henri had been, with a raging boner and tears in his eyes, at, oh, about quarter past. 'Anyway, he looks at me like I've caught him with his pants down when I drive in, shoots off in his car, and then I go into the house and there Marguerite is, head virtually dunked into a bunch of wild flowers like a Disney princess, all glowing, and I'm just like, no, actually, I've had enough of this. This is too far. I worked, and worked, and worked to bring friendship to that little girl and then she passes that friendship straight over, at the first opportunity, for a man she *knows* rejected me—'

So he did reject her, he thought. But before or after they'd had sex?

'Anyway, okay, I know it all sounds ridiculous and petty. Like I'm at school. But it's just, not *again*, you know? There I was thinking she couldn't open up to a single human, but no, it was just me. It's just the same bloody story everywhere: rejection. Occlusion. *Ex*clusion. Gossip and bitching and hatred in one direction, total blank indifference in the other.'

There was silence as they both drank.

She laughed, a little fake laugh. 'I thought I'd made a friend.'

'So – hang on a moment. Back up just a little.' He could feel his heart beating, firm, hard, against his thorax. 'What exactly happened between you and this guy?'

Stay calm, stay normal. Get the full picture. Get the full picture while you can before you nail the fucker to the cross.

Loveless, sexless marriage with Brigitte – it didn't have quite the same tragic ring to it when he factored in affairs with young women. Had he alternated between them and Edgar? And what about all that bullshit, his self-loathing because he just couldn't make himself want women as he'd been told he should? Had he just been playing Edgar for a little alternative fun this whole – fucking – time?

'A lady never tells,' she said, but raised an eyebrow.

'It's funny,' he said then, and he let the words come out, and he heard them coming out and he didn't care. 'Awfully strange.'

She looked at him, sharply. 'What?'

'Because, darling, you're not the only one who's had a little fling with our handsome farmer.'

'Who else?' she asked. 'Tell me.'

He bit his lip. He felt rage, clean and deafening and very, very calm, rise up in his chest from where the rock had been.

'Tell me!'

'Yours truly, darling.'

They looked at each other for a moment; Suki blinked, twice.

'Wait, what?'

'We've had an affair. Henri and I. For years.'

She held her hand up over her mouth for a moment, eyes wide. Then she closed her eyes and opened them and they crinkled with a smile. 'I do not believe it.'

'Well you should.'

'This – makes – so much – sense.'

His anger was starting to ebb a little now. He'd done it. And he wouldn't feel bad for this, he would never. He'd simply got the sneaky bugger back.

'Oh my God.'

'I know,' he said.

'So I'm wrong about the nurse,' she said.

'What do you mean?'

'Well, I didn't actually see anything, did I? Of course he didn't go for her. He's a poofter! Sorry. He's gay. And now it all makes sense. Why, despite how well we got on, he just never actually *went* for me.'

'What?' A new sensation started to prickle up inside him then.

'Well, nothing *actually happened* between us. I thought he was maybe asexual or something. But God, I'm so naïve. How did it never occur to me? And now – yes, that explains the wife! Oh my God! Henri Brochon is *gay*!'

Her face was alive with the gossip, all her sadness fallen away. And Edgar thought, oh no. No, no, no, no, no. What have you done, Edgar? You had a secret. You had his inviolable secret and you've let it go because this woman lied. No, because you let your ego get in the way. Oh, you've really screwed it. You've really, truly screwed it.

'You can't tell anyone, Suki,' he said.

'Of course not,' she said, smiling, but her eyes didn't focus on him.

'Suki?' He took her face between his hands, turned it to face him fully. 'Suki?'

'Yes, yes, I promise.' She pulled her head free. 'Obviously I won't tell anyone.'

But her voice was vague; her mind was already elsewhere.

'Suki, I can't tell you how important this is. I told you that in the strictest confidence.' He stood up. 'Listen, if you tell anyone that, I will be seriously, seriously upset.'

'Relax!' She smiled, drained her glass. 'Relax, I won't tell anyone. Get me another glass, darling?' She tilted it towards him. 'Oh I feel *much* better now. Oh, this is seriously juicy. You've made my day, Edgar.'

As she helped him into the bath she sensed for the first time that he was afraid of falling. She thought the hard porcelain must be painful on the bones of his bottom.

'There we go,' she said as he relaxed back into position, closed his eyes.

'Very nice,' he said.

'I'll go and prep your dinner. Knock if you need me.'

'Yes, yes.'

But the dinner was already done. She went instead and sat at the bottom of the stairs in the hallway. She needed to think about Suki. All afternoon, she'd played her words back over in her mind. And she felt ashamed, because she knew much of what she'd said was right. Marguerite hadn't risen to the occasion. But then, she never did.

And Suki might complain that she'd rejected her friendship – that she wouldn't know friendship if it hit her in the face, which she thought a bizarre way of describing it – but she had never asked for a friend. She'd never wanted one.

Was that entirely true though? What was she doing now, with Henri? Wasn't that friendship? No, of course it wasn't.

But with him, she didn't have a choice. She couldn't stop this, whatever it was; it wouldn't be within her power. And now the tension and upset she'd been feeling all afternoon thinking about Suki – how she'd hurt her feelings so much that she'd made her cry – dissolved with dazzling ease. She closed her eyes, heard his voice as he sat there beside her: 'We have *marguerites* growing throughout the farm . . .'

There was that too, though. Suki eyeing the cornflower. What had she known? Why had she referred to Henri? 'Have fun with Henri, okay?' How could Suki have seen something when there had been nothing to see. Maybe it really did surround her, a physical thing, a halo. She closed her eyes again and breathed in, imagined his arms around her.

She would have to do something about Suki. Apologise, though that required a language she barely knew how to speak. She may never have asked for Suki's friendship, but she'd benefited from it. She'd sought her out once, visiting her when Jérôme's sons were here. This was always the problem, though. No one should make demands of her, because she couldn't meet them. She'd known that all along, ever since she met Suki: she'd never be able to meet her demands. Suki needed to realise that Marguerite was only half a person.

16

He didn't come the next day.

She'd started the day feeling light, and the anticipation of seeing him later gave everything an odd, different feel to it – as if she were about to go on holiday, or it was her birthday in the days when that was still a nice thing.

Jérôme was nauseous and irritable.

'Everything,' he said when she quibbled with him over which painkillers he could take, 'everything in my entire body feels like it's biting me. Can you even imagine that? Try to get your little head around that. My shin hurts, my ears hurt. Even my *gums* hurt. Everything.'

He made a fuss over the soup she brought him for lunch – 'Oh goodness, what a wonderful *rarity* to have soup' – and over her attempts to soothe his pain with massage – 'Yes, perfect, you tickling me with your twiggy little fingers is the obvious solution to the *crippling* pain *all over my body*.' When she made to fluff up his pillows he smacked her arm, turned his face away. 'Just get out,' he hissed.

None of this touched her. Yet as the day drew on, her

feeling of lightness morphed into a duller, flatter mood, and she started to think that perhaps there was a chance he might not come after all. She hadn't questioned it before that.

He didn't come the next day, or the day after, and they were long days. She went for two runs, hoping that would help her pass the time. She thought that if he came when she was out that might in fact be a good thing, and started to question why she wanted him to come anyway. If he came, if they spent time together, their friendship could only go in one direction and it wasn't a good direction. In that direction her job was in jeopardy, and his marriage, and her security, the safe quiet dull equilibrium she'd fought for years to achieve. She wouldn't be safe any more. She concentrated on Jérôme instead, pushed the stupid thoughts about the halo around her out of her mind.

But at night, as she lay in the darkness trying to sleep, she thought about the space between them as they'd sat in the garden side by side, and closing her eyes she could almost conjure up again the heavy, palpable presence of his body, and all their unspoken words beside her.

On the fourth day, she emptied every single cupboard in the kitchen. She put all the cans of beans and tomatoes and tuna in the sink, soaking them in warm water because something sticky had spilt among them. She left them while she cleaned the insides of the cupboards and then when she came back to the cans she realised all their labels had blanched and softened and unfurled in the water, so that you couldn't tell which was which, and she drained the sink, overcome with almost tearful rage, and left the kitchen in a state of chaos, its cupboards and drawers open, and the table covered in their contents like the whole room was in the midst of being looted.

She went into Jérôme's room; he was listening to the radio.

'How about going outside? It's beautiful out there.'

He looked at her, seemed to study her face for a few moments. Then he turned back to stare down the bed.

'No.'

She went upstairs and lay on her bed face down, and felt like weeping.

It was the following day, five days since she'd last seen him, when finally she heard the truck in the drive. Her stomach was gripped, tight, with apprehension; she didn't know how she could face him, and for a moment she almost hoped it was Suki instead. She turned her back to the door, bowing her head over the onions softening on the hob. And then she heard his footsteps on the paving outside, heard them slow as he stepped into the doorway. She put the lid back on, turned the gas down, faced him.

He didn't look well, she thought.

'Good evening,' she said brightly, and she tried to smile but her face felt fixed.

'Evening,' he said. 'How are you?'

'Fine, and you?'

He didn't answer. He rubbed the side of his head, and she thought that he looked exhausted, the area around his eyes

290

dark. He was as immaculate as ever, but it was as if something had come loose.

'Can I get you a drink? Would you like to see Jérôme?'

'No, thank you.'

He said nothing more, but shifted on his feet. She felt every single part of her attuned to his movement – as if the air were made of a heavier substance than usual, each flicker from him stirring it as if with a spoon.

'Can I come in?' he asked.

'Of course.'

He bent down to unfasten his laces, carefully, and then he stepped out of his boots and left them by the door and pulled a chair out from the table with a scraping sound that made them both wince. He sat and rested his chin in one hand, elbow on the table, and she saw a long cut running down the underside of his forearm. She imagined him pushing his way through long, tangled undergrowth. He looked at her, looked down at the table, looked back at her and then away again. Still, he said nothing.

She stared at the floor, saw that there was a smudge of torn parsley on one of the tiles. She bent down to pick it up. He cleared his throat, and then he stood up and walked towards her a few steps. She made herself look at him. Her mouth felt dry, she could taste metal, her heart felt as if it were hammering at the base of her throat. He coughed again, and when he spoke his voice was low and strange, sounded as if it came from far away.

'I can't stop thinking about you.'

She closed her eyes, opened them slowly and nodded. 'Me neither,' she said eventually.

Then he took another step towards her and reached a hand out into the space between them, and she reached hers out to touch it. They stood with their palms resting against each other's and she felt that it would be a physical impossibility to look into his face now, no matter what depended on it. He cleared his throat again and took a final step to close the space between them, and his other hand reached towards her face, and she let her head roll into his palm. She closed her eyes.

The kitchen was empty. He switched on the lights; nothing, no laid table, no smell of food.

'Brigitte?' Jojo panted by his side. 'Where is she?' he asked the dog. She seemed to shake her head. He went to the bottom of the stairs, called up. 'Brigitte?' But there was nothing. He went back outside and called again. Something rustled by his foot; a gecko scuttled by, fat as a cigar.

He went back into the kitchen and took a beer from the fridge. Fragments came back to him of the last few hours, and he leant back in a chair as he knew Brigitte hated him to do. He saw Marguerite's small, tidy ribcage, imagined holding her thorax in both hands. The intercostal muscles had flickered, rippled over her ribs as she'd stretched out, arching her back. He had been moved by her breasts, which were very small. When he'd run a finger underneath them her skin had risen up in tiny goose-bumps. He'd moved his hands down her stomach, over the dip of her belly button, the softer flesh of her stomach curving out directly beneath it. Had he done the right things, when he'd touched her? How could he know? He couldn't.

He heard the clink of a glass then, and stood up. He went into the corridor, waited, then walked down it and into his study. There was Brigitte: she was sitting at his desk, *his* desk, and he was hit by many things all at once: the papers she'd emptied from his drawers and stacked in piles on the table; the red puffiness of her cheeks and eyes; the glass of whisky she held, an alien thing, in one hand.

'What the hell?'

She looked up at him for a moment, then back down at the table. Her nose was swollen as if she had a cold. If he had been vacillating between anger and concern, the anger was extinguished entirely by her expression. That expression wasn't her; it was as if she'd disappeared from inside her own face.

'Brigitte, what on earth is wrong?' He went over to her, knelt beside her. She closed her eyes. 'Brigitte?' he asked again, more quietly, and he touched her shoulder with his hand.

She shrugged it off with a flinch. 'Don't touch me.'

She couldn't know – it had only just happened. Only just now, so recently his fingertips still remembered her skin.

'Brigitte, what's happening? Talk to me. You're not well.'

'*I'm* not well?'

He took the small wooden chair from the corner of the room and pulled it up to the desk, sat down next to her.

'Have you had some bad news? Tell me what's happened.'

She looked at him and then away quickly, with something like a shudder. Oh God, he thought. She cannot even bear to look at me.

'Where have you been today?' she asked, and he cleared his throat.

'At Rossignol. There are a few things around there that need fixing.'

She shrugged. 'At Rossignol, all this time?'

'Yes. Now can you tell me what's wrong, Brigitte? You're scaring me.'

Staring at her face, he noticed things he hadn't seen before: a cluster of small, raised black moles on her jaw, near where it met her right ear. An asterisk of tight wrinkles at each corner of her lips. Her eyelashes had thinned, he thought; her eyes looked very bare. When had her face accumulated and shed these things?

She lifted the whisky to her mouth and closed her eyes tight as she swallowed some. She pursed her lips through the spirit's aftershock. She wasn't used to drinking wine, let alone whisky; she hated it.

'Brigitte?'

'I heard the strangest thing today.'

Her voice was flat, as if she were about to fall asleep. She placed the glass back down on the desk with care. Something moved inside him: something fearful, starting to uncoil.

'Did you hear me?'

'Brigitte, stop this. You're drunk.'

'I'm not drunk,' she said. 'I just needed something to help me think. I couldn't think for most of the day you see, Henri.'

'I'm going to go and get something to eat,' he said, getting up and walking from the room. 'Since you seem to have forgotten about dinner.'

But she followed him into the kitchen, sat at the table behind him as he opened the fridge.

'I had a visit this morning, Henri.' There was a shrill edge

294

to her voice now. Still flat, but with a ring of something like panic. 'From your little friend.'

'What?'

'Suki Lacourse.'

'For God's sake, Brigitte,' he said. He took cheese and some tomatoes out, closed the fridge, took the food to one of the worktops. 'How many times do I have to tell you, nothing's ever happened with that woman.'

He kept his back to her, unfolding a parcel of waxed gingham paper, removing the blue cheese wrapped up inside. But he didn't want to eat. Was this it? A banal phrase banged its way into his head: 'You reap what you sow.' Was that his mother's voice he'd imagined saying it? He saw a cartoon image of barley bales.

'She told me something – something vile.'

He felt sick; he stopped slicing, let the knife fall onto the wood. Still, he didn't turn. Not until he heard a low, strangled sound, rising into a whimper like a cough. She had one hand clamped over her eyes.

'Brigitte.' He went down to sit across from her, though he didn't think he could bear to look into her eyes when she moved her hand. When she kept it there, he realised she couldn't look at him either.

'She told me – I can't say it, Henri. I can't say it.' She took a deep breath. 'I told her, of course, I told her it was nothing but wicked, nasty, filthy – *slander*, is what I said it was. Of course I did.' Still she didn't move her hand away from her face, and he dropped his own forehead into his hands. 'But then she pointed – all these – these vile *things* out, Henri, and she made it all seem – but it can't, it can't possibly be true. It isn't, is it?'

Finally she looked out from above her fingers. He didn't move, and he heard the cough-like whimper again. 'I remember,' she said. 'I remember those years back, when you used to spend all your time over there with that – with that – that filthy *faggot*, Henri, is what he is. I remember, even just a couple of times, the thought crossed my mind – and then I thought, don't be so wicked, Brigitte, what would Henri think, don't you do him down like that. They're just friends, you can be friends with a man like that and not be – be *like that* yourself. I knew – I swore it wasn't true.'

Still he didn't move and she started to murmur, 'Oh God, oh my dear God, oh my dear God,' over and over.

He felt something nudge his leg and looked down beneath his fingers: Jojo, her chin resting on his thigh.

'Won't you just say something,' she said. 'Can't you just tell me it's all a big lie?'

But he couldn't. He didn't know what she knew. He didn't know what parameters he was working within.

'I know you're not a religious man, Henri,' she said then. 'God knows I gave up on that a long time ago. But you are married. You're married, and you were married by the mayor himself. And then you made your vows in God's church.' She took a sip of her whisky, squeezed her eyes shut and swallowed, with a deep gulp. 'In front of your parents, Henri. In front of your good, kind father and mother, in front of God. In front – in front—' Her voice broke. 'In front of *my* parents. They *trusted* you, Henri.'

'Calm down Brigitte. You have to calm down.'

'And look at everything I've put up with. No children, even though I wanted them. I wanted children so much, Henri, I think about them every single day. But no, you couldn't give me those. And never so much as—' He closed his eyes. 'But I never complained, because I've always been so *proud* of you, is the truth of it. So proud. Proud to be your wife! And now – now I'm ashamed, ashamed and *disgusted* to have anything to do with you. Look what you've done to me! I'm going to be the laughing stock. I have that – that witch of a woman – like a snake in my own kitchen, telling me the most downright disgusting things, about my own husband. Just think of her now, telling every person we know, every person whose respect I've earned over all these years, and think how they'll pity me, Henri.' She was silent, then a little cry came out. 'What will Laure think! Will everyone believe it? And at church? I'll never be able to go anywhere, ever again, Henri. And it's not just that, of course. No, there's the small fact that I have been *in love* with you, ever since I was a young girl, and now I don't even know what you are. What are you, Henri?'

He didn't speak and she reached out then with one hand and shoved his shoulder. Jojo lifted her head and whined.

'Tell me,' she said, and shoved his shoulder again, as if she were trying to wake him up. 'Tell me it's all a big lie.'

He stood up, moved across the room towards the window. She started to sob again.

'What have you done to me?' she cried. 'What have you done? What have you done?'

He tried to focus. What would he do now? Go over to Edgar's. Go over to Edgar's and kill him. No, kill Suki first, then Edgar.

'And to think!' She forced a grim laugh and he turned, still not meeting her eye. 'You know what I've been thinking all this time, that you're going to go and have an affair with Lanvier's nurse!' She barked out another laugh. 'What an idiot. Yes, I'm the first to admit it. A prize idiot. Now don't I just wish that was all I was dealing with.' Something clenched inside him: Marguerite. He had to get to her right away, make sure this poison didn't reach her. Get to her, not to Suki, not to Edgar. It didn't matter if everyone else knew. 'I can't believe I'm your wife, and I'm sitting here wishing that my husband was having an affair with a woman.'

He looked at her then, finally, but she looked away, screwing up her face again.

'At least that way I could look you in the eye,' she said.

When she stood up, slowly, as if she were injured, she picked up the last of her whisky and knocked it back. He saw her retch with the final gulp.

'What now, Henri?'

They stared across the room at each other. She looked very naked, then, lost all the way over there across the kitchen. He crossed the room and took her in his arms and she leant her face on his shoulder and wept again, and he could smell whisky and sweat and the deeply familiar, home smell of her. When her sobs had subsided she pulled back and scanned his face, eyes moving back and forth over it.

'Tell me it's not true,' she whispered. He looked down and then she pushed him away and started to shout. 'You're disgusting,' she said, 'disgusting, disgusting, disgusting, disgusting. Get out. Get out of my house.'

Jojo trotted alongside him as he walked away, and he felt as if everything were watching: the trees, the farmhouse, the barns. He pushed the dog away when he got into the truck, closing the door and looking away as she barked and chased him down the driveway until they reached the gate and he turned out of the farm and was gone.

Marguerite asked him nothing when he arrived. She looked at him with a combination of shyness and concern, and he sat down at the table and she handed him a beer.

'You can stay here, if you like,' she said.

'Thank you.'

They didn't eat. She tidied things away and then he reached out for her as she passed the table and pulled her towards him, resting one cheek on her stomach. She held the back of his head there. Then he rolled his face into her stomach and lifted her T-shirt to kiss it, and she took him upstairs – they crept quietly, quietly up those stairs – to the bed they'd only left a few hours earlier.

17

He woke early and called Paul to tell him he'd be away from the farm for a week, maybe two, and tried not to listen for something altered in the tone of his voice. Then he made a cafetière and wrapped it in a dishcloth to keep it warm for Marguerite, left out an empty cup next to it, then got into his truck and drove for an hour to the conglomeration of neon-white outlets in a big clearing off the side of a motorway to buy clothes and also plants, soil, compost, seeds, tools. When he arrived he realised he was far too early, the shops wouldn't open for another hour, so he drove to a McDonald's off a grey, three-laned roundabout and sat there drinking coffee. He tried not to think about the cows, or how the skinny ewe and her triplets were faring, or whether anyone would know to call up the various stockists and chase the orders that were overdue. Instead, he imagined Marguerite waking up and getting up to wash, pushing her thick dark overgrown fringe away from her eyes, behind her ears. Pulling jeans over the rounded bones of her hips. He imagined her stepping calmly down that staircase he knew so well, and a small smile on her lips when she saw the cafetière and the cup.

She heard a sound outside – a light, insistent clinking she knew was made by him. She put the kettle on to boil, walked to the garden door and opened it. Henri was squatting on his heels, his back to the house. He had something in his left hand and was hitting it repeatedly with something in his right. He didn't turn, though she had expected him to, had thought he'd be doing something just to keep himself busy until she emerged. She thought that he looked very far away, absorbed in whatever it was he was doing. For a moment, she felt an ache in her middle; she felt, just for that moment, conscious of the dreadful separateness of things.

Then she started to walk towards him, and as if sensing her he turned his head, saw her, stood up, left his tools on the ground. He stepped towards her. His expression was so alive she forgot about feeling alone.

'I'm making coffee,' she said, letting him take her hands. He held them firmly for a moment and then tugged her towards him. They stood close to each other; she could feel the space between their faces. They kissed, lips meeting in a way that was almost formal. Then they laughed quietly, shyly.

'I'll bring it out, shall I,' she said. He squeezed her hands. Her whole body felt rigid with desire.

'Yes.' Still without looking, she turned and walked to the house a little stiffly, conscious that he might be watching her. But she heard the clinking sound again before she reached the door, and when she turned she saw he had his back to her once more, was busy with whatever it was he needed to do.

Throughout that day, she saw to Jérôme as usual when he needed her and then went out into the sunshine in the garden to be with Henri. She made him countless cups of coffee though they drank only one or two mouthfuls of each. She watched him while he worked on a wall, a tree, a plant; while he dug things up, fixed things, welded and tapped and tied together. She read, or mostly pretended to read; she was too aware of his proximity to concentrate. Gazing at a page, she saw simply a box of letters making up words, words that had nothing to do with her or the breeze on her face or the man a metre away and his moving hands and arms. After a while, she started to see the white space between the black of the print. She tried to switch off the part of her mind that waited and hoped to find him watching her. When it happened, when she felt his gaze momentarily and furtively on her, she was seized by awkwardness and tried not to blink, so that her eyes watered. She wanted so badly for him to think she did not notice.

He spoke occasionally in a low voice.

'Rosemary,' he said, touching the deep-green stripes of leaves. 'It smells—' He couldn't think of the word, or was embarrassed to elaborate. Instead, he snapped off a sprig, rubbed it between his forefinger and thumb, held it towards her. She put her book down and rose and walked forwards and knelt down and smelt it. He watched her expectantly, and then she could barely bring herself to meet his gaze.

302

'You've become a little Arab,' said Jérôme. She was filing away her notes, quietly; she had thought him still asleep. She turned and his face came somewhere near a smile. The room was filled with light; his clean pillow shone white. His eyes looked large and blank in his head.

'Your skin's got very dark.'

'The sun's very strong,' she said.

'I used to love it. The stronger the better. I could never understand the fuss people make out of how harmful it can be.' He looked as if he was about to get into the stream of a rant, but then he stopped, looked towards the window and blinked. Something had changed recently in the way he talked: his face only held form when he spoke, when ideas and words animated it. Sudden lapses of silence had started to cut into his speech, leaving his face empty and bland, its little muscles all slackened and neutral like a sleeping dog's.

He cleared his throat. 'So are you gardening or what are you doing out there all day?'

She turned, taking a glass from the table to the sink to empty it. She could feel her face colouring; she shook her hair a little to fall around her cheeks.

'This and that. Gardening, exercise, some reading.' She kept rinsing the glass, over and over, until she felt the heat subside from her cheeks, back down into her chest. She turned and smiled. 'I'm not much of a gardener, I'm afraid.'

But he wasn't listening. He was looking into the space in front of him, his head bobbing vaguely. She brought him the glass of milk and little saucer of prunes she had prepared as he slept, and when she came to the bed he seemed moment-arily surprised by her presence. He drank the milk hungrily.

She took the empty glass back from him and pointed to the prunes. 'You should eat these, they'll help your constipation.'

He had produced only the most meagre pebbles recently – black stones that took great straining and groaning.

'I hate them.'

'Do you? You've never minded them before.'

He shook his head furiously now, clamping his lips together. 'Foul, sticky things,' he said with unexpected volume. Then he squeezed his eyes shut and thrust his chin out. She took them away, glad for his energy. She started to prepare his medication but when she turned back to the bed a few minutes later he had already fallen back to sleep.

Late afternoon, when Jérôme was still asleep, they lay on the bed in Marc's old room, the biggest room. Sunlight blasted two thirds of the bed so they rolled into the strip that remained in shadow, and she lay on top of him. Their bodies were soft, heavy. She leant up on one elbow so that she could look down into his face.

'Your eyes are like marbles,' he said, and she laughed.

'That sounds scary.'

'In a good way.'

She smiled. 'Good scary?'

'Not scary. Just good.' He kissed her. 'How old are you?'

'Twenty-four.'

He groaned and she smiled again. When she looked into his eyes, he thought for a moment of Brigitte's face as she looked up at him, scanning his face for something. 'Tell me it's all a big lie.' He closed his eyes and Marguerite rolled off him, onto her back into the sunshine next to him. They lay there together watching the ceiling, and she didn't ask him any questions, and he asked her nothing in return.

He put his ear to her belly and it sounded like putting a cup to your ear as a child, hearing the sea soar. Deep inside her a bubble popped, a sound like a spring uncoiling.

He imagined what was in there, behind the complex intricacies of the colon: the womb, an empty waiting room, two snug ovaries he imagined to be like butter beans. He pictured life uncurling from her womb: light shoots tiny thyme-like leaves thickening into vines. A heartbeat like an animal's footsteps. Thick blood, like mud.

He realised he was only half awake.

They sat on the floor, opposite each other, either side of the garden door. Her legs crossed under his. They sipped wine, a white he'd bought, and the insects chattered. The wine wasn't as good as he'd hoped, and he hoped she wouldn't notice. She made him laugh when she told him stories about her past: playing tricks as a small child at home and making trouble at school, which he could barely imagine, so uncomfortable did he imagine her being in the limelight. He saw how carefully she stepped around the edges of what she'd tell him and what she wouldn't, and wondered whether she saw that he saw.

He got to know her face when she talked. Her mouth was small and oval. When she smiled, the top lip was an entirely straight line. It shouldn't have been pretty but it was. You could see the bones beneath her skin. Her teeth were small and tidy, apart from the canines, which were more pointed than most and came forward a little, as if they'd barged illicitly to the front of the queue. Occasionally he thought how strange it was that he was looking at a new face in this way – not just the face of someone new, a face he didn't know, but the face of a woman.

Sometimes she was shy again. When she felt she'd talked too much she became quiet and serious, almost formal. He told her then about the things they'd done at Rossignol growing up. She was curious about Céline, she asked about the dog, she asked what colour Jérôme's hair had been. He waited for her to ask about the sons but she never did. He would have thought she simply wasn't interested, were it not for how concentrated she became when he told her things of his own accord. In his stories, he allowed Thibault to play a starring role; he realised he wanted to show his childhood friend in the best possible light. Just as he was putting a spin of glamour onto everything, of course: the nocturnal gatherings they used to hold in the forest, far enough away for Jérôme and Céline not to hear; climbing out of the bedroom windows at night and jumping down.

She was shy, too, at initiating contact. It was always him reaching for her. But once he had, she was entirely un-self-conscious. She was decisive and instinctual, like she was listening to some physical instruction within herself. She surprised him with her strength when she gripped his throat during her orgasm, and with the concentration like anger on her face when she became close. It was so very different from how it was with Edgar – less in the most obvious, expected ways than in the whole mood and rhythm of it all. At times it was like an entirely different act altogether from what he'd experienced. He was fascinated by her orgasms, which looked more like pain to him than pleasure. He felt pride when she came – he'd never made a woman come before – and yet he also felt that he had little to do with it. She was the one in full command of those strange, sharp climaxes, which made him understand a phrase he'd always wondered at, always associated more with male orgasms than female: a little death. It was as if she were reaching through him and through herself and passing out of them both, going somewhere else entirely. At those moments, she intimidated him.

Neither of them referred to what they were doing. It was as if it were perfectly normal that he should suddenly be here, that they should suddenly be talking to each other playfully, having sex on the scratchy dry grass outside the kitchen, creeping past Jérôme's room and up the stairs to sleep in a bed together. Not yet, he thought, when fragments of the outside world crept into his mind: the farm, the animals, the gossip in the village, Brigitte. He wouldn't address any of that just yet.

She'd been dreaming of Cassandre when she woke. She rolled over to the bedside table, took a long drink of water. In the half-place between sleep and wakefulness, she'd forgotten that Henri was there. Then she saw his lean body stretching the length of the bed and she remembered. She had the urge to tuck herself in beside him, her head on his chest, but she couldn't bring herself to do it. He looked so far away, like he had nothing to do with her. She wanted for a moment to get out and sleep in another room, show him she didn't need him either.

She lay down with her back to him. For the third or fourth time since he'd arrived, she thought that Cassandre would never lie next to a man or feel him inside her. It was one thing when neither of them had been able to enjoy that. But now here she was, enjoying all the things she'd taken from her sister.

Jérôme was awake when she came in, though he hadn't knocked for her.

'Morning,' she said, and he watched her as she came in and prepared his water and toothbrush and toothpaste and flannel. He was silent as she performed his ablutions for him; she could hear nothing but the birds.

'Gargle.'

He warbled and spat. He didn't speak until she'd dried his face and taken the towel and tray away.

'That's not much of a shirt, is it?'

She looked down at her top: a loose blue vest he'd never commented on before.

'Oh,' he said, when she'd come back with his breakfast tray and was turning to leave him to eat. 'I heard some voices here last night.'

She felt heat in her cheeks.

'A man's voice, I could have sworn.'

She tried to hold his gaze, look normal. 'Oh yes. Henri Brochon came by. He was too late to come in and see you, you were already asleep.'

He raised one eyebrow. 'Sure it was just Henri?'

308

'Of course.'

'Well, that's okay,' he said. 'Ask him to visit again. He hasn't been for a few days.'

'I will.'

'I shouldn't have to emphasise that you'd be committing a gross transgression if you were to let any other men come to the house without my permission.'

'Of course.'

He tilted his chin as if he didn't believe her.

'I would never.'

'Fine.' She turned to leave, but he wasn't quite done. 'Careful not to be a slut, Marguerite.'

'What!' She stared at him but he merely raised his eyebrows, sceptical and unperturbed. As she walked towards the kitchen, she realised the outrage she should be feeling was buried under guilt.

She tried to ignore the word 'transgression' as she sat down to eat. This situation wouldn't go on forever, it was just temporary. Not enough to be breaking any code. And Jérôme trusted Henri; he'd given permission for him to be here, more or less. They must be more careful, all the same. She wondered where he'd gone already this morning, how soon he'd be back. She'd woken again to an empty bed and had the terrible premonition, for just a moment, that that was it, that he wouldn't return.

But of course he would. His body woke him up at four, five in the morning and he was programmed to get up and do things. Once he'd done those things, he'd be back. He would come in and hold her, run his hands down her waist like he did, looking over her body as if trying to memorise it. She liked the catch of his calloused hands on her flesh. She liked looking down the length of his body when they lay side by side. Looking at his penis at rest, slowly contracting, she felt both shy and emboldened.

It wasn't until she had finished her breakfast that she realised how much better Jérôme had seemed today. Careful to still be a nurse, she thought.

When he came back, she thought he looked impatient. He would tire of this, of course; it was a holiday for him, he had nothing to do here but work on the garden. But then he smiled when he saw her and she saw nothing impatient in the smile. She wondered what he was seeing when he looked at her, what it could be that made him smile like that.

'You said you wanted to grow more herbs,' he said, and she held a finger up to her lips, led him outside.

'Jérôme heard your voice last night.'

He winced.

'It's fine,' she said. 'It's fine if we keep the kitchen door closed. You can't hear a thing that way. Tell me what you've got.'

He whispered as he told her all the herbs he'd bought for her, all the herbs he was going to help her to plant and show her how to grow. She only half listened. Mostly she wondered what on earth was happening, what on earth she had done, that this man had bought all these things for her, was going to plant them *for her*. She wanted to ask him: Why are you doing this for me? Why are you here? Why do you want me?

Then he took her head between his hands and kissed her

forehead, and walked back into the kitchen. His face was ridiculous, she thought as she watched him pour a coffee. He looked like the American actor with piercing blue eyes from old movies. Frances had had a black-and-white poster of him in her bedroom with a cigarette clamped in one side of his mouth, dressed in a big padded coat like a woodcutter, fleeced collar open. His hair curled like Henri's. She must find a picture of the actor somewhere, compare their likeness. She thought that apart from the eye colour, they were twins. And then she remembered Frances saying the actor had had a plain wife, pretty enough but nothing much, and for a moment she felt reassured about the disparity in their appearance – until she thought, no, Henri already has a wife, a real wife, what are you doing? This isn't your life. You don't belong with someone in this way.

Suki answered the door swiftly, as if she'd been hovering right there.

'Hello.' She smiled, faintly.

'I'm afraid I can only stay five minutes,' said Marguerite. 'But can I come in?'

'Of course.'

They walked through to the salon.

'I've only just got up,' said Suki. She settled down in her armchair, feet tucked up by her bottom. 'I haven't even had breakfast.'

'I'm sorry.' Marguerite had thought of what to say on the way here, but it sounded too formal now, too earnest. 'I behaved – badly. I wasn't thoughtful.'

311

'It's okay, really.'

'It's not. I mean, when Jérôme's sons were there. I wanted to say something. I just – I couldn't. That's not an excuse.'

'I was lashing out. I was upset for a number of other reasons not even to do with you. It's not a big deal. Let's forget about it, okay?'

'Okay.' But it didn't feel quite okay.

'Marguerite, forget it. I just, I had to say something because I can't let things linger and fester. But it's all over now. Forgotten. I'm so glad you came by.'

'Good. I'm glad.'

'I was also, to be honest—' Finally, she leant forward to pick up a cigarette. 'I flipped out a bit when I saw Henri there. I jumped to conclusions.'

Marguerite pulled her sleeves down, took one hand to her mouth, coughed. Suki was watching her. She inhaled; the smoke disappeared somewhere deep within and then streamed out, in two steady plumes through her nostrils.

'But I was soon disabused of that idea,' she said. A smile curled her lips. Marguerite wanted to leave. 'Okay, I have to tell you something, but it's a top-level federal secret, okay?'

'I do have to go—'

'You'll wait for this. So you know how much I hate Brigitte. And what hell she's always tried to make my life here. And you know how I used to be in love with Henri, and nothing happened?'

'Yes.'

'Well . . .' She raised one eyebrow, smiled. 'I have it on 100 per cent authority that the dashing Monsieur Brochon is in fact – wait for this – a raging queer.'

'What?'

Something kicked in Marguerite's chest. She hadn't forgotten Thibault's words to Jérôme – he'd told him Henri was gay, and she remembered it had made relative sense when he'd said it – but since then she'd come to presume it was nothing, just an attempt to derail Henri's standing in Jérôme's eyes.

'He's gay.'

'You really know that, for sure?'

'I heard it from the horse's mouth. The horse being Edgar DuChamp, the poet I told you about, who is as gay as they come and has had sexual relations with Henri for years, apparently.'

'Have you told anyone?'

Suki's face stilled; her eyes flickered down to her cigarette and she took a long drag, sniffed as she exhaled.

'Of course not. Just you.'

'I think it's very important you never tell anyone something like that.'

'I know,' she said. She stubbed out her cigarette, frowned for a moment. 'God, I just thought you'd find it interesting.'

'I just, I think something like that – a secret like that could really damage people's lives if it's true.'

'It *is* true.'

'So—'

'Marguerite, relax. Why do you care so much? Because you've got a little crush on him now too?' She took another cigarette from the pack, and then put it back. 'I don't need telling that I shouldn't go broadcasting a secret like that. I'm only telling *you* because I trust you. Of course I wouldn't tell anyone else.'

'I can see it would be tempting because of everything Brigitte has done to you.'

'I'm not that petty.' She stood up. 'I'd better get my day started.'

'Thank you for having me.'

'No worries.'

'I'm sorry again, Suki.'

'Forget it.' She headed to the hall towards the kitchen, turned in the doorway. 'Can you show yourself out?'

'Of course.'

Suki disappeared into the corridor, the yellows and oranges of her dress absorbed into the gloom.

He could hear the waterfall as he walked, a gentle 'shhh' at first, building into a deep hum. There was a slight chill in the forest, the air charged with water, and as his ascent sharpened, the hum grew louder, until the trees cleared suddenly and there it was, just as he remembered it. The water was a roar. The forest had opened into a clearing and sheer rockface, the water green and fast, falling straight down into a series of pools. They used to come here, sometimes, dive into the largest pool from the wet brown rocks above.

He climbed up and when he reached their old diving point he inhaled, deeply. He undid his zip, let his pants and trousers fall to the ground. He looked down at them, spooling around his ankles, and unfastened the first few buttons of his shirt, wrestling it up past his shoulders and over his head. His stomach was taut with hunger, a pleasant feeling. He flung his clothes onto the grass behind the rocks. Then he looked around himself and up at the sky, lifting his hands up, high, letting a stretch tear through from the base of his spine up to his fingertips. He pushed his hips out a little, brought his arms back, opened his chest out until his shoulder blades slotted into one another. Then he stepped forward, wrapped his toes down over the rock ledge, bent his legs and flexed his calves and swung into a dive.

The cold smacked him around the face and then held it tight, in a vice extending all the way around his head. Back, neck, throat, all drawn tight with it. His weight was rising in the water but he tucked and dived deeper down, pushing back the wall of cold with his hands and arms until his lungs ached, and then he let himself rise up and his face then neck and shoulders burst back into the air. The sound of the water falling from the rocks into the pool, muffled to a drone underwater, was once more an exuberant roar. He lay on his back and let the motion push him towards one edge of the pool, and then he swam back into the centre, braced himself and dived back under.

When he climbed back up to where his clothes were, he was panting hard from exertion, stunned by how icy the water still was on his skin. He sat on the grass and looked down at his body: goosebumps across his chest and arms and stomach, nipples plum-dark and tiny with the cold. He wished there might be a break in the clouds but then thought, It doesn't matter, I'll come back again on a sunny day. He could come back whenever he wanted. He could do things like this, things he'd forgotten to do. He would come back here with Marguerite.

When he drove back he had to add fifteen, twenty minutes to his journey in order to approach Rossignol from the back, avoiding Saint-Sulpice. Thinking about the village, the exhilaration he'd felt in the water skidded in his chest into deep dread – as it did each morning when he woke, before he turned to look at her asleep beside him. Then he could focus on her breath, the long sensuality of her sleeping limbs, the soft place at the back of her neck where her hair started. Being back in that house again, sharing a bed and meals with this woman, getting to know a stranger's voice and her slow, smooth movements, was all so strange and enchanting that he could put all the other thoughts and feelings aside with an ease he found, in moments of dread and clarity like now, almost supernatural.

But it was still there, all the time, waiting. Brigitte hadn't come for him but she'd work out where he was, sooner or later. The farm – he couldn't even bear to imagine facing Paul and Thierry, holding his head up as he went about his day there, sensing them steal looks at him, trying to understand the man they'd known and worked for and respected in the light of that cataclysmic discovery. Perhaps by some miracle they might be more open-minded, more 'liberal', as Edgar always said, than the generations that came before them, but even then he couldn't bear for them to see him in this new light. Or perhaps they would quit their jobs, unable to feel anything but the contempt he surely deserved. As for everyone else they knew: he knew their reactions, he knew exactly what they'd make of it and how long the news would fuel their gossip. It was enough meat to sustain even that hungry pack for years to come. Not just a homosexual, he imagined someone saying in a voice not unlike his old headmaster's, but on top of that a liar, a cheat, heaping scorn on that poor gullible wife of his. And didn't we always suspect something? Didn't we always think he was just that bit too aloof, too detached – hell, even just too damn *masculine* – for his own good?

But then there was something else, of course, there was a twist in the tale. Because, he imagined saying to this faceless interlocutor, this morning I had sex with a woman. And I *like* to press my face between her thighs, I like the smell and taste of her, I like what's there. I don't like it more but, at least for now, I like it just as much.

That thought represented something like relief, and his relief too felt like a source of shame to him. Was he so closed-minded himself that he saw redemption in the fact that he might not be as thoroughly and unremittingly gay as he'd thought he was? And yet he couldn't quell it, there *was* something redemptive in the new imaginary life he glimpsed: a life that looked normal to everyone, even in a place like this, even in places far more conservative than this. He could be the man his mother presumed he'd end up being, the kind of man to drape his arm around his best friend's shoulders without worrying that it translated wrong. A man, in love with a woman.

All these things fell away as he turned the corner off the driveway. The door to the kitchen was open, and the sun had come through a little so that it lightened the stone wall of the house, flickering with the moving shadows from trees. Marguerite was in there somewhere, seeing to Jérôme or putting something away or stripping the leaves from flowers and snipping their ends to put in a jug of water. He wouldn't have expected her domesticity, even that she would know how to cook. It surprised him that she was so good at these things, she who had something unmoored about her, something calmly feral.

317

He wanted to call out when he walked into the kitchen, take her outside and hold her and tell her about the waterfall, make plans to go there one day while the old man slept. But as he walked slowly, carefully through the hallway and up the stairs, some of the thoughts he'd had in the car came back. He might be with a woman now, but still he was skulking. With sudden weariness, he thought that he would spend the rest of his life skulking, and lying, and hiding.

She was sitting on the bed, back against the wall, feet pulled up, arms hugging her knees. She didn't look at him right away.

'Marguerite,' he said. Then she turned to face him, smiled flatly. 'What's happened?'

'Nothing,' she said.

He sat down on the side of the bed, looked at her. He reached an arm out towards her but she didn't move. 'Is Jérôme all right?'

'Fine.'

She rested her head on her knees, and sitting there, with only one side of her face visible, she looked very young. He felt awkward then, as if he had made a grave mistake. He was in a room with a stranger. The thought of kissing her felt as wrong, suddenly, as kissing a child.

He stood up. 'I should go,' he said. 'I'm intruding.'

'You must go if you want to.'

He turned; she had leant her head back against the wall now, looking down her face at him. Her dark eyes were wide and thin at this angle, like slits.

'Do you want me to?'

Slowly, she shook her head.

'What's wrong?' he asked. 'Something's wrong, I can see it.'

'Where were you?' she asked.

'Just now?'

'Yes.'

He sat back on the edge of the bed.

'I went to a spring,' he said.

'A spring?'

'A spring, with a waterfall. Through the forest, over towards Pontoux. I'm going to take you there, it's beautiful.' She was watching him carefully. He smiled. 'I went for a swim.' It sounded foolish.

'On your own?' she asked, and he found himself smiling more broadly.

'Yes, of course.' He reached his hand out towards her again, but she didn't take it. 'Something's worrying you.'

She buried her face in her knees, then looked back up. 'It's stupid,' she said, and he waited. Something was rippling up inside him, something delightful, and he wanted to throw his head back and laugh. Could it be that she was jealous?

'Tell me.'

She must have sensed the laughter in his voice because she frowned, her face became serious. 'I know almost nothing about you,' she said.

'I know. I'm sorry that the situation is like this. You must tell me if you want me to go.'

She paused. 'I don't.'

'I haven't seen anyone else, not a single person. I just need to – work out what's happening, what I have to do about – everything.' There were too many things he didn't want to name: Brigitte, his marriage, the farm. There were the things he simply couldn't name, either, could never name to her:

319

that perhaps everyone he knew now knew what he'd spent his entire life trying to hide.

'I know,' she said. 'You don't need to – work anything out yet. Not on my account. You can stay here.'

'Thank you.'

She moved then, lay down on her side, facing him. He lay down too, held her hands. He looked down at them in his own hands and thought that his looked very ugly, the skin tough and aged against hers. They lay in silence for a while, and her eyes were closed. He thought that perhaps she was going to drop off to sleep, but he didn't want her to. He leant forward, kissed her, and she kissed him too but not like normal.

'I think—' she said, and then she stopped, and he watched her lips hover over the words. He waited. The room was too warm; he wanted to get up and throw open those windows, let in the day. But he knew that if he moved, her words would be lost. A hawk cried, and then she spoke. 'I think you've been with men.'

Later, as dusk approached and the clouds scattered, he stepped out into the garden and breathed in deeply. The sky was shot through with pink and grey. He stretched and then he filled the watering can from the outdoor tap, where a hose would previously have clung. He had to fill it slowly, letting the water flow gently, so that it didn't ring out in the can's metal belly.

He took the can over and then crouched down to look at the herbs. They looked shy, but healthy. When he stood and lifted the can over them and tilted it, letting water scatter over the herbs, their scents rose up together.

He picked some basil, slapped it in his hand to release the oil and held it to his nose. When he closed his eyes and inhaled, some distant childhood memory caught on his thoughts, like a torn nail on fabric. He couldn't place it but he thought it was a memory from this place. Something rose up in his chest and he turned and leant against the wall, looking out at the garden in the falling light.

When she'd told him what she'd heard, delivered it like a physical blow, he had turned from her, his thoughts wild in his mind. He'd felt not just something like panic, that she knew about him, and he'd lose her, and Suki and Edgar's fire had clearly spread, as he'd known it would; he'd been seized, too, by a deep, violent anger. He'd sat on the side of the bed with his back to her and for a moment he felt that he could turn around and shake her to death.

And then she'd sat up and rested her hand on the back of his neck and leant into his back, her face on his shoulder, and she'd told him that it didn't mean anything at all to her whom he'd been with.

'I only care – I only care if you see someone now, when you're also with me.'

He thought of her in Jérôme's room now, and knew that she would be focused on the old man, all her concentration and energy whittled down to one thing as she went about her duties. But when she left his room, she would be thinking about Henri. She'd come through to find him, like a cat, and she'd eat across from him and sleep beside him, all the time knowing what she knew.

She could see that he found it difficult to look at her. They ate dinner quietly, and there was a formality in his manner. Not just embarrassment, she was sure, but resentment, even fury. How invaded she would have felt, she realised, had he told her something he'd discovered about her. If he'd confronted her with her own past, as if he had any right to it, she would have wanted to close the whole thing down, send him away and shut the doors to the house. Hide. It was possible that she had ruined everything by forcing the conversation. They'd been separate from the rest of the world until now and she'd gone and let it in, with all its triviality and mess. She, who needed her own privacy so badly, had intruded monstrously upon his. And all because she'd been jealous, she thought; all because she'd worried he might flit between her and another lover, that the rough thumbs that ran over her hips might also stroke the poet's stubbled cheek and jaw.

She couldn't finish her food; she lay down her fork, pushed the plate away. He looked up then and he let her hold his gaze. She could see that it was difficult for him. Then he looked back down at his plate, cut a piece of the beef she'd made, pushing the fork into the meat so that the metal scraped the plate. She had humiliated him.

She needed to speak, needed to say something, but she could think of nothing that she could possibly say now. It was too late.

Jérôme called her then, and she was relieved to hear his knocks. She went through to his room, closing the door behind her, and she smelt and saw immediately that he had wet himself.

'Don't worry,' she said. 'It's not a problem.'

He closed his eyes and sighed as she lifted him to sitting,

pulling the sheet out from underneath him, pulling his soaked pyjama bottoms down to his ankles. She dried and cleaned his crotch and wet buttocks, dressed him in clean trousers. And then she dragged his chair over to the bed and lifted him up to sit in that while she wiped the plastic undersheet clean. She went out to the utility room with the wet things, threw them into the machine and took crisp dry linen from the cupboard. When she came back in, he didn't look up at her. She had unbuttoned his shirt before she'd left the room and as he sat there the two sides fell apart like curtains from his hard white belly, his concave chest. He, too, was lost and small and humiliated. Two men sitting alone in this house, the soft flesh under their shells exposed.

She took his shirt off and put on a new one, to match the clean bottoms. As she fastened his buttons, she felt his breath on her forehead and temples.

She would drive to the store tomorrow, get the new equipment they needed to match his growing weakness. A commode, nappies, convenes, a hoist for the bath. She'd been putting it all off for far too long and it wasn't fair, even if she knew how much he'd hate it all.

'Will you be able to get back to sleep all right?' she asked when she had him back in bed, and he shrugged.

'Who knows?'

She left him, closed the bedroom door. She put on a wash, and then she leant back against the wall in the semi-darkness of the utility room, closed her eyes. She'd allowed herself to think, just for little snatches of time over the last few days, that she wasn't alone. But of course I am, she thought. Everyone always is.

When she came back through to the kitchen, Henri was

323

standing tall in front of the sink, hands in his pockets, staring out into the falling darkness, and she saw the anger in his stance. He didn't turn around straight away; she sat down, held her head in her hands. Finally she felt him turn, and she dropped her hands to look at him.

'You're upset,' he said, as if he couldn't believe it.

'I feel like I've destroyed something.'

'That's what I feel,' he said, and frowned. 'How can you not care – about it? I need you to tell me, honestly. I can't understand how you could really not care.'

'I don't,' she said. 'I can't understand why you'd think that I would. All I care about is that I've ruined something.'

He blinked impatiently. 'But tell me honestly.' His face was hardened now, and she realised he was bracing himself for something. He stood even taller. 'Tell me. Don't you think less of me?'

'No,' she said, and she heard that her shock rang out in her voice and saw that he registered it. 'How can you think that?' She got up and walked over to stand in front of him. 'You must think very little of me to think that.'

'I don't,' he said, 'but you have to understand what it's like for me. How it's always seemed to me.'

'It doesn't seem like that to me.'

'You almost make me believe—' He paused, and she waited. 'That there really might be another way of seeing it.'

'But I don't see it in any way,' she said, and when she looked up at him again he didn't look away. 'It just doesn't seem any single way to me.' She stepped forward, unsure whether she could dare to touch him. She reached a hand towards him, tugged the fabric of his sweater. 'It changes nothing.'

He stepped forward, closed the gap between them, and pulled her into his chest.

'Nothing?'

'Nothing, not a single thing. I'm sorry that I brought it up. I didn't have the right to.'

'You did,' he said. 'You have the right to know everything about me.' Relief washed over her, and a little thrill at all those words might signify if she let herself think about them but it was cut short. She was still hiding everything from him. She didn't know how she could ever start to let him see.

Jérôme barely slept that night. He called her to him so often that, after the third time, she could no longer bear to wake Henri when she opened and closed the door to their room, or sank back into the bed beside him. She spent the rest of the night sitting in Jérôme's chair, dozing when he slept.

His temperature was raised, his voice hoarse.

'Does your throat hurt?'

'No.'

'Do you feel hot or cold?'

'Neither.'

He moaned occasionally, as he slept. She didn't know if he was dreaming or in pain.

She woke in a room filled with early daylight, and she saw that he was awake, watching her. She sat forward, stretched her neck. It felt rigid.

'You're like that blasted dog,' he said in his new husky voice. 'Grenouille.'

'Why?'

'He used to follow me around the place. If I'd let Céline have her way, that dog would have slept in our room with us and I would have woken up just like this, to find the bloody thing at the end of my bed. Waiting.'

She smiled. 'Do you miss him?'

'Grenouille? No. I couldn't stand him.'

She stood, stiffly. She was cold, felt as if she were made of wood. She took his temperature. 'You're back down to normal,' she said.

'Good.'

She poured him a glass of water, and as she did she thought of Henri. He would be awake already; perhaps she'd find coffee waiting for her in the kitchen.

'He never liked me,' said Jérôme. 'It drove me mad.'

'Who?'

'Grenouille.' He cleared his throat, a deep scratchy noise. 'He was suspicious.'

'But you said he followed you everywhere?'

'Yes. To check up on me.'

'It sounds like you're the suspicious one.'

He grunted. 'I'm tired.'

'I'm not surprised.'

'All this time you spend thinking . . .' He looked at her, twisted his mouth. 'Lying in bed, just thinking and thinking. You remember the oddest things.'

She sat down, waited.

'Before you woke up, I was just thinking about a set of

326

handkerchiefs Céline made for me one year. For my birthday or Christmas. Beautiful things. Expertly sewn.'

'That's a nice present.'

'I don't think I ever told her how much I liked them.' He closed his eyes, opened them, nodded. He smiled a grim smile. 'Age is turning me soft.'

She watched his hands as they clenched and unclenched, slowly.

'Still. Always make sure you tell someone how you feel about them. Always make sure you've said everything you wanted to say. In case they die.'

'I know,' she said, and he eyed her, sharply.

'Yes,' he said. 'Yes, I suppose you do.'

She leant back in her seat, on the passenger side. She turned her head to face him and he looked at her and smiled, moved his right hand from the wheel to her thigh. She was almost dazzlingly happy. She wanted to say something but instead she reached out and ran her fingers into his hair, and he turned to her again.

'I've never met anyone like you,' he said. He looked back at the road, and they drove in silence again. But then five minutes later, he continued as if there had been no pause. 'You're the quietest person I've ever met.' She laughed, getting ready to deprecate herself, but then he said, 'But you still communicate. I feel like you have your own language.'

How could she respond to that? She couldn't, but she needed to tell him something, anything.

'I feel—' She looked down at her feet, flexed her toes in her trainers, tried again. 'I feel comfortable with you.'

Boring, she thought, what a boring thing to say, but then he slowed the car and pulled up at the side of the road, stopped the engine. He turned to her and pulled her towards him, kissed her, and she climbed over the gearstick and handbrake and sat astride him. He held her body as close to his as he could. Then he pushed her away so that he could look at her face.

'Tell me more about how I make you feel,' he said, and she leant forward and rested her face against his. She spoke into the space beneath his ear, into the warmth of his neck.

'You make me feel—' His head pushed heavily against hers, as if he were drunk. 'Like nothing else matters. Like it doesn't even exist.'

'That's how I feel with you.'

Cramped, quiet so they could listen out for other vehicles, constricted by the car's tiny dimensions and low ceiling and the wheel behind her back, they came together, quickly. After-wards, she leant onto him, her face in the crook of his neck and shoulder, and kissed him as he held the back of her head in his hands.

'I love you,' he whispered, as she realised she'd known he would.

'I do too,' she said.

18

There was something in the silence that felt wrong. She went straight through to Jérôme's room and there she found him, on his front on the floor, one hip hitched up as if he were crawling. His eyes were half open. There was blood, a lot of it, spooling around his face and neck.

She realised she'd screamed and that she couldn't move, couldn't bear to check the extent of the damage. Henri had rushed in and he was picking Jérôme up from the floor, and she saw him standing with difficulty and carrying the old man in his arms like a sleeping child. She looked down at her right hand, gripping the table. She wanted to move it but she couldn't. She was saying please, please, please, please.

Then Henri was in front of her with his hands on her shoulders, shaking them. 'Marguerite.' His voice was hard and harsh. His green eyes in front of her face. 'Pull yourself together. He needs you, right now.'

He needed her. That woke her up. So he was alive, if he needed her he was alive. She approached the bed. 'Jérôme.'

'Where were you?'

The blood was all over his face.

'I'm calling an ambulance,' she heard Henri say and then everything clicked into place.

'Don't do that,' she said. 'Not yet.' She held Jérôme's face, very gently, and he winced. 'Tell me what hurts.'

'I tried to find you,' he said.

'Get me a bowl of warm water and a load of towels,' she shouted out to Henri.

'I was trying to find you,' he said again, dragging his voice like a tired child.

'Jérôme? Listen to me. I'm here. You're fine. You're safe. I'm right here. You've had a fall but you're fine. You're safe and you're fine.' She was running her hands up and down his body now, watching his face as she did so. Legs and feet fine, hips fine, thank God, thank God, his hips were fine. Gently, she took each hand and moved it around, watched his face. By a miracle, his wrists were too. Then, gently, very gently, she held his face and rolled it a little to each side. He groaned.

Then Henri was there with water and towels and she fastened one to his chin, the source of the bleeding. 'Hold this here,' she said, and she dipped another towel in water and started to wipe his cheeks. She rubbed the blood away, let the rosy water drop down into the pillow. He closed his eyes.

'My head hurts so much,' he said, and then tears ran down from beneath his closed lids.

'Lift him a little,' she said to Henri. 'He needs to sit up to swallow pills. Gently. Support his neck.'

'No, no, no,' Jérôme whined, and the tears came again, more now.

'Put him back.'

She prepared an injection instead. She saw that Henri turned away when she gave it.

The cut was small and deep, not the gash she'd thought it might be. He'd fallen onto his chin and nothing was broken, not one of his brittle little bones. When she'd dressed the cut she gave it two small stitches and then Henri helped to hold him as she changed the sheets around his body. Clean, dry sheets and pillow. Clean, dry pyjamas. They'd only been gone half an hour, she kept thinking as she worked. Forty-five minutes, perhaps. They'd not been gone so long. She took his blood pressure, fine. She hadn't abandoned him. Forty-five minutes, maximum, they'd been gone. But she'd been in the throes of another orgasm, she thought, while Jérôme cracked to the floor on his own. The fear he must have felt, as he lay there and realised he couldn't move. All of that fear while she nuzzled her stupid face into Henri's neck.

The diazepam had kicked in and he was mostly asleep, eyes flickering open now and again, the odd word coming from him, a little separate from him. She turned and saw Henri standing in the doorway, and the look on his face made something unbearable happen in her throat. The pain of it was startling. She turned back to Jérôme, watched him lying there clean and peaceful now, a bandage covering his chin, and she felt her shoulders moving independently of her. A sound came out through her throat: a clean, deep sound she didn't recognise. Henri's arms were around her then; she turned as he pulled her into them. She wept, and she was surprised by the sound her throat gave to the pain. She'd almost forgotten that pain could have a voice.

He carried her through to the kitchen, laid her down on

the sofa with her head on his lap. He ran one hand over her hair, slowly and heavily, over and over. Like she was a small child, or an animal.

'I thought,' she said.

'Shh,' he said. 'I know.'

But he didn't know.

'I thought I'd done it again.'

'Done what?'

'Killed someone,' she said, and his hand stopped stroking her head. She felt her shoulders shake again. The tears stung as they slid out of the side of her eyes, collecting hot in her ear. He hadn't moved, hadn't pushed her away from him. His stroking had started again. One of his beautiful, rough hands, heavy as a paw on her head.

When she'd stopped crying she kept her eyes closed and told him about Cassandre.

She rose quietly from the bed and dressed. She opened and closed the door very carefully. Then she walked down the stairs in the full dark, letting it close in around her. She thought about her lack of fear now that Henri was here. All those nights she'd spent alone, terrified of everything outside.

Jérôme was asleep, his reedy fragile snore creaking in the room. She settled into his armchair, her legs tucked underneath her. Sitting was a little sore, as if she were bruised from Henri's attention. It was a pleasant kind of pain.

'You weren't responsible, surely you see that,' Henri had said.

'But I was. Everyone said so.'

'Who said so?'

'My mother, for one.' In the weeks after Cassandre had first been rushed into hospital, phone calls had battered the eerie stillness of their apartment. The first time her mother had confirmed what Marguerite had already known was just a few days in. She hadn't known who was on the other end of the phone – she'd been trying to work it out when her mother had said, very plainly, in that new low voice she'd had since Cassandre had gone in, 'The dreadful thing is that Margo knew she was ill. If she'd only woken us up, we could have got her to the hospital in time. These things are all about timing, stopping the swelling before it's had time to damage too much. If we'd known even just a few hours sooner – if Margo had had the sense to wake us up – the situation would all be very different.'

Frances had looked up from the newspaper she was reading; Marguerite could still remember the wild look on her face. She'd stretched both hands out to clasp Marguerite's.

'It wasn't your fault,' Henri had said again, so firmly that he sounded angry. 'How could you have known? You don't even know if they could have stopped it at that stage.' He'd shaken her shoulders. 'Marguerite?' He'd made her look him in the eye. 'It wasn't your fault.'

But it was. Everyone knew it, though most didn't tell her directly. She'd lost track of how many times she'd overheard people: friends at school, teachers, family friends. 'Poor Margo, I don't know how she'll ever get over that.' 'Did you hear she knew Cass was ill? If only children knew these things, if she'd known they could have caught it in time.' 'I've told mine that they're always to come to me, right away, if they ever know that one of the others is unwell . . .'

She would have preferred them to tell her directly – to punish her as she felt she deserved. But there was no punishment, no recrimination, in anything but her parents' increased coldness and silence. They divorced four months after Cassandre was hospitalised, as they'd been trying to do for so long. Finally they felt they had an excuse. Frances, who had come back from England to stay with them as soon as Cassandre was admitted, was let go again. She had her own life now anyway, in her own country. Marguerite was too old for an au pair. Once Frances had left, there was no one who didn't avoid Marguerite, slide around her, shrink back to make way. She had become an ill omen.

But Henri hadn't pushed her away. After she'd told him, he hadn't let her go, and they'd gone to bed and drifted into sleep together, with her still there in the space he'd made between his arms.

'Where were you?'

His voice sounded rubbery, untested. She opened her eyes; she hadn't realised he was awake.

'When?'

'When I fell.'

She stood up and went over to him, poured water into his glass. 'I had gone to the shop. I was only gone about half an hour.'

They looked at each other and then his eyes slid past her and she handed him the glass, helped him take it to his lips. He drank, staring ahead of him.

'Does your chin hurt?'

'Yes. Everything hurts.'

'It's almost breakfast time. I'll get you some food.'

'I hadn't called for you, actually,' he said. She looked at him lying there, blinking at her. With the bandage on his chin, his face looked crowded: its big nose, the watery eyes and full lips.

'What do you mean?'

He tutted, sighed. 'Yesterday. I didn't need anything. I hadn't called you to me.'

'So why did you get up? Where were you trying—'

'I—' He stopped, looked away, looked back at her. His mouth opened, he made the shape of a word, but he didn't speak. He closed his eyes and she waited, but still he didn't speak.

'I'll go and get some food.'

He opened his eyes then, but he couldn't quite look at her and she realised that he was embarrassed. 'I wanted to see if I could,' he said, and she waited. 'Walk on my own. For some reason I got it into my head that I could.'

How could he have thought that? she wondered. She hadn't thought he could even sit up on his own any more. She couldn't imagine how he had mustered the strength to get himself to standing.

'No, I got my answer,' he said. 'I'll never be able to walk on my own again, that's the end of it,' and she thought that she couldn't bear the look on his face, that she would do anything to be able to distract him from those thoughts.

'I'm sorry I wasn't there.'

'Well, me too,' he snapped, looking up at her, and she remembered that he'd told her something about woodlice, once, and a dream in which he'd fallen and she'd been right

335

there to pick him up. She wanted to hide her face from him. She turned, walked to the door, opened it, and then he said, 'Lucky that Henri happened to visit at that moment.'

She nodded, tried to hold his gaze. 'Yes.'

'He must have got quite a fright.'

'I'm sure—'

'It's good of him to make these visits.' He blinked, eyes wide, and she nodded again. 'I do hope he'll come again.'

He came into the kitchen from outside, flinching briefly in a shaft of sunlight, and it occurred to her that she must look terrible. He stepped forwards and took her to him, and his body was warm, smelt of something particular she thought she was coming to learn. She was seized, then, by the fact that she would lose him too.

'I wish I could make you happy,' he said.

She detached herself from him, went to wash her hands at the sink. 'Do you think anyone's really happy?' she asked.

He thought for a moment, looked out of the window into the garden. The sound of birds and insects, the pretty fluttering of light and shadow on the grass under the olive trees, all seemed to her to belong to a different world.

'No, I suppose not.'

She realised her question hadn't been kind. She reached for his hand, hooked two fingers onto his. He looked at her, smiled faintly, looked back out of the window.

'But I've been a lot happier over the last few days than I can remember being,' he said, and she wished she could feel the giddiness she knew that should make her feel, but instead all she could feel was dread. It wouldn't last. It never did. She mustn't think that it would. He was looking at her, and she realised she must say something, but she couldn't.

'You've gone away somewhere,' he said. He held her waist, kissed her forehead. 'I'm going to go back to the garden. There's coffee.'

She watched him walk out across the scrubby grass towards the olives, and she wished she could call him back and tell him how happy she'd felt too. But putting words to it felt like a curse. Happiness for them wasn't possible, she thought. Surely it was only a matter of time before Brigitte worked out that Henri was here; and then she'd call Jérôme's sons, and they in turn would call the house, enraged, telling her to leave. She thought of Jérôme with his bulbous bandaged chin and felt sick. She couldn't leave him to die in someone else's care, not now.

Henri had gloves on already; he was squatting close to the ground, doing something to a mound of soil. She wanted to ask him, What do you think's going to happen? Do you think you can just sit there making this garden beautiful again? Do you think we can just stay here playing at husband and wife, uninterrupted? And she wondered, did he know something reassuring that she didn't know, or was he just ignoring the great calamity surely bundling their way? Was he less in command of things than he seemed? She felt a sharp little whistle of pity, then, and she wanted to run out to him and pull him up from the soil and tell him that they needed to face the truth: that they should run, now, before it was too late.

As Jérôme ate his breakfast she was tense, listening out for sounds from the garden, the clinking and tapping of Henri as he worked. She hadn't thought you could hear from this side of the house, but then she thought about Thibault and Marc playing football, the hollow thud of the ball hitting a tree, their occasional shouts. And again when she thought of Henri in the garden she thought that there was something terribly, self-knowingly futile in his work there. She didn't want to think of him like that.

'You're all locked up in there,' he said, and she looked at him and tried to smile. 'I wonder if I could guess what you were thinking.'

'I don't even know what I'm thinking most of the time,' she said.

'You're pathetic, you know. You don't fool me one bit.'

He was chewing carefully, she saw; it must have been pulling the cut on his chin. 'Let me just make one thing clear,' he said then. 'When you go to the village, you're not to spend a single moment longer than you need to.'

'Of course not.'

'I'm your priority here.'

'I know that.'

'I'm why you're here.'

'Of course.'

'I'm paying you to be here, absolutely and 100 per cent *for me.*'

She took a deep breath. 'I was gone for half an hour yesterday.'

He swiped a hand at her, the other shaking as it gripped his toast. 'Oh, forget yesterday. I'm talking about now.'

'I know that you're my priority. You're my only priority.'

'Make sure of that.'

She nodded. 'I will.'

'Good.'

'But I do have to go further than the village today,' she said. 'I have to go to Pontoux, and that might take up to an hour.'

'What on earth for?'

'I need to get you some new things.'

'What new things?'

'I think convenes would be helpful now.'

'The pan is fine.'

'There are certain things I can get that will make you more comfortable, make things a bit easier.'

'I only fell because I tried to walk. It was my fault for being stupid, I don't need any new contraptions. As long as I don't try to walk on my own again I don't need anything.'

'The bath,' she said, and he groaned.

'The bath is fine.'

'It's getting unsafe.'

'It's been unsafe for God knows how long. It's no less safe now than it's been all along. That's the beauty of getting care in my own home: there are no health and safety inspectors here.'

'We can just get you things to make you more comfortable.'

'Please,' he said, and his eyes became wide, theatrical, a child pleading not to go to school. She wanted to laugh, for a moment, only it wasn't at all funny. 'Let's just give it another week.'

She sighed. She was too tired for this. 'We'll review it in a few days, not a week.'

'Fine. We'll review it then.'

'Okay.'

When she left his room, she left the tray at the bottom of the stairs and walked slowly, heavily up them, and then she went into her old room, Thibault's room, the small room where she and Henri didn't sleep, and she closed the door and pulled the shutters to and lay face down on the bed.

She woke with a shock when he opened the door to the bedroom, confused for a moment as to where she was. It was very dark and hot, and she remembered she'd closed the shutters. He crouched by the bed; he looked wounded, she thought.

'Tell me honestly,' he said, and she pushed herself up to sit. 'Do you want me to leave?'

'No.' She pushed her hair away from her face, shook her head. 'I don't want that.'

'Why are you in here?'

'I don't know.' Her head throbbed. 'What time is it?'

'Four o'clock.'

'Oh God,' she said, getting up from the bed, and he stood.

'He hasn't called for you.'

'He can't still be sleeping.'

'He must be. I've heard nothing.'

She went to open the shutters, let the air and light in, and then she sat on the bed and he sat down beside her.

'I don't want you to go.'

'I don't want to,' he said. 'Tell me what's wrong.'

She stared at his hands, tanned and beautiful resting on his thighs, the veins etched across them, the clipped, broad nails. She wanted to kiss them.

'I'm scared,' she said.

'Don't be.'

'We can't go on like this. I'm going to lose my job.'

'That won't happen. I promise.'

'How won't it happen?'

'I won't let it.'

She sighed.

'I want to show you the herb garden,' he said. 'I want – I want to run us a bath. I want to have dinner with you outside, in the olive groves.'

'That doesn't answer anything.'

'I know, but we're okay. I haven't been here long. She won't know I'm here, she—' He blinked, looked down. 'She'll think I'm somewhere else.'

'Where?' He didn't look up, and she wondered whether Brigitte knew about the man, the poet. 'In any case, we're on borrowed time,' she said.

'We'll work something out.' He made it sound much easier, much less complicated. He looked at her, took her hands in his. 'But one request. Can we work it out tomorrow?'

She sighed again, nodded. 'Yes.'

'I want one more evening with you when we don't face any of that. And then I want you to have a proper night's sleep.'

She nodded. 'Me too, badly.'

'And then tomorrow we can work it all out.'

'Okay.'

'Please don't sleep in here again,' he said, and he was smiling, teasing. 'It's gloomy.'

'Okay.'

'But since we're here, now,' he said, and he leant towards

her, took her head in his hands, kissed her, and she let herself go into the strange foreign familiarity of him.

They took chairs and a side table outside into the garden and ate dinner there, as he had wanted. She made a very simple tomato sauce with pasta. She asked him if he ever cooked and he was embarrassed, he said he simply didn't know how, and she thought she caught a glimpse of him as a young boy. Then he grinned and told her he'd been shocked when he'd first met her and she clearly hadn't known how even to change a plug, and she smiled ruefully and told him that wasn't something they taught nurses or city girls.

'They don't have electricity in the city?' he asked, smiling, and she pushed him with one hand. His expression was very young, and she wished for just a moment that she'd known him sooner. 'And do they teach "nurses and city girls" to cook this well?' he asked, and she shook her head.

'No, they don't teach that either.' And she told him about Frances, laughed when he teased her for taking cooking lessons from an Englishwoman, of all people.

They drank a soft, velvety red wine he'd bought, and they talked about nothing important at all during dinner. When they'd finished the pasta he cleared it away, quietly, and she broke up chunks of black chocolate into a bowl with strawberries and torn basil, and they went back outside and picked at that and didn't speak much any more. The basil was as fragrant as she'd smelled, plucked from the herb garden he'd showed her so proudly at dusk after she'd given Jérôme his dinner.

'You'll want to water this one assiduously,' he'd said as he showed her all her herbs, laid out beautifully in semi-circles reaching out from a rosemary plant at the centre, and she'd thought, *You*, he'd said *you*, not *we*. 'This will last all the year round,' and she'd thought, This garden will only last as long as Jérôme does, it's not going to see the winter, and then she looked at his very green eyes as he spoke and the creases etched at the sides, curving over the tops of his cheekbones, the freckles scattered across his nose, and she tried to shake all the negative thoughts away. She concentrated instead on this man standing next to her, and the fact that he'd done all of this, bought and plotted and planted this tiny little garden, just for her. Silvery sage and crisp, buoyant basil and dark rosemary, it was all planted for her. He knew about Cassandre and the great, irreversible error she'd made, and he'd still done this. He still had his hand resting on the small of her back, was still smiling at her as if she were something very different from what she was.

It was only later, when all the food was eaten and gone, that he brought up Cassandre, though she saw that he did so very carefully, touching on Frances first and then reaching through her to Marguerite's youth.

'I was thinking, today,' he said. 'I'd like you to try to think of a young girl you know. A fifteen-year-old, or a girl around that age.'

She found herself thinking of the abysmal fête she'd been to in Saint-Sulpice, and the siblings who had manned the *beignets* stall. She couldn't remember much about their faces but she thought she remembered the girl handing over her change, her awkward combination of shyness and pride, taking her job seriously and clearly feeling older than she looked.

'Do you have someone in mind?'

'Yes.'

'I need you to try to imagine that girl, then, suffering the tragedy that happened to you.'

Marguerite stiffened. 'I know it's not easy. But please try.'

And so she tried to imagine the girl, whose face she couldn't remember but whose long drab hair she could picture hanging down from each side of her face, and she imagined someone pointing at her and saying, That girl's lost her sister. And then she thought, no that's not enough, and so she had someone tell her, and she realised she pictured Suki saying it, That girl's lost her sister. Her little sister came to her when she was ill and the girl didn't realise it was serious. So as a result her little sister's in a coma, and she's going to be very badly damaged when she comes out of it, and then a series of seizures will batter her relentlessly, like waves in a storm, infections chasing her in and out of hospital, so that it feels as if she's never given time to recover. She'll become depressed, slowly suffocated by her repetitive new life's total lack of incentive – so that it seems often to those around her that she becomes worse and worse and worse with each passing year.

'Do you think it's the girl's fault?' he asked. 'Do you blame her?'

She couldn't think that far. She thought that no, of course she wouldn't blame her, but she needed to have time to think about it fully, give it close, rigorous attention. To work out what she would feel towards her, and what that meant.

'I can't think too much about it right now,' she said.

'Of course.'

She would turn it over in her mind in a safe, private place.

It already felt risky, discussing the whole thing with someone else, having someone bring it up uninvited – as if it were in danger of being normalised, of seeming like it belonged to the rest of the world and the things that happened to other people.

'I won't mention it again,' he said. 'That was just the one thing. I just wanted you to try, very hard, to see yourself as someone else would, not as this criminal you think you are.' He rested his hand on her arm. 'But I promise not to talk about it any more. I understand, it's a sacred pain.'

She took her glass and drained the dregs and squeezed his hand and nodded. It was extraordinary that he could know that, understand so entirely what it was. Sordid, but sacred.

She felt light by the time she looked in on Jérôme, listened at the door to check he was sleeping, pulled the door to and made her way up the stairs. Perhaps she should just let all of this happen, stop pulling away from it. If Henri wasn't worried, perhaps she didn't have to be.

19

He had been standing in the pasture looking down over the farmhouse, about to speak to someone, when he woke, sharply. A gun.

Marguerite was sitting up next to him, her form vague in the moonless dark. 'What was that?'

He didn't answer. He sat up too and the silence felt deafening, rushing around his head. He thought he heard the very distant howl of a dog.

'It sounded like a gunshot,' she said.

'It was a gunshot.'

'Fuck.'

He got up, stumbled towards the chair, took the trousers hanging over the back of it, pulled them on quickly. He grabbed his shirt, made for the door and then went to the inky shape of her on the bed.

'Get up and go to Jérôme. Wait in his room. Don't turn on any lights.'

He tugged his shirt on as he ran down the stairs quietly, his feet bare, and he found he couldn't think of much but he didn't feel very shocked, either. It was almost as if this had happened before.

She heard Jérôme knocking as she fumbled in the dark for her clothes but they seemed to be strewn everywhere and she couldn't find her top. This is a joke, she thought, a complete joke, and she managed to get her jeans into a coherent shape and then tug each leg through them, fasten them. Jérôme knocked again. She took Henri's sweater and pulled it on, felt it scratch dumbly against her breasts as she crept down the stairs.

'I heard a noise,' he whispered when she came in, and she went up to the bed, crouched beside it to try to look into his face.

'Me too. A bang, perhaps a loose shutter.'

'It sounded like a shot!'

'I'm sure it was nothing.'

'Turn the lights on, for God's sake.'

'I will,' she said. 'I will.'

He was silent then and she could hear his breath, hoarse and shallow.

'Well turn them on now.'

'I will, in a moment. But it's okay, we're okay, let's sit like this for a moment.'

'What's going on?'

'It's just a noise, these noises happen.'

'They're no good for an old man like me.'

'No, they're not. Can I get you some water?'

'I don't need water. Why won't you turn on the light?'

'I'm just waiting to see if there's another bang.'

She could make out the white of his bandage and his eyes, the shadows of his face.

'What can I do to relax you?'

'Turn the light on.'

'Yes. In a moment.'

Her knees ached from crouching, but she couldn't bear to move in case she missed a sound. They stayed silent, both of them listening, braced for some other noise over the thumping in their ears, the orchestra of insects outside. After a while, she shifted her weight, knelt down on the hard stone floor. Henri was out there, she thought then, for the first time. He was out there and there had been a gunshot.

'I'm not as nervous as I'd usually be,' Jérôme said eventually, and she nodded, even if he couldn't see her.

'Good.'

'Henri will take care of it.'

She took a breath, waited, and he said nothing. She must speak, she realised, but she couldn't think of a single way to do it.

'I've told you before,' he said, his voice a little louder than a whisper. 'I'm not an idiot.'

'Of course not.'

'You'd do well to remember that next time.'

'Yes.'

She waited and he didn't speak again for what felt like interminable minutes, and she thought again of Henri outside and the old man beside her and she wanted, more than anything, for all of this to be a joke after all, to be back upstairs asleep in the safe, warm bed.

'Not going to say anything?'

'I'm so sorry,' she said, because that was the only thing she could think of.

'You should be. You should be desperately sorry, you should be racked with remorse. You should be afraid, too.' She heard him lick his lips. 'I'm sure I could make certain you never worked as a nurse again.'

She closed her eyes. All the horror, she thought, slithering up inside her but also pounding at her from the outside, a gunshot, Jérôme, the end of everything she and Henri had been doing.

'What can I do?'

'Nothing,' he said. 'I'm not going to do anything about it, *for now*. That's not because what you're doing isn't a shocking violation of your contract, of your duty of care.' He paused, and she waited while he found the words he wanted, could almost imagine him picking each one out, one by one. 'It is gross misconduct. Incomprehensibly stupid, worlds beyond unprofessional.'

'I'm sorry.'

'But there are two things. One, and this is the really strange one, I can't seem to care too much.' He barked a little sharp, whispered laugh, a fake laugh. 'If it were any other chap, my God would I be furious. But as you know, I really am fond of that boy. Even if he's a damn fool to have done what he's done. Irresponsible, unspeakably stupid. Disrespectful to me, irresponsible with you. If he cared one jot about you, as I'm sure he claims to, he wouldn't have let this happen.'

He waited again, the horrible silence coming back in to fill the space between them.

'And the second thing,' he said finally. 'Luckily for you, I don't actually want you sent away. Even though God knows you deserve to be sent scuttling off to some desperate little life elsewhere, I don't necessarily want that.' He sniffed. 'I don't want a new nurse, not now, I need someone who knows me. And you owe it to me, I think, to stay with me until the end now.'

'I want to stay here,' she said.

'I'm sure you do.' His tone was a jeer.

'For you,' she said. 'For the job. Not for anything else.'

'Hmm.'

'I – want to stay here, as your nurse. I would be very upset not to be able to care for you.'

'Well, don't be a bore,' he said. 'Don't overdo it.'

'I'm not.'

'Well,' he said. 'One condition then.'

'Of course.'

'Actually, two. One, you've got to be less of an idiot. Stop courting disaster and make sure my sons don't find out about any of this. God knows what his wife thinks. And more importantly, don't you dare drop your attention for one moment. You're here for me, not for Monsieur Brochon. I'm your patient, I'm your employer, I'm the one you're here for. Don't you let your care for me suffer one single drop because of him.'

'I won't,' she said, 'I would never, I promise, you're my entire focus.'

'Yes, yes,' he said. 'But words are easy. Just don't for one moment forget why you're here.'

'I promise.'

He sighed, deeply, shifted his head a little on the pillow.

'The *stupidity*, though,' he said. 'That's what I really can't believe. You, fine, but Henri . . . How could he be so unspeakably stupid?'

She closed her eyes; she wanted to beg him not to say that. But he was right. Henri had been acting like a child, she thought, and the pain of that thought was searing. She couldn't bear to feel pity for him, to think less of him. She wanted to see him as the calm and handsome and intimidating man he'd been to her.

But they had been like two children, she thought, like children in Neverland, in some ridiculous made-up world. She of all people knew that world didn't exist; she'd known it all along.

There wasn't a single star. He stood in the door from the kitchen, trawling the garden from side to side with the beam of the torch. Someone had just been here.

When they had sat outside for dinner, the turquoise of dusk had been mingled with clouds; now they squatted, a dark lid over the house, as far as he could see. The black bin in which he'd been collecting up weeds and detritus from the garden was lying on its side, sickly, spewing shrivelled leaves. A scarf of Marguerite's lay like oil on the ground; the chairs on which they'd sat to eat had been knocked forward like suppliants, genuflecting, heads locked together. He closed the door behind him, letting it click quietly. Still looking out at the garden, sweeping the torchlight back and forth, he turned the key in the lock and then crouched to slip the key beneath his bare foot in its boot. Moving the torch into the crook of his elbow, he used both hands to tie the laces tight. He would need them tight if he had to run.

Then he stood up and stepped out into the garden, turned onto the driveway, sought out its corners with the light. He thought of the lighthouse in a book he'd read as a child, how eerie a symbol of homecoming it had always seemed to be. And how lonely a home, that one sweeping light amidst acres of stormy ghastly black.

Surely whoever had just been here had left, he thought as he stepped forward, gravel crunching and popping underfoot. People don't wait in the shadows with a gun, not in real life. But still he felt watched. He moved so that his back was to the house but he didn't feel protected, there was still the bottom-right corner of the driveway, behind his right shoulder, where he knew the intruder had recently been, had recently pushed over the bin, the chairs, held the scarf that had touched Marguerite's skin. He swept it quickly with light and then moved the torch back to the driveway in front of him, the little green car of Marguerite's, his own silent truck.

He approached his truck first. He hadn't locked the doors, he never did. He swung the torch quickly down onto the seats, the spaces at the foot of the seats, the boot he had always taken pride in keeping so ordered and tidy. Its empty space blinked back at him, and he moved past it with a small exhalation, looked in the tiny spaces of Marguerite's car, found emptiness there too.

And then he moved further forward, and the torch caught something dark and straight lying in the space between those once-grand gates, opening out onto the empty road beyond. He moved closer and saw that it was one of his own shotguns:

352

dark, diesel-coloured metal shining now in the torchlight, laid out like a gift for him against the gravel. He ducked forward to grab it, eyes and torch on the road ahead.

He opened it up, eyes darting between the gun and the road. It had been fired, and now it was reloaded. The skin prickled around his neck, something curling around his ears. Who could have done this, have crept in here and fired a gun and reloaded it and left it here like an invitation. He knew who it had to be, and yet he couldn't recognise anything he knew, not even the remotest trace, in the lunacy and abhorrence of the act. He advanced slowly, steadily, running the torch into the tracts of forest either side of the road, and he thought he could smell an engine on the air. But the night was silent, and he turned his back to the road and forest and strode back to the house, refusing to run and refusing to turn back, refusing to show his fear.

He righted the chairs and bin swiftly, grabbed the scarf, unlocked the door as quietly as he'd locked it. Then he stepped into the kitchen where the refrigerator was humming, rattling very slightly, an inane sound, and he shut the door behind him and locked it and leant for a moment against the table, breathing in, breathing out. He crouched down, took off his boots and crept through the house, past the utility room and Jérôme's room and the bottom of the staircase, round to the forbidden rooms they'd explored furtively as children, the study and dressing room and the grand, large ground-floor bedroom where Jérôme and Céline had slept. In the torchlight, he looked for a place to hide the gun.

'We need to leave here,' he told her when he woke her. She fixed the one dark eye not hidden by the pillow onto his, and he saw her pupil contract, noticed the naked pink flesh of her caruncle.

She blinked. 'What?'

Then she turned, both eyes closed again as if she were in pain, the back of her head on the pillow. The half-light washed over her face.

'We need to leave.' He'd been waiting to say it for what felt now like hours, lying there filled with fear and resolution and rage towards Brigitte as Marguerite dozed beside him, marvelling at how she could sleep at all. When he'd come in, crept through the dark to hide the gun, every muscle in his body still alive with adrenaline, she hadn't even asked him what the noise had been. She had just held him when he'd told her there was nothing out there, and then she'd slept. 'We need to go.'

A frown passed over her forehead, and she opened her eyes, stared up at the ceiling. Then she sat up and turned to look down at him, very sadly. 'We can't go.'

He felt acutely embarrassed then, he realised, under her gaze. He sat up too, stared across the room and out of the great wide windows, to the dark cypress just ahead. But he wasn't exaggerating things. Brigitte had come to the house and fired a gun, laid it down fully loaded in the gateway. An oblique, violent warning of bad intent, of the violence she could do them.

'It was Brigitte who came last night,' he said. When he turned to look at her again, he saw just how tired she was. Her face was grey and drawn, its bones sloping down from dark rings under her eyes. 'She disturbed things in the garden. Knocked chairs over, messed things up.'

'I'm sorry,' she said.

'Why?'

'Because—' He saw her think for a moment, and then she closed her eyes, shook her head. 'I don't know.'

'It's not your fault. But she's worked out that I'm here, obviously. She'll come again.'

She nodded, and he was amazed for a moment by her equanimity, but then he saw that without the gun it didn't sound as urgent as it was.

'She had a gun on her,' he said, and her eyes widened.

'*What?*'

'It was a gunshot we heard.'

'You said it was nothing.'

'I didn't want you to worry.'

She shook her head, dumbly. 'Where was she? Did you find her?'

'No,' he said. 'But I found the gun.'

'Has she gone mad?'

'I don't know,' he said. 'I wouldn't have thought so, but yes, it seems completely insane to have done this. And she'll come again.'

'She can't.' Her voice was firm, even strict.

'She will if I stay.'

'So you can't stay,' she said, and he was chilled by the blankness in her voice.

'I want us to leave here together,' he said, and he heard that his voice wasn't firm, that it didn't sound how he wanted it to. She closed her eyes, shook her head slowly, and when she opened them she didn't look at him but stared ahead.

'I can't leave Jérôme,' she said.

'Why not?'

'I won't leave him.'

'He'll find another nurse.'

'I won't let him down. I promised him I'd stay here until he died.'

'But he'll be fine with someone else.'

'No,' she said, he saw that there was anger there. 'I'm going to nurse him until the end. I promised.'

He leant back against the wall, then, and for the first time he envisaged the only other real option available to him: leaving Rossignol on his own, taking his things, driving back to the farm, to a crazed Brigitte he no longer knew. He didn't see how that would be possible, how he could possibly leave what he had here. And Marguerite – she would resume that life she'd had before all this. She'd wander around this great empty house, lonely and sad, in servitude to the worthless old man in his bed, this tyrant who wouldn't let her go.

She sat back then too, laid her hand on his, and the look in her eyes was kinder. 'He knows about us,' she said. 'He told me last night.'

'Shit.'

'I know.' She twisted her lips, and they were very pale, very dry. 'But he's sort of okay about it. I mean, he's not, but it's all relatively okay. I promised I would stay here and be with him until the end.'

'But—' He had to look away from her to be able to say it; he felt as if he were shouting across a great gulf, so different from when he'd said it in the car just two days ago, and again, last night, after they'd made love, before they'd drifted into sleep in each other's arms and then the gunshot had woken them. 'I love you. I'm in love with you.'

'So am I.'

'So—' And he wanted to say, so how can this old man be more important than that? and as he searched for the words she stopped him, resting a cool hand on his face to turn him towards her.

'I'm not going to leave Jérôme. I need to be there with him until the end, I would never forgive myself if I wasn't.' Then she closed her eyes and kissed him, twice.

'And then what?' he asked when her face pulled away. 'After he dies.'

'I don't know.'

'Then we must be together.'

'Maybe.'

'Why maybe?'

'What about your wife?' she asked.

'This is more important than her.'

'Where would we go?'

'Anywhere.'

She sighed again, rubbed her hands over her eyes, and he wanted to shake her shoulders, wake her up, make her engage with what was happening.

'I need to sleep, Henri,' she said, and her voice had a keening edge to it, as if she were begging.

'Okay.' She stared at him, waiting for more, and he nodded. 'Okay.' He smiled, touched her face. 'It's okay. You need sleep.'

She let her head slide down the wall to rest again on the pillow. He leant down to kiss her, and as he did so he was aware of a quite dazzling pain at the very pit of his chest, at his sternum, as if something had been lodged there. He felt as if all he could do with the pain was lie down, panting, knocked flat by the extremity of it. But he rose and dressed, quietly, and he didn't turn back to look at her when he left the room.

Jérôme was precious and tricky all morning. He kept her in the room with him, didn't want to finish the bread and butter he'd asked for, tried a pear, didn't like it and asked for a peach. He snarled when she said they were out of peaches – 'All eaten up by a *visitor*, no doubt' – and as she read to him, he frowned frequently so that she found she stumbled over certain words, mixing up prepositions and missing out connectors.

'It feels old and filthy in here,' he said when she put the book aside, making to leave. 'Give it a clean.'

The room was as clean as it always was, but she saw that he would do all he could to keep her there, and that she would have to do his bidding. She opened the windows wide, scrubbed the sink and mopped the floor under the bed. He had the radio on, and its droning commentary drifted in and out of her mind as she worked – odd phrases about something that was happening in China and something else in Poland, analysis of a recent football game between Lyon and Troyes – but she couldn't hold on to them, found her mind instead moving between some banal and senseless memory from school or nursing college, and then the incomprehensible, preposterous image of Brigitte standing wild-eyed in the dark with a gun.

By the time she had cleaned everything she could, his eyelids were drooping but she saw him try to fight to sit upright, look awake. She gave him a few pills and he didn't swallow properly and choked, vomiting a jet of garish pink froth onto his chest and the sheets in front of him.

'Blood!' he exclaimed.

'It's the coating of the pill,' she said, and with a great roll of exhaustion she left the room to get pyjamas and clean sheets, came back and went through the long palaver of changing them around his immobile body.

'I'll have lunch soon,' he said when she was finished, and she nodded.

'You didn't eat much breakfast.'

'Quite.'

'Will you sleep first?'

'Barely. Bring me lunch very soon, I'll just close my eyes for a quick moment. Half an hour, no more. Then I think you should stay in here for the afternoon, read your book or something.'

She nodded again and took the sheets up in a great bundle in her arms out of the room and into the utility room. She dropped them onto the floor and then she leant back in the cool dark of the room and closed her eyes. All she wanted in the world was a day of total silence.

Henri was standing in the kitchen when she came in. He had his back to her, staring out of the window above the sink. He didn't turn, and she looked at the breadth of his back and felt frightened by the strangeness of him, by how little she knew about him. She shook the kettle to check its weight for water but it was empty and she didn't want to disturb him by filling it at the sink. She closed the door, shutting out the rest of the house, and finally he turned but he looked at her only for a moment.

'Do you want me to leave?' he asked eventually, his back to her once again.

She sat down. 'Of course not. But you have to.'

'I know I have to. But I'm asking whether you want it. Whether it'll be a relief to you.'

'No, it won't be a relief to me, Henri.'

She looked at the back of his neck above his collar, brown against blue cotton. She imagined standing and crossing the room, reaching up on her toes to kiss the skin there, and it felt like an impossibility.

'She destroyed the garden,' he said. She looked outside, unsure what he meant, and then stood and went out, walking over to see the little herb garden he'd shown her so proudly the night before.

The herbs had been flattened, others tugged from the earth so that great clots with little stones littered the mess of green. She knelt down and rested her face in her hands on the earth, like a child, like she was praying. The smell of soil and basil and rosemary and mint rose up to meet her face as she held it in the dark space of her hands, her elbows sinking into the damp softness. The tidy, beautiful little garden he had made for her, spent hours over the last few days planting with care, as if it was something she deserved. They would never grow another one, she thought. It was destroyed forever, and she thought of Cassandre, of her broken green eyes, her broken gaze.

20

He heard Jojo howling as he turned onto the track leading up to the farm. The sound was unlike anything he'd heard from her before, it was like a wolf: plaintive, unbreaking. It was only when he turned in through the gates that it broke into barks, the shrill, chest-deep barks she gave when she was afraid.

She threw herself against his legs, wove in and out of them repeatedly, irritatingly, so that walking up the driveway towards the farmhouse was difficult and slow. He pushed her aside but she came back, hitting herself against him. When he left her in the kitchen to look through the house for Brigitte, she started to whine again, and her howl followed him around as he stepped into each empty room.

'Where is she?' he asked her when he got back to the kitchen, and she barked twice but didn't turn to lead him anywhere. 'Where is she, Jojo?'

He held her face between his hands and she jumped up, paws on his stomach, gazing up with her dark, blank eyes.

He'd been collecting his things together slowly at Rossignol, stalling, when Paul had called the house. He'd thought he might find Henri there, he'd said; Brigitte had mentioned something about it. But she'd been behaving strangely, and now she'd gone. He was sorry to call, but he was worried. Henri had stood by the telephone in the corridor outside the kitchen, his head dipped, and it had occurred to him for the first time that the gun might not have been a warning of the violence she could do them, but the violence she could do herself.

He went to the chicken house first, but he knew before he got there that she wasn't inside. The hens were insolent, he had trouble rounding them up and locking them in for the night. He didn't look in the milking parlour yet; he didn't want to see Paul or Thierry if they were still there. He kept moving and his goat barely noticed him as he passed, Brigitte's pigs indifferent as he made his way towards the root cellar. The farm – his farm, his family's farm, his world – seemed eerily the same, as if he hadn't left it for almost a week. Its indifference was like a reproach. The place wasn't his any more, not at that moment. A child he'd chosen to leave, who'd decided it would be just fine without him.

The root cellar was empty. The idea of Brigitte hiding in that place was preposterous to him in any case, but then the idea that Brigitte had disappeared was preposterous, too. To be playing hide and seek with this woman he'd known, peripherally, as a child, but now couldn't imagine ever to have been one. He couldn't try to get into her mindset, to wonder where she was most likely to have gone, because her mind was, he realised, a closed and one-dimensional place to him: somewhere he'd never really tried to explore.

He had trawled most of the fields and outhouses before

he thought of the stable in which he'd killed Vanille. He had avoided it since then. Now he looked over the nodding cows towards it, lonely and pretty in the dusk, facing out at the edges of his land, and he felt something hard hit him in the gut, a metallic taste release onto his tongue like shot. He imagined Brigitte, her hair and clothes in disarray, looking around, wildly, in her new grief and humiliation and stumbling forwards towards the old stable in which – in one quick, heartless motion – her stranger of a husband had dispensed with another old female. That was surely too metaphorical for Brigitte, he told himself as he strode towards it, grass tugging with long wet fingers at his boots. But then he thought that maybe it wasn't, that in fact it was just literal and emblematic enough for her, and he quickened his step until he'd reached the stable and stood before its wide, open doorway, looking into the gloom.

She wasn't there. He breathed in, smelt mildew and the unmistakable stench of decomposition. A dead rat, most likely, decaying under the piles of rotting hay. When everything was okay again he would raze this place.

Marguerite lay on their bed, the sinking sunshine on her body. She held both hands over her stomach and looked down at it, much paler than her hands and arms, and imagined Henri's face as he kissed it, his eyes closed, brown eyelashes flecked with blonde. She imagined him leaving life in there, something that would germinate and blossom into a bud under her skin and flesh. Then she looked away, turned onto her side, felt the tears slide, warm, onto the pillow.

'I feel sick when I think of what I'm going back to,' he'd said before he left.

'I feel sick all the time.'

'I don't feel sick when I'm with you.'

'No. Nor do I.' She'd stroked his face. 'It's the only time I don't.'

She lay there as the light dropped further, as if her limbs were bound to the mattress. Then she got up quickly and walked down the stairs, stars blinking around her vision. She had wanted to hold him to her so that he wouldn't leave, but she couldn't do that because their reckoning had come now, their little period of calm had expired. It wasn't just the two of them any more. The world had come in.

As she prepared Jérôme's dinner she saw the long evening stretching out before her, silent and empty, and she filled a glass with wine and drank it down in three long gulps. The light was low, but the air still warm. She could see through the window the cleared stretch of soil that had been her little herb garden. Henri had pulled everything out, put it in bags, tied them carefully, taken them out to his truck.

After he'd got the phone call he'd been tense and distant and he'd left in a hurry, his thoughts far away from her already. He'd held her head to his face for a moment, tight, and kissed the side of her forehead, and then he'd left, slamming the doors of his truck hard as if he'd forgotten all about Jérôme. They hadn't had sex one last time and now that struck her as a terrible thing, and a great snake of dread rose up, uncoiling inside her so that she had to go to the kitchen door and lock it in spite of the evening's warmth.

The phone rang once, a sharp exclamation, and then the silence snapped back in on them. She waited for it to ring again and when it didn't she turned back to Jérôme and tried to smile.

He sneered. 'Changed his mind,' he said.

She looked back down at the page and kept reading, though she wasn't convinced he was listening. She herself was barely paying attention to the words, they merely formed shapes in her mouth. As she read she thought of herself yesterday, which felt now so very far away, and how as she had dozed in Jérôme's chair she had half dreamt of a house that resembled this one, just much smaller, with a happy dark-haired little child who looked like Cassandre standing next to her at the stove. Henri walking in from outside, stamping his feet on the mat. A vignette from an old children's book, a fantasy. Now she felt the truth surrounding her, slinking over her shoulders, hissing in the empty space around her. There was no route for them to take together. And not because theirs was a star-crossed love, forbidden for some noble reason, but because of a web of inexorable, quotidian reasons. He was married. He ran a farm, his wife was part of that farm. He could never leave it. Jérôme would die soon enough, and then she'd have to leave this place. And even if she stayed in Saint-Sulpice they would never be welcome here, not together. She would have to move on somewhere else and he wouldn't be able to, couldn't be asked to.

And then even if they found a way, against all the odds, to carve out a new life for themselves, their love for each other would wane. It might feel now the only true answer to any-thing, but she knew enough to know how these things go. Boredom would seep in: he'd grow tired of her, resent her for the farm he had lost, start seeing her shortcomings. Now he liked her quietness, he had said how he liked it, but in time he'd become frustrated. He'd want someone cleverer, more vital and full-blooded, more like he was. And there would be men. Men, perhaps even other women.

Then she thought of him now, back at his farm with a wife who had turned up at this house in the middle of the night with a gun, and the dread clattered afresh around her. Henri would be safe, she was sure, because in her mind she realised that somehow he was congenitally safe, she couldn't imagine that he wouldn't be able to protect himself. His wife surely wasn't a real threat to him.

But tonight she and Jérôme would be alone again here. She would lie in the dark waiting for sleep without Henri's long, warm body in the bed beside her, unable to fit her own body into its crooks.

'I think I've had enough now,' said Jérôme.

She stopped reading. She put the marker in, set the book to one side. His eyes were closed as if he might sleep again. But then he opened them and looked at her. 'I don't suppose we'll reach the end after all.'

'What do you mean?'

He rolled his eyes. 'You know what I mean. We should have chosen something shorter.'

'We'll choose something shorter for the next one if you like,' she said. 'This is very long.'

'There won't be another book.' He looked at her, nodding. 'Isn't that funny? *The Count of Monte Cristo* will be the last book I ever read.'

'I don't think—'

366

'Oh, don't try.' He smiled dryly, lips pale. 'I've told you before. You don't need to pity me.'

'She's been all right,' said Paul when he called him. He tried to listen out for something changed in the tone of his voice, some sign of what he might have learnt about Henri, but there was nothing. 'We knew something had happened, obviously, between you two, and we didn't want to poke our noses in or anything; we just wanted to make sure you were both all right, but she's – well, she seemed fine enough until yesterday I suppose. It was just, Thierry saw her yesterday evening and he said she seemed pretty bad then. And then nothing this morning, no sign of anything. Which I thought was a bit unusual anyway but especially as we had the fitter from Montpellier coming to talk us through the new baler and she said she'd be there.'

'What do you mean by pretty bad yesterday evening?'

'Oh, I don't know.' He paused. 'You'd have to ask Thierry.'

'He didn't tell you?'

'He said – I guess he just said it seemed like she was pretty upset. With all due respect, obviously, he also said she might – and he wasn't judging or anything—'

'What?'

'She seemed quite out of it.'

'Drunk?'

'Yes. Very drunk.'

He had never seen Brigitte drunk, couldn't even imagine it. Nor could he imagine her being visibly upset in front of anyone but him or perhaps Laure, their employees least of all.

He thought of her face when she cried, the way it crumpled, ugly and naked, and he felt like a monster.

He would wait until night fell, he thought, and then he would call the police. He bathed and changed and then he went down to his study and made his way through great piles of paperwork, and for a little while it took his mind off Brigitte. He switched on the desk lamp and it threw a warm puddle of light over the papers as he went through them, closing in bit by bit on the gap he'd left in their records and accounts over the past week. He felt the familiarity of these tasks like a balm.

When Jojo's barking broke the silence he stood and went through the kitchen and outside, and it was as if suddenly he could breathe again when he saw his wife walk up from the driveway, her gait straight, not drunken, no gun in her hands, no wild hair or wild eyes. His fists unclenched. Their eyes met briefly when she neared him and then she looked away again and walked past him, pushing the door into the kitchen.

'Where have you been?'

She snorted. 'Where have *I* been?'

She looked tired, he thought, but hard: her eyes, her mouth, the set of her jaw.

'Paul was worried.'

'And you?'

'Yes, I was worried too, Brigitte. Extremely worried. I thought you'd gone mad.'

She looked away, busied herself clearing the table to sit down. 'Yes, well. I didn't know how else to get through to you.'

'I can think of other ways than that.'

'The truth is, I did go a bit mad. I did what you do, Henri, when you're really het up about something: I drank a lot of alcohol. For a few days. It's no way to fix a problem, it's sordid and stupid, but I didn't know what else to do. I was beside myself, Henri.'

'And now?'

'I'm stronger than all that,' she said. 'I remembered that you just need to pray when things seem unbearable. Talking to God: that's where you'll find your strength, not in the bottom of a bottle. No, I won't have another drink. I'm not like you.'

'And what did God make of your behaviour?'

She blinked, slowly. 'You don't seem to feel very sorry about any of this.'

'I stopped feeling sorry when you turned up with a gun, like a psychopath.'

'And how would you have had me react?' she asked, staring at him so that he found he had to look away. 'Five days ago I'm told that my husband is a deviant. A deviant and a liar. He's been having an affair, and not just any affair but the most sordid kind.' She crossed her arms. 'And he doesn't deny it when I ask him about it. No, he just runs off, leaves me at my moment of need, without a word about where he's going. Not a word.'

'I'm sorry for that.'

'Oh, are you? And what else are you sorry for? The next thing I know, his truck is parked up at Rossignol – he hasn't even bothered hiding it. He's having another affair, a real affair this time, with some – some *slut* half his age. And he's shacked up with her! Behind Lanvier's back, I presume, so that he's not just lying to me, his wife, he's also lying to a sick old man!'

'Brigitte—'

369

'No, I think if we're going to talk about God's *interpretation* of anyone's behaviour around here, it's going to be yours, Henri, not mine.'

'I'm sorry, for all of that.'

'And what about the fact you've left me childless, Henri?'

He looked down, ran one hand over his face. 'I didn't do that on purpose.'

'But you didn't give me a – a normal experience of marriage, did you, Henri?'

'We had sex, if that's what you mean.'

She barked out a little laugh. 'I think we both know enough about breeding animals to know you need a little more than that to bring children into this world.'

'Not necessarily.'

'Oh come on, Henri. You didn't do it nearly enough, not like a man, a husband should do. Even though you *knew* how much I wanted a family, I told you for years and years. Just sitting there watching my friends have children, watching Laure build up her brood of four, and me with none, as if I was barren. Trying to avoid everyone's questions.'

He shook his head. 'I'm sorry about that, Brigitte. I really am.'

'I worshipped you, you know. I always did.'

He couldn't respond to that. A wood pigeon called out nearby, gentle and sad.

'I've put up with everything.'

'It hasn't been a perfect marriage for me either.'

'Oh, don't think I don't know that I bore you. That you're *unfulfilled* by me. I'm no intellect, I know that, Henri. I don't always share the same interests you have. But I've been loyal.

I've run this farm with you. I've worked so hard. You couldn't fault the work I've done.'

'I know.'

'I've been patient, I've always let you go off when you want to.' She sniffed. 'To do God knows what. And I would have defended you to the last, if anyone had spoken badly of you.'

'I'm sure.'

'Even now, I've defended you.'

He looked up and she nodded, blinking fast.

'Yes, I've spoken to that little witch,' she said. 'Lacourse. I've made arrangements with her so that her filthy rumour doesn't go anywhere else.'

'What do you mean, arrangements?'

'She had all sorts of complaints to throw at me,' she said. 'Stupid complaints about unfair behaviour over the years. She made me promise to do certain things, pathetic things, to increase her standing in the village. Do you think I enjoyed swallowing all of that, Henri?'

'No,' he said.

'I should say not! But I did it, for you. Even after everything. No one else will be hearing about your so-called affair with that faggot.'

He took a deep breath. 'What do you want me to do?'

'Stay here,' she said, without a second's pause. 'Don't do anything rash with that—' He watched her struggle for the word, her mouth mean with it. 'That wretched little whore.'

'Don't call her that.'

'Don't you dare defend her, Henri.'

'Don't call her that.'

'Look at what she is,' she hissed, and then she stopped herself and looked away and breathed in, out. She turned back to him. 'Stay at home, see to the farm, don't let any of this get out. Make sure that no one else finds out about your little fling.'

He closed his eyes for a moment and it was only now that he realised he hadn't slept, apart from perhaps twenty minutes at his desk, since midnight.

'Why do you want that?'

'I want a normal life,' she said. 'As far as I can have one. I want things to be like they were before. I went half mad, I got drunk, I lost my way. But today it's all changed. I see everything much more clearly. Our reputation's still intact; Suki won't be telling anyone her vile stories about you and the poet. And now at least you and I know that you're not a faggot after all. Even if I'd rather you hadn't proven it by having an affair with a girl half your age, it's still a good thing, isn't it?'

He watched her face with interest, then. The same denial he'd been living with for most of his life, playing out in the intently bright expression on her face, the intently bright words.

'Well . . .' he said, and she frowned.

'For God's sake, you're clearly not a homosexual. Unless you've been playing brother and sister with that nurse for the past five days, which I very much doubt. So we can just forget about all of that.' She took a deep breath. 'Will you stay?'

He looked down at his hands, waited for the thoughts to still in his mind.

'You know that girl will lose her job if you don't?'

He looked up.

372

'Oh yes. I'll make sure of that. The only reason I haven't got her sacked already is because I'm trying to keep a lid on that rumour, too. For your sake.'

'Jérôme already knows.'

Her head pulled back a little, like she'd been slapped, but then she shook her head.

'And his sons? They don't know yet. The nursing agency doesn't know. She'll be sacked in an instant if I make a call. Those boys already want to get rid of her.' She saw, then, that she'd got through to him; her eyes widened, she nodded quickly. 'Oh yes. Jean-Christophe called after their recent visit, asking all sorts of questions. He said he didn't trust her; he said that he was looking into something dodgy about her past, something about getting a medical lawyer involved.'

'I don't want to hear your poisonous rumours, Brigitte.'

'Well, just so you know. She's not the pretty picture you no doubt think she is. One phone call, Henri, and she's gone. And I very much doubt she'd be able to get another job in a hurry with this on her record.'

He shifted and Jojo barked, once. Brigitte was watching him.

'So will you stay?'

'I'm going to be back at the farm, for now,' he said, slowly, and he saw the relief pass over her face like a shadow. 'Whilst we work everything out. I need to go to bed now so I can get in a full day tomorrow. I'll sleep in the spare room.'

He didn't wait for her to respond, and as he made his way up the stairs he thought of her tearing Marguerite's herbs from the ground with her large pink hands, but his anger was tempered now. She was right: his crimes were surely worse.

Only there had been no option; none of it had been a choice. It was all he could have done.

Marguerite would sleep well, he thought, without him to keep her awake. She'd sleep, and each of their bodies would lie untouched these few kilometres apart. He settled into the stale spare bed and looked through the darkness at the room he'd slept in as a child, as a virgin. He'd been born in this house, within these walls, just as his father had, just like all the thousands of creatures on the farm that had been birthed and born breech and been stillborn or had lived and reproduced and gone on to die.

Marguerite had told him he wouldn't be able to move somewhere else with her, and she was right. He'd known it, really, when she'd said it, and now he felt the knowledge like a weight against his chest. Tomorrow he'd wake up at first light and he'd walk out onto his land and work, and he'd keep doing that until he'd seen out his useful time here, just like one of the animals. Then he'd die, where the soil still smelt like home.

21

'Come on then,' Jérôme said when she came into his room with his lunch. 'Tell me what you bought.'

She placed the food down on the tray over his lap, watched his fingers shake as he grasped the spoon.

'They're all just things designed to make you more comfortable,' she said, and he nodded and rolled his eyes.

'Yes yes. So bring them in then.'

She went out and with dread she carried in the boxes of things she'd bought in the great hangar-like store outside Pontoux.

'You'll be using this for your toilet,' she said, her hand on the box containing the commode. 'We won't—' She stopped. They wouldn't have to stagger to the bathroom together each time he needed to shit, she could have said, her neck twisted under his arm, or use the too-small bedpan when he couldn't make it in time. But he didn't need to hear that. And he didn't look up; he had lifted the spoon full of rice to his mouth and as he waited his hands shook and most of the rice fell down his front. He dropped the spoon to the tray, didn't try to push any more food onto it.

'And these look scary but they're not,' she said, holding up the box of convenes though he still wasn't looking. 'They're convene catheters; they're much better than what you might have experienced in the past.'

'Funnily enough, I haven't experienced a great many catheters in the past,' he said.

'We'll try out the bath seat this evening.'

'A veritable treat,' he said, trying now to shovel a new pile of rice from the plate to the spoon. It was slow work. 'How *will* I be able to contain my excitement?'

She pulled the chair near to the bed, sat down. 'Would a bigger spoon be easier?'

'Yes, yes,' he said, 'and you may as well just feed me while you're at it. Or no, whizz the whole thing up into a milkshake and give me a straw.'

He caught her eye and she saw fear in his face, for all his deadpan bravado. She knew that look intimately now, the very same as when he looked out of the window each night, into the darkness outside.

'I've got no appetite for this dross.'

'Can you at least try?'

'I can't face it.'

'It would be good to have just three mouthfuls.'

'No.' He folded his lips over each other, and she noticed the burst veins on the tip of his nose, little purple stars like sea anemones. She took the plate from him, stood up.

'Well, I've got just the thing then,' and she left the room, coming back with the coffee-glazed éclair on a plate, and he smiled in spite of himself.

'Making me fat,' he said, and she looked at the hollow

scoops under his cheekbones, the rubbery tendons of his neck, the bulbous clavicles beneath, and nodded.

'You have me sussed,' she said.

He ate almost the whole thing, slowly, and then she lifted him with difficulty into a sitting position so that he could piss into the pan. Then he slumped back down into the bed and looked up at her, face yellow-grey against the white of the pillow.

'Look at you,' he said. 'Brown as a nut.'

'I should get out of the sun.'

'It suits you,' he said. 'You've never looked so well.'

She felt the faint beginnings of a blush, and looked away. 'There's some post for you here,' she said, and put a few letters down on his bedside table, including one with a handwritten address – surely the only handwritten letter, she thought, he'd received for some time.

He nodded and closed his eyes. 'I'll sleep now. You go and do whatever it is you do now he's gone.'

He opened one eye then, studying her face, and she turned, the weight of it all like a stone in her stomach, and left the room.

When she came in to check on him in the afternoon, she found him wide awake, staring ahead, a torn envelope in his hand. He didn't look at her until she'd crossed his line of vision, standing at the sink at the foot of his bed, and then he studied her face, eyes wide, and it was as if he'd never seen her before.

He was silent and watchful as she took him to the bath using his new stick for support. He kept his silence as she put him into the new bath seat; he didn't complain as she lowered him down clunkily, knock-kneed and naked, nor when, back in his bedroom, she fixed the condom of the convene over his penis. His docility was unsettling.

When she had got him back into bed she lay a towel out under his lower legs and massaged oil into them, his short straight calves, almost hairless, and the bulb-like ankle bones and knuckles of his toes, swollen and distorted with arthritis. As she massaged him she found him watching her again, mournfully, eyes large and watery in his head, so that she was moved to ask him if he was all right. He didn't respond, looking away and staring down towards the end of the bed, his mouth drawn down into a crescent like a sad puppet.

She read a few pages and then finally he spoke: he asked her to stop, said he wasn't in the mood, and she put the book aside, prepared his room for bedtime.

'The post you gave me,' he said when she was at the sink. 'Some of it was five days old.'

She turned her back to him, rinsed out his glass. 'That's often the case. I only collect it once a week or so.'

'Well, I wish you'd got it to me sooner.'

She rolled her eyes, she didn't have the energy for one of his tirades, but he didn't follow up on it and took his pills in silence, the mournful look in his eyes again as he watched her, and she started to feel uncomfortable in his silence.

'Are you all right?' she asked him, wary that he would snap as he always did when she asked questions like that, particularly for a second time, but he simply shrugged and looked away.

She switched off his bedside light, left him to sleep. When she'd eaten she went upstairs and ran a bath of her own, Jérôme's watchful silence still beating like a physical presence around her. She looked down the length of her body in the water, the body Henri had made his, and she closed her eyes and felt tears slide from the corners of her eyes, into her hair and her ears.

She hadn't yet got to sleep when Jérôme knocked for her.

'I thought you were asleep,' she said when she came into his room, his bedside lamp already on.

'No,' he said, 'I couldn't.'

'Do you want to take something?'

'No,' he said. 'Sit down.'

She sat at the chair by his table, and he looked at her, took a deep breath. 'You're going to have to leave,' he said, and she felt her chest kick.

'What?'

'I don't want you to,' he said. 'For God's sake, it's the very last thing I want.' He lifted his shaking hands, rubbed them over his face, the short white hairs covering his cheeks and chin and jaw where he needed a shave. 'If I could have my way,' he said after a while, hands dropping to his sides, 'I'd say nothing and try to have you stay here until I die. Don't think I haven't considered that. As I'm sure you know by now, I'm no saint. But I've thought about it, and I've realised I just can't let that happen.'

'Let what happen?' she asked. 'What's happening?'

'You'll have to read the letter I opened this afternoon,' he said. 'It's from Jean-Christophe, the little worm.'

She watched him, feeling sick, and then she stood up and opened the drawer of the table where he'd let her put away the post he'd read and didn't want thrown away.

'Wait,' he said, before she took the handwritten letter, and she held it in her hand and watched him, felt her hand shake like his. 'Before you read it . . .' He waited, looked away, folded his lips inwards as he thought. 'No, don't worry, best to read the thing first.'

She sat back down and looked at the page, felt him watching her as she read. *Dear Father*, it started, *You'll forgive the formal nature of this letter but what I'm writing about is, as you'll see, of a particularly sensitive nature. After our last visit to see you at Rossignol, I left with a deeply uncomfortable feeling about your current nurse, Mlle Demers, whom I am of course aware I hired in the first place – something that now gives me cause for great regret, and again I do ask your forgiveness . . .* She felt the heat rise to her face and something else rising up from deep within, up from her stomach through her chest, into her gullet and onto her tongue so that it felt heavy in her mouth, metallic, as if she couldn't have spoken. She was calm, and horrified, and the words she read – even 'her sister, a patient there who was, by all accounts, most severely damaged' – felt like something she'd read before or known she would read in her future, so that they weren't a surprise at all but the intimate words of a document read and examined and re-examined.

. . . I simply had to have a few questions asked, via a contact I have through work who specialises in clinical cases of this kind – the kind that actually wind up in official proceedings, that is – and deeply concerning accounts arose. It appears the manager of the care home passed the official line that Mlle Demers had had

no involvement and so all was put to rest and indeed buried, on paper, but as with all these things there was still a number of individuals whose suspicion and discomfort had persisted long past the inquest . . .

She pictured those individuals – she knew them exactly, and she felt hatred rise like a pulse in her neck. *I have contacted the manager, and do think that with some legal pressure and on the insistence of the nursing agency with whom Mlle Demers is currently filed, there's a strong chance they'll be persuaded to re-open the investigation. Of course, I (and, I am sure, you too) hope to find that absolutely nothing untoward went on, but I think you'll agree that the circumstances do seem simply too convenient for words, and that in a country in which euthanasia is rightly – given the grave ramifications it would have for the security of all the nation's most needy and vulnerable – categorically illegal, a serious criminal offence, one can almost imagine how a desperate and unhinged young woman might take it upon herself . . .*

She couldn't look at him. She let the paper rest on her lap, and she gazed at the floor just past her feet in her scuffed slippers, looked at the little chips in the stone from years of use. She imagined those three men as young boys, running past her feet and back out of the room, and it was not difficult to picture Jean-Christophe's chubby face as a little boy, his rosy cheeks and fair hair, a child with the power within him to reach into the future and lay a snake into the pit of her past.

It is not, needless to say, my usual wont to get involved in something of this nature, and you'll appreciate that if the matter didn't have the most severe implications regarding your own safety and wellbeing . . .

She heard the paper start to crunch in her hand, and

loosened her grip, lifted the letter and let it rest on the table beside her. She wouldn't speak to Jérôme, she thought. She couldn't bring herself to say a word. She would simply pack up and leave. She stood and felt the room spin and adjust, not unpleasantly.

'Marguerite,' he said, as she made to leave the room, and she stopped in the doorway, one hand resting on its frame, her head bowed. 'I would have left that poisonous letter to rot in the desk,' he said, and she let herself meet his eyes then. 'I hope you know that.' His eyes were wide, more serious than she'd ever seen them. 'But I can't let it rest because I'm afraid you might be in serious trouble, and for all I'd like to let you risk it and stay with me until the end, I'm afraid I've had to reckon with myself and I simply wouldn't be able to countenance it. You deserve more than that. Please sit down.'

She sat again, held her face in her hands.

'In any case, if we're going to be honest, I'm not at all sure your agency won't be following up pretty soon with a letter of their own. If there's an investigation, they'll suspend you until it's carried out. They'll be watching their own backs.'

They sat in silence for what felt like many minutes. She couldn't get her thoughts straight yet but she knew she would, she just needed to wait for the adrenaline to recede. Right now it was like waves at high tide, lapping relentlessly at her chest and distracting her from the letter's shiny reality so that she felt alert and muddled and calm all at once.

'I'm not going to ask you about what he's referring to, because I don't want to confuse things in case anything gets asked of me, but all I will say is that—' He paused, waited. 'I in fact, contrary to what Jean-Christophe says . . .' He cleared his throat. 'I don't want to pass judgment on what you may or may not have done. I trust you.'

She leant back in her chair, stared up at the ceiling, exhaled so deeply that she felt physically lighter.

'So we're at a deadlock,' he said. 'Except actually we aren't, because the one thing we do know is that you're going to need to go away from here.'

'I can't escape an investigation,' she said.

'You certainly can. And if you don't, you're the idiot I suspected you were for a long time.' For the first time that evening, she recognised the expression on his face. 'Yes, you're an idiot if you don't get the hell out. Go on a very long holiday. Out of the country, I'm talking about. You think they'll let you go anywhere once an investigation's open?' She felt the horror stir within, and she wished he'd stop talking just for a moment. She wasn't ready to formulate thoughts, a plan. She wasn't ready to accept that this in any way resembled an externally quantifiable reality, that she might wake up in the morning to find that the letter still existed when the sun was shining and the day well underway.

'You've presumably got plenty of money set aside after working here all these months, living like a monk. And in any case . . .' He looked down at his hands and up again, his mouth twitching with something smug, proud. 'I was going to wait but I'll let you know now that I've had a decent amount of cash set aside in the house for a long time now. I don't believe in keeping everything tied up in the bank, never have. I've already mentioned to my lawyer that I was intending to leave most of it for you, was going to confirm it with him next time we spoke.'

'You can't—' she began, and he shook his head.

'Don't try to persuade me, or thank me.' He sniffed. 'I'd already decided on it. I don't want those vultures getting hold of it. They're getting more than enough already through shares and assets, including this place, of course. No, I'll speak to Monsieur Richoux and I'll tell him I've given it away in various anonymous charitable donations, otherwise they'll think you've stolen it of course. You could do without that extra trouble.'

He was almost making jokes, she thought, and, as if he realised the same thing, he frowned, serious again.

'So you'll take the money and get the hell out of here until you know they're not opening an investigation. And to be honest, they might well not be able to. He thinks they will, but he's not an oracle. It's what, years in the past, and you'll know better than me but it sounds like the only thing they've got on you is a couple of suspicious co-workers. So you might find all of this blows over and you can come back.' He smirked. 'Perhaps I'll still be alive, even.' He looked away and the smirk drooped. 'No, I won't be. But I'm just going to have to get used to that. I'm not going to have you nurse me till I die after all. I'll have to go with some brainless idiot beside me.' He nodded, slowly. 'I'd be angry with you if I didn't realise part of this is my doing, of course.'

'What do you mean?'

'Oh, come on,' he said. 'We both know I wound them up, didn't I? I knew I was doing it, I did it on purpose, talking about wills and lawyers and pay rises. I just didn't know Jean-Christophe would be able to open this can of worms.'

'I'm sorry,' she said, quietly.

'Oh, don't bother with that. It's too late for all that. I wish you hadn't done it, because you're going to have to leave me at the very moment I need you the most, but that doesn't mean what you did – or didn't do, of course – was wrong. Now go on, get out of here and leave me to sleep. And start thinking, hard. If you'll take my advice, which you will unless you're a total cretin on some kind of suicide mission, you'll act quickly.'

She rubbed her palms against her legs, tried to dry them, and she stood up. 'Thank you,' she said, 'very much. For—'

But he shook his head. 'Don't bother. Let's not be too soft. What's done is done, it's time to move forward. Now get out. Let an old man get some sleep.'

He reached out his hand, grappled slowly with the switch of the lamp, and she stepped forward to switch it off for him.

'Goodnight,' she said, as she left the room, looking back at the dark shape he made in the bed, but he didn't reply.

Marguerite had joined Cassandre's care home as a member of staff in spring, just five days after Cassandre's sixteenth birthday. They'd celebrated in the usual way, the day room spruced up with balloons and a garish cake most of the patients, who were fed via endoscopic tubes just like Cassandre, couldn't eat. After the carers and nurses had gathered to sing happy birthday and the cake had been cut, Marguerite wheeled her back into her room and she and her mother sat there opening her presents for her: a ladybird lamp that projected colours onto the wall, a pink blanket to spread over her knees, a few CDs, new leggings and sweaters and tracksuit bottoms. Cassandre watched, something like a smile carved into one side of her face. She wasn't speaking. The latest seizure had been one of the worst so far, apparently fifteen minutes long, and although at the hospital they had insisted that her degradation in speech was temporary – a symptom not of the seizure, but of depression and fatigue – she hadn't yet said anything distinct. Marguerite knew rationally that the doctors must be right, but she realised that part of her didn't really expect Cassandre to speak again. Giving voice to her needs couldn't change them.

When their father arrived and mother left, Marguerite made two cups of coffee and they sat listening to an audiobook until Cassandre fell asleep. They watched her, her sixteen-year-old face, overweight and misshapen, its contours much smoother in sleep, and Marguerite imagined they were both thinking the same things: conjuring up images of the other sixteen-year-old existing somewhere else in some abstract place, a young woman whose illness hadn't taken hold of her. One who'd be having her sixteenth birthday party that night, with friends and boys and a grown-up new haircut.

Marguerite stayed when their father left and Cassandre was taken out of her chair and put to bed. She turned on the new ladybird light, and in the dark of the room it cast spots of light that turned and twisted like dust motes across the wall and onto the ceiling, spectral. Cassandre wasn't in pain tonight, she had had a relatively painless day. She gazed into Marguerite's face as she sat there, and her eyes looked inky, as fathomless as wells.

'I'm coming to work here,' Marguerite said. She'd told her so many times, never getting a response. Without words Cassandre could reply in a whole host of ways, a language that Marguerite knew as intimately as her own thoughts, but to this she still hadn't responded and Marguerite thought that per-

386

haps she just couldn't understand the implications. 'It means I'll be here nearly every day.' She held one curled-up hand in both of her own. 'We'll see each other nearly every day. I'll make sure everyone looks after you even better than they already do. When I'm on night shift I'll be here all through the night, so you'll never be lonely.' And she could make sure none of the men touched her, a thought that paralysed her sometimes during the night, when she herself was alone, safe, in control in her own bed in her mother's quiet apartment. She knew enough about this industry to know that, even in a care home as humane and well managed as this, the patients without real language suffered the most. No one could watch everyone. There were unexplained bruises, urinary tract infections. Two female carers had been fired overnight just a few months ago, and Marguerite had heard that they'd been found 'messing around' in the room of one of the unconscious young males on the ward.

'I'll be here nearly every day,' she said again, and Cassandre's eyes continued to gaze into hers, and she felt the pain cleave her chest, straight down the middle. She kissed Cassandre's hand and rested her face on it.

Marguerite hugged her knees to her body, feet up on the ledge underneath the wide open space of the windows. Tonight, she didn't feel afraid to have them open; she let the darkness of the drive, the solemn cypress tree and fat wedge of moon spill into the room. She understood now. No one would come to harm her and Jérôme in the darkness; they were going to come in different ways, with official letters and investigations and the delayed, long-overdue tumbling out of consequences she'd been half awaiting for over two years.

She thought of Ottilie, the manager of Cassandre's care home. She had been contacted already, the letter had said. She would be worried, compromised. Ottilie, whom Marguerite had called five minutes after she'd driven the fine needle into the flesh of Cassandre's thigh, whose face had registered a moment of disbelief and then knowledge, had become serious and firm as she came towards Marguerite and held her tight in her arms for a moment. Ottilie was small and Marguerite had had to lean down to rest her head on the woman's bony little shoulder. She'd breathed in the thick smell of cigarettes that shrouded her, permanently, felt the heavy rings on Ottilie's little bird hands pressing into her back. 'Sit down,' Ottilie had said then, pushing Marguerite firmly towards the chair. 'Tell me how you found her.'

And Marguerite had recounted the lie she'd practised, the lie Ottilie knew to be a lie but accepted with brisk nods, wide eyes: she'd just come into the room on her rounds, it must be cardiac arrest, the patient wasn't responsive, the patient wasn't breathing, the patient was filed as DNR: *Do Not Resuscitate*. Marguerite had taken, then, just a moment to look at the patient, whose face had been puce but was rapidly paling now, and then she'd looked away again and stared at the floor while Ottilie went to report the death and call the next of kin. Marguerite's mother.

Ottilie had allowed her to work there in the first place, an obviously unconventional arrangement, a controversial one, and she'd helped to smooth the way whenever it became clear, as it often did, that other members of staff didn't like that the new nurse was also a relative. Ottilie, in her inimitably tough way, had insisted that the personal connection would not affect professionalism and indeed it largely hadn't, a few hiccups notwithstanding; Marguerite had been, by and large, the example of professionalism. She'd been allowed no special allowances or favours: Ottilie had given her short shrift when she'd voiced her concerns about Richard, the carer whose hands and sideways glance disturbed Marguerite, whom she watched closely when he was on duty, didn't like to let turn or change or touch Cassandre. Ottilie had come down hard on Marguerite when some of the carers had complained that the new nurse insisted on sitting in on them when they washed a certain patient. She'd treated her firmly and fairly, like any other member of her staff.

She'd also been the one to advise the family, some months into Marguerite's time there, to consider changing Cassandre's status to DNR. Cass had suffered a seizure so prolonged that neither time nor medication could stop it; only in hospital under general anaesthetic had her body finally stilled, the seizure soothed into abeyance. She'd spent weeks in intensive care, and when she was finally stable enough to return to the care home, to Marguerite's care, she was once again an altered creature. Sustained low blood pressure and sepsis had worked together to spread further damage through her beleaguered brain. She was tortured by the jolts of her spasticity, alert to nothing but immense, immeasurable pain. Face twisted into a rictus, she groaned and shouted through the new confines set on her voice.

Marguerite had started to struggle to give all of her patients equal attention, now that all the usual sounds of the ward became absorbed into the almost-constant howls of her little sister. She'd seen with pain and calm fury how the rest of the

389

staff clearly found the sound intolerable, exasperation etched into their faces, even if she did too, even if Cassandre's wailing and shouts grated against her nerves so much that sometimes she wanted to shake her to get her to stop. In agreement with the doctor, she'd been generous with sedatives and pain relief, but Cassandre's tolerance was high, the capacity for relief limited. Her sister's latest incarnation was inhuman, an abomination of what it could mean to be human.

'You must pray,' she was told more than once, by more than one of the staff. Others told her, kindly, that they prayed every night for Cassandre and she responded – to these people she liked, and respected – by saying that they shouldn't pray to the devil, that his was the only power that could possibly be playing a part here.

Cass had become, more or less overnight, the home's most demanding patient. It was Cassandre they all dreaded, Cassandre whose voice made that ward feel like bedlam. The girl who'd once been that clean-faced, elfin child enthralled by her older sister – even the girl who had half-smiled at them, peaceful enough, on her sixteenth birthday – was now a creature stretched out on a rack. Marguerite's dreams of taking her out of the care home had dissolved. It didn't matter any more whether Marguerite was her nurse, or could be with her every second of the day and night, or even whether they moved into an apartment of their own. Everywhere would be the same hell for Cassandre.

She stood, leant forward to breathe in the cool summer-scented air. Nothing else could have happened; there was no other path she could have taken. She'd done the only thing a sister and nurse and human being could have done for Cassandre, release her from the torture chamber her existence had become. They would just have to accept that.

She lay down on the bed, expecting to stay awake, but she slept in pockets, her waking thoughts merging into dreams and back out again. She decided she wouldn't leave, that she may as well wait until the agency contacted her. Then she decided that she would leave, and that she'd go straight back to Paris to face the worst of it, speak to Ottilie, find out what evidence anyone thought they had. Next she decided in a dream that she'd go to a police station and tell them she'd killed her sister; then she dreamt that she was in hiding on Henri's farm, among the sweet stench of pigs. When she finally woke properly, a little past four, she stood up and went back to sit in front of the window, cold in the almost dawn. She couldn't bear to go back into the labyrinth of her half-conscious plotting. Unable to find any clarity, she couldn't decide how serious this situation was, how high the stakes. Her instinct was to think that Jérôme was overdramatising it but then she thought of what it meant if she'd been found to have administered a lethal injection, to have killed a person, and saw that perhaps he was simply being realistic about the scope of the consequences.

The light was rising, birds and insects stirring and calling, her cool face bathed in the wet fragrance of dawn. One particular bird started to trill now, insistent, like a high-pitched drill in the copse outside the driveway, and she realised, standing up from her chair, her skin raised in bumps along the underside of her arms and at the back of her neck and shoulders, that she was deeply, viscerally afraid.

22

He was sitting on the single bed, stretching his neck where it was stiff from the night, about to get up and dress for the day, when the phone rang. He opened the door and when he got to the top of the stairs, where one of the handsets was placed, Brigitte was there too, her mouth set grimly, face creased from sleep. Together they reached for it and she tried to pull his arm away and he shook her off and took the phone in his hand, ignored her low command that he must not dare to answer it.

When he put the phone down he went back to his room and dressed as she stood there, watching him.

'You must not go,' she said. He fastened the zip and button of his jeans, pushed past her, and he tried to close the bathroom door but she came in, stood beside him as he brushed his teeth.

'Henri,' she said, 'you *will not go.*'

His eyes met hers in the mirror and then he bent his head, spat out the scuddy white foam, rinsed out his mouth and splashed water into his face and over his hair.

'If you go, Henri,' she said as he combed his hair quickly,

watching the lines the comb carved in hair darkened with water, 'you can forget this arrangement now. You can forget me covering your back. I will tell everyone everything. Paul, Thierry, the village, everyone who thinks you're the great man you pretend to be.' He placed the comb on the shelf, buried his face in the stale cool of a towel. 'Thibault will know,' she said, and he turned to look at her, and for a moment he had the most fleeting impression that perhaps, in spite of everything, they in fact shared some great understanding, that really she knew him far better than he'd ever realised. 'Everyone will know what you really are,' she said.

He heard Marguerite's tense voice again in his head, *I need you*, and he passed Brigitte in the doorway and walked down the stairs.

'Then everyone will know,' he said, and he let Jojo greet him in the kitchen and then he shut her in, closed the door behind him and inhaled, the great mineral wetness of dawn filling his lungs as he strode down the driveway towards his truck.

He loved the sound of the gravel under his tyres, loved the smell of the forest around Rossignol at this time. He closed the door of the truck gently, went around the side of the house to the kitchen door and tried it to see if it was locked. It opened, and as he passed through the room the kettle battled out its clumsy crescendo and clicked, exhaling long plumes of steam. He stepped quietly out into the corridor to find her emerging from Jérôme's room. He thought that something like relief passed over her lovely face, but she also looked tense, afraid, and she gestured to the kitchen and followed him back into it, closed the door behind her. He made to step forward to take hold of her but she shook her head, held a piece of paper up in the space between them.

'You have to read this,' she said, and he took it and sat down. As he read, anger and then horror filling the spaces inside him, he was no longer aware of her. When he'd finished it he read it again, and then he laid it down on the counter and watched her back as she plunged the top of the cafetière slowly, as if it were very heavy to push. He waited, but when she was finished she didn't turn around. She was a stranger, he thought. He felt afraid of her. And yet as she stood there, listening, he thought that her neck looked fragile, like it could snap, like his own in the photos of him as a small child.

'Jean-Christophe is atrocious,' he said, 'a bully,' and he could think of nothing else to say, unsure whether to refer to the letter's accusations as a truth or as something outrageous, a gross misrepresentation.

He watched her take two cups and fill them, but still she kept her back to him. He didn't know what he had permission to say or presume, and he picked up the letter again, laid it back down.

'He is trying to scare you,' he said. 'What does Jérôme say?'

'Jérôme says I have to run away,' she said, and her voice was so small that he couldn't stay sitting, he stood up and walked around the table that stood between them, taking her in his arms, and she buried her face against him but there was no elasticity in her grip, as if she didn't know whether to hold him or not. He held her tight, breathed in the smell of her. She wasn't a stranger, he thought, she was this young woman he had come so quickly to know, kind and human and devoted to her sister. But Jérôme was right, she had to run away, and the realisation was both terrible and oddly reassuring in its clarity. A relief, somehow.

'What do you want to do?'

'I don't know what to do.'

'Do you—' He paused and she loosened herself from his arms, took her cup, walked away and sat at the table. 'Do you think that there is any risk that anyone could pin anything on you?' he asked, and she pushed the cup away and sank her face onto her arms. He saw that he needed to show her that she could break out of silence, that the crime levelled at her in the letter was not in fact a crime in his eyes, whether it was true, as he now suspected it was, or entirely unfounded. He trusted her, he realised – and the thought was a great relief to him – to have done something this extreme, this unthinkable, only under the most unthinkable of circumstances.

He turned to look out at the garden. The stubborn, un-stoppable beauty of a summer's dawn turning into morning.

'You have to remember that I'm a farmer,' he said finally, spying the way that he might open up a path to break through her silence. 'To me, life and death aren't what they are to most people. I've never been very good at sickness; I don't have an instinct for how to care for people or animals.'

He thought of his mother when she'd been close to the end, and how for all the pain and sadness of her vulnerability he had felt something remarkably close to impatience as he watched her struggle to hold on. He'd vowed that, like his father, he would simply close his eyes and wait for the end, once it was time, that he'd not fight against it.

'On the farm, if something is healthy – a crop, or an animal – it works, it thrives. If it's not healthy, it no longer thrives and it no longer has its place amongst the rest of the farm. Of course, I know that's not the same for human life, I'm not saying that it is. Humans don't have to fulfil a purpose in the same way, or do a job, they don't have to be healthy to thrive, they don't have to thrive to justify their existence. But—' and he cast around, unsure for a moment what he did mean, unsure of how to make her understand that to him, very simply, forcing life beyond its natural extension didn't make any sense.

'But just because we're human doesn't mean we should live at any cost. We shouldn't live at the expense of life. Once we've got past the point where life is being lived, we shouldn't have to cling on to it as if it has absolute value, in and of itself. When someone has come to their end, their real end, then it's no longer life we're giving them by keeping it going. It's not life, it's not death.' He thought for a moment of Vanille, her sagging jowls in his hand, the dull desperation in her eyes. 'It's punishment.'

He turned, and she was sitting upright now, staring at the cup of coffee in her hands.

'I'm not being articulate,' he said, and he hated that he wasn't. 'I'm not making sense.'

'You are.'

She picked up the coffee, blew into the cup, put it back down.

'I have no knowledge, no idea about the medical world, about your job and the intricacies of disease and injury. But what I'm trying to say is that I trust your instincts for understanding the point at which life ends. I trust that you would

396

have known, would have acted only out of love and kindness. As a nurse, and as her family. Even,' he said, and he came to sit down next to her, 'as a human.'

He watched her profile, the straight nose and mouth that he thought painfully lovely, and he was going to try again, to cast around again for the right words, force some meaning into them that might unlock her, when she spoke.

'I've thought so much about what it means to be human. Sometimes I've thought that it is having autonomy, just the ability to make choices and decisions. Sometimes I've thought that it's communication. And maybe that's right, maybe without communication – not words, I mean, but anything; the ability to show your pain, or fear, or hunger, in some way, even just with your eyes, or hands, or whatever it might be – maybe without that you find yourself cut off from living among humans. But Cassandre *could* communicate, still, even long past when she stopped speaking, and yet even when she was communicating, so loudly it seemed to tear her lungs and no one could bear to be in the same room as her, even then I could see that humanity had been snatched away from her. It had been stolen. By the end, the place she was occupying was a place you or I have never been, even in our worst nightmares.' She met his eyes then, and she looked furious. 'Whatever we think we've suffered, it's been nothing, *nothing* compared to that.' She looked down, her expression calming, and he saw that that fury was her confession. She tugged her hands so that two knuckles cracked. 'It was no longer a human place. It was a place of the very purest suffering. Worse than Christ.'

Henri watched her face, her straight lips closed gently now into silence, and he wanted to say, *how beautifully you speak*, wanted to tell her that she could be so much more than she was, this creature of silence, if only she'd give herself permission. Instead he stroked the side of her face with his hand, pulled her head forwards so that he could kiss her forehead. It was very cool. He rested his lips on it and closed his eyes, trying to cast the feel of her skin into his memory.

'You're remarkable,' he said, and he felt her shake her head. He forced her chin up with his hand so that she looked at him. 'You are. You have to promise me that when you go away from here you'll make a life for yourself. I think you've been serving out a sentence you set yourself when you were fifteen. I think everything you do is in some way penance. I can't tell you how important it is that you stop doing that.' She looked at him, unspeaking. 'You don't have to cut out joy from your life because of what your sister suffered. I would say, even, that you owe it to her to go and live properly, a proper life.'

'I don't deserve it,' she said, shaking her head again.

'But you do. You never did anything wrong. You've been paying the price for a random, cruel illness that had nothing to do with you.' He wanted to shake her into understanding that, but he could see how obstinately she'd made herself believe that it was her fault. Perhaps that was an easier way of understanding what had happened than the knowledge that it was a simple, meaningless tragedy, the kind that happens everywhere, all the time, to anyone. She couldn't accept that even her sister was not special enough to evade it; no one was. He thought that perhaps if he had years to spend with her he might start to break down her obstinacy, the devotion with which she'd betrothed herself to this belief. But they didn't have that time.

'If you won't believe it wasn't your fault,' he said, and he pulled away from her a little so that he could really focus on her face when he said it, 'you must at least believe me when I say I think you did the bravest thing for your sister that any human being could do.'

Because it was, he thought. It was a truly horrifying thing to have done, a horrifying act of love and courage, something he didn't think he would have had the strength to do himself.

'But Jérôme is right,' he said. 'You have to go away.'

'I'm scared,' she said, and her eyes filled slowly with tears, until she had to close them and they ran down the sloping plains of her face. He held her head in his hands, her forehead once more against his lips, and he said that she mustn't be, that she was very strong and that she of all people could do it, and he wondered whether they were talking about the running away or the thing he imagined she found most terrifying of all: trying to live a proper life, for herself.

After she had taken Jérôme his breakfast, Henri asked to go in and see the old man and she left them in the room together. She didn't know where to start preparing for going away, still couldn't understand that this could be real, so instead she left the house and turned out of the driveway and broke into a slow jog, building up her speed gradually as the track darkened with forest. A few minutes in, she heard a rustling among the trees to her right and she thought she saw movement and was overcome with terror, turning and sprinting back to the gates of the house.

Back inside she took sprays and unguents out from under

the sink and she went about cleaning the kitchen, sorting the cupboards, throwing out the spongy stubs of vegetables from the fridge, scrubbing the spaces of the hob, the sticky grease of the extractor fan. Next she cleaned upstairs, ending with the old room of Thibault's she'd occupied at the beginning. When she'd finished, she sat on the edge of the small bed in that room and she looked at the broken chair and the detached wardrobe door resting against the wall and thought of the version of herself that had sat there so many times before Henri had started visiting the house, and she saw clearly that something had changed in her between now and that time. Looking back at the interminable days and weeks she'd lived in this room before him, she had the feeling of looking at something murky, something half in shadow.

She stood and went down to him then. He wanted to speak to her about Jérôme, about logistics, but she didn't let him just yet. They had sex, the air still pinched with the smell of bleach, and as they did she thought that one day she would look back at this, this ability she once had to take him inside her without a word, and she would see the self that she was at this moment as something out of shadow; that for all the terror she felt in the woods and the pain with which she thought of the old man down the corridor, she became fleetingly, as Henri's body was locked into hers, a thing in the light, at last.

They had worked out a plan, between them. Jérôme had given orders and Henri had made phone calls and from tomorrow morning there would begin a rotation of visiting nurses, no one person to live there all the time but a revolving team of

400

them, overseen by the village doctor, who would come to Rossignol to assess Jérôme the following afternoon and twice weekly from then on. She was to call her agency, hand in her notice, pretend to see out the notice period in the hope that the agency didn't hear anything from Jean-Christophe or anyone else before it expired. Jérôme's lawyer would be visiting, too, in the coming days, and Jérôme would tell him he'd given away the cash he'd held in the house – to diffuse, unnamed beneficiaries – and he would have Monsieur Richoux type up a reference for her, dictated by Jérôme, which would be sent to her so that she could practise again in future if the worst didn't come to the worst. That was a kindness she couldn't have anticipated, she thought, something she would never have imagined from Jérôme. And it continued: she must keep the car, she must take the cash, enough to keep her going for a good while, said Henri, and she couldn't bear to hear how much. Then he looked down and said that she must do her handover and leave immediately the following morning, and stay away until all talk of investigations was over.

'And Jérôme?' she asked.

'What of Jérôme? Jérôme will be fine. He'll have all the medical attention he needs.'

'He wanted to die under my care,' she said, and Henri took her hand in his.

'He does,' he said, 'but he doesn't want you to be taken away from here. He wants you to leave while you can. He thinks, we both think, that all of JC's fear-mongering is baseless, that there's nothing that can touch you. But it's best to be safe. He wanted you to have that money anyway, and the car. This is just you taking it earlier than you were going to, and going away for a while just to make sure that you don't get stuck in something pernicious and unpleasant, something dangerous.'

And you? she wanted to ask but couldn't, and so instead she asked him if he would stay until she left in the morning and he smiled, the hushing sound of the start of a laugh in the back of his throat, and he blinked slowly and said of course he was going to do that, but only if she promised to feed him because he hadn't been able to stop thinking about her cooking since he'd left the house. She smiled and nodded, and she was glad that they were pretending everything was going to be all right when they both knew that it wasn't, for either of them – even in the best possible scenario, in which she was never held accountable for what she'd done to Cassandre.

Sitting at her place at the table in his room, watching again as he tried to negotiate a spoon between shuddering fingers, she said, even though she felt sure he would not let her continue, 'I'm very grateful, and very sorry.'

He dropped the spoon. He was tired, she thought. Weary to his bones.

'You're not to bother with all that,' he said. 'I'm not helping you out to be kind or because I think you're special.' He frowned down towards his feet at the end of the bed and, with his chin bowed to his chest and neck slumped forwards like a turtle, his broad mouth stretched wide, sulky, he looked immensely ugly. 'I just don't want the money going to my sons, they've got enough what with this place and shares and savings and what they already got when Céline died. Yes, the

Napoleonic law has me in a bind, otherwise I'd be divesting them of some assets too.' He stared at his food, looked at her, looked back down the bed. 'No, you're not special. I'm not helping you for any other reason than that you probably don't deserve to go to prison, which is frankly where you've got yourself headed without my intervention. God knows you don't deserve my help – you're a bloody fool, and reckless to boot – but no, you don't quite deserve prison.' He took up the spoon again. 'So do what I say, take the car and the cash, get going as soon as you can tomorrow morning and let some more competent professionals take over my care.'

She swallowed, felt the blood burn underneath the skin of her cheeks. He could still hurt her.

'I won't take it, then,' she said, and a flash of fury crossed over his face.

'Oh, for God's sake don't be noble,' he said. 'It's too late to pretend you've got morals. Take the bloody cash. You're doing me a favour: I don't want it, I've got no use for it. I'm telling you to take it, that's my command and God knows you at least owe it to me to do me that last great service. Since you've been having an affair under my roof, and since you're leaving me just as I make my final, shabby crawl into the ground.' He licked his lips with a pale tongue. 'You either take it or you burn it. Now get out of here, take this foul food with you, and go and spread your legs for Henri like you're so fond of doing. You may as well make yourself useful to someone.'

She wanted to spit in his face as she took the tray from his lap. She walked from the room and slammed the door behind her, something she'd never done before, the whole time she'd been here, however hard she'd been pushed. Her hands were shaking just like Jérôme's as she tried to clear the lunch things away, and when Henri tried to hold her she pulled away.

'He's a monster,' she said.

'Yes, he can be. Don't let him get to you.'

'The things he can say,' she said.

'He wants your anger,' he said. 'He wants this response. It's his way of coping with you leaving.'

'He's desperate for me to leave. After all of this, after everything I've put up with—'

And he had got her into the situation with Jean-Christophe, with the care home. If it hadn't been for his vile games, for the way he'd used her to goad his sons, there would have been no investigations, no medical lawyers, no one going to the care home to pick around among the bones she'd left behind. That was surely the only reason he was doing anything to help her now: he knew that all of this was his fault.

'I'm not going to take his money,' she said. 'I can't.'

'You must. You need it.'

'I have money of my own.'

'Enough to keep you going for a while?'

'No.'

She looked out at the sunshine outside and she wanted to shake the house away from her, shake the old man's sour air from around her shoulders.

'I'm going to take some now and buy us champagne,' she said, looking at Henri. 'Champagne and lobsters for dinner.'

He smiled, and she loved the way his flesh crinkled at the sides of his eyes, this stranger whom she suddenly knew and would just as suddenly not.

She hadn't been able to find lobster. They drank champagne in the garden, sitting on the grass among lanterns filled with candles, as the darkness fell, until Henri confessed that he didn't like champagne very much, and she took his and drank it for him. She thought that the delicate flutes that she'd found and dusted off looked odd in his large cracked hands, and she felt sad that he looked embarrassed when he admitted that he preferred wine. They ate monkfish and it was good but not perfect, just a touch overcooked, though he said he didn't think it was, and then they set their plates aside and lay back on the grass and lay there together, head to head, for a very long time, insects creeping in the grass by their ears and under their necks. He talked a little about his childhood, about the boredom of his teenage years on the farm, and she wanted to ask about how he had discovered his feelings for other boys and whether he had had them for girls, too, and whether he'd been in love with Thibault and whether anything had ever happened between them, but she didn't. Instead, she listened, and avoided her own childhood, and let the lovely, glossed-over memories he had of this house and this garden float around between them.

When they were tired they cleared away their food and went upstairs. They made love for the last time in the big bed they'd shared and she felt shy under the pressure of momentousness, as if it must be different from how it had been before, a summation of everything that had come before. Of course it couldn't be and for the first time she felt glad when it was over, when she could lie with the back of her body fitted into the front of his and wait for sleep. She didn't think she'd sleep, and for a while she lay while his breathing changed, listening

405

to the rich, rustling night outside the windows that she'd spent so many evenings dreading, but then she too became overwhelmed with tiredness, the tiredness of a child.

It was the thickest, blackest part of the night when she awoke to Jérôme's knocks and went downstairs. He was pallid, his temperature raised, his forehead dankly damp, and he was in very great pain, so much pain that his face was contorted with it. He was sick, heaving drily over the plastic bowl she pulled under his chin, vomiting water and the foam of undigested painkillers. He writhed, turning his head from side to side on the pillow, and in one of the moments in which the convulsions had abated just a little he grabbed her arm, the strength of his grip surprising, and looked up into her face with very wide eyes, his breath acrid as eggs, and stared, breathing sharply, as if he were looking for something in her that he'd lost.

'I don't want to die,' he hissed, his pupils large in his eyes. 'I don't want to die, I'm not ready, I'm not ready,' he moaned and then his head sank back into the pillow and his face creased like a child and tears slid from his eyes as he wailed. It was a quiet, high-pitched sound, like the creaking of a door, and it continued until the pain rose again, silencing his voice into nothing more than panting breath. She watched him, holding his hand, its grip at times so vice-like that she winced as the knuckles of her fingers were squeezed together – until finally, so precariously and gradually that she felt she had to hold her breath, he had fallen asleep.

She tucked her body back into the folds of Henri's and lay there, his breath warm and rhythmic on her neck. She dreamt of nothing.

IV

VI

23

They called him when it was time; he'd asked that they did. He had promised Marguerite, in the still cool of dawn when they'd lain awake together, facing each other on that bed for the last time, that he would be there when Jérôme died. She'd looked grey and drawn in the morning half-light, her expression very solemn, as it had been the first few times he'd met her.

'You promise you will.'

'I promise.'

'You don't mind?'

'I don't mind.' Even though he hated sickness, had no desire to see another old man die.

And he didn't mind, he found, as he washed himself in a cool bath at noon, his duties for the day cut off early and left for Paul to take over. He dressed in a crisp blue shirt, one of his smartest. Brigitte eyed him as he came into the kitchen, wet hair cool against his temples.

'So you're going to go and watch him die?' she asked, her voice low.

'I promised I would.'

'Don't worry about the farm, of course,' she said. 'Just leave me and Paul to pick up where you left off, we're used to that. God forbid we get in the way of your sacred duty.' He didn't answer, drank a glass of water down. 'Perhaps you should just get a job as a nurse yourself,' she said, and he put the glass down. 'They do have male nurses, you know,' she continued. 'Especially your lot. You'd fit right in.'

'Goodbye, Brigitte,' he said, and he bent down to take Jojo's silky face in his hands, kissed her between the eyes.

Jérôme seemed scarcely to have spoken, ever since Marguerite had left. Henri had visited him twice, but the old man had barely registered his presence. He was concentrating on dying, Henri thought. It was his time. He had nothing left to keep him going.

He could smell how imminent it was as soon as he entered the room. The nurse left him and he pulled up a chair, quietly, and sat a little way from the bed. She had opened the windows wide, and as he sat there he watched the branches of olive trees moving lightly against the sky.

Occasionally he looked down at Jérôme, lying like a small creature in the bed. His breathing had taken control of him. It was separate from him. He spoke occasionally, grunting form-less words and gurning, his jaw pulled down so that it showed how long his bottom teeth were. A scum mark of dried blood marked his teeth halfway down, like the line of seaweed left on a beach by the tide. The smell of his breath was strange: it was something oaty and old, something that no longer had anything to do with food. His irises were faded and misty, his

410

eyeballs mustard-coloured. There were large purple bruises on his hands and wrists, just under the skin, like clusters of grapes that had been trodden underfoot.

'I promised her I'd be here,' Henri said loudly, leaning forward as if his words might better penetrate the gulf that seemed to stretch out between the old man and him. 'She wanted me to be here. She cared very much.'

The old man mumbled, bottom lip pulled right down. His eyes slid over Henri's face. Henri leant back in the chair and he looked back out of the window, at the trees he used to climb, the odd cloud passing by, very high overhead. He thought of the pride with which Jérôme had spoken of Marguerite, when Henri had asked to see him, to make arrangements for what she should do about Jean-Christophe's letter.

'A queer little thing,' he'd said, 'but she's got backbone. I'd have liked a child like that.' He'd spoken of his own children, the sons who'd disappointed him. 'I don't care what people achieve at work, how much they earn. I don't even care what they do in their private lives.' He'd eyed Henri then, and for a moment Henri had wondered what he knew about him. 'What I care about is: are they reaching their moral potential? Do they have *mettle*? That's why that boy drove me so mad,' he'd said, and Henri had known he was speaking of Thibault. 'His potential was sky high, but he never met it.'

Henri had thought then of how badly Jérôme had gone wrong, because mettle wasn't the only way to measure people. By that metric, Jérôme would be a great man, but there were other things, surely. Kindness, humanity, things he associated with Marguerite far more than just backbone.

But he was right that she was a far greater person than the

sons he had poisoned with his skewed metrics, his impossible standards. And then he'd been vile to her, made her hate him, and Henri had never told her the good things he'd said.

Jérôme grunted, mumbling again, an urgency to the jumbled words he squeezed out between the long, scum-marked teeth. His head rolled from left to right on the pillow every few minutes, eyes searching the ceiling. His hands kept rising up to grasp something; they'd settle on the rails of the bed, he'd grip those. Or he'd pluck restlessly at the sheets. It was all as if there were something he must try to remember, something he'd lost or forgotten, something that was just there, just there – if he could only catch it before it slipped away.

Henri left the house, let the nurse do what she needed to do with Jérôme's body. He took a cup of coffee down to the stump of the oak tree he'd felled with Thierry and Rémy, the stump he'd pretended to examine for signs of disease as an excuse to stay a little longer with Marguerite, before they'd put a voice to what was happening between them. In that quiet, funny time – just days, he thought, before they'd had the courage to acknowledge the pulsing cord stretching out from one of them to the other, binding them together, invisible.

He thought of Jérôme's hands as he plucked at the sheets, and then for a moment he thought of the young girl Marguerite had nursed, imagined her small hands, smooth and perhaps a little square, like her sister's. Her life had become a prison at the end, Marguerite had said, unnatural. He thought of Marguerite's face, the cool skin of her forehead under his lips, tried to imagine her expression as she reached forwards to release her sister.

He would not live imprisoned, not any more. And he would not live like Jérôme, dogged by anger and regret. He wouldn't spend his final moments like that, searching wildly for all the things he hadn't said and hadn't done. He wouldn't die still grasping.

He sat down on the stump of the tree, placed his coffee down beside him. He watched as the cup fell dumbly onto its side and the liquid spread, slowly, into the prickly grass, into the dark soil, and he didn't try to stop it. He watched it and then he closed his eyes and inhaled, heard a great rush of air gathering in the forest behind him, smelt the pine and earth and whatever else it was that laced the air here, ripe and dark and beautiful. He felt it cool his face, wash the stale smell of death right away. He wouldn't live like Jérôme. He had a choice, of course.

He could hear the water as soon as he cut the engine, that distant hum. It got louder as he strode upwards through the forest, his legs light and quick, and by the time he reached the clearing it was all he could hear, a constant roar.

He climbed up to the diving spot and he undressed, let his clothes fall to the ground beside him. He ran his hands over his body. His chest, alive with breath. His taut stomach, the hair that started at its base. For most of his life, he'd barely allowed his body what it had needed. He'd fed it, kept it clean and exercised and strong, but he'd only very sporadically let it take what it wanted. All those years upon countless years of privation, of shame and guilt. At least recently he'd put an end to that.

He crouched carefully, squatted, breathed in the air rising from the rocks and water beneath him, air charged with moisture. Wet and electric as the earth, the soil of his farm, the roots of plants and herbs, the warm breath that shoots from the nostrils of an animal.

This had always been his favourite time of day, the light falling, earth cooling. Time for a beer, for a bath. In that sliver of life he'd allowed himself at Rossignol with Marguerite, it was the time when she'd come into the kitchen with Jérôme's tray, clear away his dinner things and pour them each a glass of wine. The beginning of their time. He hoped that right now she wasn't alone, that she was happy with the English woman. Every day for the last few weeks he'd followed her in his mind, imagined going to meet her somewhere in England, seeing whether they couldn't just make something work. And always he knew that the thought wasn't a real thought; that it was relegated to the most purely hypothetical, a half-worn fantasy. It was too late for him to make a new kind of life. But not for her, he thought. She didn't have her own soil; she could plant herself wherever she wanted to. She just needed to learn how to live properly, as he had never done.

The spray beneath him cooled the still-warm evening air so that he felt goose-bumps ripple across the skin of his forearms, up his back. He stood and looked around him and up at the sky, lifting his hands up, high, letting a stretch tear through from the base of his spine up to his fingertips. He pushed his hips out a little, brought his arms back, opened his chest out until his shoulder blades slotted into one another. Then he stepped forward, wrapped his toes tightly over the rock ledge, reached down for the shotgun Brigitte had left as an offering in the darkened driveway, lying in silent vigil under Jérôme and Céline's old marital bed ever since. He straightened, carefully, taking care not to fall before it was time. His hands were shaking, he noticed, and it was as if he were looking at someone else's hands, not connected to him. Slowly, he brought the cold nostrils of the thing to the soft flesh under his jaw, one finger curled around the metal of the trigger. He closed his eyes, inhaled deeply, felt the moisture-laden air uncurling in his lungs. This was his place. This was his time, now.

24

She had grown accustomed already to the smell of the place: a cold smell, somehow, even on days like this, when there was barely a cloud, the sun high in the sky. The walk from the village to the house was hot, so that she could feel her T-shirt grow damp under her backpack. Summer would be coming to an end soon, she'd heard someone say in the village: there were storms forecast for the weekend. But for now it was every bit as warm as it had been.

As she turned onto the final stretch leading up to the house, the sea emerged, flat and dull green-blue. There was the thundering of footsteps behind her and she hugged the wall to let a little squad of children run past, rubber sandals and trainers smacking the pavement, their cheeks puce or sunburnt, hairlines wild with sweat. They found the narrow opening in the wall that divided the pavement from the beach, like water will find an opening, and then they jumped onto the sand, momentum skidding momentarily to a stop in this new medium. Then they were off again, running more awkwardly now down to the sea, their feet sinking as they went.

That smell, like gulls and fish and netting and seawater and damp, salty towels, all at once. It was strongest when she pushed open the light glass door that led into the hallway, mixed with the whiff of damp masonry, and then when she opened the second front door it receded a little, competing now with whatever was cooking in the kitchen, or sun cream if the kids were getting ready to go outside.

She went through to the kitchen. The radio had been left on and was murmuring a gentle torrent of foreign words she couldn't bother to decipher. She pulled the backpack with relief off her back and onto the table, pulled the damp cotton of her top away from her skin. She poured a glass of water from the tap – she still didn't like that it came out a little red with rust, though they assured her it did no harm – and drank it down in four breathless gulps, and as it went down, that new, low-level nausea curdled again in her stomach. She wiped sweat from her temples, held the glass to her cheek. She heard stomping upstairs, liked the way it felt as if the house was rattling when people moved.

The youngest came into the room with his busy steps, fish-white torso bare, speaking to her in English until he looked up and saw that she wasn't his mother. He retreated again, still speaking, nonplussed, and she heard him plod back down the corridor and shout up the stairs.

The kids would need their lunch soon. She put water on to boil, took a box from the fridge. Frances was teaching her new recipes, fuelled by the vegetables she and Mark grew in their garden: big pots of stew and curry, largely, full of chickpeas and lentils and spices, things that might have tasted crude and simple without Frances's touch. It was a meat-free household, the eldest child had explained proudly, but they all ate fish, and often Marguerite would find the sink full and stinking with cockles or winkles or death-grey prawns.

She still thought of Jérôme most times she prepared a meal, imagining what he'd say if she brought him what she was making: slick houmous or yellow, turmeric-rich curry with paneer. He might be dead already, and it was strange to know that she wouldn't know if he was. It might be happening at this very moment, as she dug a brush's bristles into the black pockmarks of a potato. At some point he would cross over into that other place, into nothingness, and she would be busy with something here, loading the dishwasher or tying a kid's shoelaces.

Frances came in then, the youngest marching in front of her, and she pulled the top of Marguerite's backpack open with one hand, peered inside.

'Milk, wonderful,' she said in French and the middle child, trailing into the room with a bundle of swimming towels in her arms, parroted her with an elaborate accent, rolling her eyes into her head as if she were someone very grand. Frances smiled at Marguerite, rueful. 'Stop washing those,' she said. 'I can do it. Go and cool down outside, take a break. You're going to have to start taking things a lot easier now,' she added. 'Trust me, I've been there. Three times.'

The nausea was rising up again, oily, slippery, an animal presence at the bottom of her gullet.

'Are you sure?'

'Very.'

'Thank you.'

She put down the brush and potato, turned off the tap,

stepped carefully around the little girl and into the cool damp of the pantry, then out onto the patio. She sat on the step, felt its pebbly stone under her palms, closed her eyes, took a deep breath. Then she lifted her face so that the sun was on it, beating like blood.

She took off her trainers and socks and stood, stepping onto the grass, feeling its cool wetness under her feet as she walked forwards into the garden. There was a clinking sound from the other side of the fence, a neighbour doing something, and she ducked a little as she walked so that she wouldn't have to say hello. She walked the length of the garden and then she lay down at the far end under the apple tree, took another deep breath in. That smell: salt, and water, and wet holidays. A cold smell, not unpleasant.

And something else, too, as she lay there, the very faint breeze tinged with it. Rosemary, she thought. Lemon thyme. She opened her eyes and she looked over at all the herbs, bushy and splendid and messily efficient like the rest of the garden, banked in rows against the back wall. She closed her eyes again, rested her hands on her stomach to calm it, the curve where her belly had already started to swell. If she lay still enough she could imagine that he was lying next to her, head to head, his limbs straight as railway sleepers, warm body solid under the soap-clean cotton of a shirt.

Acknowledgements

My thanks are owed:

To early readers Albi and Will Kemp, Karen Raney and Miriam Robinson.

To Blake Morrison, Francis Spufford and Erica Wagner for their valuable guidance and encouragement.

To Johnny Goring for patient, amusingly worded instruction on all things agricultural, and Katie James at the National Sheep Association; to David Mitchell and Dr Nicky Thomas for advice on medicine and nursing; and to Dr Richard Perry and Dr Fergus Rugg-Gunn for their generous counsel on neurological issues. All errors are entirely my own, and in spite of their expert advice.

To Clare Alexander, who didn't just trust in the book but whose astute understanding helped to shape it as I wrote. To Anna Kelly for her sensitivity, support and insight, and to Helen Garnons-Williams, Luke Brown, Katy Archer and all at 4th Estate. To Kathryn Court, Victoria Savanh and all at Penguin US.

To Mum and Claudia, for your indispensible wisdom and patience with the book.

To Petra, for keeping me silent company during the final months of writing.

And most of all to James: for making it possible – in so many different ways, big and small – to write at all.